PRAISE FOR MADDIE DAWSON'S
MATCHMAKING FOR BEGINNERS

"A charming read . . . For fans of Liane Moriarty's *What Alice Forgot* or Aimee Bender's *The Particular Sadness of Lemon Cake*."

—Library Journal

"A delightful, light-as-air romance that successfully straddles the line between sweet and smart without ever being silly . . . The novel is simply captivating from beginning to end."

—Associated Press

"*Matchmaking for Beginners* is lovely from the inside out."

—HelloGiggles

"Infused with the kind of magic so frequently lost as we become adults, this one-of-a-kind novel pushes the boundaries of coincidence and connection by asking us to believe in fate and, possibly, magic once again. The characters jump off the page with their quirky habits and capture hearts with their meaningful development and interactions, leading to moments that will bring readers to tears one minute and having them laughing out loud the next."

—RT Book Reviews (Top Rated)

A HAPPY CATASTROPHE

A HAPPY CATASTROPHE

A Novel

MADDIE DAWSON

LAKE UNION
PUBLISHING

Text copyright © 2020 by Maddie Dawson
All rights reserved.

Published by Lake Union Publishing, Seattle

www.apub.com

Amazon, the Amazon logo, and Lake Union Publishing are trademarks of Amazon.com, Inc., or its affiliates.

ISBN-13: 9781542006460
ISBN-10: 1542006465

Cover design and illustration by David Drummond

Printed in the United States of America

To Jimbo, for all the love and the laughter,
forever and ever

CHAPTER ONE
MARNIE

Patrick is late meeting me for dinner, which is good because it means I get a few minutes to sit by myself at our favorite table in the back of LaMont's, where I can sip my merlot and practice how I'm going to ask him my big question.

Patrick and I have been together for nearly four years, and I can talk to him about every little thought that might come into my head, but this—*this* is one of *those* questions, you see. Life-altering stuff. And Patrick is a man who has already had enough life-altering situations to last him a hundred years. He would prefer decades of some good old status quo.

But . . . I just can't.

So I take a gulp of my wine and close my eyes. I left the flower shop early so I could rehearse. Luckily, this is Brooklyn, so people on the subway didn't seem to notice that I was practicing out loud and enumerating talking points on my fingers.

Here's what I've got so far. "Patrick," I will say, "I love you more than anything. You, my love, are the flap in my flapjack. The cream in the center of my Oreo cookie. The monster in my monster mash. *And* you are the horizon of all my longing."

Sappy? God, yes, although that part about the horizon of my longing *might* be considered poetic if I use the right tone of voice. If I'm lucky, he'll laugh. And once he laughs, it'll be easy. I'll just blurt the question out, and then it will be done. Yes or no.

"Yes or no, Patrick," I'll say. "Take all the time you like, my love, but please remember that I am already thirty-three years old, and that loud banging noise you hear—well, that thing is my heart."

For God's sake, get a grip, Marnie.

I smile, recognizing this voice in my head. It's Blix—or not really her, since she's dead and all, but it's what she *would* say if she were here. I can squint and pretty much see her essence sitting across the table from me right this minute, all floaty and light, in her bright scarves and necklaces and long skirts, with her wild Einstein white hair sticking up everywhere, shaking her head and yelling at me to stop stressing about the question.

Just lighten up! Trust in the goddamn universe for once, will you?

Blix was always going on about the universe, and frankly, she and that *universe* of hers are what got me here. She was a one-of-a-kind matchmaking wizard, and she always said she knew two things from the moment she met me: I was a natural-born matchmaker, *and* also Patrick and I were meant to be together. (Never mind that I was engaged to be married to Blix's grandnephew at the time; she and the universe already knew *that* relationship was a lost cause.)

I wasn't so sure I believed her. In fact, I was stunned when I found out soon after she died that she had left me her Brooklyn brownstone, having apparently decided that I, Marnie "Nobody Special" MacGraw, was the one to follow in her matchmaking footsteps and inherit her ongoing projects, as well as all the charming misfits she cultivated.

I had no intention of actually doing anything that crazy. By then, I was divorced from her grandnephew, and I was back living with my parents in Florida, heartbroken and blindsided by life. After months of listlessly dating my ex-boyfriend from high school, I may have accidentally agreed to marry him. I had *zero* plans to become a matchmaker in—*Brooklyn? Are you kidding me with this stuff?* So I came here intending to sell the building and go back home . . . only it just so happened that there was this guy Patrick living in the basement apartment of that brownstone.

And, well, Patrick turned out to be . . . my true home.

Okay, if I'm being honest here, he was not the man I would have chosen. That's when I learned that love doesn't always come in the package we might expect. He's a reclusive introvert, for one thing, and I'm always working out plans on how *not* to be alone. But he's smart and funny and possibly the tiniest bit crazy in all the good ways, and he knows how furnaces work and also he senses exactly what to say when I'm feeling lost or sad. He bakes the best pies from scratch, and he's the only person I know who likes to have all his conversations about world events in the bathtub, and besides all that, he lets me eat the centers of all his Oreo cookies. From the very start, even when I was a big whiny pain who knew nothing whatsoever about city life, he took care of me and made me laugh. And I fell for him in a way I'd never known I could love anyone.

Which just goes to show that we don't know everything about ourselves, because this was definitely not the way I saw my life going, being the live-in girlfriend of a brooding but funny artist, and owning a flower shop where I did matchmaking on the side. By the age of thirty-three, I was supposed to be a suburban mom married to Blix's handsome grandnephew, living next door to my parents and spending Saturday afternoons lolling around the pool with my sister while our husbands manned the barbecue pit and our kids napped in their strollers.

The only big question I'd planned to be asking at age thirty-three was should we have potato salad as a side dish, or would corn on the cob be best.

But you know what? Blix had some serious magic to her, and somehow she transferred that to me, and right now I hear her whispering in my ear, *Oh, for heaven's sake, Marnie, stop with this. You're going to get everything you want. Just trust in the universe.*

So I'm sitting there practicing my speech when I get distracted because at the table next to me, a sweet-faced hipster in a plaid shirt and a fedora is being yelled at in a most entertaining way by a blonde-haired older woman dressed in white and gold. His mother, no doubt, since they have the same nose. Any person from around here could tell exactly what's going on. A Florida mom has come to Brooklyn and has now had quite enough of us. And her unsuspecting son, not reading the signs, has gone all irresponsible on her and ordered himself some food, just as she's planning to make her escape.

And she's furious. "If *you* think I'm going to be running through that *damned* airport because *you* had to eat something called a quail egg slider that no doubt takes *thirty* minutes to prepare, you've got another think coming!" she says. "I'm not putting up with any more of your thoughtlessness. I've called me an Uber, and I'm leaving. You will *not* be taking me to the airport."

Normally not having to take someone to the airport is like a huge, amazing gift. But the guy takes in this news with the glazed look of a man whose mom has been visiting for far too many days. He's quietly mumbling that it's four whole hours until her plane leaves and also, just as a point of information, quail egg sliders are quick to prepare.

I am beaming over to him the message, *You can make it, dude, we're all here for you,* when suddenly my hand jerks and knocks my glass of merlot into my lap, and red wine spreads everywhere, splashing the tablecloth, my skirt, the floor. As I'm standing up to escape it, the guy leaps into the air with the kind of alacrity a firefighter might display upon running into a burning building and hands me a fistful of napkins.

"Oh, thank you," I say. "That's really very kind."

"Here. You might need more," he says, now grabbing bundles of them.

"No!" yells his scary mother. "Stop that, you're spreading it. Here, I can fix this."

And then, in one quick motion, she stands up and tosses white wine all over the front of me. Like this is a real thing that civilized people do.

I gasp and blink in surprise as it slowly occurs to me that the entire front of my body is freezing cold, soaking wet now with two kinds of wine.

"OH MY HELL WHAT JUST HAPPENED," says the guy.

"White wine takes away red wine," says his mother. "Believe me. She'll thank me later."

"Mom!" he says. "You can't go pouring wine on a stranger! How is it that you don't know this?" He turns to me. "I am so sorry. Really! Please, Mom, sit down. You're making things worse." He's grabbing for even more napkins. Soon he'll be going from table to table taking them out of people's laps, I'm afraid.

"Oh, stop it, Graham. This will take the stain out," she says, her eyes huge and insistent and maybe just a tad insane. "White takes out red. Everybody knows this."

He says to me in a low voice, "You might want to run to the restroom before she starts ordering whole pitchers of pinot grigio to drown you in."

"Oh, for God's sake!" she says, laughing. "This son of mine! He always makes me out to be a lunatic, when *he's* the one who can't figure out how to be on time for dinner when he knows I have a plane to catch. Thanks to him, I can't even finish my glass of wine because my Uber's coming for me. Anyway, honey, your skirt already looks better."

"I'll go to the ladies' room and get the rest out," I tell her, ducking in case she's going to now start dousing me with other liquids she finds around the restaurant. "But thank you."

"No, no!" wails Graham. "*Don't* thank her. We don't want to encourage this."

"Why shouldn't she thank me?" she says. "I did her a favor. And now kiss your old mother good-bye, you rapscallion, because I've got to go."

She holds his face between her two hands and kisses him, the loud, smacking kind of kisses, and then she turns to me. "Are you married, by any chance? Because this delinquent of mine is *very* available. Unfathomable, I know, but true."

I decide I like these two, just as Micah, the waiter, glides over with a fresh white tablecloth and some setups and a new glass of wine for me.

"When Patrick gets here," I say to him, "would you please tell him I'm in the restroom?"

"Well, *are* you married?" the mother says.

"She's married to Patrick," says Micah, and I can't resist correcting him. Patrick and I are not exactly married, I explain, but we are committed, living together, here forever, all that.

"It's never forever until you get the ring," warns the mom, and Graham rolls his eyes and picks up a huge suitcase she'd stored under the table, and begins ushering her out, his hand at the small of her back. She's waving to all of us like a beauty queen on a parade float—and all I can think as I hurry to the restroom is that I hope he comes back.

Because something momentous has just happened. There are sparkles forming in the air all around that guy, and I know what that means:

6

he's about to fall in love with somebody, and the reason I'm here is because the universe needs me to help things along.

Sure enough, as soon as I get to scrubbing my skirt in the ladies' room, a woman comes out of one of the stalls, and bingo! Right away I know she's the one. The air shimmers around her, exactly the way it did around him.

It happens like this with matchmaking sometimes. I've been doing this gig for more than four years now, and there are times when I'll be on the subway or walking down the street, and I see two people who aren't even *looking* in each other's direction, and suddenly I know I have to engineer them into each other's path. I've jumped out of coffee shop lines, redirected cab drivers, and embarrassed myself by racing across parks, leaping over small dogs and picnic blankets—all so I could accost strangers who were in danger of walking away and missing out on love.

And it works. That's the most amazing thing: the shimmers don't lie.

But *this* time! Oh my. This woman is tall and red-haired and, despite the sparkles twinkling around her, is sort of theatrically sad. I watch as she leans toward the mirror and sighs, like her face might be a disappointing used car she's considering buying. I keep stopping my skirt-scrubbing to see what she's deciding about herself. Is she going to buy this face or not?

"Wow," I say. "Would you look at my skirt! Can you believe this? I spilled red wine all over myself. How bad does it look? Is it really terrible?"

She drags her eyes over to me. "It looks fine to me," she says. Her voice sounds close to tears, which is a little bit of a setback for my plan for her. In the past, I've had to bring weeping people to meet the person they're going to fall in love with, but I'm not going to lie: it's a harder path.

"Funny thing," I say. "I'm the one who spilled the red wine, but then a woman sitting at the next table stood up and threw her glass of white wine on the stain! Just tossed a whole glass on me, because she claimed that everybody knows white wine takes out red wine stains."

"Yeah, I think everybody might be a little crazy these days, don't you?" she says sadly. "I've just been stood up by a guy who sent me thirty text messages telling me I'm the one for him, and then we make a date, and now he texted me that he changed his mind."

"What a jerk," I say.

"I even shaved my legs for this dude," she says, "and now he's texting me he's not *coming*?"

"Listen to me," I say, all in a rush. "It's awful, especially the leg-shaving part. And the texting part. Thirty texts is too many, a red flag, actually. But I have to tell you something. There's a man out there in the restaurant right now, and I think he is going to be the love of your life. No, I know he is."

She blanches. As anyone would.

"I think you should consider going out there and meeting him," I say. "Your call, of course, but it might be something you'll look back on and be happy about."

She stares at me for a minute like it's now confirmed that I'm part of the conspiracy of crazies, and then she turns on the water and starts washing her hands. "How am I supposed to believe that you know who I'm looking for when you don't even know one thing about me?"

"I know. I'm just a woman in a public bathroom with wine all over her skirt. But don't you believe that things can work out in mysterious ways? That everything is kind of just up to luck—like whether you get into a certain subway car where someone you need to meet is waiting, or whether you enter a shop and start talking to a stranger that you end up loving for the rest of your life?"

"That has *not* happened to me," she says with a bitter laugh.

"It's happening to you tonight," I say. "Just go out there. He's a very nice man in a very tasteful fedora with a little feather on it—I was sitting next to him. In fact, it was his mother who threw the white wine on my skirt, but now she's gone and he's eating all by himself."

"A fedora with a feather?" she says and laughs again.

"Don't be like that. The feather is entirely removable," I say sternly. "And anyway, I'm aware that it sounds crazy, but I'm a matchmaker. I know things by intuition. I read energy. You know how it is that you can feel when people are looking at you across a room or something? Well, I can feel when people match up."

She stares at me for a long time, and then I feel something kind of shift in her, like maybe she remembers that she does believe a tiny bit in intuition and fate. Most people do.

"Well," she says and sighs. "Okay, but I want you to know this is nuts."

I coach her a little: hang with me, be patient, don't get upset by any early signs of awkwardness. Sometimes the universe takes a bit of time setting things in motion. Be cool. Don't worry. I tell her my name is Marnie MacGraw; she says her name is Winnie.

"Oh God," she says. "Why am I doing this?"

Because, I want to say to her, because the universe has gone to a great deal of difficulty to line all this up for you. Just to recap: It required me coming to the restaurant early to rehearse how to ask Patrick a question so major I didn't want to do it in our house, and then spilling my red wine just so a woman visiting from Florida, who had once seen some household guru explain how to clean up wine, could jump up and embarrass her son by throwing her white wine on me. And you had to endure thirty text messages from a man who wasn't going to turn out to be anyone important in your life but was just there to somehow get you to come to this very restaurant at this very time. *And* if we go even further back, it required me moving to Brooklyn because a man jilted me on our honeymoon, which caused his magical matchmaking great-aunt

Blix to be so mad at him that when she died that summer, she left me her brownstone in Park Slope along with all her unfinished matchmaking projects, and that's where I met and fell in love with Patrick, who lived in the basement and was the least likely person for me to love in the whole world, and who I never would have met in a million years because he hates leaving the house. Do you not see how stunning and miraculous this is? And we haven't even had to go back to all the eggs and sperms that had to meet up since the beginning of time in order to create the humans that are participating in this little dance of ours.

"You're doing it because it's going to be great," I say, and we walk out into the dining room.

In the dining room, everything has changed, as though the air itself has softened and become more flexible. People are chatting and drinking cocktails. Patrick is there now, sitting at our table, and when he sees me, he smiles and does his signature ironic wink, which always makes my heart speed up. At the table next to him, the guy, Graham, is sitting alone and scrolling through his phone and picking at an enormous salad and quail egg sliders. When I squint, I can see that he still has the sparkles hovering about him that I saw before. I hold up one finger to Patrick: this may take a second. He nods.

"You didn't tell me the guy's name," she whispers.

"I heard his mother call him Graham."

"His wine-throwing mother?"

"The very one."

"So, according to you, this may all turn out that I someday have a mother-in-law who's nuts? Maybe I don't want that." But she's smiling. She's into it now.

"On the plus side, she does know how to get rid of stains. And she lives in Florida, which is very far away."

"Oh my God, oh my God. What am I doing?"

"Be cool. It's showtime." I intercept Micah as we get closer to the table, and I take him by the elbow and turn my body just so. I want to talk confidentially. I have a whole plan. "Listen, Micah. A favor. Could you move Patrick and me to another table, please? And let this lady sit at our table instead?"

He's shaking his head no. He has a whole list of people waiting for tables, he says; she has to put her name on the list, can't make an exception, blah blah blah.

"See?" says Winnie. "This isn't going to work. Thanks, but I'm just going to go."

"You stay put," I tell her. I try to reason with Micah, but he's not budging.

Patrick comes over then. He puts his arm around my shoulder and leans in and stage whispers, "Why are we having a high-level conference here? Are we contemplating a pitching change? Or overthrowing the government?"

"Marnie is being a little impossible, insisting on rearranging the restaurant."

"She is quite impossible," Patrick agrees. "But maybe you needed to have it rearranged, and the universe hadn't informed you yet."

"Listen," says Winnie. "I'm going to leave. You're all very nice and very weird, but this just isn't my night."

"Stay here," I growl.

Graham now gets up and joins us. "Um. Not to be paranoid, but is this about me, by any chance? And my mother's bad behavior earlier?"

"Your mother?" says Patrick. "Who are you?"

Both Graham and Winnie turn to look at Patrick, and I see how they slide their eyes away immediately upon realizing that his face isn't quite what they were expecting. *This* is why Patrick is an introvert. He was in an awful fire eight years ago or so, and his face is scarred from skin grafts, and his right eye is maybe a little bit crooked. I always have to re-realize how it is that he lives with this every day, with every new encounter—people looking and then flinching. They don't know how to react to the scars, the pinched, too-shiny skin near one eye, the jawline that's not quite symmetrical. They are sorry, I know they are. They don't mean to be cruel, but they're caught by surprise. They look away. I ache for Patrick every time it happens, and I always want to tell him they don't mean it, that they can also see the light that shines out from him. That he's beautiful. Incandescent.

The moment is over quickly. Graham has recovered. "Oh, sorry. I'm Graham Spalding. And my mother threw some wine on your wife before you got here."

Patrick doesn't explain that I'm not his wife. Instead he just introduces himself, and then he looks at me. "You have wine on you?"

"It's better now. Winnie here helped me clean it up."

Winnie is looking at Graham Spalding very carefully. "And where is your wine-throwing mom now?"

"In an Uber, thank God, on the way to the airport," he says.

The universe holds its breath . . . one . . . two . . . three . . .

"Maybe," Graham says, "since there are no tables, you'd like to share mine?"

. . . Aaaaand it exhales. We all go to our rightful places. I can almost feel Blix smiling at me from a spot near the little twinkling fairy lights strung behind the bar.

Now you need to ask him. You've got to set this thing in motion, girl.

I swallow, suddenly nervous.

Patrick is watching me and smiling. "Here's to the James Bond of matchmaking!" he says and lifts his glass. "Another successful exhibition of some of your best tactical maneuvers! This one was kind of epic, suspense-wise. I rate it a ten."

"You're too generous. I thought for a while there that Winnie was going to have to come sit with us until Graham noticed how much he needed her. It was a last-minute save."

He rolls his eyes. "Sure," he says. "Just do me a favor and let me know if you see anyone else needing to be fixed up before dessert and you need to go sit at another table, okay? Or if M calls you into headquarters, and you have to leave."

I put my bracelet up near my ear and tilt my head like I'm getting a message. "All clear for now. All the romances in here seem to be intact for the moment."

He leans forward and whispers, "Nice work. They look like they're hitting it off. Mission accomplished."

"Sssh. Don't look. It's too early to evaluate."

"Not in this case. He's complimenting her on her shoes. He's a goner."

"Patrick. We don't speak of people in love as goners."

He smiles at me and reaches for my hand. "Nonsense. We're all goners here. Happy little goners."

Andre, our favorite waiter, comes over. Patrick says he'll have the lemon aioli squid and I say I will, too, and then we're quiet, and he's staring at me expectantly, so I drink about four gulps of wine because I know it's time to say the thing. Patrick is smiling, with his head tilted to the side, waiting. And my heart is beating ridiculously loud. They can hear it across the room, I'm sure.

"Okay, MacGraw, out with it," he says. "I can't stand the suspense."

"I can't. We need to make polite conversation for a while first. What did you do today?" I fold my hands in my lap.

He exhales. "Okay. What did I do today? Well, let's see. I went to my studio and I stared at the empty canvas I've been staring at all week. And then, let's see, your mother called."

"My mother?" This makes me happy. My mother and Patrick both love to bake, and they're always exchanging recipes.

But then I see that he's frowning. "Yeah," he says. "Not to be alarming or anything, but she said kind of a weird thing. She wanted to talk to you about it, I think, but I guess when she called your number, you couldn't pick up . . ."

"No. I couldn't because—get this, Patrick—there was an old man in the store who hadn't talked to his daughter in five years, and he heard that she had a baby last week, and he wanted to send her flowers and also tell her that he is so sorry for all the times in her life when he wasn't there for her. We all worked for an hour on the note. Everybody in the whole place was in tears by the time we got it written."

"Nothing like a day when the whole shop bursts into tears."

"Oh, stop. You know. It's the best possible kind of tears. Everybody was hugging the old guy and giving him tips on what he could say. It was like pure joy, the whole community helping him." I take a sip of wine. "So, what's going on with my mother? Did I do a terrible thing not picking up?"

"No, I think it's probably fine. She says your dad won't get off the couch. She wants to travel and go places, and he says he's too tired for all that. She sounded a little sad, is all."

I am sure this is no big deal. My parents have been married for forty years, ever since they were teenagers, and they live in the suburbs of Florida (they happen to be actual Florida natives and not transplants), and he likes to play golf and she swims at the Y and they finish each other's sentences, and bicker in the irritating way of people who have long ago turned their differences into what they consider a kind of amusing road show, for the benefit of an audience, usually my older sister Natalie and me. My parents are fine. Their marriage is an example to all their friends. They're an institution.

"Tell me what else you did today. Did you take Bedford for a walk?"

"Oh God. It was awful." He laughs. "We went to the park, and Bedford dragged me over to the playground, where he took a kid's sneaker and ran off with it. So when I brought it back, the kid started screaming bloody murder at the sight of my scary face. And then the mom got all upset, and she yelled at the kid, which was terrible because he has the perfect right to be freaked out by my frightfulness. And then Bedford took the opportunity to grab the *baby's* shoe out of the diaper bag, and he runs off with it, and she and I both start running after him, but then the kid starts crying to be picked up, and I don't even know how it happened, but suddenly the mom just handed over her baby to me and picked up the older kid and went to get the shoe back!" He shakes his head. "Can you imagine? She just gives me her *baby*, and you know me—I don't do babies, and I didn't know how to hold the baby right, and so it stared right at my face in shock for about ten seconds and then it just let out this bloodcurdling scream and started wailing like the end of the world, and then the mom came running back without the baby's shoe that Bedford took, probably realizing what a crazy thing it was to just hand a weird man her most prized possession—so *I* had to go find the baby shoe, and bring it back, which made everybody start crying again at the sight of me, and my new position is that dogs and babies are the *worst*."

My heart sinks. I put down my wineglass.

"Um, so . . . what just happened?" he says. "What did I say? Tell me."

There's no choice. I have to come out with it, even though my voice is suddenly clogged in my throat, and my heart is hammering away something awful. "Patrick," I say, "I-I want a baby. I need to have a baby."

He stares at me. "Wait. So *this* is what you were going to ask me?"

"Yes. Listen to me. I need us to have a baby, Patrick. And you would be such an amazing father, and our lives would be so full and wonderful, and I can't imagine *not* having a baby with you, and I'm thirty-three, and I want this so much, so very much."

I'm ignoring the fact that his eyes have gone opaque and that he has put his napkin down.

He laughs, one of those hollow laughs that makes me want to hide my head. "*What* is this ludicrous idea you have that I would be an amazing father? You should ask the woman in the park today how amazing

I am with children. Marnie, honey, I am useless when it comes to kids. Beyond useless."

"You know that's not true," I say. "That one baby was not a referendum on you."

"No. It is true," he says. "It is definitely true. You love me, and so you choose to overlook a million things about me that are ruined. But look at me, Marnie. Honestly. Look at my face and my arms and try to tell me I'm a person who should be a father. I'm not father material. And the thing is, you really do know this. Which is why you're so nervous."

"I know the opposite." I reach over and take his hand, which makes him flinch just the slightest bit. His hands are scarred and they hurt him, because when the fire came, he ran toward it, holding his hands out, trying to save his girlfriend. He is the best person in the world. "Patrick, please. This is so important to me. It's everything. All the magic, all the possibilities of life—it's all right here for us. I need a child. I need us to be parents of a child. I want to do this with you. You'll be a wonderful father. You have so much to give. You'll see. It's *life*. It's us—it's you, coming back to life. Affirming what's good—"

He interrupts me. "But I'm happy, Marnie," he says quietly. "I like our lives just the way they are. I don't need another affirmation of what's good. I have what's good."

I lean forward, as if I can persuade him by getting closer. "But this will bring us so much more happiness! Think of it. We can take this next big step. I know we can do it. I just know we can."

He's silent for a long time. "I-I don't know what else I can say to you. I can't do it."

"I haven't ever led you astray, have I? We'll be together through this. It'll be wonderful. Trust me."

He picks up my hand and kisses it. Kisses every knuckle while he looks into my eyes. My heart is like a trapped little bird in my chest; it thinks—it hopes—that there could be a shift, just like earlier. That the universe can show up at the right time and bring light to a situation, to an impasse. I can't be the one to convince him, but something else can.

And then, wouldn't you know, the molecules do shift, and suddenly Graham and Winnie are standing there, looming like happy idiotic bobbleheads right at our table. They are leaving, and they are just so happy and they want to thank us for making sure they got introduced—and oh, they couldn't help but sense that something special was happening at our table, too! What is it? Can we talk about it?

"Not sure we should discuss it just yet," says Patrick in a low voice, "but we may be considering running for president. Or buying the Knicks basketball team. One or the other."

Winnie's mouth makes an O, and Graham laughs and pulls her to him. "In other words, Win, it's none of our business."

Win. He calls her Win already. You see? They'll be engaged by tomorrow night, the wedding will take place next Tuesday, and by a week from Saturday they'll own a house and she'll be pregnant. With twins.

I beam them over some scraps of love that seem to be floating around the table, and she leans over and gives me a quick hug and whispers, "Thank you, I'll never forget this," and I tell her I have a flower shop, Best Buds, and if she ever wants to, she should come and tell me what happened—and after they leave, Patrick and I ask Andre to pack up our food, which we now know we cannot eat.

It's a hot, humid night outside, almost like a jungle, and we decide, without even talking about it, to walk all the way home to Park Slope. It's as though we know that all these intense feelings can't fit inside our house. We need to work some of them off before we get there.

He holds my hand, but his back is stiff and his eyes look straight ahead, and I'm not at all sure if he's holding my hand like he's going to change his mind and be the father of my child, or if he's holding my hand like he's comforting me before announcing once and for all his final answer that he can't give me what I want.

I know deep down inside me that I am going to need to be able to live with whichever this is going to be, which is something that I really, really hate about life. The way you know exactly what would make you happy and what you need, but you still might not get it. This just doesn't work for me at all. That's where Blix was such an expert: she said you just have to keep going toward what you want and being open to surprise—because maybe, just maybe you're really not the expert, and there might be something better you haven't thought of.

Still, I would just like to put the universe on notice that I might not be able to give up the idea of having a baby and remain a mostly pleasant person.

When we get home, he goes upstairs and runs a bath, and while I'm brushing my teeth, he comes in, strips down, and gets in the tub.

"Wait," I say. "I want to get in, too."

"You should." He pours in some divine-smelling bubble bath. Lavender, I think.

I set up little tea lights all around the edge of the tub, turn off the overhead light, and then climb in next to him—it's a huge claw-foot tub from probably 1900, so we both fit—and I lie back against his strong chest, my hair drifting in the water, fanning out around my shoulders. This is what I like about Patrick—the way that when things are tough between us, he doesn't look for reasons to keep things bad. He wants to find the place where we can be okay again. His heart is beating underneath me, and even just the sound of it is so lovely and reassuring.

We don't talk, but after a bit he soaps my body and his touch is silky and sure. He bends his head down and kisses my shoulder and I laugh because he's taken in a mouthful of bubbles. I twist around and fashion them into a beard for him and then kiss him on the mouth, which fills my own mouth with bubbles, too.

Afterward, we stumble our way to bed, sleepy and calm at last, and he pulls me to him, and we make love very carefully—like we're making up for something hard that we might not be able to recover from. He is so loving and sweet, so warm and familiar.

At the crucial point, he reaches over to get a condom, as usual. I admit that I had entertained a tiny bit of hope that maybe he would skip it, but nope. I close my eyes and try not to be disappointed. It's okay.

It's not until we're all done and he's getting himself all put back together, that he turns to me with a shocked look on his face. "It broke," he says. His eyes are wide.

"What broke?"

"The condom. It's completely ripped."

I get up on one elbow. "Are you kidding me? It broke?"

"Oh my God. Did *you* do this? Is this some of the Marnie magic at work here?"

"You think I have powers over latex?"

"Marnie," he says. "I think you have powers over everything. I haven't yet seen the thing that you don't seem to know how to control."

He flops down on the pillow. And I'm relieved to see that he's laughing, even though it's not altogether a happy laugh. "You are a minx of the highest order," he says. "And oh my God, if we end up with a baby because of this . . ."

I sock him in the arm. "If we get a baby from this, it'll just mean that there was a baby out there who was waiting for us to agree to be its parents, and it saw a way to make that happen, and it will be this wonderful, magical baby that was supposed to come to us."

"Marnie."

"What?"

"Could you just . . . not? Please."

Long after he's asleep, I lie perfectly still for a long time, and I have to admit it: I am watching the full moon through the wavy glass in the window, and I am visualizing all the little sperms energetically swimming toward my hopeful, patient little ovum, who is no doubt jumping up and down and cheering them on. "You did it!" she's yelling. "You broke through! Hurry! We've got so much work to do! I'm going to get right to it, drawing up the blueprints for some arms and legs and a heartbeat. But first—implantation, here we come!"

The universe has so many tricks up its sleeve.

And now—well, I just hold up my hand toward the ceiling, where there might be the slightest little bit of mist forming up in the highest corner. Is it Blix, smiling down on us? Blix, who knew from the beginning that we were supposed to be together.

She had a mantra she lent me. I pinch my fingers and say it over and over again:

Whatever happens, love that.

CHAPTER TWO
PATRICK

It's nine o'clock in the morning, and Patrick, who has been awake since four thirty, is in the living room, busily hyperventilating. The front door just closed behind Marnie, who was tripping off to the flower shop practically singing, swishing her long skirt, leaning down to kiss his coffee-soaked lips, ruffling his hair, kissing his nose and the tops of his ears. The whole happy dance bit.

He should perhaps go look for a paper bag to breathe into before he falls over on the floor.

Did he just get her pregnant? He did, didn't he? It would be just his luck. He should write a letter to the condom company. *You should be ashamed of yourselves, making such a stupid, flimsy latex product. Where is your pride in your work? Do you care nothing for those of us who should not be permitted to reproduce?*

Instead, he just sits there, his head in his hands. *Patrick,* he thinks. *You are the world's biggest idiot. She wants a baby, and, dude, you know she's going to MAGIC the whole world until she gets one.*

Oh God, he is so doomed. He loves her so much, but he is not, and never has been, fatherhood material. He has never once looked over at a baby and thought, *Wow, I wish I'd made that kid! How do I get me some of those toothless, drooly kisses? How fun would it be to see if I could get by on four hours of sleep every night for the next eighteen years?*

But he's watched as she flirts and coos over babies in public and rhapsodizes about the ones who come into her shop. He once listened, mystified, while she described a scene of a baby rubbing a banana into his own ear. She was laughing so hard she could barely even get the story out. So what kind of denial had he been living in, thinking that this subject would never come up? That she'd never look at him across a table with her big eyes and her trembly voice and beg him to have a baby with her? That he'd never have that uncomfortable moment of telling her no?

That then a condom wouldn't break that same night?

He looks over at Bedford and Roy, her dog and his cat, who are curled up together on the rug, having their usual midmorning nap. They've forged an unlikely friendship since Patrick moved upstairs to live with Marnie; they even have their own Instagram fans for their interspecies cuddling, @BedfordlovesRoy. But cute as they are, it has to be noted that they have been abject failures as baby substitutes.

"Guys," he tells them. "I'd like to believe that you really tried, but I'm afraid you didn't even come close." Roy doesn't bother to respond, of course, but Bedford wags his tail. "Nope. Don't bother wagging now. None of us has done enough to keep her from wanting a kid. Not a single one of us."

He rubs his face, hard. He needs to get hold of himself. Go take a shower, stop drinking coffee, switch to water, and get himself to work. Work might take his mind off this situation, if he ever did any of it, that is. He's supposed to be turning himself into a painter, now that the fire ended his career as a sculptor. At least that's the plan. He hasn't been able to do much. He sucks at painting, is the truth of it.

He and Marnie even converted one of the apartments into a studio for him last year when he decided he was mentally well enough to do art again. Not sculpture, because of the damage to his hands. But he should be able to paint. Marnie made that decision for him, really. She eased out the tenants who were living there—they needed to be on their own anyway, she said—and then the two of them cleaned out the rooms and repainted the walls and installed shelves for his supplies. Art tables appeared. Easels. Lighting. A studio futon. It was his own space, with the perfect light coming in from the north-facing windows.

Nothing, nothing, like the studio from before.

The studio of the fire.

Anneliese briefly rises up in his head, as she does whenever he thinks of anything having to do with that day. He sees her tilting her face up, catching the light, smiling at him playfully.

Not screaming today, as she usually is when she shows up.

He wonders briefly if he and Anneliese had ever talked about having a child. He doesn't think so. They were young though, so maybe it simply hadn't occurred to them yet. Maybe it would have eventually come up. And, you know what, maybe he could have been a father back then if that's what she'd wanted.

But now. No. There are a million airtight reasons he doesn't want a child, reasons that any person possessing a shred of sanity would agree with.

Number one: He looks scary. Children shrink from him. One of his eyes looks like it was installed crooked from the factory, and besides that, the skin on his face is stretched out and shiny, the result of the thirteen surgeries he had. His mouth is crooked. His jaw isn't symmetrical anymore.

And number two: Even if the baby eventually got used to the wonky look of him (which he assumes it would because people can get used to anything), he'd have to go out in public all the damn time, at first to push the baby carriage because he's pretty sure the law requires that people air out babies from time to time, and then the next thing you know, he'd be hauling himself to playgrounds, and every damn day he'd have to endure scenes like the one in the park yesterday, when he took down both a toddler and a baby with his freakish appearance.

Number three—and this may be the worst of all—the well-meaning public. God, he hates this one, when he gets used as the example for the lesson on "Why It's Important to Be Polite to the Abnormal." (Or what's the politically correct term now? Atypical? That's probably it. *Atypical.*) He can envision his own child's well-meaning young teacher saying in a sweet singsong to her class of monsters: "Now, children, Mr. Delaney can't help it that he looks butt-ugly and is so very atypical. But we, the beautiful, need to be polite to him, because he's still a human being. We have to be tolerant and pretend he's like us."

No, no, no, no, and NO.

Of course Marnie doesn't get any of this. She calls him luminous. She says no one sees him the way he sees himself. She says he doesn't even know what he really looks like, that he's beautiful, which of course is a crock of shit, some lie she tells because she loves him, and frankly he could spend a thousand years and still not figure out how *that* even happened, that she started loving him. Apparently Blix's matchmaking had something to do with it; Marnie believes that Blix, who rented the downstairs apartment to him long before she'd even *heard* of Marnie, somehow arranged the whole romance between them. He's never been sure he believed in all that. But whatever. Doesn't matter now. He's in love with her. He's become comfortable with being part of a couple again.

Oddly enough, they don't really have that much in common. She has about ten times the number of emotions he has, for one thing—she cries and laughs and sighs and smiles and yawns and complains and leaps up off the couch and performs impromptu dances—and each emotion catches him by surprise as it comes careening in. Who has the energy to feel that many feelings?

The truth is, when he's around Marnie, he can mostly shut out Anneliese's screaming in his head. He can even get himself to *almost* believe in the narrative of the culture: that everybody has some tragic thing to carry, and that you're supposed to take your tragedy and drag it deep into the compost pile of your heart, where it can eventually germinate and allow something new in you to be born. Besides that, he also knows that he came back to life, and that Blix and then Marnie carried him most of that distance.

But—here's the thing—he has come as far into life as he can come. He cannot go farther. The baby thing—no, no. No. Absolutely not.

Because what he knows but what she doesn't seem to get is that deep down he is still broken. He watched his girlfriend die in front of him, and he knew then and he still knows that it was his fault.

He lives this every day—the sound of the explosion, the way Anneliese was immediately engulfed in flames, and he remembers staring at her, his mind trying to put it all together, and then time slowing down, and him running and running toward her, holding his arms out to catch her, and she was screaming—he could see her screaming rather than hear her—and she was lit up, her long black hair was now only a flame, and he remembers noticing that he was on fire, too, even though he couldn't feel anything, and then he fell and squares of black filled in his field of vision, replacing the bright orange ball of light that burned into his eyeballs.

No one will say this—not the doctors, not the fire officials, not the therapists who tried to help him—but he knows he should have stopped it from happening, that he simply wasn't paying attention when he should have been. Why didn't he notice the smell of gas? Why wasn't he the one who got up that day to make the coffee, the one who turned on the burner that lit the spark that caused the explosion? Most mornings he did the coffee while she set up her easel, but this one day, the day when it mattered most, where was he? Across the room, doing some stupid task he doesn't remember for a sculpture that would never get made.

So he has to live with Anneliese's screams. It's the price he owes for what he did.

There's something worse. He knows he should have called her parents—Grace and Kerwin Cunningham are two of the finest people he ever met, and he was there when their daughter died, and he hasn't been able to face them. He was in a coma at the time of Anneliese's funeral. He received a note from Grace while he was in the hospital, a few shattered and heartbroken sentences. She didn't *say* it had been his fault, but he knows she must think so.

Just about eight years ago now, and every day is another day he's doing the wrong thing by hiding. He keeps their cell phone number folded up in a box with things he's moved from place to place. A couple of times he's punched in two numbers, maybe three, and then hung up.

And now there is this woman in his life who sees sparkles, and for whom every story is a love story. He has to be very, very careful not to risk his entire heart again. He loves her, but he has to hold something back. He could lose her, too.

His phone dings, and he leans over and picks it up.

It's Marnie texting him.

OMG! I have seen 15 babies just since I left the house. FIFTEEN ADORABLE BABY HUMANS.

He is reasonably sure this isn't an over-the-top number, not in Brooklyn on a summer day. Instead of answering, he sighs and googles "How often do condoms break?"

Google instantly replies that studies show somewhere between eight-tenths of 1 percent and 40 percent of men report condom breakage at some point in their lives.

Very helpful statistic, Google. Why did you even bother?

He types in: "And can you get pregnant if the condom breaks?"

Google says of course you can. What are you, some kind of dunce? Don't you know *anything?*

Okay, so Google didn't say that last part, but he can picture it chuckling at the hopelessness of the question.

Bedford comes over with one of Patrick's sneakers and drops it onto his stomach. Time for a walk.

"Today," he tells Bedford as they head out the front door, "we are enacting a new policy. We are not going to the park, and we are not going near any children."

A text dings. Marnie.

Also, Patrick, just FYI. I now think we are undergoing an INVASION OF INFANTS. There must be a store somewhere handing them out. #BabiesRule #HereComeTheTots #EvenTwins.

He stops by a lamppost and types: *You may be in a scene from Night of the Living Dead with babies as the zombies. You should run. Proven fact: they WILL eat your brains.*

"Actually," he informs Bedford, who wags his tale in agreement, "they already have eaten her brains."

CHAPTER THREE
MARNIE

You know how it is when you get a new car, and suddenly every car you see zooming down the road is the very brand you just bought?

Well, that's what is happening to me with babies today.

I'm on my way to work, and I swear there are babies everywhere: spilling out of strollers, being cuddled in front carriers and backpacks, riding along freestyle on their mamas' hips—and several are even perched on top of men's shoulders and are using their fathers' skulls as makeshift bongo drums. Oh, I can just *see* Patrick with a baby on his shoulders. Both of them smiling down at me, the baby grinning toothlessly and reaching down to grab his daddy's ears, while Patrick laughs.

This calls for another text.

It's got to be some kind of sign, all these babies, I write. *Just saw #16. Cutest one yet!*

This shows that the universe is obviously on the side of me having a kid. First, it destroyed a perfectly adequate condom, and now it's *throwing* me into the paths of all the cutest babies and parents.

As soon as I walk into Best Buds, Kat, my business partner, looks up from the counter where she is cutting the dead stems off of yesterday's flowers and says, "Oh my God! Look at you. He went for it, didn't he? You look radiant! I'll bet you're probably already pregnant!"

I give her a big smile and do a little shimmy. Kat and I had spent the day before practicing my speech for Patrick, which she was sure was going to go just fine. "Amazingly enough," I tell her, "I just might be."

"See? I told you, didn't I? He wants a kid as much as you do."

"Welllll," I say. I put my purse down in the cubby under the counter, first taking my phone out and slipping it into my pocket for when Patrick texts me. We write to each other all day long. "Actually, he thinks it's an insane idea. In fact, he said no."

"He said *no*?" She tilts her head, adjusts her smile wattage downward. "Then how are you possibly pregnant? Did you find some other dude overnight or something?"

"Perhaps you've heard of condom failure."

"Noooo! Get out of here. That did not happen."

"Oh, but yes."

She stands there staring at me. "I have never been so in awe of you as I am at this moment."

I laugh. "Why? I didn't have anything to do with it."

"Of course you did. Marnie! I would bet my whole month's salary on your ability to somehow manifest a condom breaking. I've watched you up close. I know your powers." She smiles and lowers her voice, even though there is no one else around to overhear her. "Also, that's how I got pregnant with Jazz. Though not intentionally, of course. But the condom did break."

"Really," I say. "I did not *intentionally* break the condom. But it is possible that there's some baby out there wanting to be born, and that that's who broke it."

"Thank you for not saying that the universe broke it," she says.

Kat is my age, but she already has two adorable middle schoolers, Jazz and Tish, who spend half a week with her and half a week with their dad, who is remarried and lives on the Upper West Side. She started working here last year when she dropped by the shop one day and noticed that I might not be using, shall we say, all the best business practices. I was bungling several important tasks of owning a business, like for instance, billing, ordering, paying bills, knowing how to get the right people for maintenance, and figuring out taxes, just to name a few things right off the top. I was also a little bit flaky with the flowers, which a lot of people think may be Job One when you're a florist.

But that's just it. I like the flowers just fine; they're pretty, and they please people and give them an excuse to drop in. Sometimes the flowers even make us some money. But make no mistake: I'm here for the community. I love the people who seem to gravitate here, hanging out telling their stories, laughing, eating, juggling oranges, drinking tea, polishing their toenails, practicing their marriage proposals or their job interviews, writing books, writing notes to people they love—and I don't much care whether they need a bouquet or not. I've turned the back room into kind of a salon for them—I put in thick lavender carpet, painted the walls white, strung some fairy lights, and bought a soft, squishy rose-colored sectional sofa and a wicker desk, some beanbag chairs, candles, bookshelves, and about a million pillows.

Naturally people started showing up—Lola, my neighbor and Blix's old best friend, comes in to knit several times a week; a guy named Ernst brings his laptop and works on his screenplay there because he says the vibe is so good for his characters' dialogue; Christine sits cross-legged on the floor and writes letters to her old boyfriend who doesn't want to take her back (we're waiting for a match for her to show up and get her to leave this old BF alone)—and then there are a group of three high school girls who regularly come bounding in with such panache and swagger that Kat and I have taken to calling them the Amazings.

Kat, a former accounting major who only took the job if I promised to stop using the word *universe* in her presence, at first didn't see the point of my little back room salon.

She was all like, "Aren't we a flower business? This back room side hustle you've got going on will not pay the bills. It's what my grandmother would have said was just frippery."

I hugged her. "That's it! Frippery is the perfect name for it." And I painted a little sign, THE FRIPPERY, for over the archway. It matches the words on our frosted glass front door—BEST BUDS painted with little vines and buds weaving through the gold letters.

"But can't we at least suggest that people make a purchase every once in a while?" she whined, and I said, "It's all going to work out fine as long as people are having fun; it always does." Which she said was the most ridiculous thing she'd ever heard a business owner say.

But you know what? It has worked out just fine.

Anyway, Kat is now a believer, and she even permits me to point out the accomplishments of the universe once or twice a month now. This is because I fixed her up with the UPS guy one slow afternoon. Of course, it wasn't me fixing her up; it was the U, that word that we do not utter. Whenever he was around, she was covered in sparkles, and he was just the same. Now that she's in love, she's less irritated by all the wacky talk about energy and spirits. Love does that to people, I notice. Improves their outlook on life.

"By the way," she says, as I'm heading into the Frippery to fluff the pillows, "did you happen to see a woman and a little girl out there when you came in?"

I've been studying myself in the mirror to see if I can detect any signs of first-day pregnancy, but I come back out. "Scads of them. Women and baby girls everywhere you look."

"No. This is a middle-sized girl, maybe seven or eight. They were looking for you."

"Nope."

31

"I told them you'd be in later, and they said maybe they'd go get some breakfast. They flew in from England last night, and the mom looked like she could really use some caffeine. I sent them to Yolk."

"England's a long way to come for a bouquet of roses," I say.

"Maybe your reputation as a matchmaker is now international."

I wave her off. "The important question of the day is: Do you think I could really be pregnant?"

"You really could be pregnant."

"Huh. And I suppose Patrick would eventually get used to the idea, wouldn't he? I mean, he wouldn't leave me or anything."

She stares at me. "Good heavens, what's happened to you? You're the one who'd be telling somebody else that hell yes, everything's going to work out! I can just hear you now: 'It's life, it's meant to be, it's'"— she makes a face—"'the *universe* doing what it does so well!'"

"I know, I know. It's just that I want this so badly. I've never wanted anything this much. It makes me scared I won't get it."

She rolls her eyes. "Did you talk to Toaster Blix about it?"

"Didn't have a chance this morning," I say. I once made the mistake of telling Kat how I sense Blix's presence near her old temperamental toaster, an appliance that insists on throwing bread at me on a regular basis. And how, in times of trouble, I can simply go stand near the toaster and feel her energy there. Kat, of course, finds this hilarious.

"Well, go into the Frippery then and see if you can summon her from the dead. She'll set you straight. Remind you who you are."

CHAPTER FOUR
TESSA

It takes all her willpower, but Tessa Farrell makes a point of not checking her cell phone all the way through breakfast, even though it's been vibrating in her bag the whole time she and Fritzie have been in the restaurant. (If you can refer to this too-precious little sliver of real estate as a restaurant—it's called Yolk, according to the name burned into the piece of wood over the door. If you want to be technically correct, Tessa thinks, this place is actually closer to being a pretentious little closet that somehow got crammed with six tables.)

It's Richard, of course. The phone. Sending erotic messages and texts, then trying to follow up with a phone call to say dirty things in her ear and make her laugh. And although she'd give anything just now to hear his liquid, chocolaty baritone transmitted through the transatlantic satellites, she won't allow herself that.

Good God. How has this happened to her? This stupid aching need. She hasn't ever had one moment of sentimentality her whole life, and now she can't think of anything besides how much she loves Richard and how much she wants to be in bed with him. It's beyond ridiculous. She always thought that the whole business of falling in love was merely a hoax perpetrated by the movie industry to get people to feel bad about their own dull lives. Or, worse, propaganda to get people to consign their lives to perpetuating the species. She'd lived her whole life resisting all of that rubbish.

And now it's all she can do to keep from running out into the street and throwing herself in the path of the nearest Uber, making the driver take her to the airport, so she can catch a plane and fling herself into Richard's arms. Richard, who last time they were together stopped her anxious yammering on about something by simply leaning over her and smiling and saying, "Will you fucking shut up and kiss me?"

She wants so much to talk to him that her head throbs with the need for his voice, but Fritzie is watching her closely, and Fritzie hates when she's absorbed with the phone or with Richard. She has an eight-year-old's razor-sharp instinct for sniffing out a rival for attention, and so she despises Richard. She puts her hands over her ears at the mention of his name, and over the past few months, whenever Tessa would leave Fritzie with a sitter so that she and Richard could have a date, Fritzie would scream bloody murder and then do some horrible thing. Once she threw out the new lacy thong Tessa had guiltily bought for herself, casually tossed it right in the dumpster, laughing. Another time she poured Tessa's perfume down the sink—Chanel No. 5, which Richard had given Tessa for their one-month anniversary. When he gave it to her, he said she reminded him of Coco Chanel, and for a whole week he called her his Coco.

Tessa sighs and regards her plate of golden-yolked eggs and the multigrain toast, buttered so precisely to the edges that it looks almost surgical. Fritzie, slouching in her chair, is pushing her food around the plate. She won't eat. She knows her mother wants her to eat.

Outside the window, all of Brooklyn—weird, crowded, hot, overcast, Augusty Brooklyn—tramps by. So different from their home in San Francisco.

And oh so different from where Richard is—gone away on a year-long fellowship to teach poetry in Rome, living in a little *pensione* over a tavern. She doesn't even really know what a *pensione* is, because she's not the sort of woman people invite to *pensiones*, but he wants her to come. He wants her. That's what all these texts are about. He wants her. In the fever dream of the last months, kissing in doorways, making love in the shower with the water running so Fritzie couldn't hear them, they'd worked out a plan to be together. She was meant to be already on her way there. Instead, she's in the overcrowded, godforsaken Northeast, barely able to breathe, and since he's been out of her sight, everything between them feels to her as though it could fall apart at any moment. All her plans, so carefully stacked up in her head, are like dinner plates that have all started to wobble at once.

"You *know*, I think you're supposed to be talking to me," Fritzie says, leaning on her hand with her elbow propped on the table. She's exhausted from the flight, a red-eye that got them into JFK at midnight, New York time. That would have been bad enough, but they were still on England time, so it felt like it was five a.m. They caught the flight after taking a train to Heathrow from the countryside, where they'd been staying with Tessa's mother, Helaine. Plan A had been that the visit would go so well that Helaine would be thrilled to keep Fritzie for the school year and allow Tessa to go to Rome—but Helaine had been horrified at the idea. The whole visit had unraveled rather suddenly and there'd been a terrible row, and Tessa and Fritzie had left in a huff.

So that meant Plan B: New York. And the guy she hadn't talked to in nine years.

By the time the plane landed at Kennedy and they'd checked into the Hyatt, Fritzie was too keyed up to sleep. Jumping on the bed and turning the lights on and off. This morning her eyes are puffy and the skin underneath them looks smudged, and her straight brown hair, always tangled, is truly a wild bloody mess, and her personality has gone to hell besides. She screeched when Tessa had tried to comb her hair, cried when she had to brush her teeth. So, fine. Tessa is just going to try to get through the day. Today and then the next day and the next, and by then, maybe by then she'll have scoped everything out, decided how to proceed.

"Gaia's mum says that mealtimes are very valuable times to be together, because that's when you can teach me about life," Fritzie says.

Tessa has heard enough about Gaia's perfect mom to last her entire lifetime, and she particularly isn't having any of it right now. She says, "Well, when I figure out life, you'll be the first to know. Now finish your eggs."

Fritzie sits up straighter and makes her eyes go round. "You always say that people should just eat what their stomachs tell them to eat and they don't have to finish the food on their plate just because some people think wasting is a bad thing. You *said* that. And now you're telling me I have to finish my eggs. So which is it?"

Tessa feels her jaw aching. "Fritzie. Please. Just stop."

"Stop whaaaaat? What am I doing?"

"Stop being so bloody ornery." She puts her fingers on her temples. Fritzie slumps back in her chair, chewing on a lock of her hair, and swinging her legs against the table leg, and watches the cook and the waitress, who are flirting with each other.

When Tessa feels calmer, she smiles and says the thing the counselor said she should reiterate often: "Listen, Fritzie, we're on the same side, you and I. We're both tired, but let's try to have a good day, all right?"

Fritzie picks up a spoon and tries to get it to stick onto her nose, her newest obsession ever since she'd seen it done on YouTube.

"Why did you have me anyway?" she says in a dangerous voice, and as soon as she starts to talk, the spoon falls to the floor with a clatter. The waitress looks over, startled.

"Well. I wanted you," Tessa says slowly. Which is not altogether precisely true. Fritzie was actually the product of a drunken night, a little mistaken encounter really—and actually Tessa was forty at the time and stupidly didn't think she could get pregnant, and then—oops!—there Fritzie was, thumping around in her uterus a few months later like she owned the place.

Fritzie is shaking her head. "Nuh-uh. I heard Grandmum telling Pearl that you had me by accident, and that *you* thought it was going to be fun raising a kid, but now you think it's too hard and you don't like it anymore." She doesn't look at Tessa while she says this, simply keeps rearranging the flatware, moving it all around. "It's okay if that's what you think," she says, thrusting her chin out. "I don't care." Her fingernails are dirty, her face has a smear of jelly on it, and there's something sticky tangled in her hair.

"That is not true," Tessa says. "I love you very, very much!" She feels her blood pounding in her head. It's horrifying, the things her mum says. And within earshot of a child! In the thick of the fight, Helaine accused her of being the worst mother in the world. And, who knows, maybe she is. It certainly doesn't come easily for her. She loves Fritzie, she does, but she's just no good at handling everything.

Motherhood has so many stipulations and rules, and so many people with opinions about how you're doing. Even before Richard came along, she had trouble paying attention to everything. She gets caught up in her own projects—the maths problems she loves to work on, and her grad students she needs to advise, and she forgets stuff. Like dinnertime. How is it that there have to be three meals made and served every damn day—seven days a week? Who made *that* the norm? Life has become a series of commands she is required by law to say: Eat your food, do your homework, be quieter, get away from the stove, stop talking, hurry up, not that channel, take a bath, go to bed.

And Fritzie seems smarter and tougher every year. Only eight years old—and already her huge saucer eyes are exhibiting a wounded, blaming expression that Tessa finds alarming. Has she somehow caused this in her child? Has she already ruined her? Not given her a proper family?

"Tell me about my bio-daddy," she'd demanded one night, and Tessa had had to take a deep breath. *Him.* What was she supposed to say?

"Well," she said slowly, "as you might imagine, he was very handsome, and he was younger than I was, and so charming."

"Why isn't he with us then?"

"I knew him for just two nights. And that was it between us. We went our separate ways."

"Two nights? Why didn't he want to stay with me?"

"Well, he didn't know about you."

"How come he didn't know about me?"

"Because I didn't tell him."

"Why didn't you tell him?"

Tessa found herself launching into the biological explanation about sperm and eggs, how it was the woman's job to carry the fetus, (they had a tiresome, protracted moment about the weirdness of the word *fetus*) and that the man can escape scot-free, never knowing what his contribution was. In fact, men needed to be told. Women had to tell them.

Fritzie was bouncing on the bed on her butt. "Why didn't you tell him you had a fetus?"

How to go into this? "Because it wasn't that kind of thing. It wasn't a forever thing. It was just two very, very lovely nights."

She stopped talking then because Fritzie had gotten mad.

"He should know about me! Why didn't you tell him? He might *want* to know me! Did you ever think of that?"

No. Actually, Tessa *hadn't* ever thought of that. But when Helaine said she wouldn't keep Fritzie, the idea of sending her to her father seemed like a plausible plan. Why not? He'd been a nice guy. She'd been friends—or acquaintances, really—with his sister. Elizabeth. They were good people. Maybe he *would* like to know his kid. Just for a while. Not forever or anything.

She just wants a bit of time off. That's all she's asking for. One little tiny academic year away from responsibility. Richard wants her to come, but the place he has is small, he says. Too cramped. It's no place for a child. Tessa knows that what he means is that he isn't interested in being a father figure to Fritzie. And she doesn't blame him. She can't imagine him becoming a proper stepfather, and, even worse, she can't imagine herself worrying about Fritzie in some Italian *pensione*.

Still, it's a crazy plan. One of her craziest. She'd been so sure Helaine would want to keep Fritzie that she'd gone ahead and taken a sabbatical at work and arranged for one of her grad students to live in their flat.

And then . . . no. Just no.

Fritzie is standing up, tracing the ring from the water glass around and around on the table, sliding packets of Truvia into the wetness and soaking them.

"So what are we going to do now?" she says, her voice pitched perfectly into a whine that shreds Tessa's nerve endings. "Are we going back to that place to see if the matchmaker is there yet?"

"No, I don't think so." They'd come from a little shop, a florist. Where his girlfriend worked apparently. Elizabeth had told her that. Elizabeth, whom she'd reached—amazingly enough—from her mum's house after the row. She'd made it sound all casual . . . Is he still in Brooklyn? Still doing art? She didn't mention the kid.

And as soon as she'd gotten off the call, she'd booked the plane tickets to New York. She had to pay the highest possible fare for such late notice, of course. But it was worth it, to sweep out of Helaine's house with no further explanation. And now here they were, on their way to finding him. She had his cell phone number, but she should do it in person. And maybe it would be best, she'd decided, to see the matchmaker girlfriend first. Pave the way, you know.

But then the matchmaker hadn't been in. It was too early, the person there said. And now Tessa is feeling too dispirited to go back. She needs to take some time and think things through—not simply careen from one possible solution to another. Take a few deep breaths, try to get a grip.

"What is a matchmaker, anyway?" Fritzie asks.

"She's somebody who helps people who want to fall in love."

The waitress, gliding by with the check, smiles. "Oh! Wait! Are you going to see the matchmaker? You don't mean Marnie, by any chance?"

Tessa nods.

"She is totally amazing," the waitress says. She has eyes that look like Bing cherries, so dark and shiny, and a charmingly messy bun on the top of her head. "Omigod. You'll totally love her. She got me together with Barney here. One day she came in here to eat breakfast with a friend, and I was working, and Barney was just this guy passing by in the street, and all of a sudden she jumped up and ran outside and chased him down. It was insane! Brought him back here, too. She said she saw sparkles that meant we were supposed to be together. And now here we are. When she's on her game, there's nothing she can't do." She looks over at the cook. "Isn't that right, honey? We owe her big-time."

Fritzie is looking from the waitress to the cook and back to Tessa. Her eyes are wide. The cook, handsome with a face that looks so perfectly stubbled it's as though he might have painted on his whiskers, is snapping his towel and grinning self-consciously.

The waitress says, "So tell me, are you looking to get matched up with somebody? Because Marnie is the absolute best. I literally don't know how she does it, but she's super good."

"No, no," says Tessa, flustered now, like she's been caught hoping for love. "It's not that. I'm not looking to meet anybody."

"She's not looking to meet anybody, because she's already got a Richard," says Fritzie. And for once, she says his name in a nice way. She puts one hand on her hip, thrusting out the other hip like an adult would do. "My mum's in love with Richard, you see, but he's moved to Italy for the year and she wants to go and be with him, but the trouble is, he doesn't have room for a kid. So we're not really sure what we're going to do with me. We have a lot to figure out."

Tessa feels a pulse of shock.

"Wow," says the waitress. She blinks in surprise. "Well, good luck with everything. I'm sure Marnie will help if she can." She looks at Tessa and smiles.

Tessa busies herself with getting cash out of her purse. Bills are stuffed every which way into her bag, a function of traveling and buying airport snacks. She grabs a wad of cash and gives it over, and the waitress takes it and moves away. Tessa feels a buzzing in her ears.

"Wait," says Fritzie. "We came all this way to see a *matchmaker*?"

It's time, she knows. Time to tell Fritzie the real reason they've come to Brooklyn.

But she just can't seem to bring herself to do it. Not yet. She doesn't want to blow it. Instead, she says, "It's a surprise. You'll just have to wait and see. No more questions."

CHAPTER FIVE
PATRICK

Two days later, Patrick is out walking Bedford—the third walk of the day, if you please—and he is dedicating this walk to wishing he could be a different sort of man. The kind of man who could simply go into his perfectly nice studio and start creating something that could pass for *art*.

Also the kind of man who didn't spend twenty-three hours of the day wishing that the properties of latex were more reliable.

And . . . the kind of man who could bring himself to smile during conversations with his girlfriend about life-changing events like pregnancy and childbirth and fatherhood and how they might turn his life around into something unexpectedly marvelous.

It's one of those leaden, oppressive August days when the air smells like exhaust fumes and is so thick and heavy it's like something you're wearing rather than breathing. The Weather Channel is predicting thunderstorms tonight, and Patrick thinks they can't come soon enough for him. Across the street from the house, the morning regulars are at

Paco's bodega, grizzled older guys lounging against the building, mopping their foreheads and drinking bottled water and soda. They salute him, holding up their plastic bottles—"Howya doin', Patrick?"—and Patrick salutes them right back, waving Bedford's leash at them.

He clomps along, stopping as Bedford lifts his leg at all the usual spots. He takes time out from thinking about condom breakage to ponder the usual question he has during dog walks, which is how any one physical beast could possibly hold so much liquid.

He remarked on that once, and Marnie said, "Oh, he's not really letting much out. Basically he's just leaving text messages for the other dogs," as if this was something everybody knew but Patrick.

"Really? Text messages?" He'd been astonished yet again at the way she sees the world.

The truth is he can't get over how she lives her life, bouncing from thing to thing with the most open heart of anyone he's ever met. She actually *looks* for complications to concern herself with, which baffles him. She will stop all their forward progress just so she can dig through her purse for money to give to homeless people on the street; she often carries cookies she's baked (both the wheat kind *and* the gluten-free kind) to give to strangers—and, oh yes, she talks about the universe like it's a personal friend of hers, as in, "Well, we'll have to see what the universe has to say about that." And when people are maddeningly late, she shrugs and says Mercury is probably in retrograde, and when objects are lost, she has this chant she says, and 90 percent of the time, the lost things obediently come right back from wherever they were escaping to. She says you sometimes have to "beam energy," like that's a thing. As near as he can tell, she actually thinks that Blix's spirit hangs out near the toaster in their kitchen.

He can't quite believe how much he has let himself love her. He can't help it. Being loved by Marnie feels like he's stumbled out of the attic where the crazy person lives, and now he's allowed to go outside and breathe in the fresh air. He can smile. Make love. It's like experiencing color again, after living in a world that had mostly faded to gray.

But then, once he finds himself basking in it, even the smallest bit, the bad thoughts show up in his head.

Hi, Patrick. Have you given any thought to the fire today? You haven't? Well, try thinking about this, you with your happy, satisfied little life. All of this, may we remind you, can be taken away from you in the flash of a nanosecond. Every single shred of happiness—poof!

Her name was Anneliese Cunningham.

It's a name he doesn't ever say aloud anymore. No one says it. She had long black hair and big green eyes and one dimple, and she was an artist, and she wore black leggings and long black T-shirts and a silver chain with a crescent moon every single day along with ballet slippers, except in the winter when she wore furry boots. And she was twenty-four years old on the day it happened.

She didn't believe in magic or Mercury in retrograde. She believed in art and in hard work that might pay off over time but probably wouldn't. She had silences he couldn't penetrate.

And now those silences stretch out inside him, like they have become a big nothingness existing among his organs and muscles. A black hole at his center.

He woke up in a hospital. He will always remember the way the room smelled and how the light felt like knives when they told him that Anneliese was dead. He politely asked if they could kill him, too, but they ignored that because they wouldn't, and he couldn't figure out how to change their minds. It would be so easy for them to do it, a little overdose, a willingness to look the other way. No one would report them. And he would be so grateful to them. But no deal. He had to get up; he had to learn to walk again, and there were painful surgeries and therapies to get through, and he couldn't even move his face, couldn't cry. But then—and he was supposed to be happy about this, everyone said this was wonderful, the miracle he'd been waiting for—he got a big settlement check. A payoff. What a rip-off, to take away his girlfriend's life and his livelihood and then think that money could make up for even one second of it.

Here, my son. Here is what your girlfriend's life was worth. Here's what your well-being was worth, your joy, your *face*.

Die, he said to that face every day and every night. The face in the mirror.

He had a therapist for every part of him. Body, mind, and spirit. He went through the motions. And later, when the whole medical establishment said he was well enough—or as good as he was going to get anyway—he moved into a luxury hotel, because he was rich and so why not, and he ordered room service whenever he thought of it. He didn't go outside for months, just ordered the filet mignons and the salmon mousses because he could afford them, and he threw most food away and spent his time watching daytime television and late-night movies and trying to figure out how to die without doing anything truly violent to himself because he didn't have the stomach for that. People from his old life came and tried to reach him—even Anneliese's parents, Grace and Kerwin—but he turned them all away. He couldn't face them. He feels bad about that now; he should have summoned the courage to face them, and now it's way too late. He wanted to be alone while he waited for death.

But when he didn't die, when eons had passed and it looked like he was so incompetent at wishing for things that he was going to have to stay alive forever, he took a little research job, writing descriptions of diseases for a medical website, a job as distant from art as possible. He was irrationally angry with art, like that had been the thing that betrayed him. He wanted a job he could do from his hotel room, without any conversations with human beings. The website was designed for people who had some kind of distressing symptom, who were probably up in the middle of the night typing in things like: "black mole on armpit" or "headache after sex." Patrick's job was to get them to seek medical attention, so he wrote things like, "Possible malignancy" or "Possible brain infarction." He took a kind of pleasure in ringing the warning bells for others. "This could be a sign of serious disease. You should see a medical professional immediately," he would type. "DO NOT LET THIS GO UNTREATED."

He could make anything sound dire, because to him, everything was dire: an ingrown toenail can lead to an amputation, a twitch might be a stroke, and a young woman in an artist's apartment might turn on a stove to make a simple cup of coffee and that little surge of gas might trigger an explosion that kills her.

That is the world we live in, folks. Get used to it.

He can't really explain the thing that happened next. He ventured outside one day, called there by a force he still doesn't understand. As he stood there blinking in the sunlight, unsure of what to do, suddenly there was an elderly hippie woman walking toward him, smiling. She was wearing all kinds of scarves and jewelry and a pair of embroidered pants that looked like they'd once belonged to either a toreador or Liberace. She said her name was Blix, and she greeted him like she'd been waiting for him, as though they might have been old friends. He wasn't used to people coming up and talking to him, particularly ones who didn't look at all surprised by his appearance. He didn't really want to talk to her—or anyone—but she wasn't having anything that sounded like no.

So that was the day he learned, over a cup of coffee in the darkest corner of a New York deli, an elemental fact about life: that there are certain people in the world who find you and lather you up with so much love that you don't even realize how it is that suddenly you belong to them in ways you could not have predicted. Like it or not, they get underneath all your carefully built defenses, and your whole fort just crumbles at their feet and all your foot soldiers hang up their weapons and retire. You try to call them back, and they say, "Nah. We're good. See ya."

She somehow wormed out of him the whole sorry story of his life, and then insisted that he come along and live in her building, a brownstone in Brooklyn. Hotel life was getting monotonous and boring, and Blix was very persistent. Much to his own surprise, that next month he gave in and moved into her basement apartment with a newly purchased bank of computers, and he adopted a ferocious cat who was hanging around the garbage cans. Most days Blix would come pounding down the stairs, ignoring every single signal he gave to her that he did not want to talk, and when he'd give up and let her in, she'd sit on the floor and tell him her philosophy of life, which mostly included a whole lot of fantastic swear words as well as some fairly insane talk about love and forgiveness and the universe and souls. The swear words were colorful and made him laugh. He had forgotten the sound of his own laughter. She had a book of spells, which he did not think she was serious about, but she told him she made good use of them, especially when people needed a little assistance in finding the right person—a concept he rejected. There is no right person, he told her, and she said that there absolutely was. Someone for everyone. Maybe several people. Everybody could have love. He just had to wait. In the meantime, she said, they could dance and eat great food. She had spectacular friends, including her boyfriend, Houndy, who was a lobsterman. There were times they all ate lobsters for breakfast, lunch, and dinner up on their rooftop looking out over Brooklyn—just like Patrick preferred it: close enough that they could watch the city unfolding but with enough distance that he didn't have to interact with it.

He would protest to her that he was ugly and wretched and that he hated what his life had become, and she'd say, "So what, Patrick? We still have to dance."

But then the very next year, Blix had to go and get cancer, and she did *not* consult medical professionals like Patrick advised because she had magic spells that were supposed to heal her, and besides, she said she was eighty-five years old and that was enough of a life for anybody, and maybe the whole planet needed to accept the idea that life ends and when the time comes to say good-bye, maybe folks could just throw themselves a big party instead of spending all that precious dwindling time chasing down a painful cure and having parts of themselves frozen or amputated. It sounded so plausible when she'd say it that way. She wasn't one little bit afraid of dying. And he helped her. He was there with her when she died, holding her hand.

She left this beautiful, rundown brownstone building to a stranger who turned out to be Marnie, a person who seemed to come parachuting in from out of nowhere. She was the jilted ex-wife of Blix's truly horrible grandnephew—and just when Patrick had figured out how to cope without Blix, there Marnie was, barging into his life, banging on his door with her problems and her secrets and her laughter and klutziness and tons of bad boyfriend stories. *Go away,* he wanted to say. But Marnie needed his help fixing things. She needed advice about the neighbors. She was from Florida so she was baffled by the noises the radiators make and what a cellar was for. She didn't know about taxicabs, bodegas, or winter boots.

It was like a firecracker in his life, meeting her. Just the way she pulled him out of himself. He began to suspect that Blix might have sent her. Yes, it's preposterous, but he has found himself believing in some impossible things over the last few years.

But now he knows for sure: he's come as far as he can come. It may have been magic that brought him into this new life, and if that's true, he's fine with it. But he personally is at the end of what he can do. And he doesn't want or need to go any further, thank you very much.

He stops walking now while Bedford investigates an old bagel that's lying on the sidewalk, and Patrick has to pull on his leash to get him to leave it alone. Take that little struggle and multiply it by millions, he thinks, if there's a baby. If there's a baby—oh God, he can't even go there.

His phone dings. Marnie.

I'm watching two guys playing with a toddler in the shop, and I have to say it again: you are going to be such a wonderful father. He waits a moment, and she sends a photo: two smiling male-model types, playing peekaboo with some towheaded kid. It looks unreal, like an advertisement.

He tries not to answer, but then he can't help it. *These guys may think they've conquered parenthood, but we must not overlook the horrors that await them. Three words, Marnie. REPORT CARD CONFERENCES.*

She replies immediately. *LOL. What about them?*

Right now we have none of those in our lives. This is a blessing we fail to appreciate enough. Sitting in a little classroom hearing the news about disappointing test scores, uncompleted homework, tardiness. Tardiness! Does anybody ever use the word "tardy" unless it's about school? I could go my whole life without ever hearing the word "tardy" again.

Done! I'll go to the conferences!

Also. Sleepless nights, Marnie. Those will affect the entire household. All of us. You, me, Bedford, Roy. If nothing else, think of poor Bedford.

There's a long silence. He goes into Paco's. He needs a bottle of antacids and another cup of coffee, and he hangs out for a bit to talk to Paco about the Mets, who are perhaps showing a little bit of promise this season. Back when Patrick first moved here and was so screwed up he couldn't even go outside, Paco used to take care of him. When Patrick couldn't face meeting people, Paco would bring him ready-made meals, knock twice at the door, and leave the food for him. Some things you never forget.

His phone beeps. Marnie again.

Only eighteen years of sleepless nights. We'll be fine.

It's time to be serious, he thinks. His tactics to discourage her aren't working. *Aren't our lives perfect as they are? Child-free? We go up on the roof and nobody goes over to the edge and falls off. We sleep soundly all night long. We complete most of our sentences. No one needs a sippy cup. Or a Boppy, whatever that is.*

She starts typing right away. Typing and typing and typing. The three little dots go on forever. He's talked baseball scores with the guys, and he's tasted a sample of Paco's newest creation, a guacamole quesadilla, admired it and encouraged him to make more, and is back at home by the time she's come out with her latest message.

A Boppy is a special baby-holding pillow, Patrick, and I want one in my life. In fact I want it all. Sippy cups and Boppies and the whole messy life! I want the family bed and the way it feels to smell their little sweet baby heads, and the little snow boots lined up next to our big ones, and I want the smooshed-up banana on the couch, and I want the day's THIRD milk spill, and I want to sing lullabies when I'm too tired to hold my head up, and I want to fill out field trip permission slips and I want soccer games and bath times, and all of us cuddling on the couch watching Disney movies, even the ones that make us cry. OH, and I want dinosaur Band-Aids and Girl Scout cookies and those scooters that terrorize people on the sidewalks. And sleepovers where nobody sleeps, and also those little socks that have lace around the edges. And baby strollers! And car seats! THAT IS WHAT I WANT. And, Patrick, it is possible that there is already a baby coming for us. Don't forget that. Our lives will be perfect either way . . . but I think even MORE perfect with a baby! So there. Full stop. End of story.

There is no answer he can give to any of this, of course, so he puts his phone away and stares out the window. And when it rings an hour later, he winces. *Oh my God, has she thought of ninety* more *horrible things she wants to endure?*

But no. It's Elizabeth, his older sister. Elizabeth still lives in Wyoming in their hometown, and she's never married because she's even more of an introvert than he is.

"Hey," she says in her midwestern twang. "So how's it going there, ya big lug?"

He says it's fine. Is everything all right with her? They make the usual polite small talk: summer's hot, she's had to put in air conditioning in the front room after resisting for so long, the apple orchard looks like it's going to be a good crop this year, she's playing Scrabble online now, and can he even believe it's come to that? She's read over one hundred books since the first of January.

Then the point.

"I wouldn't call you long distance on a weekday, you know, but something kind of strange happened the other day, and I thought to myself, 'Well, I should tell Patrick about this.' Do you remember that acquaintance of mine from years ago? The one that came to town and . . . well, you knew her, too? Tessa?"

"Tessa . . . Tessa . . ."

Then he groans. Of course. That Tessa.

"I'll refresh your memory," she says, and now he has no choice but to sit and listen. You can't ever get Elizabeth out of a paragraph she's already started. "You were in town for an art show, and she was here hoping I'd help her get a job at the college, so she came to your art opening, and I *think* you two—well, I kind of know actually, so why am I pretending that I don't know? It was plain as the nose on your face, it was."

"Elizabeth, it's fine. I remember Tessa." One night—no, two. He's not proud of this. Never talked to her again. Just one of those things.

"You *do*. Well, good for you for not trying to deny it. Sexual intercourse is nothing to be ashamed of between consenting adults these days, so we'll just go on with life, shall we? Although I will say, I was a little surprised. Her being so much older than you and all."

"Yes," he says and waits for her to get to the point. He does not want to get into defending an unwise testosterone-fueled decision he made when he was twenty-eight years old and full of the dickens at his first hometown art show. He thought he was a big deal back then. The former cheerleaders were smiling at him, for Christ's sake. People who didn't look at him twice back when he was a nerdy kid who didn't do sports and just wanted to hang out in the art room were now circling around him, smiling and asking him questions. He had reached a level of coolness he could only have dreamed about when he'd been in high school there. And there was sophisticated Tessa, wearing a short black dress and stiletto heels. Looking out of place, and grateful to talk to him about his "process."

Later, there was a hotel room, kissing in the elevator, and his surprise that a woman his sister's age, a grown-up, would just invite him up to her room.

"So Tessa called me up out of the blue," Elizabeth is saying. "Wanted to know if you were still in Brooklyn." She stops talking.

"Okaaaay, so?" he says. His head may be starting to pound just the slightest bit.

"And I'm sorry, this is out of character for me, don'tcha know, but I got to talking about you, and when she said how she might look you up, I said that, well, you were involved with someone, and she said how of course you would be, you were so handsome and talented, and so before I knew it, I told her about th-the *fire*, and all the operations you'd had, and I'm afraid I went on some. And she wanted to know—well, she wanted to know how it all ended up. Were you okay? She wanted to know if you were, um, disfigured"—he has to close his eyes for a moment to ward off the way his stomach lurches at that word—"and if that had interfered with your ability to, you know, *get along in life*—and then I told her the truth, that you'd had a rough time, but you'd met someone anyway, because that's just the kind of person you are, a survivor, because you are, Patrick. And she said you were a hero. And I said that you weren't really. I don't like that kind of talk. The hero talk."

"You're right. I'm not a hero," he says. "I'm just living my life." *And I am currently banging my head against the wall. And my game shows are starting soon, and I need to stop talking about the past.* "But why are you telling me all this?"

He can feel her debating how to break the news to him. "Well, I gave her some information. The name of Marnie's store and your cell number and your address. I hope I didn't do a bad thing," she says in her flat, ironic voice. "Like, you know, maybe if Marnie is the jealous type and gets mad about your old . . . *whatever* showing up. But *then* I was thinking—and what do I know about love, so don't pay any attention to anything *I* say—maybe if Marnie *did* get jealous, that might actually be a good thing since it could get you to step up and do what needs to be done and marry her."

She lets out a bona fide cackle at this. He remembers now that his sister is an aficionado of romance novels. And apparently now she's dreamed up a little romance novel of her own, starring him as a reluctant bridegroom; Marnie, his jealous live-in girlfriend; and Tessa, a siren, "the other woman," blasting into town to shake up their world.

He rolls his eyes. When exactly did the world lose its collective mind?

"So please tell me I didn't do something awful," Elizabeth is saying. "Maybe she won't even contact you. I couldn't tell if she was hoping to start something up with you again, but I think I discouraged her from doing something embarrassing like that. Still, it would be amusing at least, wouldn't it? You, with two women wooing you. Give you some stories to tell yourself in your old age."

"Elizabeth," he says, aware that he needs to cut this off before the conversation goes completely off the rails. "I'm sure it'll be just fine. She probably won't even call. I've got something burning in the oven, so I've got to go. Nice to talk to you!"

Bedford is looking at him, wagging his tail, when he hangs up, always up for a good story. Roy sniffs and leaves the room. He's never cared much for Patrick's romantic exploits.

CHAPTER SIX
MARNIE

I'm at work, but in between texting with the overly neurotic Patrick and waiting on customers, I have checked myself in the mirror about five times today, because it is possible that four days after the Great Condom Failure, I'm beginning to show some signs of pregnancy. I think my hair is beginning to look shinier and more lustrous, which the internet says happens to pregnant women. I also may have just the slightest glow to my skin. Just saying.

Anyway, I'm happy for the distraction when the Amazings come swanning in.

Usually they talk about their friends and all the problems everybody has: a guy they like named Mookie just lost his dad, and Justin doesn't have the money to go to college. All of them seem to have something they're recovering from. Their teenage lives are complicated, and hard. But today's topic seems to be how many people it's possible to fall in love with at one time. Ariana, their ringleader, who is wearing torn leggings and about four tank tops simultaneously along with multiple necklaces

strung around her neck, is arguing that the number is infinite, depend-
ing on how big your heart is and how much "soul energy" you have. The
one called Dahlia isn't so sure. She has choppy purple hair and bangs that
are only about one-eighth of an inch long, and she thinks you should
pick one person and give everything you have to that person.

Kat looks at me over the top of her glasses. I hide a smile. It's hard
to explain how much I adore these conversations.

"No, no, no," says Ariana. "It's the opposite. There's no *one person*
for everyone. That's a bunch of propaganda to keep women in their
place. The truth is that the more love you give out, the more comes
back to you, and then it just keeps going and going. So you can have
lots of people in your life simultaneously, and people will just gravitate
toward you because they feel you loving them." She's got huge blue,
sea-glass eyes and wild curly yellow hair that I swear she dips in pink
ink, which makes her seem even more sincerely wacky. I love hearing
her talk. "People can tell, you know, how you really feel about them. I
read something about it; it has to do with microscopic eye movements
that we feel even if we can't quite see them. It's science."

The quiet one with a shaved head, who is always partial to wearing
camouflage and lace—Charmaine—laughs and says, "God, you're so
super ridiculous, Ariana. You get in so much trouble if you don't just
stick to one at a time! People get so mad at you if you do that."

"Who cares if they're mad?" says Ariana. "They need to let go of
their expectations that everything is all about them. Anyway, that seems
crazy getting mad about love. Love is like a physical place, an energy,
and like, it's open to everybody and it's all unlimited, and you even have
to work to push it away, to keep from being hit by love energy. Because
it's the way you're meant to live. You give it all, and it all comes back."
She waves her hands in the air. Beautiful long, tanned arms with a tiny
rose tattoo right near the wrist. How do you already have a tattoo by
seventeen? I was barely allowed to get my ears pierced by then.

"Wait, what are we talking about? Like, sex?" Charmaine again.

"Anything. Everything," says Ariana seriously. "Give it all." She gets up and goes over to her bag in the corner and takes out her video camera. Lately she's been taking videos. She likes capturing expressions, she told me once, especially the way people look when they're talking about love, so she might do a whole documentary on that. She has a theory that people can fall in love with anyone at all, simply by looking into their eyes for fifteen whole minutes without speaking. She'd like to do a documentary about that, too.

As usual when I listen to Ariana, I'm reminded of Blix, who would likely have felt exactly the same way. Blix danced with every single person at my wedding to Noah, her grandnephew—men, women, children, waitstaff, potted plants. I can still see her glowing face as she spun around on the dance floor—dressed, in fact, a lot like Ariana, now that I think of it, all those layers of colors and fabrics. (Maybe not as much bare belly showing.) The day I met Blix she told me quite happily that she had walked away from two husbands on account of them boring her. No other reason. I told her I didn't know you were allowed to do that, leave somebody simply on the grounds of boredom—and she said that *of course* you were; why, being bored for your whole life would be the worst thing that could ever happen to a person! You couldn't live like that! You had a responsibility to at least save your own life, didn't you? Didn't it improve the planet if you were happy?

That might have been the moment I fell in love with Blix. The moment that changed the course of my life.

Later, I'm standing at the counter, clipping thorns off a new shipment of roses, when my mom calls. The Frippery is filled today with some of the regulars: Anxious Toby, who is adorable in spite of the fact that his forehead is always lined with worry and also that he wears his hair in a man bun, and Lola, who comes in to pile some of her abundant love on me, and Ernst the Screenplay Guy. The Amazings are now doing some yoga poses while a woman in a turban and a long dress, a newcomer, is playing the flute.

"Hey! How are you?" I say to my mom. "I'm just here at work, trimming some roses. I was going to call you later."

"Oh, no, I get it that you're busy. I've heard about people who have to work for a living. Not that I have ever had the pleasure—I've always been 'the kept little woman at home!' As you know. Holly Housewife. Or something. Donna Reed maybe."

There is something so weird about her voice, all this angry cheer. I keep silent. She liked staying home, didn't she? She was one of those moms who did everything for my sister and me. Drove us to baton-twirling lessons and cheerleading lessons and band practices. Folded laundry. Knew how to make little packets of the bedsheets before she put them in the linen closet, curling the ends together just so, smoothing them so tightly it was almost like they'd been ironed. She sewed our clothes, whether we wanted her to or not. (We mostly did not.) She made our friends welcome. She always said she felt sorry for the moms who had to work.

"Oh, come on," she says. "Laugh. I'm telling jokes."

I fake a laugh. "So. How . . . are you?"

"I'm fine, I guess. So listen, you're busy, but I just wanted to hear your voice."

"Well, here it is. Hi. My voice. La, la, la, la."

"I also need to hear about what you do."

"What I do? The flower shop, you mean?"

"No, not the flower shop! I understand what a flower shop is. I want to know about the magic. The matchmaking."

She lowers her voice when she says the word *magic* like it might be overheard by her minister or, worse, some of her neighbors. Millie MacGraw is a decent, law-abiding Florida woman, fifty-nine years young (as she would say), and she's known for her loads of friends and her meat loaf recipe and the fact that she can swim a mile without even getting winded. She has let me know time and time again that she doesn't think much of magic—she's more a believer in hard work and letting time pass because time heals all things—and she certainly doesn't believe in *match-making* magic. She's a down-to-earth woman who gives practical advice to strangers in grocery stores and is always the first one to take over casseroles and coffee cakes when any of her many friends is having trouble. Her superpower is that she can talk cops out of parking tickets. Which she is always getting because she parks with impunity wherever she likes.

"Oh," I say. "Well. The magic. Not sure I can explain the magic, you know." I peek through the door at the sun beaming into the Frippery, where Lola is rolling oatmeal-colored yarn into a ball, and where Ariana is now doing a handstand.

"Well, then, any of that love stuff you do. You know. I know that that woman, Blix whatever, left you her house because she had the sight or some such thing, and I assume she thought you did, too, and that's why she just gave it to you out of the blue, really. And Natalie said something the other night about how you've really become a sought-after matchmaker now. She said you even introduced her to Brian, way back when you were in college."

"Oh," I say lightly. "Really? Natalie said that? Well. Yeah. That happened."

"So . . . who do you make matches for? Besides Natalie."

"Oh, various people. People who need to know that somebody's out there for them, I guess."

"And . . . so how do you know?"

"Well, I guess I see sparkles."

"You *guess*?"

"No, I know. I see sparkles."

"You see sparkles."

"Yes."

"In the air? In your head? Where?"

"In the air, I guess. All around the . . . people."

"Huh," she says, and then she falls silent.

"Yeah, so that's pretty much it, Mom. So what's going on?"

"Well," she says. There's a pause that is borderline alarming. "I don't know. I think I might be a little bit in need of something just now. Can you send any sparkles my way, do you think? I don't know what's wrong with me, but I just—" Her voice breaks off.

"What? Oh my goodness, Mom, what's wrong?"

"Probably nothing. I'm just a little down, I think. Your father and I—well, you know how he is. Never wants to do anything, never wants to go anywhere. Just wants to sit in his easy chair every night falling asleep to the news. I shouldn't bother you with this. It's just that—Marnie, I don't think I can do this for the rest of my life. I'll tell you the truth, if I'd known this was what marriage was going to turn out to be about, I never would have signed on for it in the first place."

"Oh!" I say.

Then she apparently realizes what she's said, because she backs up a little. "Not that I regret having you kids," she says. "But now with everybody grown up and gone and even Natalie's kids not needing me so much since they're in day care, I tell you, I just want to get the hell out. I'm sick to death of making meat loaf for that man. Forty-something years of meat loaf every Thursday night! What was I thinking, signing up for a lifetime of that?"

"Well." I pause. I can't think of anything else to say. Is this where I confide that I think I might be pregnant? And that I would really appreciate it if she would figure things out with my father because he's my father, and she always acted like she *liked* taking care of him and making meat loaf? And that, by the way, all I want right now is to get married and have a family, and I'd like it if she would please stop making it sound so terrible.

"Well," I say again.

She makes a sound that is probably technically a laugh. When she speaks again, her voice sounds defeated. "You're stunned. Okay, I get it. I've vented. Thank you for listening. Go back and do your interesting little magic things, and don't worry about me. I'm really fine. Just a bored spoiled brat, that's me."

"Mom, wait—"

But it's no use. Now she's back to being Brisk Mom, the one who used to make us clean our rooms on Saturday morning before we could watch cartoons. "No, no more. Anyway, you're at work, so I'll let you go now. Just . . . wanted a nice little chat. Maybe someday you'll really explain what you do. I can take it, you know. I'm open to magic. Might even need a little for myself. But you take care. I love you."

"Mom?" I say again, but she's already hung up.

I wander back to the Frippery, and because I'm a hopeless over-sharer, I flop down on one of the beanbags and tell Lola and Kat and the Amazings about my meat loaf–making mama and that she's saying she's done with putting up with her life as it now stands. They make sympathetic noises about how my mom is probably just going through a little bad spell, and that she'll be okay, which is what I think, too.

And *then*, now actually high on oversharing, I tell them all about how I *might* be pregnant, and that I've been googling symptoms of pregnancy, and already I think I have at least three of them. Including some very nice shine to my hair, even if I do say so myself. And yesterday I was *craving* a chicken taco with sour cream, which I hardly ever want.

"You should start taking folic acid like *immediately*," says Kat.

Ariana eases herself right side up and looks at me, squinting a bit. "Your hair does look phenomenal," she says. "My friend Janelle just found out she's for sure pregnant, and her hair is, like, *gorgeous*. Really super shiny."

Charmaine says, "*Ariana!* You're not supposed to be telling people!"

"I can tell people because Janelle is telling *everyone*. Besides which, Marnie doesn't even know Janelle." She looks at me. "It was supposed to be a big secret because Janelle is in our grade, and so when she first found out, there was a lot of drama around what to do about it, but now she's decided to keep the baby and she's even super excited about it. I think she's crazy, frankly, but she's got all that mystical stuff going on—you know, bringer of new life and all that. She says she feels like a goddess."

Lola clears her throat. "Well, Marnie dear, how is Patrick feeling about you and him having a baby?"

"*Possibly* having a baby," I say. "It's definitely not anything official."

"Have you taken a pregnancy test yet?" she asks kindly.

"Oh! Oh, no. It's waaay too soon for that."

"Oh," she says. She lifts her eyebrows.

"Yeah, it's just since Monday," I tell her. "Four days ago. Not that pregnant yet. Even if I am. You know."

"I see," she says kindly and looks down at her knitting again, probably embarrassed for me.

"This is a very premature announcement," I say, clearing my throat. "A lot of people probably would have kept quiet about it at this stage."

Kat says, "Say! Not to change the subject or anything, but did that woman with the kid ever come back? The one from the other day? Remember? She was from Great Britain, and she so wanted to talk to you."

"Nope," I say. "Can't say that I talked to anybody like that this week."

"Weird. She seemed so downtrodden. It was like nobody ever needed a matchmaker more. I was sure she'd come back."

"Well," I say. "She didn't."

When I look up, all of them are looking at me with pity in their eyes. Like maybe I'm hopelessly misguided or something.

And here we are: there's been a little shift in the atmospheric conditions. Nothing really, really major, you see, but before long, I spill my cup of tea and my favorite mug breaks, and then later, Lola's knitting unravels when she puts it down. The Wi-Fi goes down, and the cash register stops working. A customer comes in and complains that some flowers she bought *last week* aren't still fresh, like she would have expected.

CHAPTER SEVEN
MARNIE

All the way home on the subway, I try different techniques to keep myself from feeling bad. It's like there's a dark mood hovering over me, waiting to settle into my bones and tissues. Maybe it's hearing about my mom's unhappiness, or maybe it's talking about the might-be pregnancy with my Frippery friends and realizing how much I want this to be true and how sad I'm going to be if my one-time-only condom breakage didn't miraculously lead to a pregnancy.

Or maybe—although I hate to admit it—maybe sometimes there can be a mood heading for you, and you have to simply stand there and face it down.

Blix would say to make friends with it, not to fight it. She'd say moods have something they're trying to tell us, and to let them come over you and settle into you, unflinching. That's what she did with her cancer, I've heard. Which is a much harder thing to do than simply avoiding a bad mood. She didn't go in for all those warrior metaphors about fighting cancer, not Blix. She did some spells to suggest it might leave her, but when the cancer gave her a sign that it was staying and that this was the end of her life, she didn't fight anymore. She lovingly gave her tumor the name Cassandra and meditated on the fact that eighty-six years might be the life span she was allotted here on this Earth, and that death was simply a change of address anyway, and she was ready for some new digs.

Anyway, just in case there was something I could do to head it off, before I left Best Buds, I took a peek in Blix's book of spells. For good measure, I put some eucalyptus leaves and rose petals in a little silk sachet and tucked it into my bra. A little protection spell. Couldn't hurt.

I text Patrick when I get off the subway and am turning onto our street.

Almost home, I write. *Any interest in a chicken from Paco's for dinner?*

The three dots show up like he's writing to me, but then they disappear.

I wait. Nothing for a long time, and then they show up once again. And disappear again.

Oh, for heaven's sake, I think. Is he so upset about this baby talk business that he can't even send a proper text? I cross the street and go into Paco's and grab a chicken from the rotisserie oven. Paco is in the back, so Dunbar rings it up and gives me a smile.

"Paco wants me to tell you that if you need more food tonight, we can bring some over," he says. He has a funny look on his face. (Of course he does because everything is a little weird today.)

"No, this will be fine, I'm sure," I tell him.

It's seven thirty when I get back outside, and the sky is looking threatening. The last rays of the sun are breaking through some fairly ominous clouds. The weather is in a mood, too.

I'll go home, I think, and I'll try not to bring up babies or condom breakages or teacher conferences. I'll be chill. Patrick and I might have enough time to eat the chicken up on the rooftop before the storm hits.

Maybe I'll phone my mom later and see if she's really okay. This day needs to shuffle on out of here. I should go to bed early, call an end to it.

It's dim in the hallway when I open the door, and I hear the soft murmur of voices. When I go into the living room, a silence falls. It takes my eyes a moment to adjust. And then I see: there, sitting on the living room couch is a woman with curly black hair and a serious look on her face, wearing a frilly sundress and stiletto high heels.

And Patrick is standing by the fireplace looking pale and rather like a specter of himself, formal and uncomfortable. He casts me a miserable look, but I can't study him now, because my eye is caught by a little girl who is sitting next to Bedford on the floor, a child wearing a blue sunsuit and a backward Yankees baseball cap, who now leaps up and starts jumping up and down, rather like there's an invisible pogo stick attached to her, and she's singing some tuneless chanting thing.

A little girl! I love little girls.

But this one. It takes me a moment to realize that there's something even more interesting about this one, and then it hits me that—oh my God, she is the spitting image of Patrick.

I can't stop staring at her, and I'm smiling so hard my cheeks are hurting. I might be just about to drop the rotisserie chicken. I actually feel a bit wobbly, I think, and Patrick moves swiftly across the room, and he takes the chicken out of my hands, and he puts his mouth next to my ear.

"This is the very craziest thing," he says. "You're not going to believe . . ."

He stops talking because the little girl is hopping over toward me on one foot, and Bedford follows her, wagging as hard as he can.

"Hi, hi, hi!" she says, jumping up and down, her cap flying off. A bunch of Patricky brown hair flops against her forehead just like his does. "Are you Marnie, the matchmaker lady? Do you want to see me do a cartwheel? I can do twelve in a row! And guess what we just found out: Patrick is my real bio-daddy! And that's why we're in Brooklyn, which I so did not know until one hour ago. I thought we were here to go to Coney Island and see the Statue of Liberty, but that was just what we were doing while my mom figured out what to do! So that means I have known for one whole hour that I have a real daddy who is alive! And I already texted my friend Gaia and she texted back NO WAY all in capital letters because that means she's yelling."

"Fritzie," says the woman on the couch. "Sit down."

I swivel my eyes over to the woman, and she looks back at me without smiling.

"This is Fritzie," she says with a dry little laugh. "And I'm Tessa. Sorry for the surprise here. I'm from the past."

"Would you like some chicken?" I say.

CHAPTER EIGHT
PATRICK

Why, yes, just as Patrick suspected, they would like chicken. That would be so nice, Tessa said.

And oh, she then wanted to know, had Marnie gotten that chicken from across the street, by chance, because she and the kid had just been over there. Such nice men running that store. They'd told her which house was Patrick's.

Patrick couldn't believe all this was happening, all this comfortable chatter. Chicken? Seriously? This proved what he'd always suspected, that women were four steps ahead of men when it came to knowing what to do, even in untenable situations. Like this one.

So apparently, when you were facing your former accomplice from a meaningless two-night stand and her daughter, it was food that was needed. Chicken, then.

He was almost always clueless. When the doorbell rang, he'd actually thought maybe Marnie had forgotten her key, or perhaps Paco was running over, as he sometimes does, with some new creation for Patrick to taste.

Instead, he'd flung open the door—he might have even been smiling—and there was Tessa Farrell standing in front of him, looking at a kid who was hanging off the side of the stoop, swinging her bare, mosquito-bitten legs back and forth and fighting to hold on to a small pink rolling suitcase and a piece of dirty white fluff.

"Patrick!" Tessa said. She turned and smiled at him. "Surprise!"

He was caught off guard. He said hi and then didn't know what to say.

"Do you know who I am?" she said. She crinkled up her eyes at him, enjoying her moment of power here.

He nodded. But would he have recognized her if he hadn't heard from Elizabeth that she was in Brooklyn? He's not sure. Their association had been so brief, after all. And mostly in the dark. He remembers the curly black hair and thick eyebrows that looked like they might have been painted on with a magic marker, and the English accent. She still had all that, of course. But she'd changed. She looked more upholstered somehow, and older. Perhaps a bit gloomier. She hadn't changed as much as he had, of course, a fact that he saw in her face even as she tried to hide it.

"You're in shock," she said. "I've startled you. But—well, here we are. This is my daughter, Fritzie." She smiled and gestured to the little girl to come over to her. The little girl—a blur of blue with a slim pale face and straight brown hair—stuck her fingers in her mouth and leaned against her mother and regarded him seriously.

"This is Patrick, honey," Tessa said. She was giving him an appraising look, followed immediately with a big, artificial smile. It was Reaction Number Four of the reactions he could not bear: the one that said, *You look absolutely tragically horrifying, and I feel so sorry for you that I'm simply going to pretend that everything is normal, and I hope you will, too.* But there was another way, too, that she didn't seem shocked by his features. That's right: Elizabeth said she'd told Tessa.

They seemed to expect to be invited in, so he let them inside, which meant that he had to pick up the little pink rolling suitcase and guide it over the step. It had a decal of the Little Mermaid on it.

"Do you like *The Little Mermaid*? " he asked the little girl. Frisky? Frenzy?

"No," she said and looked right in his eyes. Unlike her mother, she didn't seem sorry for him, not in the least. "I think she was very stupid, what she did."

"What did she do?"

"She gave up her whole voice so she could get a pair of legs."

"What?" he said, startled. "Why would she do that? I thought she was a Disney princess and therefore smart and beautiful."

"Yeah, the Disney princesses do dumb things. She gave up her voice just so she could get some guy to like her."

He led the way into the living room and placed the suitcase near the door. "Well," he said, amused in spite of himself. "Disney has some explaining to do on that one. Voices or legs? You don't hear of guys having to make that kind of choice, do you?"

"No, you don't," the kid said. "Lots of Disney stories are like that. I'll show you them if you want."

He felt a little pulse of alarm. Were they . . . staying? Had he missed something in the conversation with Elizabeth, zoned out at the part maybe where it was being explained that Tessa had a kid, and that both of them were intending to stay with him and Marnie? Or maybe he had somehow been signed up to take them around Brooklyn. He absolutely would not be a tour guide. No way. He'd explain, if necessary, that he is in the first stages of working on a painting, and now he needed to go back across the hall to the apartment containing his studio and get back to it. But here they were, in his living room, looking at the books on the shelf, the art on the wall (much of it his). Bedford came out from the kitchen, wagging all over, but wise old Roy made a beeline for one of the bedrooms. He hated company almost as much as Patrick did.

"Sit down, sit down," Patrick said, because it was unbearably awkward just having them stand around looking at stuff, and Tessa plopped down on the couch, saying something teacherly to her daughter about famous Brooklyn brownstones and the granite they're made of. She seemed a little grayer and tireder than he remembered. Having a kid could do that to a person. She'd be, let's see, forty-nine by now. Forty-eight? He felt a little flick of embarrassment, remembering that night, those two nights. He'd been so full of himself over getting a write-up in the local paper and having his work displayed in his hometown. "World premiere art opening of a brand-new talent!" That's what the poster said.

"Have you been living here long?" she said and looked around the room like maybe she was totaling up how much money a person would have to earn to live here.

"Over seven years," he said, clearing his throat. The kid put down a porcelain orange he made years ago. It made a sound when it went back on the shelf, and he tried to hide the shudder he felt.

"Since the accident, then?"

He turned his eyes back to her, and she said, "Oh, I'm sorry, are we not supposed to talk about the accident?"

"No. It's fine," he said. "I talk about the accident nonstop. It's my favorite topic." *Let's see,* he thought, *if she understands sarcasm.*

The child—really, was she called Frisky?—was walking around the room picking up objects, and several were, like the orange, pieces of actual art that Patrick had made and which were very delicate. And which he could not duplicate. On account of the accident and his hands.

"I'm sorry, but you shouldn't . . ." he began, and hoped that Tessa would get the hint.

"Mommy said you were in a big fire," said the child.

"Elizabeth told me," said Tessa.

The kid pointed to her own face. "It looks like it kind of melted you a little bit, right around your eye. Does it hurt?"

"No," he said. He never minded when children asked him about the accident. That was so much better than when they just looked scared out of their minds. This girl, however, regarded him with a coolness he found unnerving.

"It doesn't hurt," he said, "but you're exactly right. It melted me. That's very perceptive."

She nodded solemnly and then started dancing around the room—humming and spinning herself in a circle. A whirling dervish of a human. He was staring at her long tangled brown hair, hanging straight down her back in a way his sister would have said was messy and needed to be tamed. And then she stopped spinning and fell down on the floor, laughing, and he saw there was something about her eyes—the shape and the size and the color—and except for the fact that both of hers were exactly where they were supposed to be, and the skin around them was a healthy pink color, he saw that he could have been looking right into his own face.

She looked just like school pictures of him. He did a little math in his head. Nine years ago . . .

He swallowed hard and looked up at Tessa, who was watching him with a kind of satisfied smile on her face.

"Yep, she's yours," she said.

He didn't want to meet her eyes, to see her slightly supercilious expression, that knowing smile that came from seeing him be shocked. But he couldn't look away.

He didn't know what to say. The top of his head seemed to be growing warm. He wanted to excuse himself and go outside. Maybe start walking and just continue on, perhaps take a little discreet vomit break over by the tree on his way out of town.

The child had been petting Bedford, who had lumbered over to see what the fuss was about when she fell to the floor, but now she got up and came over and stood close to Patrick. He could smell her breath and her shampoo and some undefinable kid smell that made him uncomfortable. How is it that all children manufacture that certain smell—sort of a mixture of socks, hair sweat, crayons, macaroni and cheese, and something close to slightly rancid butter?

"Did you know that you're my bio-daddy?" she said. He saw she was missing one of her front teeth, and the other one was only half grown in and had a jagged edge. He remembered that phase, when new permanent teeth looked like jigsaws.

"Before now, I mean," she said. "My mum says you didn't know because she didn't tell you when I was growing in her uterus, and anyway you weren't around, and also, she said that you and her were just not really friends or anything, so you didn't know. But I thought maybe you did think about it."

"I didn't know. No." He was dizzy from hearing her talk, so he just fixed his gaze on the top of her head, unable to quite turn away. And, just by the way, he wondered, what the heck is the world coming to if *bio-daddy* is a word kids use now?

"Give Patrick a moment," said Tessa. "You're crowding him. Come over here."

He felt a flash of gratitude. The crayon and macaroni smell *was* truly overpowering, and he couldn't have those jagged teeth so close to him right now. Also, he felt like his brain was short-circuiting as it flailed around, trying to work out the news flash that because he slept with this woman two times nine years ago, that the result was . . . this.

He got up and went to stand next to the mantel, inexplicably. Maybe he thought it could hold him up when his brain completely shut down and he crashed to the floor.

And that's when Marnie walked in. He watched her face, and he could tell by her expression as she looked from one face to another that she figured out the whole scene in a matter of seconds. Knew who everybody was and probably how they got there and what they wanted and how it was going to all turn out. That was the way women were. They just got stuff. And that's when Marnie invited them to stay for chicken, and after that, the evening was out of his control, just like his life was probably about to be.

Once in the kitchen, after the introductions have been performed (and not by him), he opens a bottle of wine when Marnie says he should, and he stands back and watches as Tessa walks around, admiring the refrigerator, which Blix had painted turquoise (always a crowd-pleaser), and the scarred old oak table and the view of the water towers from the window, just now losing color with the black clouds looming overhead. She has questions about Brooklyn. Do they like living here? Are the schools good? It seems like such a lively place. Hot and humid, though. Does Marnie like owning a business? Fritzie had thought the little shop was so cute.

Fritzie, not Frisky. Thank goodness for that, at least.

The last light glints from under the storm clouds on the windows of apartment buildings down the street as he pours the wine into three bowl-sized glasses. Marnie puts on music—easy jazz, her favorite for dinner parties, which this is possibly becoming, a celebration of sorts, the weirdest one ever—and then she phones Paco, who bops right over carrying a container of mashed potatoes and broccoli rabe and some snowflake rolls. He comes in and has to shake hands all around, and he cannot seem to wipe the big, pleased smile off his face every time he looks at Patrick. Like Patrick has gone and accomplished something amazing.

"You gonna introduce me to your new family member?" he says, beaming at the kid, who is cartwheeling all over the place now, dodging people and chairs except when she gets going too fast and crashes into the adults. Patrick can't believe that Tessa doesn't stop her. Paco is saying to him, "They were over at my place earlier, and I saw her and when Tessa here asked me if you lived nearby, I got it. I said, 'This girl is a little Patrick.' Dunbar and George—we all saw her. We all thought the exact same thing." He turns to Marnie. "I'm sorry we couldn't tell you. But a big surprise, no? Patrick's life before you? You not upset by this, I bet. You open to everything!"

Marnie is smiling, loading up the mashed potatoes into a bowl. "Yessir. That Patrick sure can keep secrets," she says, and Tessa says, "No, no! He didn't know! I'm the one who kept the secret. I never told him I was pregnant. We were"—she smiles coyly—"just ships passing in the night. Well, two nights, actually. He was such a youngster! It was when he had an art show—and I was in town interviewing for a teaching position, and I slightly knew his sister . . . Hey, remember our trip to the boys' locker room?"

Patrick can feel himself groaning inwardly. Why give Marnie an image? She's already rolling her eyes at him, and when she passes him on the way to get her purse to give money to Paco, she touches his arm and whispers with a deep chuckling laugh, "You got a lotta 'splainin' to do when this is over, you youngster you."

But he finds himself wondering: Will it be over? Why are they really here? What is his role supposed to be? He eyes the Little Mermaid suitcase, over in the corner, being sniffed at by Bedford, and feels a bit uneasy.

During dinner, he is placed next to Fritzie, who animatedly resumes talking about Disney princesses again. "Why do we even have them?" she says. "Boys don't have movies about a prince, do they? And also in the movie *Cinderella*, did you ever notice that the prince has to have a big dance so he can find somebody to marry him? Like, why can't he just talk to women he knows and find out if he loves them or not?" She is gesturing with her dinner roll. "And doesn't he totally know everybody in the kingdom already?" She shakes her head like this is the most ridiculous thing in the world. "What's he gonna learn about girls at a dance?"

"I have to agree," he says. "So maybe he shouldn't have looked for Cinderella with the glass slipper, then?"

She nods. "The glass slipper was the worst idea *ever*." And then she laughs, such a delighted little laugh. "Like, every time you would step on it, it would probably crack. I bet her feet were literally bleeding all over the place!" He's struck by how the word *literally* sounds like *yiterally* when she says it. He doesn't think he used that word when he was eight.

"I can see your point," he says, the slightest bit charmed. He's less charmed, though, when she picks up two of the snowflake rolls and starts tossing them into the air and catching them again. "Here! Patrick! Can you catch a roll in your mouth if I throw it right to you?"

"No, I'm sure I can't," he says. But then he has to anyway, because she tosses one at his face. It hits him in the eye, and he reaches up to grab it.

She stares at his hands. "Ohhhhh," she says. "The fire hurt your hands, too."

"Yes. I had surgeries to fix them."

She looks at them appraisingly. "Let me see them. I bet it was hurting for a long time." She reaches out to touch his hand, and he lets her, even though he hates his hands being touched and every fiber of his being is yelling out for him to pull his hand back. The nerves never healed right, and now he knows they never really will.

"You know," she says, and her face is so serious that he thinks she's going to come out with some from-the-mouth-of-babes observation, even though he doesn't really believe in that kind of thing. Still, he's heard from people who like children that it happens. She doesn't, though. She says, "I kind of wish I had a Spider-Man suitcase instead of the mermaid one. It wouldn't be pink, it would be red or black. And when I fly on an airplane—and ohh! Did you even know I just came from London? It is five whole hours LATER in London, and we were staying with my grandmum." She's bouncing up and down on her chair, and now she takes on the voice of a much younger child, singsongy and possibly bratty. "You don't know her, but she's nice. 'Cept she doesn't want to keep me. She can't, 'cause she's mad at Mommy. That's the only bad thing. The fighting. So we came here. To see you. Only I didn't know that's why we were here. I didn't even know about you!"

Tessa, who is talking to Marnie, suddenly looks up. "Fritzie," she says warningly. "Let's not get into all that, shall we?"

But Fritzie is too manic by now. Even Patrick, who knows nothing about children, knows that he's watching a situation spin out of control. Fritzie laughs and gets to her feet and cups her hands around Patrick's ear and whispers into it, loudly and wetly: "So. My mommy is in love with Richard, and they want to live together in Italy, but the trouble is, Richard doesn't want a kid. So we hope I can come and live with you."

Marnie and Tessa stop talking. "Oh my God," says Tessa. "This is *not*—"

"What?" says Fritzie to her mother. "That *is* what we're doing. We might as well tell them!"

"Oh, well," he hears himself say over some unpleasant buzzing in his ears.

Tessa starts to laugh. "Fritzie! I can't believe—" She looks around at the silent, shocked faces that are looking back at her. He can see that she's embarrassed almost beyond excruciation. He's actually fascinated with the whole scene, as if it has nothing to do with him, as if it's a television show about human beings who had a crazy, madcap plan, and he wonders how they'll resolve this and what will happen next. Tune in next week, folks.

Tessa stands up. "You know what? Never mind. This is such a stupid idea. I'm out of my mind, and I just realized I probably sound like I'm the worst mother in the world. Come on, Fritzie. We should go." She glares at Fritzie, who bursts into loud, uncontrollable tears.

"Come on," her mother says. "Stop it. You're just overtired. Let's go. NOW."

Patrick, for one, is all for letting them go. It is dawning on him that *this* is what this oddball sitcom was leading to—having Fritzie *live* with him and Marnie. Huh! He doesn't even know this kid that's supposed to be his, and she doesn't know him. How was he supposed to be able to raise her? And exactly what kind of mother would plan in advance to drop off her kid with strangers, even if she believed one of them might be the "bio-daddy"? Because he is fairly certain that a man doesn't turn into a father within a matter of seconds, and he certainly has no intention of even trying. He'll be reasonable about sending checks and presents, he supposes, if that's what's called for—but when he looks at this presumed daughter of his, he's not feeling a requisite desire to give her fatherly advice or correct her homework or walk her down the aisle at her wedding.

In fact, he's all for cutting things short right this minute, shaking their hands, rolling out their Little Mermaid suitcase, and saying goodbye. He might thank the child for giving him some things to think about with regard to well-loved fairy-tale stories and Disney princesses before he closes the door.

He stands up, too.

"Wait," says Marnie. "No, no. Stay right here." She's looking at Tessa with an expression on her face that Patrick knows all too well. Oh God, she is seeing a love story. Her eyes have lost focus. "Tell us what's happening. Tell us what you need," she says, and she reaches over and touches Tessa's hand. Fritzie stands next to Patrick, her fingers in her mouth, looking contrite, and then she slowly settles herself against him. Nestles, really.

Marnie says in a dreamy voice that makes Patrick almost groan out loud: "Start from the beginning. You're in love with somebody? Tell me the whole story."

And then Tessa, dabbing at her eyes, sits back down next to Marnie and starts in talking about some professor poet named Richard, and blah blah blah . . . Italy . . . never in love before . . . overwhelming . . . just a year . . . and she goes on and on, until Patrick, frankly, can't take any more of the embarrassment of it all. He looks over at Fritzie at about the three-minute point, and says, "Hey, kid, why don't you and I go up on the roof before the storm gets here and see if we can see all the way to the river?" It's lame, but it's the only thing he can think of, and she considers the option for a moment, cocking her head, and then she looks at her mom and Marnie and accepts, but only if Bedford comes, too.

And there it is. He knows, watching the storm clouds roll in, that when he goes back into the kitchen, everything will be different. And by the time the first flash of lightning and crack of thunder happen, Marnie comes up to the roof to tell him he's right.

CHAPTER NINE
MARNIE

"So can we go over this one more time?" Patrick says to me three days later. We're alone at last in the kitchen of the basement apartment—his old apartment, where he lived when I first came to Brooklyn—and we're cleaning it because Tessa and Fritzie are going to be staying here for a few weeks. And then Tessa will go on to her tryst in Italy, and we'll have Fritzie for an even longer, longer time. Through the school year.

There had been some talk about how ten months was perhaps too long for a child to be away from her mother—but I found myself making the argument that if Fritzie is going to be left with us, at least she should be allowed to complete the third grade in one place. When I said that, Patrick went into a coughing fit and almost had to be revived.

"Tell me just so I can explain it to the part of my brain that is still not understanding," he says. "Why, again, are we doing this to our lives?"

"Because it's the right thing to do," I answer him cheerfully. Then, rather crudely, I point to the general direction of his penis. "Mostly because of that guy."

He comes loping over and leans against the counter, thrusting his hip out, with his hand against the cabinet above my head. He's grinning down at me. The provocative sexiness of this pose is not lost on either of us. "*That guy*, huh?" he says.

"Well. Yes. And it *is* the right thing to do," I say, looking up at him. "You dog, you."

"Yep. That's me, the guy leaving a trail of unintentional babies. How's our own little situation going, by the way?" He reaches over and touches my abdomen. "Any news from that front?"

"Won't know for another week," I say. "Although, just as a heads-up, the consensus around Best Buds is that my hair looks particularly lustrous lately, which is a sign of pregnancy hormones. So brace yourself. Just saying."

He groans and buries his head in my neck. "How is it that in the space of one week, I've possibly become the father of two? Tell me that."

"Um, because you're just ridiculously lucky? As well as devastatingly handsome and virile? And women can't resist you?"

"Marnie," he says, and his voice has turned serious. "You know, don't you, that I never had any interest in Tessa? It was just an idiotic mistake, my hooking up with her. So . . . you're not insisting we keep Fritzie because you're trying to show how magnanimous and forgiving you can be, are you?"

"Are you kidding me? Patrick! I know you didn't love her. I'm insisting we keep Fritzie because she's your child, and she needs a home. And she needs you. And also her mother is involved in some kind of epic love story—"

He's shaking his head. "Aha, that's it! You've sniffed out what is possibly the Greatest Matchmaking Project of All Time."

"Patrick, that is not—"

"Oh, yes, it is. Don't forget I've seen you run across restaurants and leap through dog parks to make sure two people get together. So I can see where an intercontinental love story would be just your thing."

"No. No! I'm doing this for Fritzie. If anybody ever needed a family, it's her. It's heartbreaking what's happening to her. And she's like a little adult, trying to manage her feelings. It just kills me, how she's trying to be so brave when her mom is going off and leaving her."

"What I want to know is why can't this Poetic Giant Among Men get a larger *pensione* in Italy if he wants to take up with a woman who has a child? You'd think that would set off some alarm bells for Tessa. She should say no."

"Patrick, she can't say no. She wants what we all want in life—for somebody to hold us in bed and say they can't live without us. And she hasn't ever, ever had that. So maybe now that she's found Richard, *this* is what's going to make her a better person. Love might save them both."

He rolls his eyes so hard that he falls to the floor pretending he's dying. That's when I know I really have him.

So I sit on him. "And maybe, you old cynic, she'll have more love to give to Fritzie and end up being a better mother. Isn't that what love does for all of us if we let it in? Maybe this was meant to be. Set up by the universe . . ."

At the mention of the universe, he closes his eyes and folds his hands on his chest, corpse-like.

"Yes, Patrick. Yes! Deal with it. *Set up by the universe.* Lots of things are going to be set in motion that we can't see the end of. That's the way the whole system works." I put my face up against his and kiss him five hundred times across his cheeks and nose and forehead.

"So *fine*," he says. "But how did *my* life get tangled up in this? I don't even like her."

I laugh and poke him in the arm. "Oh, really? The evidence would indicate that you must have been quite fond of her for at least two happy evenings of your life."

"Oh God, Marnie. She wasn't interested in me, and I was a jerk. Just showing off."

"And, if I may ask, oh careful one, was this another condom breakage situation?"

"No. This was all stupidity. I figured she was forty years old, so she must have the birth control situation all figured out. I think I was probably embarrassed to bring it up."

"And see there? You got a great kid out of it. Proof once again that the universe works in mysterious ways."

He makes a face and I roll off his chest onto the floor next to him. "I like the kid," he says in a voice that means just the opposite. "No, I do. I like anybody who's not above criticizing the Little Mermaid's wimpiness and who's bold enough to throw a dinner roll at a man's face at dinner. But if you ask me if she feels like mine, if I feel any connection to her, I'd have to say no. I just don't. You and Tessa say she looks just like me, and I suppose she might have some resemblance. Maybe. And Tessa says there was no one else. So—she's mine. But it's not ringing any bells for me, to tell you the truth."

"So? Maybe that will change. Maybe you're supposed to change in all this, too, Patrick. Get to know a different kind of love. You know? It's possible. The fates . . ."

"Nope," he says. "I'm the one who gets to be in control of my fate." And he pulls me over and starts kissing me.

We really get into making out and are just starting to think about removing clothing, when we hear Bedford barking outside, and it's time to go greet Tessa and Fritzie, who have returned.

"Patrick! Patrick! Where are you?" Fritzie is yelling.

"See?" he groans as he hauls himself up off the floor. "This is the kind of thing we're not going to be able to do anymore."

"We'll find ways, trust me," I say. And he shakes his head mournfully.

There's just one little thing that flattens me, I think, after he's left to go upstairs. Tessa is a total wreck and she may have a life that's never going to work out the way she planned it. But, damn it, she *did* have a baby with Patrick. Her cells and his cells mingled and created this walking-around, talking human girl who is a perfect genetic combination of the two of them, and who looks especially like him.

And I may never know what that's like. I put my hands across my middle, where maybe, possibly, somebody's in there, right now just a little ball of cells dividing and growing every day.

But what if there isn't? And what if there never is? Then what?

"Marnie! Marnie!" Fritzie is yelling for me. "Marnie, come look at what Bedford found in the park! Somebody's gross old boot!"

I go upstairs. And I'm smiling by the time I get there because the truth is it's been a long time since Bedford brought home an old boot and had somebody think that was great.

A few days later, I take Fritzie with me to work. I've told her about the flower shop, of course, and also about the Frippery and all the fun people who come there, and the things they do. She marches along next to me, in torn denim leggings and a *Purple Rain* T-shirt and red flip-flops, and she oohs and aahs when we unlock the door of Best Buds and go in. I see it through her eyes: all the twinkling lights and the buckets and baskets of flowers, the cooler filled with roses and tulips and daisies, the long counter with its marble finish, and the sound of the alto flute music I put on. It's a paradise in here, and I'm so pleased to see that she agrees.

She immediately sees the Frippery for what it is: a place for cartwheels among the pillows and beanbags. Then she runs over and writes with the markers at the desk, decorating a piece of construction paper to say: FRITZIE'S FRIPPERY.

"Marnie!" she calls while I'm talking on the phone to Patrick. "Can I call it Fritzie's Frippery? Would you put up my sign? Fritzie's Frippery! Because I never had a frippery before! I didn't know anybody who has a frippery! We could put on the sign: 'Come frip out at Fritzie's Frippery!'"

"Yes, we could," I say, and Patrick on the other end says, "Oh, dear God in heaven. This morning she came into my studio and wanted to know if we could sit together and do some oil paintings. She's taking over, isn't she?"

"What did you say to her? Please tell me you didn't push her out of there."

"Do you have any idea of the extent of the damage one eight-year-old girl could do with oil paints?"

"No."

"Well, it's epic. So I gave her some watercolors. I let her paint. She lasted fourteen seconds, and then she was wandering around wanting to know if, when you and I get married, she could be the flower girl, and what should she wear in her hair that day. And also if Mister Swoony could be in the wedding, too."

I laugh. Mister Swoony is the stuffed animal she carries around with her, really just a piece of dirty, stitched-together fluff. "And what did you reply to that?"

"I said there were no such plans, and she could wear whatever she wanted in her hair any day of the week. And that Mister Swoony can make his own arrangements."

After I get off the phone, she says to me, "It's such a good thing you and my bio-daddy are going to keep me. Do you think he would mind if I called him Daddy? I always thought that Daddy sounded like a cool name. I never get to call anybody Daddy. Some people don't have daddies. Of course I could use Dad or Papa or Father. Is he the type to like Father better? Maybe I should call him PapPap. That's what my friend Asia calls her grandfather, but I think it sounds cool for a father, too. I think probably he's going to have to get used to me before I ask him. Don't you?" I'm at the counter trimming the stems of the flowers from the cooler, and she has the broom and is sweeping up, waving the broom rather dangerously around the counter area.

She suddenly does a cartwheel and when she stands up she says, "Can I tell you a secret? My mom and I came here the other day, before I met you. I didn't know why we came here, but I think she wanted to see if you knew Patrick."

"Oh," I say.

She goes on to do five more cartwheels. "She's kind of different from the other moms, did you know that? She isn't really good at knowing how to do a lot of stuff. It's because I am a surprise girl. She and my dad didn't mean for me to happen, you see, and she told me she didn't ever play with dolls so that's why she doesn't know how to be a mum. So she says we are really like friends in the world. That's what she calls us: friends in the world."

I feel my hands shake just a little. "You know, your mommy is lucky to have you being so understanding and all. A lot of kids—well, when I was a kid, I would have had a hard time, I think. And I want you to know, it's okay if sometimes you have a hard time. You don't have to be brave all the time, you know."

She takes Mister Swoony out of her backpack and sets him up next to the cash register. She keeps licking her lips, like she's nervous. "I'm okay," she says and cartwheels herself over to the cooler door. "I think that cartwheel was my best one today," she says, when she's upright again. Red-faced and smiling.

I tell her I once could do a pretty decent series of cartwheels myself. I think my record might have been twenty-two in a row, but that was on the beach, and I was ten years old.

She regards me seriously. Then she says, "I need to see you do them! Let's go to the Frippery!" and so I put down my cutting implements and the roses and we head to the back room, where she folds her arms and insists that I show my stuff. I do about two really, really lame cartwheels.

She frowns. "Hmm. You need some practice. Straighten out your knees, and then you'll be good. We'll work on it."

Later, the Amazings drop in, and Ariana and Charmaine immediately take to Fritzie and show her how divine it is to put glitter on everybody's cheeks; even Lola gets a dose of purple sparkles right across her cheekbones. Lola is knitting a long scarf, and she crooks a finger and beckons Fritzie over to ask how she likes Brooklyn so far. And if she'd ever want to come and live here.

"I do live here now," Fritzie says. "This is my new home because Patrick is my bio-daddy, and he gets to keep me now while my mom goes to Italy." She says this and then she gives me a big smile. "I belong with Patrick and Marnie now. And Bedford! Oh, and Roy! Roy is still getting used to me. Actually, Patrick is, too."

"Oh, how exciting," says Lola, startled, but then she turns her shock into a twinkle and smiles at me. "How interesting things are at your house these days, my dear. Where are you thinking of enrolling her in school?"

Ah, yes, *that*. There will be so much to think about, but I particularly have to give some thought to this school business. Unlike where I grew up, enrolling in school isn't an easy situation in Brooklyn. From what I've heard, you can't just go down to your neighborhood school building and sign up. I've been a witness to enough passionate, ferocious discussions from Park Slope moms to know that there are about a million choices, and many of them are god-awful and some of them are bearable, while one or two might be absolutely perfect, but you don't know which is which until you've researched and explored and talked to everyone involved.

I have not done any of this. I have a moment of being swamped with panic, but Lola puts aside her knitting and places her hand on my arm.

"Dear, call Emily Turner," she says. "She'll know who you should talk to."

Emily Turner is known around here as Mom Extraordinaire. She sometimes shows up at Best Buds in the afternoons, often wearing magenta yoga pants and carrying a huge thermos of green tea and trailing a contingent of little girls. So I call her, and describe Fritzie as best I can, and she tells me that Brooklyn Kind School is the only place I should consider sending a child who is coming from elsewhere and who may have, um, tendencies toward shocking mic-drops and spontaneous series of cartwheels.

"Also, she needs friends, like immediately," says Emily, and so the next Monday I arrange for her to come in with her girls—Sierra and Autumn and Blanche, who are six, eight, and eleven—to meet Fritzie. I get some cookies from Cupcake, and some lemonade from Paco, and Emily and I stand in the doorway and watch as the four of them play. I feel the same way I used to feel on first dates, all that nervous jumpiness in my stomach. But Fritzie seems blissfully nonchalant.

All I can think of is: What if this doesn't work? What if they hate her?

But it does work. Fritzie is a little bit bossy, but in a charming way if there is such a thing. She demonstrates her cartwheel technique, of course, and then shows off how cool it is to dust their faces with purple glitter, and then she sits down with her Little Mermaid suitcase and starts unpacking her treasures for their enjoyment.

There's a hair clasp that looks like one that Taylor Swift once wore, and an empty tube of Ridiculously Red lipstick that Tessa once let her try on when she dressed up like a witch two Halloweens ago. There's a two-dollar bill that her friend Gaia gave her, and a penny that got flattened by a train, and a love letter a boy named George wrote to her in first grade that just says "I thik you R GRAT." She has a fuzzy pink fur notebook with a lock on it, and a tarnished gold earring that her grandmum gave her. And then, at the bottom, a bottle of candy sprinkles.

The other girls pass everything around and seem to understand the value of each of these promising treasures. But when she pulls out the bottle of chocolate sprinkles, Blanche says, "What do you carry that around for?"

"Duh!" says Fritzie. "Because what happens if you run into some ice cream, and you don't have any sprinkles?"

"Wow. This sums her up perfectly," I say to Emily Turner.

"I love this kid. And poor thing, it looks like she's really dealing with her abandonment issues so bravely," Emily whispers—which is when I have to whisper back that I'm not really sure Fritzie is aware of any abandonment issues. If I had to characterize her, I'd say she is mostly relieved to be getting free of her mom. She's mostly the kid carrying around candy sprinkles in case she happens upon an ice cream cone.

"Oh, she has them all right," Emily says. "You don't get to skip abandonment issues if your mom is going to Italy and leaving you with virtual strangers. You just don't. I'm talking to Yolanda at the Kind School. We've got to make sure this girl gets in."

CHAPTER TEN

MARNIE

My period does not come on time, and so I buy seven pregnancy tests. As any person might do. I am now entering a new phase of life, and I want to be prepared.

Well, to be clear, first I buy only the one, and I dash into the bathroom between customers at work and test it out. I am stunned—beyond stunned—when no line appears in the little window. This test is obviously defective because, although I have many irregular things about me, my menstrual cycle is not one of them. It is spot-on. On time. Every twenty-eighth day by nine a.m.

And now my period is a day late. Clearly, therefore, I am pregnant. But just the same, I would like some outside confirmation.

So, at lunchtime the next day, still with no period, I go out and buy another, much more reliable, truth-telling test. This is the kind of test that spells out the words, either *PREGNANT* or *NOT PREGNANT*, in case hieroglyphic line-reading isn't doing it for you. In case you have the kind of hormonal system that wants everything spelled out.

NOT PREGNANT, it says, like a slap in the face.

Okay then, I think. *This is not going to be as easy as I thought, navigating the world of pregnancy testing.*

I consult the internet, which thinks that sometimes in early pregnancy there's not yet enough of something called hCG in a woman's system to register as a pregnancy. So, fine. The internet thinks I could still be pregnant and suggests that I do the test in the early morning, when this hCG is in abundance.

So I buy another brand of pregnancy test for test number three, and I get up extra early the next morning and creep into the bathroom to check.

Negative.

So this is war. My body and the pregnancy test industry are at odds.

It's stress, says the internet. *Wait a few days and take the test again.*

Sure enough, I do have some stress. Besides the stuff that's obvious—Fritzie cartwheeling through my life, Patrick looking more and more like a shell-shocked accident victim, Tessa mooning around the house like a lovesick teenager who's been grounded from seeing her true love—my mother has also called again and reported that she and my father went away on a trip together at her insistence, and he fell asleep in the hotel by seven o'clock every night. "It wasn't even dark outside yet!" she yells. She wonders if this is grounds for divorce.

Pregnancy test four: negative.

I buy three more tests for good measure, and I space them out, trying one every day. New stressors show up: Tessa tells me that she may simply leave for Italy without waiting to see if Fritzie likes her new school. Patrick says that he's lost the will to paint with so much turmoil in the house. Bedford throws up on the rug three mornings in a row, and each time I find mangled plastic doll shoes in there.

Ariana teaches me a new yoga pose that supposedly brings all the chi into a person's body. Kat serves me raspberry tea, for no other reason than she heard raspberries are good for pregnant women. Lola tells me to put my feet up and stop worrying about whether or not Fritzie will be admitted to the Brooklyn Kind School.

Patrick says maybe the tests are correct, and I'm not pregnant and that I should count my blessings since our lives are crazy enough right now, aren't they? Because I really do love him, I don't hit him. By deep breathing, I'm able to control myself by not looking in his direction.

After he leaves, I go over to the toaster and consult with Blix. I tell her I want a baby so much. That I am *insane* over the need for a baby. She is silent for a long time, but then I hear her. Grudgingly.

For heaven's sake, stop wasting your money on pregnancy tests. Go look at sunsets. Drink a cup of tea. Take a hot bath. And how many times do I have to tell you? Whatever happens, love that. Because maybe, just maybe, everything is perfect.

I do all these things, and still my period does not come, which surely means my body is pregnant but wants to keep things a secret.

"Tell me the truth," Tessa says to me one evening as she joins me in taking Bedford out for his last walk of the day. "Are you for real a matchmaker, or are you just making it all up? You can tell me if you're faking it. I don't mind."

"Well," I say, smiling. This is so Tessa. "It depends on what you mean by for real, I guess. I can tell when people belong together. Sometimes."

"Okay, just tell me this then. Am I doing the right thing going off with Richard?"

"Well," I say slowly. "Nobody can answer that question perfectly."

"See?" she says. She lets out a sigh that sounds a little bit triumphant. "I knew it. If matchmaking was for real, then everybody would be with the right person, because someone could just tell them who they belong with. And you'd look at me and know if Richard and I are going to last. Maybe it's like my mum says, and I don't deserve to even think about love for myself."

"Tessa, Tessa. Everyone deserves love." I try to imagine what Blix would tell her—Blix, who believed in people finding their own paths. "Let me ask you this: Can you maybe believe just for a moment that everything is going to be okay no matter which way it ends up? Whether you're with Richard for the next fifty years or just the next fifty days? How about that? Can you accept that maybe you just have to let yourself live it?"

She scowls harder. "I need to know if loving Richard is *real*, and if he's going to be the person I can depend on for the rest of my life. That's what I'm asking you. Is. This. Real. Love."

"But maybe it's worth it even if it's not permanent. Isn't it? Maybe with the spark of this love in your life, everything is going to be changed in ways you can't right now fathom."

By now Bedford has peed on nearly every object he likes, and we start back to the brownstone. When we get there, I sit down on the stoop and motion for her to sit beside me. "Let's think about it this way," I say. "Your life was truly miserable. You weren't having any joy at all. You've been raising your child and everything has felt impossible. Is that right?"

She nods.

"And then you met someone. And you fell in love, because maybe something in you knew that this is the thing you needed in order to stay alive. And so you took some really brave steps: You made a plan, which was to go to him, and then you took action. You applied for a sabbatical, you started thinking of where Fritzie could stay, and now you're asking for help. Help from Patrick. And from me. Which is a *huge* step for you, I bet. You probably hate asking for help."

"I never thought I would do this," she says, and I think she may be crying a little. "Leave her."

We sit quietly, both of us watching Bedford ambling around at the end of his leash. Looking for gum wrappers and cigarette butts he can eat. After a while I say, "You don't have to worry, you know. I'm going to take care of her for you. I will love her for you."

I put my arms around her rounded, sad shoulders. I would like this to be one of those moments, when she sees she can let down her guard, that we can maybe trust each other. I'm even thinking words like *sisterhood* and *co-parenting* and I know that any second those words are going to come leaping out of my mouth. Then, thank goodness, her phone rings. It's Richard, and she gives me a longing look.

"Talk to him," I say. "It's fine." And Bedford and I go in the house. When I look back, I see the sparkles around her, almost dazzling in their brightness.

CHAPTER ELEVEN
PATRICK

Patrick has never been one for houseguests. Even before the fire, even back when he was an up-and-coming, promising sculptor who moved in regular social circles, he liked it best when everyone he knew mostly stayed at their own lodgings. On the subway, in airports, he's happiest when he's assuming that the people he sees are all on their way back home.

Mainly this has worked for him. His parents are long deceased, and his sister never ventures out of Wyoming, and Marnie's mom and dad have come to visit only once, staying for two very polite days before they obligingly vanished back to Florida. Her sister Natalie came with her husband and two kids one time and stayed at an Airbnb and came over only for meals.

But now here is a whole new category of houseguest: an interloper who considers herself already home. And this is the kind of person who calls his name a thousand times in a row, with escalating intensity—as in "Patrick! Patrick! Patrick! *Patrick!*"—and when he finally can take it no longer and says, "What? What do you want?" this person says, "If dogs could talk, do you think they would speak English?" or "Do you think it's true that squirrels can fly?" or "What's that thing on your throat that goes up and down when you talk?"

She's up before him every morning and sticks by his side as much as possible throughout the day. Clearly, she's on a campaign to win him over. She wants to go into his studio and use his oil paints and would like to tell him a million stories that have no point to them whatsoever, some of which may even be the plots of obscure television shows that are only shown on the internet and involve characters named Dora and SpongeBob. He doesn't know what the hell she's talking about most of the time.

Aaaaaand . . . she is going to be here for nearly a whole year. Which is unimaginable. He feels the life force seeping out of his body whenever he thinks of it. His teeth hurt. His *hair follicles* ache. He feels the beginnings of an ulcer forming somewhere.

He has accepted that she's his daughter, which really, if you want to be technical about it, only means that she shares some of his DNA. Frankly, he has never felt sentimental about his DNA. He may be missing some basic drive, he thinks, the one that makes humans want to spread their seed and track their progeny, some nebulous force that sees creating family as the be-all and end-all of human endeavor.

Not Patrick. Having contributed some chromosomes to Fritzie is strictly a chemical kind of thing in his mind, not something that makes somebody a dad. How could he be connected to her, when he hasn't awakened with her when she was a baby and walked her around the house through earaches and bad colds? He hasn't put Band-Aids on her scraped knees or comforted her when she's sad or done any of the twenty kazillion things he would have done had he planned for her existence and participated in raising her over the last eight years.

He. Does. Not. Know. Her. And yet everyone acts like he should be so amazed to find himself a father. Even Paco said to him yesterday, "So you're one lucky duck! This is sure the easy way to being a father, eh? Ehh?" And he actually came out from behind the counter to give Patrick a good-natured poke in the ribs, like he'd really pulled off something of a coup.

"I am not a father!" he wants to scream about ten times a day.

He doubts he can turn into one either. Oh, he knows what Marnie is imagining. If his life were a movie, he'll be the sad, hopeless guy who is taught the Meaning of Life by a grimy-faced, obnoxious little street urchin who happens to be his daughter, and by the time the final credits roll, he finally throws off the shackles of his unhappiness and learns to embrace life and love.

He loathes that particular plot. If he has to keep her for a year—and apparently he does—then he will do it. He will spend the year the way prisoners do: marking off the days until it's over. And then he will hand her back to her mother and resume the life he's come to love: dabbling at art in a nonserious way, heading over to Paco's once or twice a day for chips and cheese, reading the paper for hours on end, sitting on the couch watching television game shows with Roy on his lap and Bedford at his feet, taking Bedford out for long walks, baking pastries when it suits him, waiting for Marnie to come home from work so they can go up on the roof together and make a fire in the firepit, drink some wine, and then head off to bed. He is fortunate in that he doesn't have to work; the settlement from the fire made sure of that. So in a very real way, he has earned—with his sorrow and his scars—this carefully curated way of life. And he intends to maintain it.

But in the meantime—well, it's not great. He feels as though a hive of bees has moved into his head. Instead of watching *Wheel of Fortune* and *Family Feud* with Bedford and Roy, he is forced to ponder whether anteaters should be called eatanters. And whether he thinks there is another solar system where another Fritzie and Patrick are doing *the exact same thing*, only *he* is Fritzie on that planet, and she is Patrick. And how would *that* be, huh? And did he ever hear that he could turn into a girl if he kissed his own elbow?

Then one day he's home and he's just made lunch for Fritzie when the Pierpont Gallery phones him.

Would he like to have a gallery showing of his work in January?

Well, you see, he would not. God, no.

But it's a fine, prestigious gallery, and Philip Pierpont himself is on the phone, doing the asking, in his cultured tones. He's up-front about the request, too: there's been a cancellation. Another artist was scheduled for the month, but something came up.

Of course, Patrick thinks. He wasn't their first choice. Someone more famous and well-adjusted, someone without burns on his face was supposed to take the slot, but couldn't—and all because a writer from *Inside Outside* magazine knows somebody who knows somebody who's an admirer of Patrick's past work, the gallery owner is wondering if perhaps Patrick has some work he could show.

Patrick says he needs to think about it. He's pretty sure he doesn't want to do this. After all, he doesn't really have much work he could show. Any, really. But after he hangs up, there is Fritzie, sitting there at the table, swinging her legs and eating a peanut butter and marshmallow sandwich with her mouth open, and she has a strand of marshmallow in her hair, and she's saying, "Oh, you're off the phone now. Wouldn't it be funny if you had a whole bunch of kids you didn't know about, not just me, and we all showed up at your house one day, and—"

"Fritzie," he says. "Trust me. I don't have any other kids."

"Well, but you might. I mean, you didn't know about me, so you might have some others, too. What if all the other moms showed up, and they said, 'Here is your son, and here are your twins, and here is a little girl . . .' Wouldn't that be funny if you had, like, eight kids?"

He doesn't let her see how much this thought makes him shudder. "There aren't any more. Maybe you should go and wash that marshmallow out of your hair."

Later, Marnie calls and he can't seem to help himself: he tells her about the gallery. She thinks it's a fantastic idea, just as he knew she would. She is all for forward motion, for progress, for life, for stretching oneself. For Getting Back Out There. She doesn't even care that he was the second choice. "So what?" she says. "It's an opportunity." Marnie loves opportunities.

He says he's not sure. "It's going to mean I'll be really busy, and, wellllllll, we do have Fritzie now . . ."

"It's fine, Patrick. We'll all pitch in to make it work. Even if you need to do a whole bunch of paintings, we can manage. She'll be in school, and she can join me at the shop if there's no after-school program she'd like . . ." She is off and running, just the way he knew she'd be. "And, if there's going to be another baby, then it'll be good for you to have your art career back in gear."

Oh yes. The other baby.

That's right; Marnie still hasn't gotten her period. The doctor she called yesterday said she'd give her a blood test for pregnancy if it hasn't come in another week. So . . . there's *that* little bug of uncertainty buzzing about in his head, too. He's kept swatting it away. He closes his eyes for a moment, feels the blackness pressing against his eyelids.

"Do it," she says.

"January is not that far away. And so I'm immediately behind. For it to be worthwhile, I'll need to get right to it."

"Of course," she says. "But I think it's worth it. This is your chance to be in the art world again. You owe it to yourself."

Later, Fritzie comes into his study and does three cartwheels before she plops herself down on the floor and stares at him.

"Hiiii, Patrick," she says after a long moment of unrelenting eye contact.

"Hi."

"What are you doing?"

"I'm thinking. What are you doing?"

"I'm thinking, too. Are you thinking about whether you and Marnie are going to get married?"

"Not really."

"Well, then, what are you thinking about?"

"Nothing you need to worry about."

"Oh. Well. Do you want to know what I'm thinking about?"

"Yes."

She laughs. "No, you don't."

"Okay, I don't."

She wiggles her toes and inspects the bottoms of her feet, which are filthy. She points that fact out to him, and he gets up and goes into the kitchen. But she follows him.

"One day my toenail fell off. Did you ever have your toenail fall off? And I thought—you want to know what I thought? I thought it was like baby teeth. That I had baby toenails and now I would get a grown-up toenail. But that's not right."

Oh God. He can't take any talk about toenails. He did not know that toenail talk came with the fatherhood territory.

"Fritzie, I am actually trying to make a big decision right now, so maybe you could go and play with Bedford or something. I'm going back in my studio now."

"Can I come in and paint?"

He looks over at her face. All shining and animated and all he can see is her mouth moving and moving and moving.

"If you can be quiet."

He gets out the watercolors and sets her up in the corner with a pad of paper and a bowl of water, and he pulls a chair over to the table, and she slides into the seat without looking at him. "I'll be very quiet, Patrick, and you can think."

"Thank you," he says. He looks at her as she dips her brush in the water and starts making bold strokes across the paper. How does she cope with the fact that her mother is just willing to walk away and leave her for such a long time? He tries to remember what his life was like when he was eight years old, and he can't even imagine what he would have done if his mom had said she was checking out. His mom—she was the whole deal! She knew how everything in his life worked. She made it all happen.

He shakes his head. Pitiful.

"Just so you know, I am very good at decisions. What are you deciding about?" she whispers.

"Nothing. Just something I have to figure out."

"But what is it?"

"You know, it's still interrupting me even if you're whispering."

"Oh. Sorry."

He feels bad. This kid's mom is leaving her. "I've been asked to show my work in a gallery."

"Oh. And you don't know whether you want to?"

"Right. And I'm not sure I have enough paintings."

"How many do you have?"

"Fritzie."

"Oh, sorry."

"It's going to be a lot of work."

"And are the people scary?"

"What? What people?"

"The ones who asked you. Are they scary? Like, if you don't have enough paintings are they going to be all, 'Grrr! Patrick! DO SOME

99

MORE PAINTINGS! WHAT IS THE MATTER WITH YOU?'" She makes her hands into monster claws. He stares at her.

"No. No, probably not that."

"Okay," she says. "Then what are they going to do to you?"

He doesn't answer. Instead he paces around and looks in a cabinet at some paintings he'd stored away. Some oils that he remembers liking. Portraits.

"There's just one thing I want to tell you, and then I will be very, very quiet for the whole rest of the day," she says, whispering again.

"What?"

"When I was in the basement about an hour ago, I saw that my mom had packed her suitcase. I think she's going to go soon."

He looks over at her, and she gazes steadily back at him. There's nothing in her face, except perhaps just a little trembling of her lip. Just a little, and then she looks down at her painting and does a wide swipe of black across the front of it.

God, he is so in over his head. Maybe he should go over to her and give her a hug, but that would be awkward when he's never hugged her before, and maybe she would be freaked out by a man hugging her, especially one with scars all over his arms and face.

"Okay," he says, and even to his own ears, his voice sounds gruff. "Well. It'll be all right. Don't you think so?"

"Probably," she says cheerfully. "Also, Patrick, why *aren't* you married to Marnie?"

"You said you had only one thing to tell me."

"But I just thought of this one, too."

He sighs.

"Don't you want to get married to her?"

"Look, it's complicated," he says. "We're just not ready yet. Okay? Now stop asking questions."

"You should get married."

"There are things you don't understand."

"What?"

"Fritzie, your limit of questions is up."

"Okay, Patrick. But I hope you'll tell me when you're ready."

An hour later he calls Philip Pierpont and says that he'll do the gallery show. Because, as he has just figured out, there are going to be worse things than needing to be stuck in his studio painting and painting and painting.

CHAPTER TWELVE

MARNIE

September 5 is the first day of school, and the lady who runs the office of the Brooklyn Kind School, Maybelle, is the picture of red-cheeked, delighted frazzlement. "The chaos will settle down in a few days," she says and comes from behind the counter to scoop two first graders into her ample arms at one time, while she's yelling out a cell phone number to a woman in the doorway. A bald, smiling school bus driver ducks in to say good morning and how glad he is that he's back because that foot surgery threatened to derail him. It's been a heckuva summer, he says. But here he is, wanting her to admire his limp.

"Yonatan, how the heck are you? You know how the first day of school goes," she says to him. "Come back and limp for me tomorrow. I'll have time for true admiration then." Then she turns back to me, giving Fritzie a wink as she hands her a name tag and a hall pass. The door to the office keeps opening and closing, with people running in waving pieces of paper and shouting hellos. Somebody drops off a plate of brownies for Maybelle, and Fritzie licks her lips and looks at me long-ingly, so Maybelle gives her one.

"Now who's filling out the health and emergency forms?" says Maybelle, and Tessa steps forward. Her face is smudged this morning with eyeliner gone awry, and her masses of curly hair are shoved up into a messy cloth scrunchie. Really, if you ask me, she looks sort of sexily disheveled, like somebody who just fell out of bed after staying up all night having sex. She's lugging along a carpetbag that she keeps adjusting over her shoulder and tottering along on boots that seem just a tad too high to be safely manageable. She's only coming along with us because I made her.

"Okay," Maybelle says to her, "you sit over here, hon, while I go over these and make sure we've got all the information we need. And let's see, Fritzie is assigned to be in Karen and Josie's class. And that is . . . yep, room 115. Just down the hall here, on the right. Almost at the end." She stops to smile at Fritzie. "Oh, pumpkin, you are in for such a good year! Karen and Josie know all the best jokes." Then she taps her temple and says to me, "By the way, if you need anything, I'm your go-to. By the end of the day today, I'm going to know where everybody is supposed to be, what their full name is, where their parents work, and the cell phone numbers of every single babysitter and grandparent. You'll see."

I look over Tessa's shoulder at the forms, where I learn that Fritzie's real name is Frances Elizabeth Farrell, and that Tessa Farrell is really Tessa Johanna Farrell, and that she will be residing in Rome, Italy, for the school year. Patrick is listed as the father and the main emergency contact.

And then, just before she's handing the papers over to Maybelle, I see Fritzie poke her mother, and Tessa grabs them back and with Fritzie standing over her, she crosses off the name Frances Elizabeth Farrell and writes in the name Fritzie Peach Delaney.

"Thank you," says Fritzie in an urgent whisper. "You said. I'm Patrick's now."

Tessa turns and looks at her, bites her lip. Then she says in a low voice, "All right. I'll go along with Peach. But legally you are not Fritzie Delaney."

Fritzie shrugs, and Tessa purses her lips and writes Patrick's last name on the form.

I want to say, *Wait, what?* What exact kind of thing is being perpetrated here?

Fritzie Peach Delaney? Are they kidding with this? I don't know which part jolts me the most—that Fritzie is choosing her own name, and it's a fruit, or that Tessa is now handing her over to Patrick symbolically. Taking his name. Of course, she *is* his child. She should have his last name. Probably. Maybe.

Tessa slides the paperwork across the desk to Maybelle, who looks it over and then tilts her head and says to me, "Marnie, are you Fritzie's stepmother then?"

And so then it has to be discussed that I am not really the stepmother, because Patrick and I didn't get married yet. And Fritzie pipes up that she asked Patrick about it, and he said we're not ready yet.

"When do you think you're going to get ready, Marnie?" Fritzie asks. "Did you decide that part yet?"

"Never you mind, it's all fine," says Maybelle.

"Well, shall we all walk down to Karen and Josie's room?" I say. "Meet the teachers and see about these jokes?"

"Okay," Fritzie says. She looks longingly at Tessa. "You coming, Mama?"

"I've got a phone call to make," says Tessa. "You two go ahead."

"But don't you want to see my teachers?"

"It's fine. They're going to be busy this morning, and the important thing is that you and Marnie see them. They'll just be confused if they see two moms coming in."

Fritzie puts down her backpack and goes over to Tessa, starts fingering her sleeve, running her hands along the hem. She puts her face up close to Tessa's and whispers something to her. For a moment their heads are together, and then Tessa pats her daughter's arm.

"You go yourself, Fritz, with Marnie. It's okay. You're going to be fine."

Fritzie hangs back. "But, Mama, when I talk to you on the phone, and I tell about Josie, I want you to know who I'm talking about."

"I'll know. Of course I'll know."

"Mama."

"You know what?" I say brightly. "Your mom can meet them on a different day. Or maybe at the pickup this afternoon."

Fritzie and Tessa just keep looking at each other. All around us people are swirling about, with their papers and their questions and their cell phones buzzing, their toddlers whining. But here they are, like they're in a bubble or something. Separate. There's something odd.

Fritzie keeps touching her. Tessa keeps looking away. "Mama, you look very pretty, Mama." She puts her hands in Tessa's hair, and Tessa tolerates it for a moment and then reaches up and takes Fritzie's hands down. She stands up.

"Okay then. Go to your classroom. And be good for the teachers. Don't make trouble the first day. You'll do your best? All right?"

"Okay."

Maybelle and I make eye contact, and she widens her eyes, like *what the actual hell is going on here*, and I shrug just the slightest bit. Fritzie is licking her lips in a manic way, and I put my hand on her shoulder and say, "You ready, honey? Let's go meet Karen and Josie."

I don't know what I've just seen, but my heart hurts.

The hallway is paved with moms and kids, all hugging and greeting each other, catching up after the summer, paying us no attention at all.

A few of the moms have fat, gurgling, chunky babies on their hips, or toddlers in tow—and I love how they pass the kids around and also how they get so excited talking about how much everybody has grown. They explain about their vacations and the catastrophes, they make plans to get together, to meet on the playground, to schedule a potluck for the end of the week, to go away for Columbus Day. They are so delightfully scary, these moms, with their shiny, just-shampooed hair, and glowing, makeup-free faces, their familiarity with each other's habits and problems and needs, their stylish clogs and skinny jeans and big leather bags. The universality of motherhood, the oldest language. Not one of them has been into Best Buds seeking a new love, I realize. No, these are the settled Park Slope young moms, the ones you see marching down the street with their Perego strollers. They have found their partners in life and are striving forward, not looking back.

"Are you going to be class mom this year? Oh yeah, well, what if they ask you?"

"Do you know if Vanessa is babysitting for Adam again?"

"Is Raven going to run the fourth-grade musical?"

"Does Maybelle have your contact info? She was looking for you!"

This is mom talk, I think with surprise. I'll get fluent in this. I'll be one of them, coming in at pickup time, sighing as I get the homework folder and ask Fritzie if she remembered her sweater or her lunch box. I'll be the one saying, "Why don't we invite Annabelle over for a play-date? And we can make some vegan brownies!"

"You know what's weird about this school?" Fritzie says to me as we thread our way between collections of parents and kids, all talking at earsplitting levels. She practically has to yell over the din: "Why are the teachers called by their first names? I think their names should start with Ms."

"It's the way this school does things, I guess. I think it's kind of nice and friendly, though, don't you?"

"Aren't they supposed to be the bosses of us, or what?" she wants to know. "Am I s'posed to say, 'Hey, Karen, get this kid to stop bothering me'? I mean, how's that gonna work? Is the kid gonna even listen to somebody named Karen?"

And then she falls quiet. I look over at her, in her blue-and-purple plaid shorts and her sequin shirt—it says HELLO in pink when the sequins are pointed upward, and GOODBYE in blue, when you mash them downward. She has her hair tucked behind her ears and she's wearing a white baseball cap on sideways and pink plastic clogs. I had some questions about this as a first-day outfit, but when Tessa didn't say anything, I realized I shouldn't either.

But now I wonder if Fritzie has suddenly caught the same trepidation I have, if I've transmitted it to her like the flu. All these bouncing children and parents, all of them knowing each other, running back and forth, tagging. A little boy bumps into Fritzie, and she yells, "Hey!" and he says, "Sorry!" and keeps going. I should think of something encouraging and positive to say, so I say that there's a lot of love in this school.

"Don't get mixed up," Fritzie says. "This is school, Marnie."

Then we get to Karen and Josie's room, or so it says on a piece of blue construction paper decorated with brightly colored hats and horns. Inside the room are tables pushed together in groups of three, and the bulletin boards are bright and festive. The place is filled with parents and kids, all talking at once. Karen and Josie are wearing jeans and identical big smiles, and they welcome the children to their colorful, busy, warm classroom.

"Ah, so you're Fritzie?" says the one called Karen, who has a blonde high ponytail and big, smiling blue eyes. "There's a chair for you over there, with a folder on it. And here's a little companion to keep you company in third grade." She hands Fritzie a teddy bear and then turns to me. "Hi—welcome to the classroom. You're welcome to stay for as long as you like, but I'm hoping to get the class all together for introductions and some games by about nine, so if you're comfortable leaving then, that would be great." She gives me a big, toothy, Miss Congeniality grin.

"Okay, sure," I say. I look around at the other parents, some of whom seem to be getting ready to say good-bye. There's no drama except for a toddler who has decided he's staying here no matter what, and his mom has to chase him down as he's starting to dismantle the cute, cheerful folders that have kids' names written on them. He's carrying a bunch of them around in his sweet little hands, and then he has a meltdown when it turns out he can't take them with him.

There's a class hamster who is doggedly running on his wheel, like that could help him throw off some of the existential angst he must feel, being surrounded by twenty-four curious eight-year-olds and their parents. Fritzie, who isn't very interested in her chair or her folder, stands and looks at him for a long time.

"You know," she says to a little boy who has come over to see the hamster, too, "I think we should let him out and see how fast he can run. Do you want to?"

"No," says the little boy.

"Come on. We could see if he runs into the coat closet or out the door, or maybe he's going to run under the radiator."

I'm about to intervene, but the little boy moves away, giving Fritzie a strange look. She shrugs and starts fiddling with the latch on the cage, and I go over and shake my head at her. I do the Mom Microscopic Head Shaking, nothing that would embarrass her. She looks down at her shoes and her cheeks get two bright pink spots on them, and I want to hug her and tell her I'm so sorry.

Just then Josie claps her hands for attention, and she gets the class to come forward and sit on the circular rug in the front of the room. "Parents, you can leave now, since you probably already completed third grade," she says, and everyone laughs.

I go out in the tide of people leaving, waving to Fritzie, who looks at me with big, round blue eyes as I'm departing.

Is she unhappy? Are those eyes about to fill with tears? Or is she going to have liberated a hamster by the end of the day, and be expelled?

I do not think I'm going to be quite the same until twelve o'clock comes when I know for sure she's survived the first half day.

Tessa and I walk back to the subway together. She is tromping along in her high-heeled boots, lugging her carpetbag and being exceptionally quiet, staring down at the sidewalk while she walks.

"Well, I think that went really well, and I think she's going to be just fine," I say. "I found myself actually getting kind of emotional, you know? Leaving her there? She looked for a moment like she felt emotional, too. What did you think of the school?"

"Yes. It was all fine." Her face is unreadable, especially since she's walking slightly faster than I am.

"Do you want to go and get some breakfast? There's a funny story about the class hamster I want to tell you."

"I can't." She stops walking, so I stop, too. The sun is blazing in a very early September way, filtering down through the green maple leaves. Tessa's face is in shadow.

"What is it?" I say.

When she looks up at me, her eyes are opaque. "Listen," she says. "I'm not going back with you."

"You're not? Where are you going?" I think she means maybe she's going for coffee somewhere by herself, or to buy something for Fritzie for school.

She looks from side to side. "Richard is here. And I'm going to meet him."

"Richard . . . came here? But that's great!" I say. I immediately start thinking of a nice dinner up on the rooftop, with all of us. I'll have time to make lasagna and I can get some of Paco's snowflake rolls and the Irish butter. Maybe a cake. It will be so civilized, us getting to wish them well. "We can all get to meet each other, and—"

I stop talking because she has closed her eyes. I think she's so embarrassed for me.

"Oh," I say, getting it. Then I look at the carpetbag and say, "Ohhhh."

"We're leaving this afternoon."

"For Italy."

"Yes." She shifts her bag to her other shoulder.

"But why are you doing it this way? You could have brought Richard around—wait, why is he here anyway? How long has he been here?"

"He showed up day before yesterday with a ticket for me. He said he didn't think I was really going to come so he wanted to come get me." She takes out her scrunchie and tosses her hair in a way I've never seen her do, like a woman in a shampoo commercial.

"Of course he didn't think you were coming. Because you've done nothing but say you were coming."

"Is that sarcasm?"

"It is sarcasm. Yes. It's the way I'm choosing to express my dismay at what you're doing. Wow. You're just . . . you're sneaking off, and Fritzie is going to be devastated, and you know it."

"No, she's not. You don't know her. She doesn't care."

"She does care. You're her mom."

"Well, but it will pass quickly. I know her. I've left her a thousand times before, and she gets over it."

"Not like this time, you haven't. Not for months. Come with me right back into that school, and let's tell her together. Come on."

"No. I'm not going to. Trust me. It's better this way. She'll be better off, not having some long, drawn-out good-bye scene. That doesn't do anybody any good." She reaches into her bag and hands me an envelope. "Here's this. Her birth certificate. In case you need it."

"I can't believe you would do this. I can't get over it."

"Listen, I'll call her tonight. My Uber is here."

Sure enough, almost as if by magic, a black Lincoln Town Car slides up to the curb, and she holds up her hand to the driver.

Then she turns and looks at me, and her eyes look just the slightest bit guilty—or maybe I am merely *hoping* she looks guilty. "Really. I didn't know he was going to do this," she says. "But maybe it's best because I suck at good-byes."

"Everybody sucks at good-byes," I say.

The driver has gotten out of the car by now. "Are you coming?" he says. When she says yes, he opens the car door, and she puts her bag on the seat and then scoots in next to it.

She looks over at me and says, "I'm sorry you're so mad at me. But I want to say thank you. The other night, when you said you would love her—that meant everything to me."

The driver walks around to his side and gets in, starts the car, and puts on his turn signal, and after a moment the car pulls away, into traffic.

She's gone. And everything that comes next is going to be up to me. Tears are pressing behind my eyes. I could honestly sit right down on the curb and start crying.

A slight breeze kicks up, sending some leaves spinning in a circle. I text Patrick. *She left! LEFT WITHOUT SAYING GOOD-BYE TO FRITZIE. She freaking just got in an Uber and went to the airport. Said she sucks at saying good-bye.*

I don't know what I'm expecting him to say—a full expression of outrage over this? Maybe he'll suggest getting in an Uber himself and racing to the airport to yell at her.

Instead, after a few minutes, he texts: *Marnie. We are not and never have been dealing with an intact human being. That is why we're in this situation to begin with. What did you expect? We'll deal with it. Somehow.*

CHAPTER THIRTEEN
MARNIE

Around eleven thirty, after stomping around and ranting and raving about Tessa's poor decision-making skills to the Best Buds crowd for nearly two hours before settling down to fill flower orders, I head back to Brooklyn Kind School.

Josie and Karen, Josie and Karen, Josie and Karen, I say on the way, like a mantra. I need these two to be everything and more. We may need to get a whole team of psychologists and social workers and play-date moms to help this little girl not feel like an abandoned child. I get off the subway and walk the three blocks to the school crossing, and uncrossing my fingers, smiling at the other moms, sizing them up for possible friendships later on. Emily Turner catches up to me when I'm about a half block away.

"Hi! How did she do at the drop-off?" she asks breathlessly. "And isn't this just the best school? Did you adore Josie and Karen?"

"Hi," I say. "Yes, it went well. And she actually seemed fine. Talked to the other kids, didn't blink an eye over my leaving, and was even looking like she was going to stage a coup to let the hamster run races around the classroom. So I'm perfecting my Mom Eyebrow Raise."

"Let's see it," says Emily.

"It's not all there yet. So no judging." I take off my sunglasses and arrange my facial expression just so, so that my right eyebrow can arch slightly menacingly. I've seen my mother silence an entire minivan carpool of screaming little girls with this trick.

"Hmm," says Emily. "I find it helps if you crook your mouth around just so, too. But you'll get it. Like this." She demonstrates by making perhaps the scariest face I've ever seen. She actually shows a glint of teeth. "Hey, so how are *you*? Do you have the first-day jitters, too? No offense, but you look a little stressed."

"Her mom left," I say.

"But that was the plan, wasn't it?"

I tell her the whole story: no good-bye, no warning, not even a visit to the classroom to look the teachers over and say nice things about what a great year it's going to be. Changed Fritzie's official last name on the forms to Patrick's and vanished.

Emily reaches over and touches my arm. "Come to the playground with us this afternoon. Do you want to? Maybe Fritzie is going to need to work off a little bit of steam."

"I'm supposed to go back to work. I have a wedding consult to do at four."

"Just stay for a little while then. We'll get treats from the ice cream truck and let the kids do their thing. I think the sprinkler system is on, and they can run through the fountain and cool off. And you can meet the other moms. We're going to be your people now. Might as well come get to know us in our native habitat: the playground."

"Thank you. I do have questions."

"I'll bet you do. Like, what the hell are we doing? Is that one of the questions?"

"That'll come later. Mainly now I want to know what everybody carries in their giant bags."

"Oh," she says airily. "Three-course meals, including appetizers and snacks. Thermoses of vitamin water. Tourniquets, antibiotics, antipsychotic drugs. A bottle or two of wine. A corkscrew. A laptop. Headphones. iPhones. A thousand dollars in small bills. A stun gun."

You see? This is why I love Emily Turner. Something tells me I may need to borrow somebody's stun gun right away.

When Emily and I get to the school cafeteria, where we parents are supposed to wait for our kids' dismissal, I see Fritzie hanging with a group of little boys, still wearing her baseball cap and hopping around like she's perfectly at home. Her face lights up when she sees me, and she comes running over, only to get stopped by one of the teachers. Apparently kids must wait in a certain area until they're fetched.

Karen sees me and frowns just the slightest bit. Which—I'm not going to lie—makes my heart sink a little bit. Did there end up being a hamster incident despite my amateur Microscopic Head Shaking? Am I going to have to resort to using words next time?

But no. She's just marking kids off from the checklist on her clipboard and struggling to put names to faces. She tells me, smiling sweetly, that Fritzie had a good day, that she's going to be "quite an asset to the classroom, a real lively personality," and I beam as though this is such exciting news, even though it could also be a euphemism for "most disruptive human being ever."

Fritzie is jumping from one foot to the next and waggling her head back and forth, which makes the baseball cap fall on the floor, and a red-haired kid swoops in and grabs it and pretends he's going to eat it. Fritzie screeches, "Don't eat my hat again!" and takes it back.

"Wow, you've had quite a day defending that hat," says Karen. She smiles at me. "Everybody loved her hat. A couple of people even thought it might be delicious to eat, isn't that right, Fritzie? Which was sort of crazy!"

And she gives Fritzie a big good-bye hug.

When we're on the way to the playground, trailing behind Emily Turner and a whole gang of moms and their kids, I say, "So was it a problem, your hat?"

Fritzie shrugs. She seems like she's in a very good mood. "Nah. It wasn't a big deal. It fell off one time, and Max picked it up and put it on his own head, and then this boy named Laramie took it and said he was going to put ketchup on it at lunch and eat it, but then I got it back, and he chased me around the classroom, and we knocked into the table of folders and they all fell on the ground. Big deal. I picked them up." Then she yells at the top of her lungs at the boy slightly ahead of us. "Laramie!" she calls, and then again. He stops and turns around, and she throws him the hat.

"Here," she says, "you can have it!"

He runs over and grabs it. "Really?" I notice he was walking by himself, looking over at the other kids with a kind of longing.

"Yeah!" she says. "It's yours. But don't eat it unless you're very, very, very, very, very, very, VERY hungry. And don't put ketchup on it!"

After he bounces away with it on his head, I say, "Wait. That's your hat. Why did you give it to him?" and she says, offhandedly, "I dunno. He needed it."

She dances sideways and backward all the way across the street, and I keep having my heart stop and restart. And once we're there, sorting ourselves out and claiming benches, the moms all open up their magic bags and hand out healthy snacks, carrots and bottles of special water and little packets of dried kelp and something called Pirate's Booty, and I get to sit on the bench next to Emily Turner and her friends Elke and Lily and Sarah Jane, all of whom are wearing the most fabulous footwear I've ever seen—clogs and sandals and whatnot—and we feed the children these wonderfully healthy snacks from sweet little ecologically sanctioned containers, and pick up their backpacks, and then someone mentions lunch like it's a thing we should have been thinking about, and so we gather up everybody, plug Sarah Jane's twins into a massive eighteen-wheeler stroller, and wrangle Elke's toddler, and off we go, to lunch down the street at a sushi restaurant, where it's California rolls and sensational games with the soy sauce bottle and plenty of happy exuberance.

There's a tension headache starting to pound just behind my eyeballs. But I try to be grateful for every moment that Fritzie is happy and carefree and playing with friends. I look up at the sky and squeeze my fingers one by one, intent on appreciating.

Patrick said we would deal with it.

It's not until Fritzie and I are making our way to the subway that she suddenly says, "Hey, where's my mom?" She's skipping from one foot to the other when she says it, intent on not stepping on any cracks. "You know why I'm doing this, Marnie? Because you can break your mother's back if you step on one," she says. "I don't know if you know that or not."

"I have heard rumors about that," I say. "But once when I was a kid, I was mad at my mom so I stepped on every single crack, and her back has stayed fine all these years. So I have serious questions about whether it's true."

"Yeah," she says. "I did that, too, one time."

"And was Tessa fine?"

"I guess so. So, where is she, huh? How come she didn't come to the school to meet me?"

"Well," I say. Okay. So here we are. I try to think of what to say. I've been trying to think of what to say all afternoon long. On the sidewalk there's a gingko leaf torn and now in the shape of a heart. I try to let it give me some courage. I believe in signs from torn gingko leaves.

She has stopped walking and is looking at me. Her eyes are guarded, like she knows what's coming and has steeled herself for it.

"Well, sweetheart, your mom left for Italy today," I say. "It was kind of a big surprise to everybody—even to her, I think. Richard showed up in Manhattan with an airline ticket for her, and so they left."

"Oh," she says. Her face goes dark, and without looking at me, she picks up a stick and starts dragging it along an iron fence, clanging it on the bars as she walks. It's like watching storm clouds coming up over the horizon: you can see them coming, but there is no escape.

"I'm sorry. It's kind of a shock, I'm sure." When she doesn't answer, I say, "I was wishing she could have said good-bye to you."

At this, she sits down on the ground, on the sidewalk. Just plops herself down and folds herself up, her arms wrapped around her knees and her head down.

I stop walking. "Are you okay?"

"Leave me alone." Her head is buried in her knees.

I stoop down and put my hand on her back, and she pushes it away.

I can't imagine what would be the right thing to say. What I want to do is pick her up and hug her and hold her and tell her that she's safe with me. But she wants me to leave her alone, so there's that. I look up and down the street, as if the answer might be found in one of the parked cars or any of the people walking by. Finally I say, "We can talk about it. Do you want to talk about it?"

"No." Her voice is muffled. Then she says, "I just thought she would say good-bye."

"I know. It sucks that she didn't. I'm really sorry."

Some teenagers go by, making a wide circle around us. Up ahead, I can see Emily Turner already at the corner, looking back in our direction. She does the "are you okay" gesture. I nod. And then I sit myself down next to Fritzie on the sidewalk. She's still all folded up, rocking back and forth, and I can hear little sad sounds coming from her. Little peeps, like a chick would make.

"Do you want to go home?" I ask her finally. I put my hand on her back, and this time she doesn't push it away.

"No."

"Okay. That's fine. We can just sit here."

"Go. Away."

"I'm not going anywhere."

"You should go because I'm going to stay here forever, and I am never going to talk to you."

"Okay then. Me, too. I'm not going to talk to myself either."

"You might as well go see Patrick, because I am not moving."

"Nope. Patrick will have to come find us if he wants to see us."

We sit in silence. She keeps her head down on her arms. I'm stiff, sitting on the pavement, so I inch myself over to the little patch of dirt and grass, the place where every dog in Brooklyn has probably peed. For a while I can't think how this will ever end.

And then—I don't know, about four eons in, I remember something I once believed about love and how it's in the messiness that all the good stuff comes, and I close my eyes and beam her over some love. And then a couple of eons after that I say, "You know, when I'm really as angry and furious as I ever could be, I like to yell and scream and run around in a circle and bang on something."

She peeks out from underneath one arm.

"Let's see," she says.

So that's how it happens that at 3:45 on a Wednesday, the first day of school and the first in my life as a substitute mom, I am on Clinton Avenue in Brooklyn letting out bloodcurdling screams and running in a circle and then banging on somebody's stone fence post with a stick. And the little girl watching me is grim-faced and serious with streaks of dirt on her cheeks where the tears were. But at least she's watching.

"Stop it," she says sternly. "You're making an idiot of yourself."

"Oh, yeah? You think you could do it any better?"

She gets to her feet and grabs the stick from me and then she zooms around and around in a circle, shrieking so loud that airplanes are probably having to be rerouted from Kennedy Airport, and then she beats on the stone wall until she's completely exhausted, and then when she's done and sweaty, she says, "*That* is the way you do it."

I say, "That was very impressive. What do you say? Shall we go meet a bride at Best Buds?"

"Why is there a bride at Best Buds?"

"Oh, she thinks she wants some flowers for her wedding. Silly of her, I know."

"Okay," she says at last. "But I am not ever going to be happy again."

"Absolutely not. Me neither."

As soon as we get home, Fritzie marches in the front door and goes to find Patrick, calling his name over and over again. I'm putting away her backpack and hanging up her sweater when he comes out from the study across the hall, lifting his eyebrows to me.

"Patrick," she says. "You are going to have to get used to me, because my mum has gone away, and I am never going to speak to her again."

"Well," he says, blinking. "Okay, then. I've been put on notice."

"I HATE THEM! Her and Richard. I HATE THEM!"

I hold out my arms for her, but she doesn't come any closer. She's like a little feral animal, not looking for cuddling.

Patrick runs his hands through his hair, and we look at each other because we have no idea what to do, except I'm thinking maybe eating dinner would be a good idea. Patrick says he would like to make Fritzie's favorite food, whatever that might be, and she walks around in a circle for a while, pondering and then says that would be hamburgers and artichokes and cherry pie and root beer. With butter sauce for the artichokes and thousand island dressing for the hamburgers.

He and I exchange glances again. He lifts his eyebrows. "It can't be pizza from around the corner?" he says. "Or a chicken from Paco's?"

"No!" she roars at him and goes over and pretends to pummel him in the stomach, only she really does get carried away and actually starts hitting him, and he has to fend her off, which almost makes her start crying. She is perched on such a delicate edge.

And you know what, because we would do anything to make her feel better, Patrick cooks the hamburgers on the grill on the rooftop, and I go to Paco's and get artichokes and cherry pie filling and instant pie crust and root beer, and I come home and make a pie. We're all hard at work, even Fritzie, who whirls around in a circle in the kitchen singing one of those tuneless songs from childhood—this one about worms going in and out of a corpse—and then I see her eyes light up as she hits on the idea of chasing down Bedford and dressing him in one of her T-shirts. He puts up with the shirt business, but apparently draws the line at wearing underwear on his head. They both come running through the kitchen and then the living room, with him barking and her shouting, and then suddenly she bursts into tears and runs and hides behind the couch and won't let either of us hug her.

But finally we get dinner ready, and she carries the pie up to the roof while Patrick and I bring everything else, and then she tells him about her classroom and the hamster and how the teachers want to be friends with the kids, and that's why you don't have to call them Ms. Her eyes are sparkling as she tells him all this, and he teases her about being friends with teachers.

Despite the slight reprieve while she eats dinner, I can see in her eyes that she's shell-shocked and sad, and that the hurt welling up inside her is so huge it is swamping her. After that, despite my efforts to have everything go smoothly, we argue over whether she needs a bath (I lose), whether she should brush her teeth (I win), and when it is time for bed (nobody wins; she argues and stalls and thinks up increasingly ridiculous topics to complain about until after ten, when we are finally all exhausted).

I lie down with her and Mister Swoony, and even though she says she's *never* going to sleep, and *never* going to be happy again, and *never* going to speak to her mother or be nice to Richard, she finally, finally drifts off. Once I'm sure that I've heard every last peep from her, I ease myself off the bed. My back is stiff, and my neck has a crick in it. And not only that, I have cramps and a headache. I stagger into the bathroom, blinking in the bright light. It's past eleven by now.

And there it is: my period.

Hi, it says. *You didn't really, really think that little rip in the condom four weeks ago was going to bring about a BABY, did you? You DID? And you think of yourself as somebody who has a sense of magic and possibility? And you didn't know I was waiting for you? Hahahahahaahaha.*

My period is always a little bit mean and capricious, but I never knew it would be this terrible.

I slide down the wall and lie on the floor with my face against the cool tile. I don't want to think about anything right now except how the fibers of the tan bathroom rug are quite irregular. It's fascinating, really, how there are different shades of beige and tan and ecru, all woven and twisted together, sticking up and leaning on each other. You might miss these if you never took the time to lie down on the floor, I think.

Should I cry? Maybe I should let myself cry. I am sadder than I think I have ever been.

Patrick comes in to brush his teeth. I don't move. I just stare at his feet in front of me on the rug. Patrick's perfect, unburned feet.

"Um. What are you doing?" he says.

"I'm feeling sorry for myself."

"Oh," he says. And then, *"Ohhhhh."* He's noticed the box of tampons on the edge of the sink. "Can I do anything?" he says. "Do you want some tea?"

"No. I think I am going to lie on the floor and cry for a while."

"Okay." His toes don't move. I close my eyes. And then I feel the warmth of him surrounding me. He joins me there on the floor, and at first he simply rubs my back and my cheek, and then he gathers me up and holds me against his chest, and he says, "You know. If tonight is any indication, we might have dodged—"

"Don't even," I say.

"I mean, just saying—"

"Patrick. I mean it. Stop."

He kisses my hair, a hundred little kisses. His heart is beating against my cheek. We stay that way for a long time. I feel tears burning under my eyelids. I am so tired and so sad.

"Marnie," he whispers. "If you really want—if this is what you need, we can try again."

I pull away and look at his face. "On purpose this time?"

He closes his eyes for a moment. "God. I must be a lunatic, but yes. On purpose. But could I ask you one thing? Could we wait? Can we get settled with this halfway-grown one first? Can we just make sure we can live through this before we embark on another?"

"All right," I say.

"I must be crazy, saying this. I *am* crazy."

"Don't overthink it, Patrick. Just take it as it comes. It's *life*."

"Okay, but can you please, please come to bed now? Because God knows we are going to need our strength."

CHAPTER FOURTEEN
MARNIE

And then the first weeks of having Fritzie go horribly. Like, the worst.

For one thing, she won't talk to Tessa on the phone when she calls. She says from the next room, "Tell her I died." Another time she yells out to me, "Please just tell her I hate her, and also I don't remember her name."

The following Thursday she says, "Tell her I'm your daughter now and she can stay away."

On the following Sunday, she's doing her homework when Tessa calls and she says, "Tell her I already grew up and left home and I'm living in my own *pensione* with a man who is handsomer than Richard and nicer."

Each time, Tessa hangs up without pressing the issue. She actually said to me the last time it happened, "Well, I guess this shows what I was saying all along. She doesn't miss me."

"No, no!" I said quickly, but it was too late because she'd already hung up. No, I would have told her. It proves just the opposite. She misses you so much she can't bear it.

Three weeks later, as September slides into October, Fritzie and I get around to painting her room a routine but comforting pale blue. I'm relieved that's the color she's picked because it seemed equally plausible that she'd go for—oh, I don't know—metallic rainbow splotches or Death to Civilization Black. I'm so happy with the pale blue that when she picks out gold foil stars to stick onto the walls, as well as gold filmy bubble curtains for the windows, I'm game. In fact, I'm game for almost anything. My heart is one big wet pulsating ball of sympathy for her right now. We go through stores like we're members of the Kardashian family, piling into the cart anything she wants: posters of unicorns and pugs and one of Dumbo with his mother as well as a large pillow in the shape of a pretzel, a lava lamp, assorted stuffed animals with enormous eyes, and an alarm clock that also tells the weather. We get a beanbag chair and white Ikea bookshelves, a new bed, a desk with a swivel desk light, a dresser, a chair on wheels, a rug with stripes, and baskets for her toys to go in.

While I'm on a ladder painting with the roller, she careens around the room, nearly stepping into the paint tray four separate times, and then insists on helping me paint the corners, which means that at one point a whole brush full of paint goes flying across the wood floor, and I have to run for wet paper towels, and while I'm gone, she steps in the paint tray and tracks even more light blue footprints across the room. When I (very kindly and patiently) convince her to stop, to never again in her life move even one muscle if there is painting going on anywhere in the vicinity, she dresses up Bedford in her baseball hat and one of her T-shirts, and the two of them run through the hallway, barking and shrieking, which causes Roy to come dashing into the bedroom, screeching, with his fur totally puffed out, and it's clear that between the paint fumes and the interspecies noise-making, he's having his well-earned nervous breakdown. He of course skids right into the puddles of paint on the floor and turns in midair and flies off down the hall making an unearthly sound. I am so sorry for him, but I have to capture him and wash his paws with water, which he hates more than anything. Then I have to wash the floor in the hallway. And the places on the wall, where he somehow touched, because I swear he was airborne at several points.

I say to Fritzie, "Do you want to take a picture of your room and text it to your mom so she can see?"

"Do you know how to spell the word *no*?" she says. *"N. O. N. O. N. O. N. O."* She says this a hundred more times, at least.

"Okay, okay, I get it," I say after a while.

We live through this day.

Patrick, who has been working in his studio, comes in from time to time, to offer consolation, wet paper towels, sandwiches, and some expertise with the Allen wrench, but we both know this is my project, not his. I'm the one who knows how important it is for her to have a haven with her own decorations, a place where she can go and shut the door, miss her mom, listen to music, do her homework, do whatever she needs to make this year okay for her.

I feel as though I'm always trying to nudge him toward her, to make him see how wonderful she is. They have a running joke about how Roy thinks he's her brother and that she's merely another cat who's always looking to take his cat treats. I'll hear her giggling while Patrick is teasing her about how Roy stashes the tuna surprise anywhere he can find.

"Roy sees you looking at that tuna surprise," I heard him tell her. "He used to hide it in your bedroom, but now you've made it so he has to look for new hiding places every day."

She giggled. "He put it in your shoes today!"

"No, no," Patrick said. "That's where you're wrong. It's under your pillow."

"No! It's under *your* pillow!"

"Not even close."

Sometimes he'll take her with him when he goes to Paco's, and he buys her gum and sour candies and those little fried apple pies that come in wax baggies. He doesn't tell me much, but I imagine that he has to be proud to have a little girl who will chat with just about everyone and who is so self-confident that she has to be prevented from going around the back of the counter and demanding to learn to use the cash register.

My mother laughs when I tell her about all this. Well, she laughs once she's gotten over the shock of Patrick having a child from a previous encounter. It has to be explained to her several times that he didn't abandon a pregnant girlfriend and then hold out on paying child support. "No, no, no," I say. "She never even told him she was pregnant."

"But, honey, didn't he *see* her?"

"No, Mom. He barely knew her. Only for that one time."

"She got pregnant in a one-night stand?" she says. "Are you sure you believe this?"

"Yes. I believe it. Because it's true. And anyway, that's not the point. The point is that the mother feels it's now his turn to do some of the child-rearing, so we have an eight-year-old staying with us for a few months."

"So you're somebody's stepmother!" she says. "I bet you can't do one thing right, can you?"

"Well, I'm figuring it out as I go along," I say. But I'm bristling at this just a little bit. It's hard to explain to my mother how much I already love this child, how this seems like some of the universe's magic at work, bringing me a gutsy little girl. There are times when I'm helping her with her homework or washing her hair for her or picking out her clothes for the next day that I feel myself floating up somewhere near the ceiling, looking down in amazement at how my life is changing.

But for some reason, everybody wants to make this a story about me getting a raw deal.

Before we hang up, I tell her a few choice details that I think might amuse her: the room decor with the lava lamp, Mister Swoony who

126

looks like he has mange, Fritzie's desire to dress Bedford and Roy in T-shirts, and the fact that, at the teacher conference I went to, Josie and Karen said she was adventurous, strong-willed, and fearless, and that she hates being left out of anything.

"Ha!" my mother says. "And you just know they mean she wants her own way all the time and is the ringleader for all the troublemakers."

"Yep," I say. "Yes, that is probably exactly what they mean."

"Does she talk to her own mother, honey?"

"Well, she doesn't want to, but I insist on making a weekly phone call to Tessa, just to keep her in the loop. So far the conversations are pretty short and awkward, but I think she needs to have contact with her mom."

"Can't say I blame her, though, for not wanting to. What kind of mother does that?"

"I know, I know. But it just might end up being the best thing for everybody. You know? We can't rule anything out."

"Do some of your magic about it," says my mother, "and then turn your magic wand or whatever it is over to me. I'm ready to lock your father in his den and throw away the key. The only thing is, he wouldn't even ever realize it. He'd just stay there!"

In the afternoons I hang out with the other moms on the playground, but I am always keeping one eye on Fritzie as she leaps from the top of the climbing structure, chases the other kids around in circles, and goes so high on the swings that my heart stops. By the time we go home, my teeth feel like I've been chewing on metal.

"Don't look," Elke tells me, when she sees me wincing. "They have to do this. It's some kind of law of nature. Nobody understands it."

The people of the Frippery point out that I've become a lot less sunny lately. Love, I want to tell them, can do that to you. It can make you downright uneasy until you find your way.

"You're jumpier," Ariana says. "Do you need me to come and babysit for you sometime? I think you're developing a twitch in your eye."

"A *twitch*?" says Kat. "The twitch is the least of it. She looks like a prisoner of war, being deprived of sleep and water. Here, my dear, at least hydrate yourself." She hands me a big cup of tea. "Go smell some of the lavender in the cooler. I've heard it'll change your brain."

"Tell us what is the very worst part," commands Lola, leaning forward, her kind eyes beaming into mine. "You've got to just say it out loud. Vent a little."

"Sssh. She won't do that," Kat says. "She doesn't want to be negative. You know Marnie."

"The worst part," I say slowly, "is that I want to show her so much love, and I can't make up for what she went through with her own mother. And the worst, *worst* part is that I want to make us into a wonderful, big, happy family, and . . . and . . ."

Lola gets up and hugs me, and Ariana declares we need a group hug.

"You're magic, Marnie," she says. "Don't forget that Fritzie landed with you for a reason."

Oddly enough, that's the day I feel the very best. As though I might be coming back into myself. When I go outside, leaving Best Buds to go pick Fritzie up from the after-school program, I look up and see the sky and notice that the leaves are changing colors and the sky is a crystalline shade of blue.

Crazy, I know, but it's like I'd forgotten all about the sky.

"How many more months do we have left?" Patrick asks me one night as we get into bed.

"Of what?"

"Of what? Of Fritzie living here."

I don't answer him, so he sends one of his long legs over to my side of the bed and pokes me with his big toe.

"Come on," he says. "Seriously. When is Tessa coming back for her so we can resume our lives?"

"I know you're joking about this, and I don't think it's funny."

He laughs. "I am so not joking. This is everything I outlined in advance that was going to be hard about parenthood. Teacher conferences. School projects. Kids' stares. The only thing I left out was that I didn't know about how a kid would want to paint a room and in the process would destroy the finish on the parquet wood floor in at least two rooms and a hallway. That I didn't anticipate."

"First of all, the finish is not destroyed. I mopped up the paint. And you, my good man, haven't had to go to even one school conference. And I think having Fritzie—who, just as a reminder, is your daughter—is opening our lives up."

"Perhaps our lives were just fine half-closed the way they were." He comes over to my side of the bed and nuzzles me, trying to get me to smile. "Come on. You know this is a hell of a thing we're involved in here. It's astonishing that people live their lives this way. Look at us. We are wrecks of our former selves, and I do not think we're even halfway done. And please don't tell me again about life's great mystery being laid out before me."

"Halfway done! You think we're halfway done? This is October, Patrick. *October.*"

He pretends to look shocked. "So you're saying this is going to be a lot longer."

I stare at him. I mean, I know this is his idea of humor, but it makes me mad.

"Patrick, this is possibly not the best time to bring this up," I say, "but I am actually the one doing nine-tenths of the work around here—both the emotional work and the physical work. So if anyone has the right of complainership, it's me."

"Absolutely. I bow to your right of complainership. Please. Go ahead. Complain away. I would *love* to hear any complaints you have about our current lifestyle."

"Yes, well, I'm not going to complain, because this is the life I expected to have. This life—with a little girl who needs us, who is brave and funny and smart and heading off every day into a world she didn't ask for, without her mother—and, well, I find that incredibly moving."

"It's very moving. And in fact, it would make a fine documentary someday. But that being said, it's a hell of a lot of unplanned work. Look at us. We're both exhausted, and now we're arguing when in the old days, we could be making love or reading or planning our peaceful tomorrows. Instead we spend all our spare oxygen talking about who made her lunch and did she do her homework, and why isn't she asleep yet, and . . ."

"Patrick."

". . . and who's going to be home when, and what if . . ."

"Patrick."

"What?"

"I know what you're doing, and I'm just putting you on notice that I still want a baby. *And*, as I may have mentioned, I am thirty-three, which is not all that young when it comes to fertility. And Fritzie is doing well so I think it's time we started trying on purpose."

He slowly slides off the bed onto the floor, as though he's oozing life force.

"Get back up on the bed."

"I have died."

"No, hear me out. I think parenthood is easier when you start with a brand-new one and work your way up."

"That is a theory that has not been proven."

I get up on my knees on the mattress and stare down at him. He's sitting on the floor facing away from me, slumped against the bed. "No, no. Patrick, listen. We'll already know so much about kids from being Fritzie's parents, that when we have a baby, there won't be any surprises."

"There are always surprises," he says. "This conversation right here is a big surprise actually."

"Well, it shouldn't be. We've had it before."

"Yes, but we agreed to wait awhile. Remember that? Your Honor, may I treat the witness as hostile while we review the tapes? You, Marnie MacGraw, said you wanted a baby. I said I didn't see myself as a father. You said I should think about it. We had sex, during which the condom mysteriously and 'accidentally' broke—" He crooks his fingers in the air.

"Do not air-quote the word 'accidentally.' You know as well as I do that—"

"May I proceed, Your Honor? Later that week, we find out we're going to be raising a child for a year in circumstances that can only be described as surprising and completely out of left field and not of my choosing. But okay. One year. Which brings me back to my original question: Is the year up yet?"

"Yes, the condom broke. But it didn't result in pregnancy, and then you said we could try again, so I think in view of the fact that I am close to being in my midthirties and you have agreed to try to have a child, that legally I am entitled to as many chances as possible. I want to buy a thermometer and start doing the charting of ovulation and all that."

"You would say this to a man who is currently lying on the floor of your bedroom, gasping for his life?"

"All I am asking is that you get yourself up on the bed and take your clothes off."

"Why are you so bossy?"

"Because I love you, and I am not getting any younger."

"You! You are killing me."

But he scrambles up onto the bed anyway, and I slather him all over with love, and by the time we're ready for sleep, I do not think he is even close to dying.

CHAPTER FIFTEEN
PATRICK

It's November, the month that Patrick thinks should include a trigger warning on the calendar page.

November was the month he was released back into the world after his hospitalizations from the fire, and each year around the anniversary of that, there is always a morning when he awakens to find the world has turned cobwebby and dusty. When he can't lift his head. The sharp smell of autumn, the particular slant of light as it comes through the windows, and the shortening of daylight settle once again into his very bones. He thinks he can even still smell the acrid odor of the smoke. His cells *know*. They are keeping records.

This year, on the anniversary morning, as every morning, he makes a mug of coffee and goes into his studio. Roy, who has decided to live in there full-time since life has gotten so busy in the main part of the house, greets him disdainfully like the fellow refugee/traitor he is. Roy sits majestically on top of the pile of unused canvases, licking his nether regions as though he's in his own private spa and the weak little sunbeam he is occupying was designed for him alone. Indeed, this studio is the place where both he and Patrick can seize even the smallest vestige of their previous life.

More and more, this is the moment Patrick waits for each day, this time of entering the studio, shutting out the world, seeking the seductive dark comfort of his pain. But today there is no comfort anywhere. He knows he's not pulling his weight in the household. He sees Marnie looking at him, measuring how much more she's doing than he is for Fritzie. She seems made for the mad dash of domesticity, while he feels lumbering and slow. He makes Fritzie's breakfast each morning, and he starts the coffeepot—and today, heroically, he was the one to locate her missing shoe, which Bedford had taken into the living room and hidden under the couch.

And then, as every morning, he was there at the front door, to see them off. Perfunctory possibly, but he does it. Each day he watches as the two of them toddle off together, heading toward the subway carrying their bags, adjusting their sweaters and their hats. Today he saw Marnie reach over and straighten Fritzie's hat, then lick her finger and clean her chin. The universal gesture of moms.

He turned away and closed the door. The piercing pain in his heart wasn't from witnessing this touching moment between two people to whom he's connected. No. It was the realization of his own emptiness. Down at the very heart of him, there is nothing. No sensation.

He knows he is not going to let himself love this child. He can't. That would be setting himself up for a heart-stopping disappointment when she is reclaimed by her mother. Anyway, it's better this way, maintaining his distance. He is far too screwed up for her to count on him. That's what nobody but him seems to see. It's like he's howling in the wilderness to the universe: *I am not to be trusted. I have a bad track record with other humans. Do you not remember that I was present at the death of one of your very best ones? I could not be relied upon to save her, and I can't help any of the others either.*

Patrick goes to the other room, where he's placed the paintings he's worked on and then put aside. He doesn't know what he was expecting them to say to him, but what he sees levels him. Here it all is, laid out before him, caught on the canvases: the smell of the hospital room, the rampaging fire, the lost self figuring out how to go on and failing at that and then failing again—all of this is right here in the work.

He sits back on his heels, staggered.

Will anyone want to see all this pain? Is there even any particle of beauty or hope in these? He examines them closely.

Goddamn. *Everything* he's done is despair. Everything. There are the two big uncompleted ones and five individual paintings that are finished, or nearly so. They are crap. How could he not have seen? How did this sneak up on him? This whole show he's doing is turning into a retrospective of his doomed relationship with Anneliese. There is no mercy in these paintings. They show only his crabbed view of the world, his well of desolation.

Anneliese, he sees, is his ghost and muse. And he doesn't know how to get free of her. She is always going to be there in his mind, jumping in when he's making love to someone else, screaming when he's sleeping, throwing herself at him when he is doing something as simple as picking up a paintbrush.

No wonder he is wrung out by the end of each day. Because every day she lives and dies again. Every day there is the fire that answered the question of who they were to each other. If he is completely honest with himself, he knows that they were an ambivalent couple. She was a difficult woman. He was a clueless man. They were locked in strife sometimes, and sometimes, even sculpting next to each other in the same room, breathing the same air, they were as far apart as any two people could be.

This is what he paints: the distances, the silences, the fire, the death. He is in that world all day long.

Hey, she says. *Would you like to paint the moment right after you woke up from your coma, when you knew you were always going to be the one who didn't die?*

Sometimes, when he breaks for lunch, he stands in the quiet kitchen, hearing the house noises and the traffic sounds from outside. The refrigerator motor comes on, the radiators scream out their protest, water gurgles in the old pipes. This old house has creaks and complaints as it settles even further into the earth. It's been settling for over a century, and yet it still sinks farther. He waits for Blix to tell him what to do. Marnie claims that Blix can sometimes be reached over by the toaster, the temperamental toaster that should probably be thrown away except that Marnie has this silly idea that Blix might be the one causing the toast to fly out of it at odd times. *You can talk to her, Patrick. Ask her a question. She's with us. I know she is with us.*

But he doesn't believe in that. Instead, he gets his lunch—a piece of chicken breast left over from dinner, an orange, a piece of Manchego cheese, and a refill of coffee—and he goes back to his studio, not even letting himself glance toward the toaster. He wonders sometimes if the spirit of Blix might rush after him as soon as he closes the door. If she might come in, with her expansive love, her laughter, and change the dynamic for him, the way she did before.

But there is only Anneliese. Perhaps Anneliese keeps Blix away.

Hours later, consumed with his work, he hears noises in the other part of the house, and he looks up. Darkness is pressing against the windows, and his neck and back are stiff. His time in the studio is up. He listlessly packs up his paintbrushes and attempts to reclaim all the pieces of himself so he can reenter what everybody else thinks of as his real life, but which he knows is really his fake life. He has to hurry because if he doesn't, then Fritzie will bound in to fetch him, her face bright with excitement. He knows Marnie tries to keep her from interrupting him, but at some point, if he doesn't appear, she spring-loads her way in, and cannonballs herself into his arms. She looks at the paintings, and he sees her face change from happy to confused and sad.

He wants her out of there as soon as possible, so they go together to the kitchen, where the warmth is, where there is music and the crazy comfort of the turquoise refrigerator, and where he grounds himself by touching objects: the vases with flowers, and stoneware pottery and the big old black gas stove with the orange teakettle on it and the worn wooden floor and Blix's old toaster. Slowly he lets himself be absorbed back into this different kind of life. He greets Marnie with a kiss, gets out plates and glasses for dinner, stirs the spaghetti sauce, pops in the pan of biscuits, pours the milk, wipes the table, smiles, asks questions, half listens to the stories of the day.

Laughs with them, even though to his own ears, his laughter sounds hollow.

How is it they don't know who they're dealing with? How do they not see his fear? It's as though every day it's a little bit harder to bring himself fully back to them. A little more of him has remained behind.

He sees Marnie looking at him sometimes before his regular personality has fully come back, sees her quizzical glance as she tries to figure out where he is. In some moods he thinks he'd like to tell her. But then he comes to his senses. No, he wouldn't. He doesn't want her to know. That would be the worst thing.

How would he even say it? *I still think about my old girlfriend. My relationship with her hasn't ended. In fact, it may be starting up again, breaking out in a new place. Also—you should be aware—I really did love her, and it was my fault that she died. You need to know that I might kill things I love. I don't think I can be what you want me to be.*

CHAPTER SIXTEEN
MARNIE

"I have a big, big, honking stomachache and I can't go to school today," Fritzie says one morning. "It's the worst stomachache I've ever had in my whole life."

"A *honking* stomachache?" I say, smiling. "Not even just a beeping one?"

She doubles over. "It's HONKING and HONKING."

The truth is I've been expecting this—the fake stomachache. I know it's fake because until this exact moment, she has been sitting at the kitchen table drawing a picture of a clown on a bicycle with a monkey on its shoulders, and three times she's needed me to stop making her lunch and go over and praise her for such an inventive drawing, and she's given me a huge, grateful smile each time. She's also had a glass of orange juice, some oatmeal with raisins, and half of a blueberry muffin. And she's told me in great detail exactly what to pack in her lunch box, detail that a person with a true stomachache wouldn't be able to bear thinking about.

Also, she just thought of this stomachache thing when it was time to put on her coat.

Believe me, I may be a rookie at this mothering an eight-year-old business, but I do know some things.

"So what's really wrong?" I say. "Tell me the truth, and I promise to try to understand. Why don't you want to go to school? Really?"

She looks like she is going to fake-cry. "Because my stomach hurts so much, and I probably have to throw up, and also I have a fever, and Blanche was sick yesterday and I played with her on the climbing thing, and it was too cold to be outside, and you can get sick if you get too cold. That's what Lola told me. She said to come in when it's cold, and I forgot."

"See? I'm going to be honest with you. That is too many things. When you're not telling the exact truth about something, and you want to be convincing, you need to limit it to just one really dazzling airtight excuse."

"What does airtight mean?"

"It means why don't you really want to go to school? What's going on?"

To my surprise, she slips off the chair and falls to the ground and rolls herself into a little ball. "I can't go to school! My tummy is killing me. If you make me go, I'll just be in the nurse's office throwing up all day, and they won't let me stay at school, and then you will look like a very bad mom."

"But you don't look sick."

"But I am. My mom would have let me stay home. So don't be mean to me."

"Here, stand up. Let me feel your forehead." I don't know what I'm feeling for, but she is now making herself look like a nineteenth-century waif who has lost the will to live.

"All right," I say at last. "You can stay home."

She brightens. "Tomorrow, too?"

"Tomorrow, too? What? Wait a minute. What's this all about, Fritzie Peach?"

"Nothing. I just think I'll still be sick tomorrow. I might not be well yet. If this is the flu, I definitely won't be well."

"Whoa, whoa, whoa. You don't have the flu. What is this all about?"

She traces a line in the floral pattern of the tablecloth, getting up to follow it all the way to the other side. She won't look at me.

"I'm on your side, you know. You and me. Against all the forces of evil."

Then she says in a low voice, "Josie says I stole some money."

I feel my heart sink at this news. Mostly because I don't have any idea of what the right thing to do is. I want to press pause on this conversation and go off to google "WHAT DO YOU SAY WHEN YOUR CHILD IS ACCUSED OF STEALING MONEY?" Do I automatically take her side, or start sussing out whether or not she did do something wrong? Why would she steal money? Is this the acting out that we've been waiting to see?

"That must be very hard," I finally say. "Why does she think that?"

"Well, she thinks that because I was the person collecting the money for the book fair. I was the one picked to take the money to the office, and when I got there, the money wasn't in my pocket anymore." She holds out her hands, in the universal gesture of what-the-hell-could-have-happened-here.

"Oh." I feel a little bit relieved. "So did you drop the money along the way, do you think? Did it fall out of your pocket maybe?"

"Maaaay-beeee."

"And somebody else possibly came and picked it up and didn't know where it belonged, and so they . . . took it home with them?" I say, like the good enabler that I am.

"Yes!" she says, brightening. "I bet that is what happened. Will you tell my teacher that that's what happened?"

"Hmm. Why don't we check with Maybelle? Maybe it's in the Lost and Found right now. Wait. How much money are we talking about?"

She shrugs, darkening again.

"You don't know? Why don't I email your teacher and ask her? Maybe we'll just replace it. This is so fixable, Fritzie. It is not a big problem at all. We all lose things or drop them sometimes. We'll just explain what happened . . ."

"It is a big problem," she says under her breath.

"I'll go email Josie right now," I say, and I get out my laptop from underneath the pile of mail on the counter. But oh dear, as soon as I power it up, I see there's an email in my inbox from Josie, with the heading, "Can you and Patrick come in?" And then it goes on from there: "There's a situation I need to bring to your attention concerning Fritzie. We are truly enjoying her liveliness and her inventiveness and her generosity to all her classmates, as I communicated at the teacher conference we had in October. But recently some disturbing things seem to be happening with missing money in our classroom, and each time, Fritzie has been the common denominator.

"We have reason to believe she's taking money from the other kids, and from the book fair envelope, and we think she may be giving it to another child she's become friends with. If you and Patrick could come in sometime with Fritzie, I'd like to handle this privately, if possible. How about after school tomorrow?"

"Fritzie," I say, looking up from the laptop. She's staring at me from across the table.

"I want my mommy."

"I know, and we can call her tonight if you want. But for right now, tell me what's going on. Please."

Her face crumples. "I want to call her right now. I didn't talk to her in a long time."

"We can call her tonight. So tell me—what happened?"

Her voice rises. "Are you going to believe the teacher, or are you going to believe me? My mommy would totally believe me, you know. But you probably don't believe me because I'm not your real kid."

"Wait, wait, wait." I can't help but laugh. "Holy moly! Don't pull that 'not your real kid' stuff before you even tell me what it is. Just tell me this: Are you giving money to another kid?"

"What she says is wrong."

"What is she saying that's wrong?"

She puts her head down in her arms on the table.

"Miss Peach. Are you giving money to another child?"

From her face, still buried in her arms, comes this: "Did you know there is a kid at my school who has to live in a shelter? He's *homeless*. Like the guy in the subway."

"And . . . ?"

She lifts her head and starts sniffling, so I hand her a tissue and wait. She looks away and traces her finger on the tablecloth again.

"Fritzie?"

"Ohhhkayyy," she says. "Well, Laramie told me on the playground that he wanted to tell me a secret, and the secret is that he lives in a shelter with a bunch of other families and . . . and . . . his dad is working somewhere far away and can't come home, and his grandma is trying to send them money because his mom can't get a job because she's got little kids and nobody can babysit them. And Laramie is so sad, and I told him it's not fair that other kids have so much money. Marnie, they have money that just falls out of their pockets sometimes. It falls on the ground even, and he doesn't even have any good sneakers. The ones he has have holes in them."

"Oh, honey," I say.

"So I don't want to tell them I'm sorry. Because I'm not. But everybody is mad at me, and Grady said I'm an idiot and he's the one who told on me, and now I don't want to go to the after-school program anymore because I hate everybody there, and Grady told everybody that I'm a stealer, and even Laramie got mad at me because everybody found out."

"Okay," I say. "We're going to fix this." I leave the kitchen and go out into the hallway, heading to Patrick's studio.

"No, no, no! Don't bother Patrick!" Fritzie calls after me. "Please! Patrick is too sad!"

She grabs onto the hem of my shirt. "Don't go in there. He's painting all the sad stuff, and we have to let him get the sad stuff out, because then he can paint good."

"Did he tell you that?" I ask her.

"Well, no, but I told *him* that. I went in there one day because I needed some peanut butter, but the jar was too tight, and he said I shouldn't come in and bother him when he's painting, and I said I needed him to open the peanut butter jar, and then I said to him, 'You should think about happy things, like about when I came to live at your house with you, or maybe you could paint about Marnie. Or taking Bedford for a walk. Any of those things would be good!' And he said he can't do that, and I said maybe it's because the sad stuff needs to come out first. Then he said I needed to leave him alone. And he opened the peanut butter jar and then I left, and I heard him lock the door."

I tell her it's all going to be fine. I say she should go brush her teeth, and that I am going to go get Patrick, sad or not, and that then we are all three of us going to the school to work things out.

And after we get the school theft stuff figured out—well, then I'm going to have to figure out what is going on with Patrick.

My phone rings just then in my pocket, and I look down and see that it's from my mom. Because of course everything always happens at once. There must be a tear in the fabric of the universe somewhere that lets everything tumble in all at the same time. But I can't talk to her now.

A few minutes later, there's a text from her.

Marnie, your father sat on the couch THE ENTIRE WEEKEND watching movies on his computer. Words he spoke to me = 2. Words I spoke to him = 250,487 approximately. Words I intend to speak to him today = 0.

CHAPTER SEVENTEEN
PATRICK

They have to go to the principal's office, which is the worst.

Just the words *principal's office* make Patrick shudder. He'd spent a fair amount of time in one of those back in Barnaby Falls, Wyoming, for petty crimes and misdemeanors he always seemed to be accused of committing in elementary school. Funny how he'd managed to push memories of all those incidents out of his head, and funny how they all come tumbling back when he walks into Brooklyn Kind School, an imposing brick building with high ceilings and checkered tile floors and that school smell, an indefinable mix of white paste, cafeteria vegetable soup, and sweaty children.

The woman at the front desk of the school, somebody named Maybelle, says, "Well, y'all are just gonna have to go wait in the principal's office," and that's when he feels his insides curdle up.

Maybelle looks at him and says with a laugh, "Oh, honey? Did I just scare the daylights out of you? You turned about four shades whiter than you were when you came in here."

He feels himself stiffen. Here it is, just as he feared: some stranger commenting on his appearance. But then Marnie touches his arm, and he calms down. Even though Maybelle *was* technically mentioning his appearance, he realizes that she wasn't talking about his scars—she was joking about him having to see the principal. That's all. He can be charming about that, can't he?

Why, yes he can, and he will.

Because something else has occurred to him. This meeting, this situation, is bigger than anything about him. Fritzie was attempting to right some injustice she'd seen, and he is here to defend her. Sure, maybe she'd gone about it in a clumsy way—certainly she shouldn't take money meant for the book fair—but as he looks over at her, sitting up straight on the wooden chair in the principal's office while they wait, trying to be brave but fidgeting and squirming around in her seat, licking her lips the way she does when she's nervous, he feels a little bit sad for humanity. Yet another little human being is about to learn the cold fact that no good deed goes unpunished.

Poor little duck, he thinks, as he watches her. She's wearing blue-and-green leggings that have little gold stars on them and a long yellowish sweatshirt that says GRRL POWER on it, and her fine brown hair is a shade too long and might be still tangled from sleep; he'd heard her and Marnie discussing that it might be time to get it cut, but obviously whoever thought it was time now had lost—and he sees that her little face is so pale and skinny, like his, and her eyes look a little red-rimmed and scared. Yet she's thrusting that chin up in the air. Defiant.

She feels him looking at her, and he pats the chair next to him, and she scoots over and sits beside him. Leans on him, actually, in a way she hardly ever does. She's all angles and fidgety action, this one, and if she touches anybody, it's likely to be Marnie. And where *is* Marnie, anyway? He can hear her out in the other office, chatting with Maybelle. Buttering up the opposition perhaps. Laying on the charm.

"It's going to be okay," he whispers to Fritzie, patting her arm. "I've got a master plan for how we can win this one. We are going into battle together against the overlords who might try to stop us. If necessary, we will invoke Buddhism and Jesus and the Preamble to the US Constitution and the King James Bible and the Kindness Doctrine, even if we have to *write* the Kindness Doctrine because life doesn't really have one."

She giggles a little. *Good,* he thinks.

Then his adversary, the principal—who goes by the intimidating name of Annie just to throw people off—comes rushing in, apologizing. She's a woman of about forty, with long, straight black hair parted in the middle, and she's wearing jeans and a harried look, and the first thing she does is stop by Fritzie's chair and give her a hug.

"Oh, honey, we have got to figure something out to make this okay," she says. Then she turns to Patrick and says, "So you're her father, I gather. And what a sweet, empathetic little soul you're raising!"

He can feel his face flush. So *this* is the way they're going to play it, disarm him first. He knows that full disclosure requires that he say something about how he's only been in Fritzie's life for two months, hardly the formative years, and he's hardly raising her. But he doesn't, because Annie winks at him and he can see that she knows it already. She says, "And you—so new to her life, too! What a gift she is!" And she smiles, shakes his hand, decidedly not reacting to the fact that his hand has scars and dry skin and is a mess.

"Now!" she says, and claps her hands. "Let's all sit down and figure out together how to fix this and make it right."

Then she plops herself down across from them in a ratty old armchair and, leaning forward, gets to the first point, which is that what Fritzie did was out of such a sweet desire to help another child, and how that is exactly the kind of spirit needed in the world and it is so good to see, especially from a little girl who is new to the school but who has already made so many friends and whose teachers think the world of her.

Patrick is aware that Marnie and Maybelle have come in and are standing near the door, watching. He sits very still, waiting with his battle plan.

"But," Annie says, "sometimes we want to help so badly, and we can't always know the right way to do things, can we, Fritzie? And so let's try to brainstorm what might be a better way of helping Laramie without taking away something from other people or embarrassing him. Because, as you already know, Fritzie, taking money from other people isn't the right thing to do. Right?"

Fritzie nods. But Patrick is pleased to see she doesn't look horribly ashamed. She's fine.

This Annie takes out some paper and a pen and says, "So let's hear some ideas. Anyone can contribute." And she looks around, waiting, her eyes sparkling.

Patrick flicks a piece of an old leaf off his jeans hem and when nobody else says anything, he says, "Well, we could pay the money back to the people who gave to the book fair."

She nods and writes that down.

Fritzie says, "I could say I'm sorry."

"Yes, and . . . ?"

"I know!" says Fritzie. "We could ask Laramie's family to come and live at our house! We have plenty of room!"

Marnie laughs, and Patrick's stomach drops. He knows Marnie well enough to know that it is not outside the realm of possibility that she and Fritzie would start a campaign to move an entire homeless family into their house.

Annie smiles. "Well, although that is very, very kind of you, Fritzie, maybe we should think of something that doesn't involve such a huge change. Is there something simpler we could do for now?"

Fritzie bites her lip. "Um, I could ask Laramie to come and play at my house after school. And he and I could do paintings with my dad, who's a painter—and then we could go to Marnie's store, which has flowers, and maybe Marnie would pay us money to work in the store. I know how to work the cash register, and it's really fun there, and then . . . and then . . . then we can go down the street and get snacks. Would that be okay, Marnie?"

Patrick's brain short circuits at the words *my dad*, just as if he's received an electric shock. *My dad?* He catches Marnie's eye, and she smiles at him.

"Well," says Marnie, "one idea would be that maybe Laramie and his mom and the other kids in the family would like to come over for dinner sometime. We could get to be friends, and maybe that would help them most of all."

Annie is beaming at them. Patrick feels his ears buzzing, no doubt a result of the short circuit.

They are still buzzing twenty minutes later, when he and Marnie leave together, walking back to the subway, after dropping Fritzie off at her classroom. He has met and somehow shaken the hands of both Karen and Josie, he has endured the stares of thirty pairs of eyes as kids looked up from decorating papier-mâché Thanksgiving turkeys, and he now feels himself to be coated in a kind of brotherly love and kindness that is so palpable it's almost uncomfortably sticky. Having kids paint in his studio? A family coming over for dinner? He is trying to get ready for a show. Has everyone somehow forgotten that? The day feels too bright, the air sharp against his skin.

Marnie takes his arm. "You did brilliantly in there," she says and hugs him. "And what did you think of the school? Isn't it just fantastic?"

He feels himself grimace for no good reason. "Well," he says. "They put on a good show. I'll say that for them."

She laughs very hard at that one.

"You are such a porcupine, Patrick Delaney! Can't you take just a moment to bask in the idea that what we just experienced was pure joy?" She pokes him in the arm, and then seeing that he's still scowling, she stands on tiptoe and kisses him long and hard and juicy on the mouth. Right there in public, two weeks before Thanksgiving, and him with his porcupine quills sticking out all over the place.

No, no, no, he thinks. *Pure joy would be having our lives go back to the way they were. No art show, no daughter I'd never known about, and no need to go visit some elementary school in the middle of the morning. It would just be me and Bedford and Roy, watching our game shows, visiting with Paco, letting the days drift by, and then calm, beautiful Marnie coming home in the evening. Alone.*

CHAPTER EIGHTEEN

MARNIE

The next day Ariana comes clomping into Best Buds after school, and I can tell right from the moment the bell sounds over the door that trouble is a'coming in. And sure enough, there she is, soaking wet from the rain and filled with angry purpose. Ariana, of course, is usually the human equivalent of a sparkly unicorn of love, so I sit up and take notice.

She jumps up to sit on the counter like she does when she wants to talk. I'm filling out an order form that's overdue, and she fiddles with the flower arrangement we keep by the cash register. Today it's lilies and mums. I wait to see what she wants to tell me.

"You should totally get more of those tulips, the ones that are multicolored," she says. "Everybody loves them so much."

"Well, it's true they're lovely, but they're out of season now, so I think I'm going to concentrate more on the mums."

"Oh! Totally! Yes. Fall is mum time. I guess you probably had to study up on flowers before you could run this place." She sighs and looks around, picks some imaginary speck off her left boot. Her curly yellow hair falls over her eyes when she bends forward. I see that the tips today are tinted purple. Without looking at me, she says, "So. I've got to do a magic spell on my dad. Any ideas?"

"Your dad? Why? What's going on?"

"He's decided that I'm a loser because I don't want to go to college next year."

"Wait, wait, wait. I've met your dad, and he doesn't seem like he's even capable of saying your name and *loser* in the same sentence. If he had had buttons on his suit the day I met him, they would have been busted off, he was so proud of you." Then I say, "And also, another whoa. Back up a sec. Why don't you want to go to college?"

"Because I have another plan for my life." She brushes back some of her stunning curls. "I've decided that I want to go on the road with my video camera and interview people about their lives and then make a whole series out of it. And my friend Justin wants to do this, too, and so we're going to get his uncle's van and do a GoFundMe thing so we can outfit it for podcasts and videos and stuff, and then we're going to broadcast our way across the country for at least a year and after that, if we're not famous yet, we'll go back to school."

"Wow," I say. It's true that she's been taking videos of all of us nearly relentlessly. And it's also true that she and Justin, a handsome, lanky guy with a killer jawline, and who slouches rather admirably, have started hanging out at Best Buds—and they have been sitting in the corner lately, their heads together, excitedly writing stuff in a notebook. I could sense that plans were afoot. But I thought we were having some senior-in-high-school love stuff. I even said to Kat one day, "Well, now we're going to be having a bunch of sparkly unicorn love action going on. We won't be able to see the flowers for the amount of love sparkles we're going to be experiencing here," and she said, "You forget you're the only one who sees the sparkles. The rest of us can see the flowers just fine, and also the dust and the cracks in the plaster and the storm clouds." (I am apparently surrounded by porcupines.)

But back to Ariana, who is now spinning out a tale of woe. "So I tell my dad this, thinking that he'll be happy that I want to help people talk about their lives—and instead I get met with this resistance." She makes a mean face. "Like, he doesn't respect creativity *at all*."

"Well," I say. "I mean, if you wouldn't mind spelling it out for me, what exactly is the creative thing you and Justin are making?"

She gives me a look of strained patience. "I told you! Videos! Podcasts! I want to give people hope, like you do. And so part of it would be just letting people tell us about the things that they believe in. Like what gives them hope."

I can't take my eyes off her. She has just a little dusting of rainbow glitter across her face today, and she obviously dipped her hair in purple Kool-Aid. While she talks, she's fidgeting and spinning some of the ten different rings she's wearing. And her eyes are glowing like crazy. I can see how her father must be out of his mind at hearing that his daughter wants to head across country with a long-haired, jeans-wearing eighteen-year-old guy with a scruffy beard and a porkpie hat and some microphones.

Then she says, "So, this is super obnoxious probably and you can say no, but do you think I could come and stay at your house? I could help you with Fritzie, and I can clean house, and I'm really quiet and my mom says it's okay if I find someplace for a while, until my dad cools off and this blows over."

"Oh, honey," I say. "Of course you can."

She lights up. "Seriously? For reals?"

"Yes. Totally. Let's just make sure it's for reals okay with your mom first."

"Believe me, she'll be grateful for the peace and quiet."

"Is she on your side, do you think?"

"She doesn't like to rock the boat. Last night she came in my room and said that I should just go to college and do my video thing on my own time, and that my dad wouldn't have to know. I should go to college for the financial security it'll bring, she said. But why should I have to go to some stupid college and hang out with kids who are drinking and doing drugs and wasting their parents' money, just because my dad thinks that's what I should be doing? I'll get my degree after all this."

So I talk to Ariana's mother, Rebecca, on the phone, and I tell her we might need some help around the house with our eight-year-old, especially where Common Core math is concerned, as well as some afternoon pickups, and we'd love to have Ariana stay at our house.

Rebecca is filled with relief and gratitude. "Teenagers!" she says. "You think you're going to be so good at raising them, and that you're such cool parents, but then—*bam!*—the very thing you didn't expect hits you right between the eyes!" Then she lowers her voice. "And have you heard that her friend Janelle is pregnant? We found *that* out by accident. It just seems that in this day and age, when they have birth control, when they have every advantage—sex education, understanding parents—no kid would have to go through this. And yet they do. I guess some things never change." She laughs a little bit. "So if it's not too much to ask, it would be much appreciated if you somehow forbade Ariana from getting pregnant while she's staying at your house. We like this boyfriend of hers all right, but I'll like him even better if they don't get pregnant for ten more years."

"Your mom says you can stay with us," I say when I get off the phone. "But she'd rather you didn't get pregnant at my house. I said I thought we could all agree that would be best."

"My mom is unreal," says Ariana. "Like she doesn't even know that I don't think I *ever* want to get pregnant. Janelle is, like, sick all the time, and it's like she thought it was going to be so super glamorous or grown-up or something, and now it just sucks for her. She's so tired and she doesn't want to hang out anymore. I videotaped her the other day, and all she wanted to do was cry." Then she covers her mouth with her hand. "Oooh, I shouldn't say that because you and Patrick are trying, aren't you? How's that going, or is that a rude question?"

"Nothing happening so far," I say. And then I get very busy doing paperwork, not looking up, and after a while of aimless wandering around, Ariana says she's going home to pack up some stuff and she'll be at my house for dinner. Is this really okay, if we start today? And do we need her to bring stuff? Should she live in the basement apartment, or sleep on the couch? Or in Fritzie's room? Anything is fine by her, just so I know. And by the way, is it really true that we need help with Fritzie's Common Core math problems, because if so, she is so on it.

"This is going to work out great!" are the last words she says as she disappears out the front door. Along with her she takes a whole bunch of the happy vibe of the place, and the happy vibe doesn't come back until an hour or so later when I look up to see a man and woman holding hands and smiling at me. The place is practically iridescent with sparkles all over the place.

"Marnie?" says the woman. She has long red hair, and she is beaming. "Do you remember me? I'm Winnie."

Of course! It's the woman from the restaurant, and next to her, smiling goofily, is Graham, still in his fedora with the feather. "Hey, how are you guys? And how's your mom?" I say. "Still in Florida, using alcohol to solve people's laundry problems?"

"We're great," he says, flushing a little. "And—well, we wanted you to be the first to know, after our parents of course—we got engaged last night!"

Of course they did. "Oh, your mother must be so thrilled for you."

"She's over the moon," he says. "Told me to thank you for spilling that wine on your skirt, or maybe none of this would have happened."

"And shall we tell her . . . ?" asks Winnie, tipping her head up and smiling at him.

But they don't have to tell me. I know. They're having a baby. You can just tell sometimes. Their auras are all crazy happy. I come around the counter and hug them, and then I pick out some yellow roses for them to celebrate everything. And they say that I must come to their wedding, and please to bring Patrick, too.

Of course, of course, I say. Sometimes being a matchmaker is just the best thing there is.

"Blix?" I say, after I watch them leave. "When is something going to happen for me?"

From up around the cooler, Blix says, *Just wait. Don't freak out. Just wait. And by the way, nice work with that Ariana. College would be a waste for her right now.*

CHAPTER NINETEEN
PATRICK

The doorbell rings, and something about the insistent ringing sound makes Patrick shake himself loose from the painting he's doing. This requires Anneliese to withdraw. *I'm sorry, but it's only momentarily, not for good. I am still painting what you say,* he feels himself saying to her. She's now his full-time muse, after all. Some days it's as though she's taken over all the rest of him, too.

Normally he has a self-protective policy of ignoring all doorbells while he's working, but today he's not completely settled in. He's having trouble sleeping, is the truth of it, so he's extra tired. At the startling sound of the doorbell, he goes over to the window and looks down at the stoop. There's a young woman with hair that looks like it was dipped in purple ink, standing there in a thin sweater, leggings, and Ugg boots, stamping her feet and looking around her.

Wait. He knows who this is.

Ah yes. It's what's-her-name. Ariana. He's seen her at Best Buds back when he used to take meals to Marnie when she was working late.

Marnie says she's the leader of a group of teenage girls who do stuff, who aren't afraid of anything. She's the one who takes videos. And please God, don't let that be a suitcase she's holding.

Great. Just what he needs: another fearless female standing at his front door with a suitcase. He's all full up just now on women who seem to be striding forward into his life, asking loudly for what they want, especially when their desires include a year of him raising their kid, the proper kind of cheese on the macaroni . . . and a baby. And what is this one going to be asking of him? Something, he is sure.

His phone dings, and he glances down at it.

Patrick. Ariana is going to be showing up at our house. She's got some parent trouble. So I said she could stay with us for a while. Will you show her down to the basement apartment and give her a key? #PatrickSheNeedsUs #YouWillLikeHerIPromise.

I am sorry, he writes. *You have obviously typed this to the wrong number. There is no one named Patrick at this number. I have never even heard of the name Patrick. Very weird name.*

LOL. Patrick. She's a kid. And it's just for a little while. You remember what it's like being a kid trying to work things out. Temporary insanity. Also, she knows Common Core math, which will keep US from having to learn it. #BrightSide

Marnie. She's at the door. #sigh #WhatIsHappening #LifelongInsanity And when should I expect the school's homeless family to move in? Will I get more of a heads-up on that one?

He wishes immediately he didn't write that last bit. She might just take it that it would be okay with him to invite Laramie's family in. He wouldn't put it past her.

CHAPTER TWENTY
MARNIE

Having Ariana live with us turns out to be great.

Fritzie and I help her fix up the basement apartment, with baskets and pillows and candles and bedspreads. And in the evenings, now that Patrick is working on his paintings in the studio, she comes upstairs, and the three of us make dinner and do homework and dance around the kitchen like wild women. We talk about love spells and the joys of videotaping people and the right way to do a math problem and how fun it is when dogs wear T-shirts.

We all have our things. Fritzie does cartwheels and draws us pictures. My contribution is that I know how to cook and also I have a million stories about life and matchmaking, and Ariana knows a hundred ways to tie scarves. She also has a skincare product that makes your face look shiny and glittery called—unbelievably—Unicorn Snot. She has no fewer than four different packages of hair chalk in primary colors, which I am so far avoiding using, but the time may be coming close when I succumb. What's a little light purple hair chalk among friends, after all?

"How is it you live in Brooklyn and don't know about all these products?" she asked me one night. We were standing in front of the bathroom mirror while she curled my straight hair into little ringlets of joy, and then she helped me massage some gelatinous sparkly gunk into my cheeks. "To bring out your inner unicorn," she said.

I tried to explain, that in my nerdish circle of friends growing up, we didn't have inner unicorns; we wanted to look natural. "Even admitting you put on lotion could be construed as trying too hard," I told her. It was important to look plain and unvarnished. Sometimes you could put on a little bit of mascara to enhance yourself, but you would go to your grave rather than admit you had done so.

"Trying too hard is wonderful!" she said breathlessly. "You think plain and unvarnished is going to bring you any real joy?"

And that is what I love about having Ariana here. She reminds me of everything I truly believe.

This is especially good for me now that I don't have Patrick around so much. I know he's doing what he needs to be doing. I know that the art show will be the very best thing for him. At night I love when he finally leaves the studio and sleeps next to me, even though we're not talking then.

I miss his texts and his jokes and his funny little dances.

My sister calls me one evening while I'm making red curry for dinner. As I'm sautéing the chicken breasts and onion, Ariana is helping Fritzie with what seems to be step twenty-seven of a routine math problem. And then there's Natalie on the phone.

"Mom's gone mad," she says without preamble.

Let me just say that Natalie and I don't talk so much on the phone anymore. She's busy with her two kids, our parents (who live in her neighborhood), her job as a very important scientist, her husband, Brian, and her obsession with housecleaning, blah blah blah—and I live in the North, a place where no self-respecting Southerner would have dared to venture, in Natalie's private opinion. According to the plan she had, Natalie and I were supposed to be having babies together and living a block or so apart, but then I inherited this house and came here.

But sometimes she calls. Rarely.

"Oh dear. What's she doing?" I say.

"Well, for one thing, she's let herself go. She's not getting her hair done anymore."

"Uh-huh." I put my hand over the phone so I won't laugh. I decide to go the impersonating-a-police-officer way. "Yes, ma'am, we're writing this down. Not. Getting. Hair. Done. Anymore. Anything worse than that, ma'am, before we arm an officer and send him over to the house?"

"Stop it! You see how you are? That is a big deal, believe me. Mom's been going to see Drena since forever."

"I always thought Drena was too heavy-handed with the hairspray, to tell you the truth."

My sister is silent, and I can tell she's seething. When she can regain her composure, she says, "Would you listen to me, please? This is serious. I think not getting her hair done is a sign of depression in a woman her age. She also won't even commit to coming to my house for Thanksgiving—when she knows how important that is to me, to have traditions for my kids. And she *says* Dad doesn't talk to her anymore, but honestly, she's so crabby I don't blame him. And last week when I asked her why she's acting this way, she said I didn't understand what it's like to turn sixty."

"Huh. So maybe this is just her version of a midlife crisis."

"It's a little late for that, don't you think? Sixty is hardly midlife unless you're going to live to be one hundred twenty."

"Yeah, but she missed the one you're supposed to have at forty. She was too busy driving us places."

"Do you ever even talk to her? I notice you don't call *me* anymore."

"I'm sorry," I say.

And I am sorry. A little bit. It's just that life is so much more interesting than Natalie could ever guess. Sweeter and messier, both.

Then I have to hang up, because the doorbell is ringing. Lola and William have arrived for dinner, with Charmaine and Justin and Mookie coming up right behind them. They're here to see Ariana—but teenagers are always hungry, and I've got plenty of red curry, so I invite them to stay. I love how they troop inside, laughing and joking and teasing each other. Mookie lifts Fritzie in the air and spins her around, and then she teaches him one of those clapping games that only third graders know.

For a while, we're all talking and laughing and doing Common Core math problems, and Lola shows me the scarf she's knitting for William. For the second time this week, Justin and Mookie try to teach us all how to do the Floss, which is a dance that looks simple but defies my attempts to master it. Fritzie is the only one who catches onto it immediately. Lola shows us how to do the Charleston, because she actually remembers learning it from her mom, and amid all the laughter, I actually have to take a moment to look around me at this delightful assortment of human beings. All of them perfect and hopeful and yet just the slightest bit sad from missing somebody who can't be there.

Sad, but soldiering on anyway. I think I might burst from how much I love them all.

After dinner, when I come back from tucking Fritzie into bed, Lola takes me aside. "What's up with Patrick?" she says. "Why isn't he out here with us?"

"He's working on paintings for his show. He grabs dinner later. Doesn't like interruptions when he's creating."

"Hmm," she says, and I can hear how weird this must sound. Patrick not participating in life at all. Like the old Patrick.

"A guy is coming soon to interview him about his 'comeback,' and I think he's trying to get a lot of work done ahead of that. He's nervous about not having enough." I make air quotes when I say the word *comeback*. Patrick doesn't like to think of it that way.

Even as I'm saying this—and Lola's eyes are searching my face—I can feel myself realize that that's not what's really happening.

What *is* happening is that Patrick is withdrawing, edging further and further away. He pretty much stays in the apartment across the hall most evenings now. I invite him to join all of us for dinner, but lately he mostly brushes me away. He has a litany of reasons he throws out:

He's working hard, he says.

He needs to concentrate.

Once he gets going on a painting, he has trouble stopping. And some days he has trouble starting.

Also: he's thinking of what he will say in the interview with *Inside Outside*. He could easily say the wrong thing, he says.

Also: he probably shouldn't have agreed to the writeup in the magazine.

Also: maybe he shouldn't have agreed to do a show at all. Who does he think he is anyway, staging a comeback? Coming back from what, exactly? People will think it sounds pretentious.

But I don't say any of that to Lola. After she and William Sullivan leave and the teenagers have gone downstairs, though, I go across the hall to his studio. "Patrick?" I call softly.

He's not in the main room. I stop at the easel next to the window. Usually he doesn't want me to see what he's working on. He says he doesn't believe in showing things in the middle of working on them. The pictures change—the light, the mood, even the message each painting has. It's all so subjective, he says, that it can be altered simply from being looked at by someone else.

But there it is. I don't understand all I should about abstract expressionism, but I feel a shiver looking at this painting. It's all browny-green algae-colored piles of paint. A minimal smear of discordant color tones—at the side. Is that an eye? It looks like an eye. I move closer and tighten my arms around myself.

"Patrick?" I say softly. I hear a stirring from the other room, and Roy comes out and trots over to me, meowing. He winds himself around my legs, and I lean over and pet him.

When I get to the back room, Patrick is sitting on the floor. There's a large canvas propped against the wall facing him, and he is staring at it, with his head propped on his hands.

His eyes slowly turn to me, and he gets up, startled. He had been so deep in thought that he hadn't heard me.

I feel my heart clutch in alarm. "Patrick," I say again. "Honey . . ."

Because what I've just realized is that Patrick's face is so sad and drawn that he hardly looks like himself anymore. How had I not noticed this before?

CHAPTER TWENTY-ONE
PATRICK

He hears Marnie calling him, and he makes the decision to pull himself together. He scrambles to his feet and composes his face into a smile, puts on an imitation of a man who's doing fine. He feels like his mouth is filled with dust.

"Hi," he says. "I was just coming back over. Is everybody gone?" His voice sounds thick and clotted, even to his own ears. He's shaky, standing up so fast.

"What's the matter?" she says in alarm and crosses over to him. Oh God. Her face searching his. It's all he can do not to tell her. Because he knows she's seeing it all anyway: how the paintings are ripping him up, how cracked he is. Maybe he's in some kind of stupid existential crisis; isn't that what people call it? He could say, "Hi, Marnie. I can hear your voice and see your face, but all around you is dust and death. I can't participate in the love story you're envisioning."

But what good would it do to tell her? What can *she* do? Instead he says in a soft voice, "It's nothing. Really. I'm just tired. Has everybody left yet?"

"They just left," she says. "Didn't you want to come over and eat with us?"

Words show up from somewhere. "I can't stop when I've got something going. I needed to get this painting under control." He can feel the edge of irritation in his voice and tries to tamp it down, but he can see from her face that he didn't manage it all that well. He turns away and goes over to the counter, puts a coffee cup down in the sink and runs the water in it. Feels the water running on his hands. Remembers falling down the day of the fire, trying to get to the water.

"And is it?" she says. "Are you unhappy with it or something? What's wrong?"

"I'm just exhausted," he says. And then he turns toward her. "Come on," he says and takes her hand. *See how I'm trying? Don't I get some points for that, at least?* "Let's get out of here. Is there any of that delicious-smelling food left? Hey, did I hear Lola and William out there, too?"

"Yeah," she says. "They were here. Lola wanted to know if you were okay."

"I got caught up with work."

She's looking at him way too closely.

They move through the studio. He throws a drop cloth over the painting in the front room, hoping she hadn't seen it.

But of course she had. He can tell by the way she recoils a little bit, just passing it. It's what alarmed her in the first place, most likely. "Is that the new one?" she says.

"Yeah. One of them."

"Patrick, it's so sad. It actually made me shiver."

"Well, that's what art is supposed to do," he says. "It's not all little flowers and puppies, you know. It's *art*."

She doesn't answer. He knows he's been too mean now. Crossed a line into being actually insulting. So he kisses her on the cheek and says he's sorry. Tells her that something smells really good.

"I think you must be starved," she says. She's made red curry, she says. She bets that his blood sugar has dropped. How many hours since he's eaten? It's easy to feel overwhelmed and not even know why. Isn't there a term now for that—hangry? He must be hangry.

He says he loves red curry, and he grabs a beer from the refrigerator and sits down at the table. He's better now. He can do this. He can eat and drink and smile. Just like a real person, one who is not seeing the world through cobwebs. One foot in front of the other. One sentence following the sentence before. An occasional smile, a tilt of the head.

"So, how are you?" he says, and the specter of Anneliese withdraws, almost completely vanished now. "How are things at Best Buds?"

"They're good," she says. She tells him about seeing the couple, Winnie and Graham, that she'd brought together the night she had the big question for him.

He grimaces a little, remembering. He will probably always think of that night as the start of a cascading series of out-of-control life events. Her wanting a baby, the condom breaking, the further question of when and if they're going to try to have a baby never quite getting answered. And then Fritzie showing up. Then there's the art show he mistakenly agreed to.

"Ah, yes," he manages to say. He tries for a smile. "So I take it they're still together then? That must make you happy."

"Yes, and they're having a baby."

"Oh, how lovely for them. I'll bet they want to raise a statue in your honor."

She is looking down at her hands. Oh God. He has been too sarcastic now, and he's hurt her feelings. What's even worse is that the topic has somehow veered over to babies again. Alarm bells sound in his brain. It's so hard to avoid all the conversational land mines when you don't see each other very much. You'd think it would be the opposite, that you could keep the subjects neutral for a few minutes of talk—but no. It's as though all the important, hard stuff naturally lies in wait, jumping out into even routine conversations, like a wild animal leaping out of a tree onto your unsuspecting head.

"Do you think much about our trying again soon?" she says.

Aaaaaaaand . . . we're off, he thinks. He drums his fingers on the table.

"You know, maybe you've noticed that I'm a bit stressed out just now," he says.

"Yeah, well, I've heard good things about sex and stress," she says.

He squints and decides to go for a joke. "You know, somehow I feel almost like we already have a kid."

"A kid, not a baby."

He feels a bitter laugh coming from somewhere deep. "Also, have you noticed that our house is pretty much filled to the rafters with humans now? How many people were actually here eating dinner tonight? It sounded like it was at least a battalion."

"I don't think we actually have rafters. Or a battalion."

"Are you kidding me? We have battalions of people living on our rafters, *swinging* from the rafters." He leans his head back and swigs his beer in an attempt to show how careless and carefree he is. But still she is staring at him solemnly. She does not read his funny mood at all. Where is her sense of humor?

He tries again. "You do know that I had no idea when I threw in my lot with you that you were going to bring in so many people. It's wall-to-wall people around here lately."

"How is this me?" she says.

"People follow you. This place is like a boardinghouse. In fact, it is an *actual* boardinghouse, now that I think of it. People come traipsing into my studio, making comments about my work. Why, even Ariana came in to borrow a pair of scissors the other day—"

"What? She did? I've told her not to bother you."

"Everyone bothers me!" he says, trying to strike a friendly, exasperated tone. Amused, even. Not as irritated as he'd felt when he'd looked up to see Ariana standing at the door. "While she was there, she said my work looked so sad, and she wondered if I had given any thought to my brand. My brand! Can you believe this? Since I was going to be interviewed, she thought I might want to decide what my platform could be. She said it looked like I was going for Sad Artist Guy. Which might not be the very best look for me, she thought."

He means to sound funny/exasperated, funny/ironic. Funny/something. Come on: children, even teenagers, talking about marketing is hilarious. But he obviously isn't getting that across because Marnie looks stricken. Why isn't she getting this?

Her eyes fill with tears, and he knows he should want to reach over and pull her to him, to comfort her, to say he understands. But what he actually wants is to go back to his studio, stop the burden of this conversation that is leading nowhere good. He shouldn't be with humans right now. Even Marnie, with all her faith and hope. He is *creating*, and the art he's doing is weird and hard and upsetting, and ohhhh yeessssss, *he* saw the look on her face when she looked at his painting. He saw how it landed inside her. Is he supposed to apologize for *that*, too? For what his art is trying to express? Does that not fit in with her all-happiness-all-the-time world view?

"Do you still love me?" she says. Quietly.

Oh God. Not this! "Do I—what?" he says. "Of course I love you. Why would you think I don't love you?"

Let her go, says Anneliese. *She shouldn't be doing this to you.*

"Because you don't look at me when you talk to me. Because you don't even really talk to me at all. Because I don't see you anymore. The last time we spent any time together was the day we went to Fritzie's school—"

"Look," he says and lets out a loud sigh. "You *know* that I'm busy—"

"Don't," she says. "I know what it feels like when people love you even when they're busy. Don't tell me how busy you are, Patrick, because I know you. And what I know is that you are in some kind of crisis."

He folds his arms in front of his chest. "I'm doing a very hard thing. It's the creative process."

"I know that, and I want to help you," she says. "Your paintings are devastatingly sad, and that's all right, Patrick, because that's what's in your soul right now, and that's what needs to come out. But in the meantime, you seem very far away from me, and every day you're spinning away more and more." She holds up her hand in the stop position, to keep him from interrupting, which he was about to do. "But whatever is hurting inside you," she says calmly, and she looks at him so directly with her blue, blue eyes filled with feeling, "I want you to know that I see you and I love you, and I'm willing to wait while you go through it, for as long as it takes. I believe in you, even if you don't right now."

He closes his eyes, tries to think of what he can possibly say—*thank you?*—and when he opens them again, Marnie has left the room.

She says these things, but she doesn't get it, says Anneliese.

Later, he lies in bed next to her and hates himself.

Maybe he should stand on the rooftop and call out to anyone who is interested—and apparently that is everyone he's acquainted with—that he knows that he is being impossible, thank you very much, but that he has nothing more to give anybody, and also for their own safety, they should get the hell away from him. Leave him to it.

And while he's up there yelling on that rooftop, he wants to say that he is shuddering right along with them. He would like very much to stop being him and try on the identity of someone else for a while.

Someone from his imaginary audience yells out, "Why the hell don't you just quit doing the paintings then, if you hate yourself so much? What's the point?"

Right. He could stop painting if he wanted, couldn't he? Even after all this time, he could call off the gallery show. He could say something's come up. He could call off the magazine interview, as well as the whole so-called goddamned comeback. He's not doing this for the money; he's not even doing it for art. He has enough of a life without art. He could just keep on hanging out in his house, watching game shows, taking the dog to the park, cooking on the rooftop, making love to Marnie, the way he had been doing before all this.

But—aha, here's the real problem—what if he called off the gallery show, what if he stopped doing these painful paintings, and it turned out he was still his fucked-up self? What then? Who would he be then? Just a guy with a bunch of scars all over his body mourning a past that he can't change; a sarcastic guy who comes across great in text messages but who's locked up in some prison, with no hope of parole. A man who hurts the things he loves.

He feels Marnie stirring next to him. So she's not asleep either.

"Patrick?" she whispers.

"I'm awake," he says after a moment.

She reaches over for him and he takes her in his arms, at first reluctantly. But then he goes through the motions of kissing her, and when he squints his eyes very tightly, he finds his way somehow to making love. He can do this. Maybe. He has to just keep reaching out for her strength to carry him through. He has to guard himself against Anneliese, who rises up in his head, wanting to make him pay attention. He doesn't have to pay attention to what Anneliese believes about him. He can climb back into his real, regular life. He smells Marnie's hair and feels her arms around him, and for a moment he does not have to live in sorrow.

But then the next morning, he goes into the studio and he hears the screams, sees the fear. He fills the canvas with everything he hears, but there's more and more and more to be painted, and he knows— Anneliese tells him—that he has to work faster.

CHAPTER TWENTY-TWO

MARNIE

We are set to have a calm, boring, routine Thanksgiving, which goes against all my animal instincts as well as my most fervent wishes. Everything I stand for, really. Thanksgiving, you see, is my favorite holiday, and the ones I like best are filled with more guests than we can sanely accommodate, as well as a lot of gratitude, mismatched plates, turkey, stuffing, and waaay too many pies. I love when the required sweet potatoes are covered in brown sugar and marshmallows and when the green beans have hard fried onions that come from a can, and it's fine with me if there are nineteen pies and all of them are pumpkin. I just like the whole idea of it.

But this year, out of deference to the Patrick Situation, I've scaled back. The guy from *Inside Outside* came yesterday and did an interview with him, and horror of horrors, Patrick told me that the guy brought with him an unexpected film crew, which may have flipped Patrick out for all time: cameras and lights, all pointed at him and at his work, work that he apparently doesn't want anyone to see. Because he's—well, he's Patrick. He's nothing if not ambivalent. And he talked to the guy for hours and hours and now he's positive he said way too much, and from the way the questions were going, he now thinks the reporter is going to make him out to be some tragic hero, fighting his way back from a devastating personal tragedy to an unlikely, desperate comeback.

"I don't want to have to be anybody's hero," he says. "I'm not a hero."

"But they have to have an angle, you know. You can't be Just an Ordinary Guy Named Patrick Who Used to Do Sculpture But Now Is Painting, and doing some good work . . . so hey, folks, come have a look. That won't bring anybody in."

"Which is exactly why I shouldn't have agreed to do the show—or the article," he says. "And why did they bring a film crew?"

"But *was* it a film crew, or just a photographer with some lights?"

"It was just a guy with one camera and one light," pipes up Fritzie. "He took my picture, too."

"Oh my God," says poor Patrick.

"You could call the reporter," I say for the millionth time. "He's a human being; he'll listen to you say what you're worried about, and maybe he could leave that part out. If you think he's going to misrepresent you, I think he'd be interested in getting the correct version."

"You don't understand. He wants me to be the sad, heroic artist."

"See? That's because that's your brand, Patrick," says Fritzie. "Call him and tell him you want to be Artist Who Paints Their Daughters They Didn't Know They Had, and then you could paint me."

Patrick looks at her and shakes his head, speechless. "You, too? I can't believe that even third graders are talking about brands these days. I think this may be the actual end of civilization. I don't have a brand. I don't even want a brand. I am an artist!" He realizes he is raising his voice. Roy runs from the room.

Fritzie is not flappable. "Ariana," she says quietly, "tells me everybody has a brand."

I just want Patrick to be calm again. So I tell him it will simply be Thanksgiving for the three of us. No strangers. No homeless people from the corner, no displaced employees from Best Buds. No Amazings. Ariana is going to have dinner with her family at her grandmother's house anyway, and Lola and William Sullivan are taking a road trip to visit her son in Pennsylvania. Fritzie wanted to invite Laramie's family, and I must admit I had thoughts about how we could help find them a place to live, but when I call Laramie's mother, Gloria, to invite her, she says they're heading up to Massachusetts to see a place Laramie's grandmother knows where they can live.

So . . . it's us.

"Thank you, thank you," says Patrick.

"However, this does go against everything that Thanksgiving stands for," I tell him. "You do know that."

"I know."

"And it might give Fritzie the wrong message about family love and community."

"Marnie."

"What?"

"Fritzie is pretty much steeped in family love and community here. Maybe this gives her a healthy message about boundaries and respecting when one member of the family is having a dark night of the soul."

"Are you having a dark night of the soul?"

"I don't know."

I stare at him, measuring the amount of light in his eyes. "What time of day would you say it is in your soul?"

"Right now?"

"Yes, right now."

"It's four thirty p.m."

"Winter or summer?"

"Late autumn, I'd say. After the time change."

"That sounds dark."

"It's getting dark, but it's not the dark night of the soul completely yet."

I study him carefully. "You're going to be fine. I have faith in you. *Blix* has faith in you."

He grimaces when I mention Blix. "No. I'm not going to be fine! I haven't shown my work in years, and I've never shown my paintings at all. I have no idea if they're even any good, and a man came and interviewed me and asked me all kinds of questions that I couldn't answer." He bangs his hand down on the counter, hard. "And it *was* a film crew. A film crew of one guy who was obnoxious and kept taking my picture. With lights."

I go over and kiss him. "So then it will just be us for Thanksgiving."

"Once again, I thank you for your understanding and appreciation. Although I might add that I don't completely believe you."

So Fritzie and I go off to buy a turkey that's not too, too gigantic (meaning it will fit in the oven), along with potatoes and green beans and the cans of fried onions, and I explain to her how you have to put canned fried onions and mushroom soup in the green beans just this one time of the year, which is a rule that she says she never heard about. Apparently it's not being properly enforced in all the states. But I want her to know about this, because it hits me that I might only have one Thanksgiving with this little girl, and forever after I'd like to imagine her stopping on Thanksgiving Eve and remembering that people have to have fried onions with the green beans. That will be my legacy to her.

And then what do you think happens? Blix would have known to warn me about this, I think. I hate to invoke the universe because people get sick of hearing that the universe is doing things—but really, we'll call it the spirit of all that is good about love and life and community decides that our Thanksgiving must be fixed after all.

As soon as we get home and are putting away the food, Laramie's mom calls me and says that her mother has had some sort of setback and they need to go the following weekend instead—and if the offer is still open, she would love nothing better than to have a normal Thanksgiving, outside of the shelter, with us. She'll bring Laramie, her three-year-old twins, Luna and Tina, and her baby, Marco. If that's okay.

So what could I say? I didn't even hesitate. I said, "Yes, yes! Come on!"

I go in to tell Patrick that, oops, there will be company after all, and he just groans. He doesn't even go crazy. "It's fine. I knew it would happen this way," he says grimly. And then he says, "What if the guy makes it sound like *I* think I'm some kind of hero? I think I could take anything but that."

"Please. Call the reporter, and tell him what you're worried about," I say. After three times of saying this, I just shorten it to "CTR."

On Thanksgiving morning, when I'm clearing the breakfast dishes and have had to say, "CTR," at least a couple of times, Fritzie gets up and takes her plate over to the sink.

"Well, Patrick, *I* talked to the reporter, and I thought he was very nice," she says.

"What? *You* talked to the reporter?" he says. "How did I not know this?"

She squirms. "I just asked him some questions, and he asked me a couple of things. He told me he has a little girl, too."

Patrick says, "I did not give permission for him to interview you."

"It wasn't an *interview*," she says.

He stares at her for a long moment. "Oh my God. *What* is this story going to consist of?" he says.

"CTR," I say. "CTR, CTR, CTR!"

"Why are you mad at *me*?" says Fritzie. "I didn't say anything wrong to him! I was nice."

Patrick staggers over to the fruit bowl, gets himself an apple, and heads back to his studio, shaking his head and clutching his heart. I would worry, except I think the apple is a good sign.

"What?" says Fritzie to me. "And don't say CTR."

"He's just being dramatic," I tell her. "Here's a little secret about people: sometimes when they seem like they're nervous about one thing, it's really all about something else instead."

"What's he nervous about then?"

"He's nervous—well, he's nervous, I think, because he's finding himself so happy to have a little girl here who belongs to him, but—" I can't believe I'm saying this.

"Marnie." She laughs and shakes her head, like she feels sorry for me, being so deluded. "Patrick is *not* used to me. I would *not* say he's all that happy about me. Yet."

She's right, of course. I shouldn't have tried to run that line on her. "Well, honey, he's scared because a long time ago he lost somebody he loved very much, and now he doesn't want that ever to happen again. So he's protecting his heart. But what he hasn't learned yet—but what he will learn—is that you can't live and protect your heart at the same time. You have to go full-out into love as hard as you can. Remember that for your future life. Give everything you have to love. It's the only thing that counts."

"You're good at the love stuff, aren't you?" she says.

I go over and kiss her for that. And then, because I'm good at the love stuff, we call her mom and do a FaceTime, and yes, it seems to me to be stilted and weird, but maybe it's only because I don't understand Tessa so well, and so when she talks to Fritzie and tells her about the buildings and the churches she's seeing and doesn't ask about the stuff Fritzie is doing—well, I take it personally. It pierces me just the slightest bit hearing her one question, which is always, "Are you being a good girl?" But, having said that, I think the occasional phone calls are important, and I wish they happened more often, but I'm good at the love stuff, so I make them happen.

Even when they hurt.

Gloria shows up about noon with her entourage. Laramie is very sweet and shy, and the twins love bouncing on the bed in Fritzie's room, and I fall into crazy, mad love with Marco, a gurgling, drooling happy six-month-old, who holds out his arms to me the minute we're introduced, as though he's been looking for me all his life. He lets me carry him around on my hip for the rest of the day, giving me his toothless, love-struck grins and at times planting wet, openmouthed kisses on my cheeks.

Honestly, it's embarrassing, the way Marco and I feel about each other. I think I am smitten. Maybe he and I are destined to be soulmates, and when he is forty-five and having a midlife crisis, and I am well into my wise old seventies, we'll travel to Europe together and I'll tell him everything I know about life and wine.

Or maybe he's just come to me so that my ovaries can get to thinking about how fun it would be to have a baby boy of our own, and that this inspires them to dust off their best egg and spiff up the fallopian tubes, fluff up the uterus. Or whatever needs to be done.

Patrick comes out of his lair and does the hostly jobs of filling drink orders and carving the turkey. He is only slightly robotic. Fritzie gets all silly and tries to drag him into the living room to dance with her, which he finally does. He even smiles at Marco and the jumping-bean twins—and then Luna, who can't seem to take her eyes off him, bursts into hysterical tears.

"His face is . . . hurting him!" she says. "It hurt him!"

Why is that what kids always think, I wonder. We all keep saying how it doesn't hurt, he's fine, he's not in pain—and finally Patrick, who is looking grimmer and grimmer like he might actually be in pain, motions to us to be quiet and he kneels down next to her on the kitchen floor. She hides behind her hands.

"Here," he says to her softly. "See? You want to touch my skin? It doesn't hurt me. It's just wrinkled up and pulled funny. But it's just skin, like your skin."

He touches her face very softly, and I hear him whisper, "Now you touch mine." But she shakes her head and won't look at him.

"Really, Patrick," says Gloria, "you don't have to do this." She goes over and sits down next to them and pulls Luna onto her lap. "Sweetie, it's okay. Look, it's just Patrick. See?" Gloria says, "May I?" and she touches Patrick's face. So then Luna peeks out from between her fingers.

"Oh, for goodness sakes," says Fritzie. "Come on, everybody. We're all touching Patrick's face! Everybody touch everybody's face!"

She runs over and climbs on him and runs both her hands over his face, and then Luna does the same thing, laughing, and so does Tina. I hold my breath. "Come on, Laramie," Fritzie says, and pretty soon all the kids are touching him and ruffling up his hair. And even though I'm nervous for him, he's smiling at them and touching their faces, and then they're rolling around on the floor, and the twins are giggling and Gloria is tickling them very gently.

"Thank you," says Gloria. "Tell Patrick thank you."

I have such a lump in my throat, because I always hope that stuff like this is going to be what heals my sweet, wounded Patrick, and I am like a little child anticipating Christmas watching him take it in. And when I can see that he's not fixed from this at all, that he's probably even annoyed some, I have to turn the music up even louder and dance around the kitchen with Marco on my hip, while I wait for the next possible healing thing to come along. When the bell rings, meaning that the rolls are browned and it's time to take the platters into the dining room, I go in and juggle the baby and the pans, and I call everyone to eat.

"Dance line!" yells Fritzie, and she, Laramie, and the twins all join in an impromptu conga line to the dining room—but of course because it's being led by Fritzie, it first goes to both the bedrooms and through the bathroom and the kitchen and is about to head out to the apartment/studio when I stop her, and at last I can persuade everybody to sit down and not stare at Patrick, so we can eat.

It's chaotic and noisy—finding enough cushions to be booster seats for the littlest ones, and then all the passing of the potatoes and the cutting up of the turkey portions and the questions of white meat or dark meat, and the explanations for why there are marshmallow things on the sweet potatoes and fried onions on the beans. Nobody under the age of ten is even going to consider eating these things.

Bedford stations himself under the table right by the twins. He knows who's likely to send some turkey his way.

I'm still discussing marshmallows when my cell phone rings from the kitchen.

"It's probably just my parents wishing us a Happy Thanksgiving. I'll call them later," I say loudly.

But it rings again after it has stopped for a second. And then the whole series starts up again. And again. And again. Patrick gives me a pointed look.

"Oh, dear," I say. "Maybe I'd better get this after all."

"When you come back, can you bring the butter?" calls Patrick.

"And the milk!" yells Fritzie.

Marco rides on my hip into the kitchen, where I pick up my phone. It's my mother's number, I explain to Marco. He gazes at me steadily, as if he already knows we're going to need to gird ourselves for this one.

"Hey, Happy Thanksgiving!" I say when I click the green button. "Are you at Natalie's? We're just sitting down to dinner, so can I call you back in about twenty minutes? We can all FaceTime."

"Marnie?" she says in a staticky voice. "Marnie?"

"Hi, Mom. Our connection doesn't seem all that good. Happy Thanksgiving!"

Marco tries to relieve me of my phone, but I twist it around so he can't get it.

"Oh, sweetie. There you are," my mother says.

"Yes, here I am. Listen. Can I call you back? We're just sitting down to eat, and I'll get everybody together in a few minutes and we can FaceTime. Are you at Natalie's?"

"What?"

"Bobobobobo," says Marco, and he now takes both of his wet hands and tries to wrest the phone away from me.

"ARE YOU AT NATALIE'S?" I yell.

"Bobobo."

"Am I . . . what? Is there a baby on the line?"

"AT NATALIE'S, Mom. ARE YOU AT NATALIE'S?"

Marco laughs at my yelling.

"No, sweetie. I'm not. So your dad didn't call you?"

"No! I mean, I don't think he did."

She laughs. "This is going to be a real shocker then, I'm afraid. But, honey, I'm outside your house; at least I think I am. I'm in an Uber. You are on Berkeley Place, right? I told the driver Berkeley Place, but then I wasn't sure. What's the number of the house?"

"Yes, it's Berkeley," I say in a daze. I give her the address. "You're seriously right outside my house?" I start walking to the front door. When I pass the dining room, Patrick gets out of his chair and follows me.

"No, no, no," he says. "This isn't happening."

I tilt the phone out of the way so she can't hear. "I think it is happening."

"Your mom is here? Like *here* here? Shit, Marnie."

"I think like in front of the house, here."

The Porcupine gathers his mental faculties and smooths out his features. He squares his shoulders and says in a stage whisper, "Okay, then.

Let's just go outside and meet her. I'll bring in her bags. You know what, though?" he says. "At some point down the road I think we really need to examine what kind of life we have going on, that people keep surprising us on our own doorstep. Like, are we somehow asking for this?"

I open the door. "I don't know why it's happening, to tell you the truth. But there she is."

My mother—wearing a fuzzy black coat, sunglasses, a black beret and leggings and boots, and with her blonde hair cut in a side-parted bob—is standing outside of a Lincoln Town Car. The driver gets out and opens up the trunk and hauls out three suitcases and puts them on the curb.

"Surprise!" she says and flings out her arms. Big smile. "Bet you never expected this on your Thanksgiving Day!"

"Hi," says Patrick, heading down the stoop, looking manly and in charge. My mother smiles at him, and then when he reaches her, she grabs his arm and poses like they're on a parade float.

"I would have called!" she yells to me. "But then I decided it would be so much more fun and spontaneous to just show up! To see the expression on your face! This is what you're all about, right? Spontaneous?"

"It's very spontaneous!" I call back down to her. "The height of spontaneity, if you ask me! Come on up!"

She gets busy talking to Patrick and hugging him. He picks up two of her suitcases in his hands and tucks the other one under his arm and comes up the steps. She waves the driver off and picks up her enormous handbag and comes right behind Patrick, talking the whole way up.

"Darling, I'm so glad to see you—and I feel like I've done the most crazy, *most* out of character thing of my whole life! Isn't this fun, though? Oh! And who are all these adorable children? Do they all live in the building, too? Now which one is Fritzie?"

I look around, suddenly aware that in addition to Marco on my hip, I have four other kids hovering around me. The twins are behind me with their fingers in their mouths, staring—and Fritzie is jumping up and down on one foot, saying, "Is this your mom, Marnie? Is this your mom? Marnie! Is this really your mom? Really? Your mom? Can I show her how I can slide down the railing all the way to the bottom? Or can I jump down the steps by threes? Which thing do you think she would like best? Which one? Do you think I can do it, Laramie? I did it four times yesterday and I only got hurt once. Look at this scratch on my leg. That's what happens if you don't do it just right."

"She's that one, the jumping one," I say. "The talking one."

"Ah," says my mother. I can feel her taking in Fritzie's tangled, unkempt hair, her snaggletoothed grin, the too-short plaid cropped pants with the star-studded leggings peeking out from underneath, the black sweatshirt that's all stretched out in the neck, the pink Ugg ankle boots, and the fact that she's standing on one foot teetering on the edge of the concrete steps. But my mom maintains a steady, accommodating smile. (I know that smile; it's saying, "Later I'll start my improvement projects on these people.")

Laramie says he can jump down in threes, too—and the two of them push past Patrick and my mom and start hurtling themselves down the stairs. She applauds them all and then chucks Marco under the chin and says the thing she always says to babies: "Well, hi there, you squeezums!" (Babies are always squeezums, and puppies are poo-zums. I've lived my whole life under these conditions.)

"Happy Thanksgiving, I am so glad to see you!" she says. "Isn't this just the most fun! It is so good to see you, darling, and my, you look like your life has gotten so busy and happy since I saw you last!" She shakes Gloria's hand. "Hi, I'm Millie MacGraw, from Florida. And I think I've just done the astonishing thing of moving to Brooklyn."

I am pretty sure I hear myself say, "You're moving here? Where's Dad?" but I can't be sure because my head feels like a bunch of honey-bees may have moved inside it. When did this become my life?

She's sailing past me into the house. "Oh, it's so lovely in here! I always just *love* these old-fashioned brownstones! The history!" she exclaims. She's come to visit before, so none of it is new, but she does always feel the need to rhapsodize about brownstones and compare them to Florida's one-story stucco houses. "Patrick, honey, don't worry about these bags. Let's just put these down here for now, and I'll figure everything out when I know where I'm going to live."

What?

"Where you're going to *live*?" I say. "You're moving . . . here?"

She turns, almost like a ballerina doing a pirouette, and looks at me with her wide, sparkling eyes. "Yes. I'm moving to Brooklyn."

What I want to say is, "Where is my real mother, and who are you?" But instead I say, "But why?"

"Because you're here," she says, smiling. "And because I'm changing my life. And I just might be in need of your services, so it seemed smart to come get them right in person rather than over the phone. So . . . I'm here, darling, and I don't want you to worry about this, because I'm going to get myself situated real soon and take care of myself."

I catch a glimpse of Patrick's face, which has an unreadable expression. He looks like somebody who might have just been hit in the head with a board.

"Have you eaten, Millie?" he says, and she answers, "Why, honey, I haven't! Looks like I'm here right on time. Is there enough?"

CHAPTER
TWENTY-THREE
MARNIE

When we go back into the dining room, I'm shocked to see Bedford standing up on one of the twins' chairs, helping himself to a turkey leg.

"Bedford!" I yell, and he jumps down, looking appropriately guilty. I wait for my mother to say something about the bad manners of poozums, but she is trying not to look scandalized. I can see it in her face. Suddenly I feel like I'm seeing the whole house—my whole life!—from her point of view. All the chipped, mismatched plates, the couch cushions stacked up haphazardly on the children's chairs, the stained Thanksgiving-orange tablecloth, the scarred wooden floor, the ratty lace curtains that belonged to Blix, the funky, colorful artwork on the wall—everything I've treasured about my own life here looks a bit shabby through the eyes of Millie MacGraw, who has matching everything and sterling silver platters and who prides herself on "making a nice home."

"Mom, here. Sit down in my place. I'll go get another plate and a fork and knife," I say. Patrick brings over an upholstered chair from the front room while Gloria moves the children over so we can squeeze in another place setting. When she comes over to take Marco from me, he bats her away and squeals. He may now be a permanent fixture on my hip.

"I have never had such a dedicated fan," I tell him and nuzzle his sweet little drooly neck. "You are pulling all the right strings with me, buddy."

Patrick grimaces. "Can you eat that way? With him, I mean?"

"Of course I can! But anyway, who needs food when I have this much love?" I glide around the table to my chair, bouncing Marco on my hip.

My mother gets herself settled in. "Ohhh, look!" she says. "You put the marshmallows on the sweet potatoes! I had no idea you still made it the Southern way."

"Well, sure I do. What other way is there? Right when you showed up, in fact, I was in here explaining about how sweet potatoes have to get marshmallowed up on Thanksgiving. Your arrival timing was perfect," I tell her.

She smiles at me. "Isn't timing always perfect? Didn't you tell me that once?" Then she reaches over and pinches my cheek. "Sweetie, you do look rather fantastic with that baby in your arms. Better watch out, Patrick. She's going to be wanting one of those of her own, I bet. First, though, forgive me for saying this, but I think y'all should have a wedding."

"Me, too! Me, too!" says Fritzie.

Patrick takes a big bite of turkey. "Wow, this is delicious."

My mother laughs.

"But you don't have to get married to have a baby," says Fritzie. "In case that's what you're talking about. I am Patrick's kid, and he didn't get married to my mom."

I let out such a big sigh that Marco laughs and pokes me in the eye with a fat, wet finger.

"Well," says my mother and helps herself to the mashed potatoes, "there's nothing wrong with that. I'm beginning to think marriage isn't such a great thing after all myself. Are you married, Gloria?"

"No—well, yes technically," she says. "We're . . . you know . . ."

"My dad's in jail," says Laramie cheerfully. "But he's getting out soon, and then we're going to move to Massachusetts and have a house. Right, Mom?"

"Right," says Gloria.

I roll my eyes so hard at my mother that she looks back at me with comically googly eyes, and then she does a pantomime of locking her lips closed to show she's not going to say another thing.

We recover. Somehow. Everybody goes back to eating dinner, my mom gives some mundane details about her flight, Gloria feels that she has to explain her situation and says she's taking the kids to visit her mother in Massachusetts tomorrow, and that by the way her husband's crime was completely overblown and nonviolent and non-drug-related, and then Laramie socks Fritzie in the arm very playfully and she socks him back, and then he and Fritzie finish their dinner and do some dance moves that Laramie learned on Fortnite, which is evidently a video game, and Patrick pours more much-needed wine for the adults. Marco gums my cheek and then stares rapturously into my eyes.

The doorbell rings again. Patrick and I look at each other.

He throws up his hands. "Your father, perhaps?"

"Or maybe it's your sister from Wyoming," I say. "We'll have all the families here."

"Maybe it's my mom from Italy!" says Fritzie. She makes a face. "I hope Richard isn't with her."

"It could be my dad, breaking out of jail," says Laramie, and I see Gloria shake her head and take another big swig of wine.

"It's probably all of them. They shared an Uber," Patrick says gloomily.

But it turns out to be Ariana, who technically didn't need to ring the doorbell since she has the front door key—but she tells me that she thought it would be more polite than just barging in. Especially since she's standing out there on the stoop with Charmaine, Mookie, Justin, and Dahlia, and they are all laughing and leaning against each other, stamping their feet, looking like an advertisement for youth. Picturesque snow flurries, looking as though they were provided by the props department, are landing on their shoulders.

"OH MY GOD! It's snowing! It's snowing! It's snowing!" Fritzie shrieks. "Marnie's mom, come see this! It's snowing!"

"Honey, you can call me Millie," says my mother. "Or Grandma Millie, if you would like." And she gets up from the table and comes to the door to admire the snow and immediately she gets swept up with the Amazings, who, once everything gets explained and sorted out, can't get over the fact that I have a mom right here on the premises.

"This is your mom?" Dahlia says. "Omigod! Guys, isn't it literally so surprising when you find out older people have actual moms?"

"I'm ancient," says my mother. "I've been around since God was wearing diapers. I used to change his diapers, in fact."

"No, no, I totally didn't mean that," says Dahlia.

Fritzie, who serves as our resident mandated reporter, is required by contract to explain that my mother showed up "by surprise" just a few minutes before, and for some reason, she has to jump up and down on one foot while she says it.

"Just like I did!" she says. "Millie and me are the Surprise Girls."

Ariana points out that she's also a surprise girl, since she didn't call either.

"And Dahlia and Charmaine," says Mookie.

"Yes. There are surprise women all over the place," says Patrick. "What we have here is an epidemic of surprise women."

I do all the introductions and go make the coffee and get out the pumpkin pies. Everybody's talking at once, and I think how

Thanksgiving might be one of those holidays that can't help but turn into what it's supposed to be about, especially in Blix's house.

I love how it feels as though Blix herself might somehow be orchestrating this from the sidelines. It's just the kind of mishmash of people that she would approve of, I think. Justin is swinging Fritzie around, which may lead to breakage of some sort, and which makes the twins also want that kind of treatment—never mind that they've never seen him before, they are in—and everybody is talking at once. Dahlia and Gloria are in an animated conversation about Massachusetts, and Mom is telling Charmaine and Ariana that she left her stodgy old hairdresser because she wouldn't do the hair-painting thing, and how *do* you get that rich purple shade? And Ariana is laughing and saying her family was hideous and she couldn't wait to get out of there, so much judgment about her life choices, like how do they expect her to want to hang around after dinner if all they're going to do is find fault with everything, and my mother—my mother!—is agreeing that family members can be the most judgmental people of all, and that it's simply terrible the way they assume they know everything about us, when they may actually know next to nothing. And then we sit down to eat the pies, and there's a small flare-up when Ariana takes out her video camera and wants to film all of us with our mouths full, but Justin takes it away from her very deftly, and kisses her on the mouth, which makes the children all go, "Oooooh," along with my mother.

The pie dishes and coffee cups seem to vanish off the table while I'm talking to Mookie, and when I look around for Patrick, so we can roll our eyes together in that companionly sort of way, he's nowhere to be found. He's gone to the kitchen and is doing the dishes, which is a nice thing, of course. Perfectly fine impulse: tidying up.

But just like that, he segues into being MIA for the rest of the evening. Absorbed back into his studio. Everyone moves into the living room, and the teenagers finally drift downstairs, and Gloria gets her brood ready to depart. Marco and I are in despair at the prospect of parting, but I tell him we'll meet again, even if I have to drive to Massachusetts to find him.

When I've gotten Fritzie packed off to bed, and it's finally just my mother and me left, she says, "Where did that sweet Patrick go?"

I find a note from him on our bed saying that my mom should sleep in our room with me. He's got lots of work to do, and this will be better for him, he wrote. He can stay up all night painting if he wishes, without disturbing anyone. And there's a perfectly good futon in the studio, too. He signed the note with a big giant *P*. No love, no hearts, no anything a person could cling to.

I stand there reading the note, and my hand shakes a little.

"Oh, this is terrible," says my mother, behind me. "Maybe you should go in and talk to him."

"No," I tell her. "He's probably sleeping by now, and anyway I'm sure it's fine. I'll talk to him tomorrow."

"Oh dear," says my mother. "Oh dear, oh dear, oh dear. I'm getting a vibe."

"You think?" I say.

"It's all my fault," she says. "Here I do the one and only spontaneous thing I've ever done in my whole life—come to Brooklyn without telling you first, and oh my gosh! What was I thinking? How was this ever going to work? How is it that you and Patrick aren't going to hate me for this? It just seemed so lovely and . . . spontaneously out of character for me! I should go to a hotel tonight, and Patrick can come back to his room. Let me call an Uber right now."

"No, no, that's ridiculous," I say. "To tell you the truth, I think he's been wanting to sleep in there anyway. It's quieter, and he can think and paint and mutter to himself. He's actually been coming to bed later and later. So he's fine, I'm sure."

"He's a moody man, I guess," she says. "Just like your father."

"Ha! Moody doesn't even begin to describe him lately. He's a wreck."

"Your father is a couch potato wreck. What the hell is it with *men* lately? Everywhere you look, they are *not* panning out. Disappointing everyone around them."

So then we stay up until three in the morning, talking. She's lively and funny and self-deprecating—unlike the mom I mostly remember her to be, who might have been the tiniest bit exacting when it came to rules and decorum and deportment. "Look! Just look at these bags under my eyes!" she says. "Now I don't mean to be shallow, and I know that how awful my skin looks is not the point of life, but I look at these every day in the mirror and I think I look just like your nana."

She said my father doesn't laugh at her jokes anymore, and he wants everything to stay put, exactly as it is. *Could we just not rock the boat*—that's his favorite expression for everything. When she told him she might want to go back to school, he said absolutely not, waste of money and time at her age, there was no need for any of that—and so even though nothing is really wrong, she says, and yes, she knows, other people have it so much worse, she just wants to live again. Look forward to something big! Gigantic!

"You know what I really want? I want to fall in love," she says wistfully, around about two in the morning. Her voice is soft and fragile, like a young girl's. "One more time for falling in love. Maybe that's why I'm here."

"Hmm," I say. I would so much prefer that she not fall in love with someone else besides my father.

"Is that so wrong?" she says, and we both laugh because it reminds us of an old comedy routine that neither of us can quite remember. "I've become the worst kind of cliché. Go ahead. I know you're thinking that. I buy every single moisturizer I see on the shopping network—wait until you see what's in my suitcase—and all I want is for somebody to look at me with a sly grin, and somebody who *wants* to listen to me, and not sit there disinterested in everything, telling me I'm too old for this and too old for that, and where's the meat loaf, and why can't we put a television set in the bedroom. If we put a television in the bedroom, Marnie, I swear that man would never get out of the room! Next it would be bedpans!"

"Well," I say. "If he wants to put a television set in the bedroom, he clearly needs some rehabilitation."

I'm being funny, but she looks at me and smiles. "Exactly! You see? Now you've never had a man suggest a television set, have you? I don't notice one in here." Then she wrinkles up her nose and says, "Of course there's no man in here either. So tell me. What's going on with Patrick, do you think? He seemed fine when I talked to him a few weeks ago."

And that's all it takes, I'm ashamed to say. I tell her about the art show and how sad he is, and how I want a baby and he isn't sure he can handle it, and how much it has stressed him out having Fritzie around. My eyes fill up with tears, and then *her* eyes fill up with tears, too, and maybe that's just because it's the middle of the night, the hour when people could weep over the last sad, neglected egg in the egg carton, but maybe we've hit upon the rock-bottom hardness of living a long life— which is that things go wrong, and you constantly have to be recasting your experiences so you can see your way forward out of despair. I try to remember what Blix would say about all this. Certainly her life didn't always go the way she planned.

She would say that Patrick is mine for life, and that I am meant to believe in him, and he believes in me—and that all these trappings of unhappiness right now are temporary distractions from the real rock-solidity of our love for each other.

"He's just going through a bit of a rough patch," I say to my mother. "He's committing himself to doing art for the first time since the fire, and I think the memories are swamping him."

Then I tell her, just in case she doesn't remember this about Patrick, that he rushed into the fire to save his girlfriend, and that when Blix was dying, he took care of her completely, all on his own, and then he rescued Bedford when he got hit by a car. In every case, he's stepped up and been the person who could be counted on.

It's *me* who is the problem, I tell her. "Here he is, holding me up time and time again, and he makes me laugh and he's so sweet and passionate and he tells me how much I've changed his life, but now I want more. I'm not contented with what we have. I want everything! More life around me, more people, and he says he needs to crawl away and be by himself. He's closing up. He said he's come as far as he can come, and he can't do any more."

"I know," she says. She reaches over and squeezes my hand and then she winks at me. "He's a great guy, but maybe he's not the *only* great guy for you. You know? Things change."

I pull back. "No. I love him. I'm not giving up on this."

"Sometimes you *have* to give up in order to save yourself," she says. "In fact, you shouldn't even think of it as 'giving up.' Call it *relinquishing*. Maybe your father is the man I was meant for in my twenties and during all the decades of raising you kids. And we had a wonderful time of it, he and I, but that doesn't mean he has to be the one for my old age, does it? Maybe after forty years we can fold this marriage up and put it in a drawer somewhere with the old silver service, and both of us can do more of what we want. I can fall in love and go to plays and join the space program if I want to, and he can sit on the couch and watch the golf channel. We'll get together with the kids and grandkids on holidays."

"With your new partners? That sounds horrifying."

"Yes," she says, laughing. "I'll bring all the men I'm currently dating at the time. Your father can give them a thumbs-up or thumbs-down. I'll take his views under consideration."

I bury my head in the pillow. "No, no, no."

"I'm shocked I have to explain this to you," she says. "I pretty much thought this would be your advice to me."

But here's what she doesn't get: he's my dad, and I know he loves her more than anything. And some things—and I count Patrick among these things—just might be worth fighting for.

CHAPTER TWENTY-FOUR
PATRICK

Patrick wakes up to find Fritzie sitting cross-legged on the side of the futon in his studio, staring at him. It's still mostly dark, with only a tiny knife-edge of gray light sticking under the shades. It was her breathing that woke him up.

"Why are you in here?" she says when he opens one eye.

"More importantly, why are you in here?" he says.

"I'm here because I was looking for you, and you weren't in your room with Marnie. Her mom is in there."

"Well, that's why I'm here. There's not room for three in a bed, is there?"

"Nope. Not unless you're going to squinch up."

"What time is it?"

"It's six thirty."

"Six thirty! Holy mother of mercy! What are you doing up?"

"I had to find you."

"Why?"

She has the look on her face of someone who didn't prepare an answer to that question. She doesn't know why she had to find him, he suspects. She likes to know what's going on, is all. She gets up off the futon and wanders around the studio.

"Fritzie."

"What?"

"Please. Don't start touching things in here. There's a lot of wet paint."

"I know."

She keeps walking around, so he lies back down and closes his eyes again. This futon is not horrible. He's pleased with himself for thinking of coming in here to sleep as a solution to the houseguest situation.

"You know why I came in here, Patrick? For reals?"

"Why?"

"Because you know how Ariana is going to go across country and ask people questions and film them?"

"Uh, yeah."

"Well, I decided that I'm going to ask people questions, too, and I am starting with you."

"And this couldn't have waited until it was daytime?"

"Patrick! It is daytime. The sun just didn't wake up yet."

"Okay. I like it best when the sun wakes up."

"It will soon. So are you ready for my questions? I have a bunch."

"Okay. Can I close my eyes while I answer them?"

"Sure. Hey, would you ever like to go with me to the planetarium?"

"Maybe."

"Haha, Patrick! That wasn't the real question for the test. I was just wanting to know. Okay, now we're starting. That question had an asterisk by it. You know what an asterisk is?"

"Yes."

"It means it's not really real."

"Go easy on me, okay?"

"Do you love Marnie?"

"Yes."

"Do you love me?"

"Of course."

"Do you love potato chips?"

"Yes."

"Okay, Patrick, none of those were the real questions either. I just wanted to know how much love you've got in ya. But you are doing very, very well. Okay, now we start. What was your favorite subject in school?"

"Art and math."

"Did you play sports?"

"No."

"Why not?"

"Uncoordinated."

"What does that mean?"

"It meant I was too busy drawing pictures."

"Who is your favorite person in the world?"

"Um. Stephen Colbert."

"Who is that?"

"A comedian."

"No. It has to be someone you know."

"Um, Paco."

"Someone in our house!"

"Oh, then you."

"Is that really true?"

"One thousand percent true."

"I don't believe you. I think it's Marnie."

"Yeah, maybe we should say Marnie so she doesn't get upset."

"Okayyyy. When you met my mom, did you love her?"

"Fritzie? This is kind of . . ."

"Just answer."

"No."

"No, you didn't?"

"No, I didn't. I didn't know her."

"Okay. No, that's okay. I get it. Okay, now, next question is: When you and Marnie have a baby together sometime, do you want it to be a girl or a boy?"

He gets up on one elbow. "Nope, nope, nope. Question time is over."

"Okay, *okay*! Um . . . what time on the clock is your favorite time?"

"I have no favorite time on a clock."

"Mine is 12:34. Get it? One, two, three, four."

"Let's go get some breakfast. Are other people up?"

"Wait. Do you like to read the end of a book first?"

"I would never. Come on, let's go see if anybody else is up."

"What are you scared of?"

He's quiet.

She looks at him. "I'm just going to read you the rest. What do you think you will say to me on the day my mum comes and gets me? Do you think you will be my dad when I'm a grown-up? Do you want more children, or just me? If you could somehow have the fire not happen, would you still want to love Marnie even if the other lady lived? Would you still want to have me at your house? What do you want for Christmas? Did you know you would be this sad? Do you think you are always going to be so sad? Do you think I am smart? And the last question: Do you really love me? Do you love me more than Roy? More than potato chips? More than painting?"

He sits on the side of the bed and looks at her. He can't answer any more questions. His throat is tight.

"Let's go make your grandmother some coffee," he says.

"Patrick!" she says, and she's laughing. "Millie is *not* my real grandmother!"

"Well, what is she?" he says. And she shrugs. She doesn't have an answer for that one.

The sun is just starting to fight its way through the dusty kitchen windows in a way that makes him feel a keen sadness about the basic grime and clutter of life.

He is so tired that it takes tremendous difficulty to undertake the necessary nine steps that are required to get cups of coffee going, which involves first finding the filters and the coffee beans, then the grinder and the coffee press, as well as the cups, the spoons, the cream. The cups are in the dishwasher. His favorite one is missing. Also, in unrelated but also disappointing developments: the pumpkin pies were left out all night, and he forgot to do anything with the turkey roasting pan, so it's sitting on the counter with turkey grease and parts congealing in a rather non-savory way.

Fritzie is dancing around with Bedford, who's on his hind legs. Roy has come along to check out what's for breakfast.

"Do you want some cereal?" Patrick asks Fritzie, and then he hears Millie say, "Well, g'morning."

"Hi," he says.

"I declare that I was up so late last night that I thought I'd sleep for days, but I can't seem to stay asleep. I'm too excited to be here. Does that happen to you, Fritzie? Are you ever too excited to sleep?"

"Well," says Fritzie. "There was one time when we were . . ." and off she goes into a long, rambling story that Patrick can't pay attention to. It is all he can do to manage at last to pour Millie a cup of coffee and hand it to her, and smile back when she smiles. She is wearing a long blue quilted bathrobe, one that moms everywhere might be putting on all over America. She is very, very suburban mommish, he thinks, with her short petals of blonde-gray hair, all tucked under and organized, as though they had attended hair training school. She is youthful-looking, but he thinks that you would never see anybody under fifty doing that precise thing—whatever it is—with her hair.

Yes, she says, in answer to a question he forgot he had asked: a piece of toast would be wonderful.

He's alarmingly distracted. He actually found himself awake at 5:14 a.m., an hour before Fritzie showed up and interrupted his catnap. He lay there with his pillow covering his face for some time, examining the new reality of sleeping on a futon in his studio while houseguests (he counts Ariana as well as Millie and Fritzie in this—the surprise women, as they were identified last night) plunder what is left of his solitude. He brought out all the facts of the matter and turned them over and over in his head, walking around them, asking himself some hard questions about how he should see this. On the one hand, he likes Millie just fine; it's not that he doesn't. He texts with her, after all. Recipes and such. She admires his baking abilities, says plenty of wonderful things about his sour cream coffee cake with the cinnamon crunch sprinkles on the top, for instance. Shares it on Facebook. And she has been known to make his Atlantic beach pie (made with a cracker and butter crust) for special occasions.

But damn it, he is busy! He's not baking anymore lately and has no need of recipes. And besides being a natural introvert, he is now a frantic introvert, in fact. And he gathers that she is having some difficulty with her husband just now (a man whom Patrick also likes, even though he doesn't know him as well as he knows Millie), which means that there will be lots of talking. Talking and planning and ruminating and problem-solving. Also there's the rather unorthodox surprise she pulled: just showing up like that without warning. He holds that against a person. And then, as if those things aren't bad enough, then there was the alarming bombshell she dropped last night, that she is moving here.

Moving to freaking Brooklyn.

Without so much as a what-do-you-think-about-this-plan to the people who might be affected by it.

Well.

Oh, he is a mess today. Cold, tired, sleepy, and his sad paintings are waiting for him in the studio, and he just knows that the multiple teenagers sleeping downstairs are going to come trooping up at some point, and Marnie will probably invite everybody for waffles or something, and Fritzie is off from school for who knows how long, and Millie MacGraw is standing here chatting about everything from the wonder of Ubers to the puzzle of whether pumpkin pie can stay out all night and still be considered nonlethal.

He realizes that he hasn't been paying one bit of attention. He drops back into the conversation, which is now something about real estate in Brooklyn and where it makes sense to look. She doesn't want to be any trouble to anyone, of course, but she had to make a move. Turning sixty, you know. Can't go on through her remaining one-third of her life span without experiencing some real life. (One-third! he thinks with a start. Somehow that sounds wildly optimistic to him, being sure you were going to live until ninety.) She's saying that a friend of theirs died last month, a person who, tragically, never even got to travel across the country. Then she shifts nimbly over to the subject of Fritzie—how adorable, how surprising, how interesting life is, just full of these kinds of unplanned events.

"That's what I'm after, some unplanned events," she says. And then she adds, "And, Fritzie, just so you know, I'm going to consider you my grandchild. You probably already have one grandmother, but you're in need of another. Everybody should have two, and I think the more the merrier in most cases."

Patrick gives Fritzie a wink. "You see?" he says.

"But that can't be right because Patrick and Marnie aren't married, and so you can't be my grandmother," says Fritzie the literalist. "Not until they get married."

"I know. But more and more I think that isn't the important thing about human relationships," she says. "Even if they never actually have a wedding, we could still have each other, and I can be the grandmother in your life. Anyway, I would like to apply for the position."

"I have a grandmum," says Fritzie, "but she lives in England, and my mum is mad at her because my grandmum said I couldn't go and live with her, because she said my mum should stay and take care of me herself. Even though my mum really thought my grandmum was going to keep me because she was family."

Millie looks at Patrick, and he clears his throat. "You don't really have to go into all that," he says.

"Oh, but it's fine," says Millie. "Fritzie, if that's what happened, then we'll just have to say it's her loss. And out of that you found your real daddy."

"My bio-daddy."

"Yes, your bio-daddy, and he's wonderful to you. Relationships change, and that's what is exciting about life. I married my husband when I was nineteen years old, and what did I know about myself back then? Nothing, that's what. And now I find I'm a person who wants to step out of that marriage, and dye my hair purple, go on dating websites, and, who knows, maybe even get a tattoo."

Fritzie looks at her in uncertainty. "I know how to dye people's hair purple. And maybe Ariana could tell you where to get a tattoo. If you really want one."

Patrick blinks. "Are you . . . and Ted divorcing then?" he asks.

"Who knows what we're doing!" She laughs. "I refuse to make any definitive statements about anything. I used to know so very much, and now I feel like I know practically nothing. It's actually a lot more fun going through life this way. At least for now."

Is it? he thinks. Frankly, he'd love to know what he's doing. To get a handle on things.

Millie is looking at him closely, and he realizes that he's been scowling.

"What is it, honey?" she says. "What's wrong?"

So he mumbles something about his painting project, the art show coming up, and his needing to learn to be disciplined again. None of this is exactly it, he realizes, but she fastens on to it just the same. She completely understands, she says.

"Your art is everything," she tells him, and she looks so sincere that for a moment he's afraid that she's going to cross the room and take him by the arms and stare into his eyes while she makes all her points. He won't be able to stand that. "It's who you are. I wish I had something like that to sustain me. My whole life was to be a homemaker. Now isn't that the dumbest thing ever, when you realize your whole purpose was keeping the counters cleaned off and the shirts folded? I can't tell you how much of a fool I feel. Nothing I ever did was worth a crap."

"What happened?" he says, glad that the subject has moved away from his so-called purpose. "That made you realize . . . ?"

"What happened? Why, I guess it was a whole string of things. Everybody left me. We forget that everything and everybody is going to leave us, and that we have to be prepared."

He feels startled, hearing her say that. It's exactly what he feels, too.

"You know," she says, "this is what I'm living for now. A happiness therapist told me that you can change your whole life by doing this one thing. Constantly ask yourself this question when you have a decision to make: Would this make me happier, or would that make me happier? It's like when you're at the eye doctor, and he says, 'Can you see better with this set of lenses, or is it better with this other set of lenses? This way or that way?' And then you have to always pick the thing that brings you the most joy. Never mind all the other stuff. Just go for the thought that feels better."

Maybe it would be an okay thing for an innocent person to do, he thinks. But what if you did something so horrible that you can never forgive yourself, and every day you're compounding it merely by seeking your own pleasure? What if it actually pains you to choose something that's only for you to feel good? That certainly wouldn't work! You'd pick the thing that feels good, but then it would make you feel worse . . . so maybe you can only feel good by picking the thing that would hurt you. But then, there you are feeling somewhat good again.

He hates the idea that there's something even called a happiness therapist, but if he had a moment with one, here's what he would like to ask: *What if you already know you can't love people because it hurts too much when you lose them?*

And what if a magazine piece is about to come out that's going to make it look to the general public like you think you're some kind of hero when you've been responsible for someone else dying, someone who had talent and who loved you? And now you're in a studio painting pictures, and in love with someone else, someone who thinks life is just all-out fun and joy, while your first love's ashes are somewhere in a vial—on her parents' mantel most likely.

Do you then just get to ask yourself: What would be the happiest thing for me to do today?

No, you do not.

He has to get back to work. A woman is waiting in his head for him to go back to the studio and work through the pain he caused her, the damage he did.

And the people standing here in front of him—they're in danger of being lost to him, too. Just because he loves them. Or he might. He doesn't think he even knows what that word means: *love. Who gave us the right to throw that word around all the damn time when nobody knows what it means?*

So here's what you have to do, he thinks: You give up your spot in the bed to the woman who *should* be your mother-in-law, and you move into your studio and sleep on the futon surrounded by your paintings. The ones that you've finished and the ones that are unfinished. The ones that are so full of screams that they frighten you sometimes when you look at them, and the ones you try to make peace with even though they came up from the depths of your longing. You tell everyone around you that you can't get ready for the show unless you live with the work for the time being. You need this, you say. Yell it if necessary, if they don't seem to believe you.

You tell the woman you love, the one who thinks she wants to have a child with you, that for you to be sleeping elsewhere is the best thing for her, too. She'll get to concentrate on being with her mother without having to worry about you.

And you say to that little girl with the stubborn chin and the lanky hair that's identical to yours, the little girl with the impulse to steal money for a cause and explore the world and the solar system, that you're watching over her, and that she's fine and lovable—and you make yourself remember that in a few short months, she, too, will leave you and be out of your life.

And you tell yourself that it's pretty smart of you not to get attached.

Because, in the famous words of Millie MacGraw, everything and everybody will leave you at some point. So maybe that's the safest plan of all.

CHAPTER
TWENTY-FIVE
MARNIE

"Your mother will be there one week tops," says my father when he calls me the next morning. He's using his manly, confident, predictor voice. The same voice he used when he told me I'd grow up to be a financial analyst if I'd just apply myself. "She's just, ah—well, your mother is going through something I don't seem able to help her with. Who knows? Maybe you can."

It's seven thirty and I'm standing on the sidewalk holding the leash and watching Bedford sniffing the ground. I am yawning more than usual because I think I *might* have gotten about two hours of sleep. As with every morning, Bedford's got himself a big decision to make about which patch of grass he'd like to pee on, but the difference this morning is that I'm in no hurry whatsoever to get back inside the house, so he's free to sniff out gum wrappers, old straws, and previously peed-on grass as long as he wants. I have my coat on over my pajama shirt and a pair of sweatpants, and I jammed my feet into my boots and came outside before anybody could find me. I could hear Patrick and my mother talking in the kitchen as I slipped away.

"I don't know, Dad," I say. "She says she wants to move here."

"I know she *says* that. But she's a Floridian through and through. She can't move there," he says in his firm dad voice.

"Are you sure?"

"Marnie. First of all, she has her life here. Me, for one thing. And her friends at the pool, at the Y. Natalie and the grandchildren. And second of all, winter. She's never lived through a winter in her life. No, she's just going through something right now. I haven't been needing her enough maybe. You could do me a favor and point out my wonderful qualities and tell her that I really do need her. Trust me, Marnie. This is a temporary rootlessness she's got going on."

My father, Ted MacGraw, is a wonderful man, a good provider, and a guy who believed strongly in his daughters' rights to excel in any workplace and to be whatever they wanted in the world. Unless what they wanted was to be underemployed, like me. Or a witchy matchmaker, like me. Or a person who moved to Brooklyn without a real plan, like me. Luckily he also had Natalie, who became a grade-A, number one scientist who had the foresight to marry a settling-down kind of man and have two children and move into a house in my dad's neighborhood.

I've always adored him, and sometimes I think it would be so cool to be as certain as he is about everything. He knows just how he feels. Good over bad, right over wrong, khakis over blue jeans, football games over soccer matches, Rotary Club meetings over sleeping late on Saturday.

"But, Dad," I say, "she doesn't seem sad. She seems almost giddy to me."

"That's an act. Don't you know an act when you see one? She doesn't know what she wants."

I am, I realize, too cowardly to tell him the things she said last night. Let *her* tell him about her desire to join the space program and fall in love with new people.

There's a silence. "We're a solid couple," he says. "Everybody envies us. All our friends. Your mom has it good, but, I don't know, there's this restlessness lately that's driving me nuts. She always wants to go, go, go. For no reason, just to get out of the house. She complains I don't get enough exercise and I won't go to the doctor for a checkup. Frankly, she's becoming a little bit of a nag."

"Dad, are you angry with her? Because you sound a little angry."

"*No*, I'm not angry," he says in the maddest voice ever. "It's just that she didn't have to pull this stunt on Thanksgiving Day. Get this. She got up very, very early in the morning and made the turkey and the stuffing and the green beans with the fried onions and the sweet potato marsh-mallow thing, and then it was all ready by noon, so I came upstairs from watching the Macy's Day Parade, thinking we'd sit down and eat, and there she was with her suitcases packed, and she said, 'I'm leaving. I'm moving to Brooklyn. Don't worry. There's a cab waiting for me, so you won't have to worry about getting the car back from the airport. And I'll talk to you soon.' And she put her house key on the table, and kissed me on the cheek, and walked out the front door. Didn't even eat the meal she'd made. Can you believe that?"

Bedford is now eating a piece of a chicken bone he found under some leaves, so I kneel down to take it out of his mouth. "What did you do?"

"What do you think? I'm a gentleman, so I carried her two suitcases outside for her and put them in the trunk of the cab. And I paid the driver for her in advance. And then I went around to the window of the passenger seat and I said to her, I said, 'I hope you have a very nice trip to Brooklyn, and have a Happy Thanksgiving.'"

"Oh, you did not!"

"I did." He laughs. "I'm chill. Isn't that what you kids say? I haven't even told Natalie yet; that's how cool I'm playing it. I want to make as little drama as possible. Give your mother some space so that in three days when she decides to come back, it won't have to be a huge deal and she feels like she loses face or something. I'm not going to beg her to come back. I'm just going to leave her to get this out of her system."

"That's probably very wise," I say.

"And, ducky, just do me a little favor, will you?"

"What would that be, oh father of mine who has missed every single signal he needed to see?"

He laughs. "Show her all the ways Brooklyn is *not* Florida. Shiver a lot! Tell her how dirty and disgusting the subways are. I don't know. Tell her you miss the Florida beaches. She's a Florida girl. She'll come home."

CHAPTER TWENTY-SIX
MARNIE

My father is dead wrong. My mother is not one bit interested in going back home. And this is fine by me. Two weeks in, and we are actually having a good time in our new capacity as girlfriends. She's asked me if I could possibly call her Millie instead of Mom. It would make it easier for us to talk about real things, she said. We sit up late talking at night, covering nearly all subjects of interest—things I never thought I could talk to her about—like bad boyfriends, men who turn into couch potatoes when you're not looking, the evidence for magic, bad hairdressers who rely on too much hairspray, the fact that my mother always thought that she and I were kindred spirits while the other two family members were too rigid, whether boredom constitutes grounds for changing one's life . . . aaaand the pros and cons of me getting pregnant.

I don't think me getting pregnant is going to happen soon, at least not until Patrick's show is over. He's getting more and more withdrawn.

I have taken to organizing what I call Jiffy Conjugal Visits when I make him sit with me in the living room under the fleece blanket—for whole minutes at a time—drinking our mugs of coffee on the couch after we get Fritzie off to school and before my mom gets up for the day. It's not ideal conditions, of course, but if a couple *wanted* to have sex under those circumstances, they could. We apparently are not that couple, however.

We sit there together, and every now and then I let my hand drift over to his thigh in a reawakening kind of way, and . . . well, nothing happens. It's as though there's a force that pulls Patrick away from the real, tangible world of feelings and love and lures him back into the conflicted world of art and misery. Sometimes it seems that there is just a little remaining bit of Patrick that's still mine, a little schmear of him that doesn't belong to this project, but it's in danger of disappearing, too.

So maybe, not to get all dramatic about it, this is nothing less than a battle for his soul. That's the message I seem to get from Toaster Blix, when I have asked. *Fight for him,* her voice says.

So one day I throw caution to the wind and get myself naked under that throw. He looks horrified, and I tell him that it's time we remembered what's good in the world. Remember making out? Remember making love and how nicely things fit together?

So I worked at it and got us started, but then he thought he heard the creaking of the hinges on the bedroom door and he leapt off of me like he'd been shot out of a cannon, and took up a sitting position, with his arm flung casually over the back of the couch. "So, how about the Mets this year? Any good prospects?" he said in a loud voice.

I laughed and whispered, "Get back on top of me; that was just the wind."

"Marnie! What if she comes in here and sees us?"

"Well, Patrick, she and I are now BFFs and not mother and daughter, and I think she'd tiptoe away back to the bedroom and silently cheer for us. She knows this is the way babies get made, and she knows we want a baby."

But uh-oh. A shadow crossed his face at that.

"Didn't we agree to wait on that plan?" he said.

"I believe the minutes would show that we decided to wait, and then *I* pointed out, accurately enough, that I am older than dirt, and that I wanted to get started on tracking my ovulation—"

He closed his eyes, shut himself right down. "Not now, please," he said, as though he was in actual physical pain at the thought. "I can't take on anything else."

"You do know that it takes nine months to actually form a little human," I said, pushing my luck. "It won't be an instantaneous new person."

"After my show," he said. And then he added, "Maybe. If there's anything left of me."

Which I should have addressed right then, except I was too scared. What the hell *was* he talking about? Did he mean that the little schmear of him that I'm getting was going to get even smaller immediately? Was he going to make it disappear altogether?

I looked into his eyes, and I couldn't find him.

That was when I actually got really frightened.

Hang on, the toaster said.

Just when I'm settling in to the new reality—being BFFs with my mom, having a bold eight-year-old to look after and a houseful of teenagers hanging out in the basement, all while trying to hold on to the rapidly disappearing Patrick—the world abruptly takes a major shift into The Holidays. I have always been a big fan of the holidays—all the tra la la stuff and the decorating and the sparkly things—but it also means that there are more flower orders coming in, more red velvet ribbon needed, as well as poinsettias filling up every available space, and along with that comes the fact that more people are likely to burst into tears in the Frippery over all that jolly deck-the-halls propaganda.

And Fritzie, who has been simmering along, takes this opportunity to go crazy.

It starts at a land mine–filled little tradition called Parent Day Luncheon held by the school. The notice arrives in the backpack one day. I see it as I'm unpacking the lunch box and pulling out the homework folder (MATH STORY PROBLEMS DUE TOMORROW: HAVE FUN WITH THESE). And there, just behind the promise of the delightful story problems, is an even *more* promising notice, printed on purple paper: PARENT DAY LUNCHEON AT SCHOOL ON FRIDAY.

"Oh!" I say. "Fritzie, shall we go to this?" I'm so on top of this, already thinking how fraught this must be for Fritzie, and how I can ask Kat if her friend Sal can help out with the orders that morning while I dash out to the school.

She's petting Bedford on the floor and doesn't even look up at me. "I asked Patrick, and he won't come because he's too busy," she says lightly, but not as lightly as she thinks. "And anyway, it's boring."

"Are you sure? I mean, *I* could come. We could make it fun, couldn't we?"

"Nope," she says, and leaves the room.

"I'll talk to Patrick," I call after her. "Maybe he could take the morning off."

"No, thank you," she says in a singsong voice.

My mother gives me an alarmed look and yells, "Say, do they ever have a grandparents' day? Because if they do, little miss, I'm giving you notice now: I'm coming to it!"

Fritzie's bedroom door closes. I bite my lip.

My mom says, "I think you should work on her." That was always my mother's way: work on somebody. But I like to think I'm sensitive to other people's needs. Maybe it's somehow worse for Fritzie if I do go—if she has to explain to everyone that I'm not her real mother; I'm not even her stepmother.

Patrick, when I ask him, points wordlessly to the calendar—how January follows December so closely. He makes a gesture that looks like a head exploding, and then he shuffles back to his studio, shaking his just-exploded head.

So I bring it up with Fritzie a few days later, as we're combing out the tangles in her hair after her bath. "Patrick is sorry but his show is just too soon. Are you sure you don't want me there?"

She looks away. "I'm sure."

"But—won't you be one of the few people there with no parent attending?"

"Marnie," she says. "Patrick should come, but you're not even my stepmother. If you got married to Patrick, you could come."

"Oh, Patrick!" I call out. He can't hear me; he's in the studio. "Oh, *Patrick*! Darling! Could we run off and get married tonight, so I can go to the Parent Day lunch?"

"Stop it," says Fritzie, and she looks like she's going to laugh and cry at the same time.

Two days later, there's an email in my inbox from Karen. Could we chat?

I call her from the Frippery.

"There are just a couple of concerns we have," she says without even taking the time for any small talk. "Soooo, Fritzie has settled down nicely, is doing her work, and there hasn't been any more stealing—or rather *borrowing* money. But . . . well, on the day of the Parent Day Luncheon, she asked if she could say a few words about her mother since her mom couldn't be there."

"I do not like the sound of this."

"Yes, well, your instinct is correct," says Karen. "She stood up and said that her mother was dead. Which I knew wasn't true, but there she was, telling a whole story about how her mom died in a big accident. She actually had some of the moms in tears. So I interrupted her and said, 'Now, Fritzie, you know that's not actually true, honey,' and she started laughing and said it was just a joke."

"She wouldn't let me come to the luncheon," I say miserably. Just in case Karen thinks I'm terrible for not being willing to show up. "Because I'm not really her parent, she said."

"I know. When we tried to talk to her about the luncheon before-hand, we told her that anyone important in her life could come. And that's when she really got upset. We never see this girl cry, no matter what happens in the playground, no matter how scared or mad she gets, she just goes on forward, like some little determined optimist—but that's when she started crying so hard and she said that Patrick doesn't love her yet, and that he's probably never going to love her, and her mum is gone for good."

"Oh," I say. I can't think of anything else. I have to pinch the bridge of my nose to keep from crying myself. "Well, thank you for this." I say we're in difficult times . . . transitions . . . knew this would be hard having her for a year . . . We do love her . . . Patrick is trying, but he has an art show coming up . . . blah blah blah. It all sounds like excuses, even to my own ears.

After I hang up, I want to march right over to Patrick's studio and tell him that he needs to shape up. Stop living apart from us! Open himself up! Emote! Love her! Love *me*! Where the hell is he when we need him?

For the first time since I've been loving Patrick, I feel like yelling and screaming at him. I stand there in the Frippery, listening to the voices of people out in the store, picking out their poinsettias, chatting with Kat about red bows versus gold bows.

And you know something? I do not care one bit about any of it. I get my bag out from under the counter, and I tell Kat that I have to go home. I need to refigure my life.

The next morning, when he's getting his second cup of coffee in the kitchen, I tell him about my conversation with Karen. I'm trying to control how annoyed I feel. It's one thing for him to be pushing *me* away, but Fritzie is his child.

He looks suitably chagrined. Or maybe it's only his basic level of chagrin-itude gone up one slight notch.

"I don't know what I can do," he says. "I'm over my head here."

"Show her you love her," I say. "Take some time off to do something with her. You are her father, you know. Kind of all she has right now."

"What are you talking about? She has you. You're far better with her than I am."

"I don't count," I tell him. "You and Tessa are the ones she needs to hear from. I'm a substitute."

"Look, I don't know the first thing about how to raise an eight-year-old girl! I told you that from the beginning. She wants things from me that I don't know how to give her, and she never stops moving or climbing on things or making comments about everything. *Everything.*"

I look at him.

He picks something off the blanket, a little piece of fuzz. "Ha! I thought the worst of having a kid was going to be the teacher conferences. But instead it's the random acts of crazy. What if she's really a lunatic?"

I take a deep breath. "She's not a lunatic. I think the things she's doing demonstrate a whole bunch of spirit and a healthy reaction to what's happened to her. She was abandoned and left here with virtual strangers. You just need to do more to show her you love her. Couldn't you do that?"

He stares at me.

I reach over and take his hand before he moves it away. "I'm in this with you," I tell him, because I think Blix would want me to throw in some reassurance for him, too. "You don't have to go it alone."

"Well, I have to do these fucking paintings alone, don't I?" he says. "*That's* the truth of it."

"When the art show is over . . ." I say.

"If there's anything left of me."

"There had better be, Patrick. There had better be a lot left of you!"

"There's already hardly anything left of me now," he says. "Also, I don't think I can have any more of this conversation right now."

And then, you know what I do? After he goes back into his studio, I stomp around for a bit, cry a little, and fling all the dishes into the dishwasher. And then I get out the book of spells that I usually keep near the cookbooks when I'm not hauling it around with me. Blix's book. I take a leaf from the African violet and a pinch from the eucalyptus leaf and some dried sage and put them in a little silk bag from the cabinet and put them in my pocket. And I say some words for a happy home spell.

Because when your heart feels like it's breaking, it can't hurt to have some eucalyptus, an African violet, and some dried sage on you.

Later, when my mother and I are walking from the subway to Best Buds, sipping our thermoses of coffee and shivering in the cold wind, she says, "I'm thinking of filling out an online dating profile. I'm ready to get out there."

"Oh my God," I say. "Can't you people just *please* do what you're supposed to do? Stop acting like you've all lost your minds?"

She looks shocked. "What are you talking about? I have not lost my mind!"

"You know," I say slowly, "not to sound all judgy or anything, but when you were talking about having flings and all, I thought that was just your charming Southern hyperbole. You really want to date . . . like people besides Dad? Strangers, you mean?"

She laughs, a new kind of trilling laugh she's adopted lately. "Yes, Marnie! Good God. I don't call it dating when you're out with someone you're married to. And also, I don't see your father here for me to go out with, so it would necessarily have to be with a stranger."

"No. I just . . . well, wait a second. Are you two getting divorced? Because that might be something you'd think about before you get all involved with another man, you know."

"I *don't* know," she says. "I think maybe you and I are thinking of different things. I'm seeing dating as something that'd just be for fun. You know. Dates. Dinner. Movies. Outings."

"I hear all the time that dating is awful. Like, seriously, ninety-three out of a hundred people will tell you it's horrible, ridiculous, painful, and excruciating."

"Not if you haven't done it in forty years."

"I think it doesn't exactly improve with age. And people expect it to lead to . . . well, sex. Maybe love."

"Oh, you," she says. "I think you're being naive. People can have little nonsexual dalliances. And that's what I want: some fun. And if I fall in love—well then, I'll make some necessary changes. It's really not something I'm deciding right now. Did I mention to you that your father hasn't noticed any haircut of mine in five years? Does that sound even slightly acceptable to you? I could use a little bit of matchmaking help."

"Mom."

"Millie. Can't you call me Millie?"

"I'm trying. It's just that I don't really see you as somebody who needs matchmaking. Not even if Dad never mentions another haircut of yours in your whole life. And by the way, if you need him to notice, I think you should tell him. You don't leave a man for not mentioning a haircut. I'm sorry if that—"

"It's not just the haircuts. You know that," she says. "I need more out of my life." She stops walking, so I do, too. She's standing there on the sidewalk, with her hair all fluffed up and her eyes full of sadness, and she looks like somebody that anyone could love. Full of the dickens, really. My mother, I realize, is actually *cute*.

"I'm invisible to him," she says sadly. "He doesn't even see me, much less appreciate anything about me anymore."

"Oh, Mom, I'm so sorry you feel that way."

"Which is why I feel like I need a fling. A little one. So how do you do this matchmaking bit, anyway? Is it always about making people fall in love with each other?"

"Making them? No. You can't make people do anything, in my experience."

"Well, that's for damn sure! So—then what? You see these sparkles around a person, and then how do you find the person they match up to?"

I sigh. "I'm sorry to tell you this, but when I read your energy, what I see is that deep down you're in love with Dad."

"You may be reading an old edition of me. The updated edition is available online."

"Really? You don't think you still love him?"

"Let me put it this way: I'm completely exasperated with him."

"Well, but don't you think exasperation can mean love, too? Love doesn't always dance around in its bright party dress, you know. Sometimes it means you're working on stuff with the person. I think as long as you're not completely indifferent to him, then I'm pretty sure it's still love."

"I don't know," she says. "I told you: I want a fling. I need to be *seen* by somebody before I get too old to care anymore."

I brush back a piece of her blonde hair that's blowing onto her face. "Can you . . . not? Can you remember that you love him and try to work it out? He still loves you. I'm sure of that."

"I don't think I even know what love is anymore. And I'm quite sure he doesn't."

"Jeez, Mom. You had forty years with the guy and about a hundred million dinners and breakfasts. You have two kids, two grandkids, a paid-off mortgage, traditions—"

She draws herself up. "Listen, you don't have to help me if you don't want to. I'm fully capable of taking care of myself," she says.

That night, after Patrick and I have gotten Fritzie and Mister Swoony tucked into bed, telling her more times than ever just how much we love her, and after Patrick has eaten his dinner in silence and then slouched off to the studio, my mom and I sit down in front of the computer. She wants me to look at her dating profile.

I groan.

"I just want you to look at it," she says. "You don't have to participate or change anything. Ariana's helping me with all that. Just let's see if anybody has answered me."

Naturally she has some prospects.

There's Hiram Putnam who is eighty-one and would love to meet a nice "young gal" and he hopes she'll click on him. He has just a couple of tiny health problems, but he sees himself square-dancing well into the 2020s. "God bless him," says my mother.

Then there's Joseph Cranston, who posts a picture of himself smiling into the camera in his bathroom mirror. He likes walks on the beach and values a sense of humor and a woman who is "fit."

"Red flag! Fit means skinny," I say. I have heard some things around Best Buds about the code words. "You don't want to go out with a guy who thinks that way."

"But I am skinny," says my mom, which is true.

"Yes, but you don't want that to be the thing he cares most about, do you? Monitoring your ice cream consumption? Counting your calories? Also, the bathroom mirror photo is a real turn-off. Shows a kind of cheapness. Or at the very least in this case, an ugly bathroom."

"You're tough," she says, patting my arm, "which is why I need you here with me."

Elliott Chase is an attorney whose wife died in a car crash five months ago.

"Too soon," I tell her.

"But he's handsome. Maybe he needs cheering up."

"Not your job. Nope, nope, nope."

"God, you're tough. If you ever lose Patrick, I don't see how you're going to get another one, not with these standards."

"I'm not losing Patrick," I say.

She's scrolling through more prospects, not looking at me. And that's when it hits me, like a blow to the stomach: Wait a minute, I *am* losing Patrick. I may have already lost him. I think of how he looked at me so grudgingly when he shuffled off to his studio after dinner, and how unmoved he is when I talk to him, and how he can't wait each day to go back over there. To be all alone. *I'm* the one who forces the Conjugal Visits. Who tries to make things okay for him.

But he's gone.

There's an ache already spreading through me, skittering across my nerve endings.

"While we're on that topic," my mom says, "if you don't mind my asking, why didn't you ever marry this guy? It's not like you to not want to get things in writing."

"I-I don't know."

"Well, do you love him?" She types something on the keyboard. A checkmark.

"Yes. Yes! I do love him."

"Do you? Then get married to him, why don't you? Frankly, you and Patrick might as well be married, with the way you're living. He's vulnerable and sweet, and you want a baby, and you're raising Fritzie and apparently a couple of teenagers, too, so I don't see what the hell the difference is. Maybe it would make him happy."

"Nothing makes him happy right now," I say before I can catch myself.

She swings her eyes over to me, looking concerned. "Yeah, I've gotten that idea. So . . . is it really just the art show, do you think? Or is something else going on?"

"I don't know," I say.

"It's like he's not even here," she says. "Isn't it?"

Something is forming in the back of my head.

"Men can withdraw so completely when there's something else going on," she says. She's not looking at me. Her words hang in the air, like little drones all pointed at my head.

A thought suddenly forms up near the ceiling. I watch it coming closer to me and settling in my head, and I realize I've known all along what's going on. I've even mentioned it, without truly taking it in or believing it.

Patrick isn't here because he's reliving his relationship with another woman.

That's it, isn't it? I think. *It's as though he's in that other room, dancing with death.*

Yes.

"Y'all should be sleeping in the same bed so you can fix this," my mom is saying, but I can barely hear her over the drumming of my own thoughts. "I'm being horribly selfish," she says. "I need to find a place of my own, and you need your time to reconnect. I feel like you're growing apart more each day, and I bet you anything, it's because you're not getting any sex. Sex holds people together, keeps them from murdering each other."

"It's not just sex," I say slowly. But maybe those words were inside my head, too.

She keeps talking. "I'm going to look for a place to live. I've been having such a good time being here with you, but this is ridiculous. You're sleeping in a bed with your mama, and your boyfriend is having to sleep in his studio. I should be sued for this."

"No, no, Mom," I say. "He wants to be there, with the paintings. He told me. It's fine. Really."

The knowledge clunks into my head like it's been floating above me and just now found the way into my brain. He is actually involved again with Anneliese. She's the one he's thinking about all the time, not me. I'm freaking competing with a dead woman, and I'm losing!

It would seem to be quite the opposite, wouldn't you think? She's already put forth all her best stuff and has no more cards to play—and I, being alive and sentient, could just possibly wow him with some amazing feat of love and tenderness that only a living, breathing human could do. I can cook meals for him, for instance. Make love to him.

But it's not that way at all. She's frozen in amber, she's perfection, and I am hopeless and real and messy, and I say and do the wrong thing, and even when I try to love him, to use my body on his body—it's pathetic. That's it. I am pathetic.

After a moment, my mom sighs and looks back at her computer screen. "And then here is young, perky Randolph Greenleaf. A medical doctor and he's fifty-four years old, and he has a nice mustache and he's never been married. What do you think the pitfalls are?"

"Gay? Misogynistic? Selfish? Crabby?"

"I'm thinking of clicking on him. Here we go!" she says. "Should I? Gosh, it's surprisingly hard to pull the trigger on these guys."

"Mom."

"Millie, if you please."

"Millie. Sorry. Are you going to go home to see Dad at Christmas?"

She doesn't look at me, just scrolls through the computer screen. "I hadn't planned on it."

"Is he coming up here then?"

"No . . . haven't heard anything about that."

"You do know this is weird though, right?"

"Christmas isn't that big a deal when you don't have children at home," she says. "You get over it real fast."

Do you? Because I have never in my life gotten over anything real fast, and now I just want to crawl into a little ball and sleep through the holidays. Sleep until I know what I'm supposed to do next.

CHAPTER TWENTY-SEVEN

MARNIE

I set out one Saturday morning with Fritzie and my mother to get a tree, which we find on a street corner in Greenpoint, and manage to drag home on the subway. Which is so crazy and ridiculous because three men have to help us get it both off and on the train because it's so big ("We are soo not having a merry little Christmas!" says Fritzie), and then we carry it home and up the stairs, and my mother says she'll be surprised if there's even one needle on the thing by the time we get it indoors. But somehow there is, and also it fills up the whole living room, having actually grown in stature on the way home. Surely it wasn't this big when we saw it on the street corner, bundled up and leaning against a box truck.

In past years, being an artist and all, Patrick has loved decorating the tree, but this year he doesn't come out of his studio. I get the box of decorations from the attic, and my mother helps me string up the lights. As soon as she gets them on the tree, she announces that she can't stay for the whole time because she's got a date with Dr. Randolph Greenleaf, who turns out to possess not all the bad qualities I had predicted. Sure, he hates restaurants and loves karaoke bars—an odd combination for one man, I think, but maybe he's as complicated as the rest of us—and my mother says it works because he's actually kind of stuffy and boring until he starts belting out tunes in the bar, off-key but at full volume.

I'm not sure how I feel about my mother going out with Randolph Greenleaf, even if it is strictly platonic as she says. And even if it technically is none of my business. I think I would just as soon *not* know him, to tell you the truth. She tells me I'd like his joie de vivre, and I tell her that I'd like his joie de vivre lots better if it was being lavished on someone else's married mother.

She laughs. "Your father would sooner cut off his arm than sing in a karaoke bar, and he would certainly never permit any friend or relation of his to do such a thing," she says. "So this is sociologically interesting to me."

"Sociology, huh?" I say.

"Perhaps it's anthropology," she answers. "I want to see how the natives of New York deal with old age approaching."

In her research, she also has joined a yoga class two mornings a week, and to blend in better with her subjects of research, she has a new haircut that is all slanted and shorter on one side than the other. The hairdresser complimented the pink slash that Ariana had put in her hair. I honestly don't know what to think anymore. This is my mom, the person who used to wear Christmassy light-up earrings and bulky holiday sweaters with reindeer on them and little white Keds with ankle socks with lace trimming. She had a pageboy haircut and Bermuda shorts.

She tells me to lighten up. "I'm shocked that you, of all people, are judging me," she says. "Not that it's any of your business, but I am not sleeping with Randolph Greenleaf. And I don't intend to."

Anyway, so my dad doesn't come for Christmas, and my mother doesn't go to Florida either. He calls me at work at least seven times in the weeks before Christmas to ask me if I think she'd come home if he sent her a ticket, and I have to tell him each time that she doesn't want to. She's not ready to go home yet.

"Are you needing her maybe too much?" he asks me, kind of hopefully. "Maybe let up on the needing just a little, so she'll come back. She's scared of snow. Maybe it'll snow, and she'll come back."

I don't tell him my mother has bought some snow boots. She's ready.

"What are you going to do for Christmas?" I ask him.

"Oh, I'll go to Natalie's in the morning and watch her kids plow through their presents. And then I'll probably go watch some golf. And I'll call you and your mom."

"That sounds nice, except for the golf," I say. "At least you'll be with Natalie and the children."

"Yup," he says. "Don't pick on the golf channel. Golf on Christmas. Lots of fun there."

It snows on Christmas Eve, which both my mom and Fritzie think is the most incredible thing to ever be orchestrated by the galaxy, and which both of them act like I somehow arranged.

"It's like Christmas in a movie! Or in a book!" says Fritzie.

She and my mother go outside on the stoop and try to catch snowflakes on their tongues. Despite my heart feeling empty, I make hot chocolate as one is required to do on a snowy Christmas Eve, and we walk down the street, scuffing our feet in the snow and admiring the big fat flakes falling under the streetlights. I try to see this through the eyes of both Fritzie and my mom. Life can be difficult, but there are moments that are beyond anything you expected. Moments of almost piercing beauty. That's what I've learned through the last years, isn't it? Be grateful for the evening, and the snowfall, and the expressions on Fritzie's face, for the warmth inside, and the tree. And send a thought to Patrick, who is fighting not only himself but also a dead woman. Maybe I should go in and challenge her to a duel. I think maybe I will look in the spell book for a potion that will banish her.

Fritzie, being crazy, naturally wants to walk backward down the middle of the street instead of forward, and she starts singing "Jingle Bells" at the top of her lungs, and then she wants to know if we can ring people's doorbells and sing them Christmas carols when they answer, just like they do in movies. I say no, but my mother says, "Really, why not?"

We go to Lola's house and sing to her and William Sullivan. It takes them forever to come to the door. We've nearly exhausted our repertoire, which only includes "Deck the Halls," "Silent Night," and "Jingle Bells."

"Come in! Come in!" says Lola when she and William answer the door. They're getting ready to head to Florida, she says. They always spend January and February where it's warm.

"I don't think carolers are supposed to come inside and bother people," I say. "We just wanted to say Merry Christmas to you."

"Oh, so sweet. And I'll miss you while I'm gone," she says. "Is everything okay?"

See? Such a small question—most people can sail right through answering a question like that. But there I am standing on her stoop trying to remember verse two of "Silent Night," and I am with my mother who wants to cheat on my dad, and Patrick is holed up in his two-room prison with the ghost of Anneliese, and Fritzie is a lunatic and I love her, and all I want is to answer the question in some kind of positive, affirmative way. I would like to answer her that everything is great; really, I mean to do that, but the trouble is that my eyes fill with tears just then, without any warning. No one notices except Lola. My mother and William Sullivan are talking about their favorite Christmas carols, and Fritzie is picking off the berries on the wreath on their door and tossing them into the street.

"It's going to be okay," Lola says softly. "Come in. We'll pretend I need to give you something. Which, now that I think of it, I actually do."

And she takes me into her house, a house that used to be so lonely and sad until four years ago when she finally gave in and let herself fall in love with William Sullivan, a matchmaking project orchestrated by Blix and then completed by me.

"Listen, you," she says and takes my hand. "I know it's hard right now. Heavens, we've all gone through this kind of darkness, haven't we? And we've come out of it. I trust in Blix's predictions, honey, and she was firm on the point that you and Patrick belong together. Okay? Just remember that. She had something real. She knew what I needed, and she knew what you needed. So you've got to just hang tight."

"Will you take me to Florida with you?" I ask her, only half kidding.

"Nope," she says, "but what I will do is leave you my house key. Maybe at some point your mother would like to move over here. I think it's going to be important for you and your Patrick to resume a real life. Moving back into the same bed could be a good start."

"He won't do it," I say.

"I bet he will," she says. "Don't forget that I've seen that man make amazing changes in his life."

"Well, not lately."

"No, not lately. But let's not give up on him, shall we? I've known Patrick for years, and if there's anything I know for sure about him, it's that he loves you very much. He feels safe with you."

When I get back home and get Fritzie put to bed and my mother situated in front of her computer, I make cups of hot chocolate piled high with whipped cream, and I take them over to Patrick's studio. I intend to say, "It's Christmas Eve, let's have sex!" or something equally jaunty and free.

But here's the thing: I get to the studio door, and it takes me approximately fifty-four deep breaths and thirty-six self-talk reassurances before I can even bring myself to knock on the door. And why do I have to knock, anyway? That's what my mind keeps demanding to know the answer to. Since when do two people who love each other find themselves having to tiptoe around?

When I finally do knock on the door, Patrick comes and opens it up. His face is drawn, but I can see the effort he's making to arrange his expression into a smile. He invites me in, and we sit and sip our hot chocolate together on his futon. We are being so careful not to stray into the territory of bad feelings that it seems like we hardly know each other.

After I've been there for a few minutes, he gets up and goes into the other room and brings back a little box. He's made me a wire necklace with a clear blue stone wrapped around and around in the wire. All I can think of when I look at it is that the poor sweet stone looks trapped by knots. My eyes fill up with tears, but I brush them aside quickly.

When I go to kiss him, it's like kissing a stranger.

Neither one of us suggests having sex. I remember then that the spell book mentions that to get rid of a ghost, you need to put salt in the corners of every room. Maybe next time I'll bring a *sack* of salt with me. Throw it around the whole damn place.

The next morning Fritzie gets up crazy early, as children all over the world are supposed to do, whether their caretakers are thrilled about it or not. I am so cheerful, I am in danger of going into Cheer Overload. Really, my cheeks actually hurt from so much fake holiday smiling.

My mother, who has made a career of creating life-enhancing Christmas holidays for children, pitches in by suggesting we play guessing games with Fritzie to keep her from insisting on opening her presents before Patrick rouses himself. I start a pot of coffee and put some cinnamon rolls and a breakfast casserole in the oven. By eight o'clock, when Fritzie can't take it any longer, I let her zoom into his studio and jump on him. I can hear her screaming, "It's Christmas, Patrick, it's Christmas!"

By the time she drags him out to the living room, I've got Christmas music playing on the speakers, and I've set the table with some of Blix's finest silver and some plates that have poinsettias painted on them. The house smells deliciously like cinnamon and butter.

If a stranger were to peek in the window and see us all there—our nodding, smiling faces, our twinkly lights, the stockings hanging on the mantel—they'd surely think we were a lovely family about to embark on a fabulous new year together.

But nothing is as it seems. And I worry that this might very well be my last Christmas with both Patrick and Fritzie—and my last Christmas having a child to dazzle—and I want to make this something Fritzie will talk about for the rest of her life.

She opens the presents that I bought for her from Patrick and me: a video game she wanted, and a box of art supplies, a light saber, and a giant stuffed sloth, which she says will be best friends with Mister Swoony. Tessa has sent her a big intriguing box that we've been wondering about all week.

Inside are two identical satiny dresses—one bright blue and one red, with lace and sashes and a sweetheart collar and covered buttons down the front.

I hold my breath as Fritzie lifts them out of the box and then puts them right back. "These can go right to the thrift shop," she says.

"They're very . . . girlish," says my mother.

"Not the kind of girlish I am," says Fritzie. Which is of course true. "I could make them into hats maybe."

Tessa calls the house in the afternoon after we are all bleary-eyed and are contemplating naps, and Fritzie talks to her very politely and in monosyllables. It is chilling to listen to, actually, how disconnected

Fritzie is from anything I can hear Tessa saying. After the call is over, she goes and sits on the couch and leans against my mother for a long time, and my mother puts her arm around her and offers to watch *It's a Wonderful Life* with her. I have to take Mom into the kitchen and remind her that that's a movie about a guy who wants to kill himself, and maybe it's not the best for today, not for an eight-year-old. And not for a man who's wrestling with his love for a dead woman either, I think to myself. Although Patrick has somehow been reabsorbed back into his studio and probably wouldn't come out to watch anything anyway.

"Okay, then, *Love Actually*," says my mother when she's back in the living room, and so then I take her *back* to the kitchen and remind her of certain elements she might have overlooked in that film, too: for instance, the couple simulating sex in the highest-production porn movie ever and the unfaithful husband and the brother suffering from psychosis.

"You're right, you're right," says my mom. "Why is it that all I remember is Hugh Grant dancing?"

This Christmas, I think, is really a big fat hoax after all. A stunning amount of work—and for what? Simply to hide the heartbreak that all four of us are feeling. I feel like I've been pushing it away so hard, and yet of course it's sitting right there in the center of my head, like a flashing red light: THIS CHRISTMAS IS A DISASTER.

In the late afternoon, when all the Christmas requirements have been ticked off, and when I am spent and bedraggled from all the effort, I stomp over to the music player and turn *off* the holiday carols and put on the music I love—the Beatles and the Rolling Stones and Bruce Springsteen. Marvin Gaye. Lady Gaga. The Supremes. My mother yells out that she wants some Frank Sinatra. We put it all on. And we turn up the volume as loudly as we can, and we turn down all the lights except for the bright-colored ones on the Christmas tree, and we dance and sing at the top of our lungs. Fritzie jumps on the couch because that's what she loves more than anything. Bedford barks and runs back and forth. My mother does dances from her teenage years, which include the jerk, the twist, the boogaloo, and some other crazy stuff, like the mashed potato. I can do the Charleston and the Texas two-step. We all fail magnificently at doing the Floss.

At one point my mother is twirling me around in a circle when I feel her move away, and when I turn back, Patrick has taken her place. He pulls me to him, and my head is against his chest. I hear his heart beating and feel his chest moving up and down, hear the bass of his voice as he sings along to Diana Ross's "You Can't Hurry Love," which is about everything I don't believe in. I think you have to hurry love because otherwise it can flit away so easily.

I've been holding myself together throughout this whole day, trying to make it festive for Fritzie and my mom, and now I'm so surprised to feel his body next to mine that I almost can't breathe for a moment. I feel like I'm melting into the soft familiarity of him.

And I close my eyes and thank whoever or whatever is out there that makes things happen. Sometimes you need a Christmas miracle, and you can already tell it's not going to come from the usual places, like candles and Christmas carols. Those all had their chance. Sometimes the Christmas miracle has to ride in on the notes of a Motown song and the Texas two-step. Dancing, I think, is almost always a good idea.

But then the song ends, and he lets me go, and when I see his eyes again, it's as though he's pulled himself away once more. But, hey, at least he tried.

CHAPTER TWENTY-EIGHT
PATRICK

Eight o'clock in the morning the day after New Year's, Patrick's phone rings. The buzzing of his cell phone yanks him out of a sound sleep. He'd been up until three, pacing and making art. Maybe it was four. Wait. No. He remembers seeing the clock say 4:20 in its huge red numerals. He can't remember all that well, frankly. Things are fuzzy and there might be mushrooms growing in his brain. Or maybe he painted mushrooms. He'll have to look.

It's Philip Pierpont. The double-edged sword that is Philip Pierpont.

This time it's the annoyingly celebratory Philip Pierpont bellowing into the phone, "Patrick! Patrick, my friend! The story is out and it's sensational. Could not have nailed this better! This is going to bring people in!" (Which does not make Patrick feel any better, for some reason. He doubts if he and Pierpont would agree on what a good story would be.)

And then there is the next prong of Philip Pierpont, lying in wait for him. His voice changes, signifying that he has a big question. So! How many paintings, exactly, was he showing? How many are ready, and when can they be packed up and brought over?

Patrick has no idea how many paintings. He doesn't even know how many he can bear to show of the ones that are finished. Or supposedly finished. Not to mention the ones he thinks he will finish before the show, which he believes is not for another few weeks. January 18, is he not right?

Correct, says Pierpont in a funny voice. "But I need numbers for wall space. You've done shows before, my artistically complicated friend. You know this."

He goes on talking and talking, and Patrick is forced to realize that Pierpont would like things quantified to a point that Patrick is not comfortable with. What if he says ten paintings? Is that too many? No, probably too few.

And now Philip Pierpont, as if he's on purpose aiming to hit all the low points, careens into Point Number Three. Opening night! There will be cheese and wine, of course, and possibly some crudités. Some more members of the press possibly coming . . . invitations sent out . . . Would Patrick agree to make a few remarks? To give a brief overview of the work? Which of course speaks for itself, but the crowd always likes a little something from the artist. An acknowledgment of the attendance perhaps. Of the honor of the thing. Gallery space.

No, decidedly not. Certainly not. NO remarks. Patrick's heart is pounding as he refuses.

The call ends badly then, the way it began. Pierpont is antsy and angry. Perhaps he has an inkling that Patrick isn't going to be the big draw he had hoped. No one remembers that he was once an up-and-coming sculptor, and they sure as hell don't care that a nobody sculptor is now going to try to be a nobody-in-every-sense painter. And one that won't talk in public, to boot.

What artist would want to talk at an occasion like this one? Well, come to think of it, he's known a few. Too many, actually. The types that wear their egos right on their chests and who slick back their brilliant artist hair and rub their brilliant artist beards and say pontificating things to the public about art and meaning and symbolism.

If he got up there, he'd say, "Art is pain. It is grief and agony and I hated my life while I painted these paintings. I look at them now, and I want never to see them again. I don't even want any of you to see them. I have—I have been skinned alive by this work." And then he would leave. Catch a cab and go somewhere where they couldn't find him and ask another thing of him.

He wonders if he dares go online and see what the article says.

He's dreaded it so much that now that it's here, he's quite sure he doesn't want to put himself through any more.

Only he can't rest. Nothing helps. He paces around, he stares at his reflection in the bathroom mirror, decides he still looks as bad as ever, he paces some more, talks to Roy who is decidedly unsympathetic. Finally, with great effort, he gets up and lets himself out the front door, goes over to Paco's, where the magazines had been delivered several hours ago.

"Hey, man of the hour!" says Paco. "Look at you, on the cover of *Inside Outside*, you devil you."

"Yeah," Patrick says. "Look at me."

"You no worry, Patrick. It's a good story. We read it out loud to ourselves here this morning. And everybody say the same thing: 'That Patrick. He's a real good guy.'"

INSIDE OUTSIDE MAGAZINE

BROOKLYN'S LATEST WORD ON ART

Scarred, Grieving but Unbowed: Brooklyn Artist Mounts a Comeback

Patrick Delaney, 36, doesn't look anything like the dashing, handsome man he was when he was considered the "Golden Boy of Sculpture" eight years ago. His face, once chiseled and with a jawline that actors would envy, is now lined and scarred by burns he suffered in a devastating fire in a New York loft—a fire that killed his young girlfriend even as he attempted to save her life.

But what Delaney has lost in his golden-boy looks, he's more than made up for in stature, as a hero and now, as an artist seeking to make a comeback in a whole new medium.

Delaney doesn't like to talk about the fire, or its aftermath, the months when he lived in a downtown hotel, contemplating his own mortality and vowing that he would never do sculpture, or any kind of art, again. He is a man of few words who grows visibly uncomfortable when asked what that turning point was like in his life.

"I had lost my appetite for art," he says.

According to police reports on file, it was an ordinary summer day in August of 2010 when Delaney and his girlfriend, Anneliese Cunningham, awoke in their SoHo loft and, as they did most days, got to work creating sculpture. Delaney was working on a sculpture called *The Fallen Angel* that had been commissioned by the New York City collector Regis Harrington—a piece that would never be completed.

Cunningham, 24, a sculptor in her own right, was working on an untitled piece she hoped to enter into a show in the fall. She went to the little galley kitchen area to start the morning's coffee. According to fire officials, a gas leak triggered an immediate explosion that killed Cunningham outright, engulfing her in flames.

Delaney raced toward her, police said, and because of his heroics in reaching for her to put out the fire, he suffered second- and third-degree burns on his face, hands and arms. He was transported by ambulance to the burn unit at Mount Sinai Hospital, where he was placed in a medically induced coma. Over the next few months he underwent several surgeries to repair damage to his hands and face. It was thought that he'd never be able to do art again.

Today, Delaney has little to say on the subject. His one statement, delivered in a choked-off voice, is, "I couldn't imagine why she had to die and why I remained alive. And I was not a hero that day. I am not the hero of this story. There is no hero."

He doesn't think of himself as a hero because he was unable to save her. In fact, medical records show that Delaney passed out from the heat upon reaching her, and he didn't even know what had happened until he woke up in a hospital weeks later with his face and hands and arms requiring numerous surgeries. The art world was lost to him.

The months and years that followed took their toll—and in talking to him today, a visitor can see in his eyes the remains of grief and survivor's guilt. He became a recluse, living in a basement apartment in Brooklyn with Roy, his opinionated orange cat, and writing for a medical website, and venturing out only when he was reasonably assured of not running into other people.

Only recently has his life turned around enough that Delaney is willing once again to create art. Over the past three years, Delaney has started painting in oils again, though not with any real interest. According to gallery owner Philip Pierpont, a friend of Delaney's, it seemed that at first Delaney had lost the will to try to penetrate the depth of creativity and strive to find its meaning.

"He was hiding. But," says Pierpont, "in a triumph of human spirit, Patrick kept at it. I always knew that deep down in him, the will to triumph over adversity would come through, and with his reentry into a new art form, I have every confidence that he will show us a return of nothing less than his very soul."

Pierpont has asked him to exhibit his paintings this January in a one-man show at the Pierpont Gallery in Manhattan, something those who know him never thought would happen.

"I have always been an admirer of Patrick Delaney's sensibility, his sensitivity, and the soulfulness of his work," says Pierpont. "I own several of his sculptures, and we have had two successful shows together. I reached out to him and said, 'It's time, man, for you to get back into the art world.' He agreed, although perhaps reluctantly, and now I can't wait to see what he comes up with. The thing about Patrick Delaney is that you know you are going to plumb the depths of feeling—all feeling—represented in his work. You come away a changed person."

Delaney was always considered a sculptor of great range and even whimsy, with his depictions of courtship in *Cupid's Arrow Misses* and *Friday Night Date Night*. His *Bird on Two Wires* received an American Post Prize and his triptych, titled *The Way of Men*, was mentioned in *Art Today* magazine as evidence that Delaney was an "artist under thirty who bears watching."

Delaney is perhaps understandably secretive about the paintings he is preparing for his show, as well he might be. After all, he was never known for his painterly abilities, especially as an abstract expressionist.

But Pierpont says he has no doubt that this will give Delaney an opportunity to stretch and grow and see what remains now that the past is behind him. "Of course we know that for artists, the past is never fully dealt with and put away," says Pierpont, "and we expect that Patrick's work will reflect the full range of his suffering. We are looking forward to welcoming him back into the art world and into a whole new range of possibility."

Delaney's personal life has taken a change of course as well. Recently, he and his current girlfriend, the florist Marnie MacGraw, welcomed Delaney's daughter from a previous brief relationship into their home. Fritzie Delaney, 8, says she is happy to finally meet her father and she loves painting with him in his studio.

"I am a surprise girl," Fritzie says. "He didn't know about me until me and my mom looked him up on the internet. And now my mom is in Italy, and so I am living with Patrick and Marnie. And I am trying to cheer him up. I am hoping he will paint about me sometime."

PHOTO CAPTIONS:

Artist Patrick Delaney, of Brooklyn, in his studio, looks over his work from the previous day. Once a sculptor, he doesn't want to show his new paintings to anyone until the opening on January 18 at the Pierpont Gallery.

A quick unauthorized peek at one of Delaney's in-progress pictures, depicting the horror of the fire that killed his girlfriend, the artist Anneliese Cunningham, eight years ago.

Fritzie Delaney, 8, the daughter of Patrick Delaney, says she has only recently come to live with him and his girlfriend. "I didn't even know him until three months ago," she says. "Now I know that he's a hero. He tried to save someone from burning up in a fire."

CHAPTER
TWENTY-NINE
MARNIE

My mother moves over to Lola's apartment the day after Christmas. No more Girlfriend Hour after we get in bed at night, complete with manicures, pedicures, and talk about husbands and flings and purple hair dye. It's just as well. I'm tired, and I don't like hearing about Randolph Greenleaf, and I certainly don't want to see my mother's tragic look when she thinks about Patrick and me.

I guess she and I both imagined that Patrick would now have the chance to move back in our room, but of course he doesn't take the opportunity.

Too much work to be done in the studio, he says. He looks haggard and stressed out when I see him in the kitchen, and I can barely reach him, is the truth of it. When I try to kiss him, his return kisses are like little pecks on the cheek, the way you might kiss an old disagreeable auntie. Or an ex who was throwing herself at you.

A woman with any self-respect would probably kick him out. But, you see, there's this child. I can't bring myself to lose her. And of course, she would have to go with him. That wouldn't be good for anybody.

Anyway, so on January 2, with school finally back in session, I come into the kitchen after taking Fritzie to the bus stop, and there's my mom cutting up vegetables for soup for dinner. At eight o'clock in the morning, but whatever. I'm a little ragged because Fritzie is upset that Patrick wouldn't walk her to the bus stop this morning, which she says is the only time he talks to her lately. He's frantic now, trying to finish up.

So she's acting out. She fussed about the need to wear her warm coat and her boots, and then she said Patrick lets her cross the street by herself, which I know is not true. He is the most danger-aware person in the world.

"You have to stop giving me so much trouble," I finally said to her, and she sunk down into herself, pouting. So then I hugged her, and I told her I loved her so much. She looked up at me with those huge, opaque eyes and then she leaned up against me, and said, "Are things going to get better again when Patrick has finished working on the paintings for his show?"

"Of course they are," I said. "Everything is going to go back to normal." And she skipped the rest of the way to the bus stop.

My mother is cutting carrots and onions with the look on her face that people must get when they are killing Burmese pythons in the Everglades, or so I would imagine. She says that last night Dr. Randolph told her that—call him old-fashioned, if you must, he said—but he doesn't much like it when women wear makeup. Or pants. His sainted mother never wore any, and she was the best-looking woman he ever knew. And she had a nice, low, calm voice, too. Sometimes, he had to admit, women's voices get on his nerves. My mother's voice being one of those, for instance, just sometimes. When she's excited. Only when she's excited.

I take Bedford off his leash and look at the table, where *Inside Outside* magazine is lying.

"Oh my goodness," I say, and my mother says, "Yes. So I won't be seeing *him* anymore," and I say, "Of course not, but ohhh, look at this—Patrick is on the cover of *Inside Outside*! And it's here! The story is out."

"Yes," my mother says. She's stirring a pot of soup on the stove for lunch. "I guess it's not very good news. At least Patrick didn't think so."

"Is he in his studio?"

"Yeah. Kind of mad, I think."

"Oh, God." Then, after I've read the story, I say it a few more times for good measure. "Of course he hates this. It's just what he feared." I start tapping on the table. "All this triumphing over adversity and the Golden Boy of Sculpture, the soul of art."

"Why is this so bad? This says only nice things about him."

"He doesn't want to be a hero, Mom. And this isn't really about him or his art. It's all about this reporter and the gallery owner needing him to sound like he's some long-suffering hero staging a huge comeback. Using the police reports. Ugh. Oh God, and they talked to Fritzie. I didn't think the reporter had permission to do that."

"But . . . well, he was a hero, wasn't he? I mean, he tried to save that woman."

"Yes, he did," I say. It's hard to explain, but I try anyway. "That woman was the woman he loved. And she died right in front of him. And this makes it sound like he's capitalizing on the tragedy. That he's benefiting somehow from being the Great Sufferer."

"Well, I didn't think it sounded like that at all," says my mom. "If you asked me, the only negative thing about it in my opinion was that they could have said a little less about how he's not handsome anymore. That would get to me if I was him."

From the toaster comes a piece of burnt toast, flying out of the holes in the top and landing on the floor. Bedford listlessly lifts his head and goes over to pick it up.

241

"Oh!" says my mother. "I don't think I'll ever get used to that temperamental toaster of yours. I'm ordering you a new one right after I finish these dishes. First I'm going to send Randolph a text message saying I won't be troubling him with my annoying voice anymore because I'm never going to see him again. And then a new toaster."

"No new toaster," I say quickly. "We love this one. And by the way, texting is considered a bad way to break up with someone."

"Tough shit," she says. "I'd hate to make him listen to my screeching over the phone."

I kiss her on her magnificent, bold, fierce-woman cheek as I head to the studio.

One time, a long time ago, when I first knew I was falling in love with Patrick and he wasn't letting me in because he was so resolutely miserable and didn't think there was any such thing as love out there for a man who had scars on his face, I accused him of living on the planet My Lover Died in the Fire. I actually said that. I was mad when I said it, and I stood there in his kitchen, the basement kitchen downstairs, wanting to make love with him more than anything I'd ever wanted in my whole life, but he wouldn't do it. I was embarrassed because I loved him so much, so I said that he'd chosen to live in unhappiness and guilt, but that he didn't have to. I said the fact that he was angry all the time meant that he was healing and that his whole problem was that he hated himself for healing. He wanted to stay stuck in his grief and let life go on without him.

Then, to put an even finer point on things, I told him that I loved him. Which I had never said before.

He said no to me that night—very sadly, but it was still no—and so I gathered what was left of my dignity and went back to my apartment—this apartment, this very kitchen, in fact—and I told myself I had to give up on him. That he would never be ready. I already knew by that point

242

that Blix had wanted us to be together, that she had done spells and magic to bring our love about. That she had peered into the future and had seen that we were perfect together. I'd seen things she'd written in her spell book: our names linked over and over again. So not only did I feel sorry for myself and for Patrick, but I felt sorry that Blix had failed, too, at the thing she most wanted.

But sometimes it hits you that you can't go about life forcing everybody to do the thing you think they should, even when it's perfect for them.

So over the next few days I made up my mind to sell the brownstone and move back to Florida. Patrick had already decided to move back to live with his sister in Wyoming. At the time we had the argument about love, the U-Haul truck was parked outside the building for him to put his stuff in it.

I don't think I can really explain what happened next, except to say that I had given up on him, and sometimes when you surrender to things, all the energy changes.

The next day we awoke to a foot of snow, and school was called off, so I took Bedford and Sammy, the kid who then lived in the apartment where Patrick now has his studio, to the park. And Bedford got lost. Sammy and I searched and searched, but it was snowing so hard, and we couldn't find him anywhere. My cell phone had no power, so I couldn't even call for help. I just kept calling and searching for Bedford, frozen through to the heart and feet of me, and fearing the worst.

But then I looked up and there was Patrick coming toward me, holding out his arms, like a mirage coming through the blizzard. It was like seeing a Saint Bernard with a keg of brandy, only better. He, who disliked dogs almost as much as he hated being out in public, had gone out looking for my dog, and he'd found Bedford injured in the street, hit by a car. Patrick had taken him to the vet in his U-Haul truck, and then he came and found me in the park.

There he was: a man with snow on his eyelashes and in his eyebrows, a man with crinkly, smiling eyes and a sad, lopsided grin, a man who loved me. Who had saved my dog.

Until that moment, I don't think Patrick really did know that he could have love in his life. Or that he could save a dog's life by striding into a vet's office and authorizing surgery. Or even that he could go after a life that he yearned for but which had seemed impossibly far away for him. But after that—well, maybe he figured out that resistance was futile, that there is love out there for all of us. He loved me. And I loved him, and I, for one, was sure that love was all it really took to make something work.

We had a talk. He said he'd make a deal with me: he wouldn't go home to Wyoming if I didn't go home to Florida. We'll see what happens, he said. Then, being all Patricky, he gave me all kinds of warnings about how hard it was going to be to drag himself permanently away from the planet My Lover Died in the Fire, but he hoped I wouldn't give up on him. And he was going to try, too, he said. He'd at least try to stop parking his spaceship at that planet's parking lot, he said.

And so we started living together. It was wonderful. We took long bubble baths together with candles perched all around the tub, and both Bedford and Roy would curl up on the bathroom rug, watching us (and each other) with suspicion. We'd sit up late at night around the firepit on the roof, with my head on his shoulder, just talking and talking. He told me all about Blix and her outrageous shenanigans. He told me how she made him believe in magic.

That first summer, we bought a hammock and two ukuleles, and we learned four songs that we'd sing at the tops of our lungs, so badly out of tune that we were sure the cars honking on the street were trying to drown us out. We read the *New York Times* in bed on the weekends, fighting over the Arts and Style sections and not getting up until noon. We discovered Blix's treasure trove of recipes and cooked them all, slow-dancing in the kitchen while we waited for the pasta to boil.

And in the classic tradition of lovers everywhere, we felt supremely sorry for anyone who wasn't us.

I'll always believe that it was Blix, who was really the champion of the two of us, who somehow made sure that things straightened out for us. He and I have laughed about all the things she had to arrange just for that one moment of a change of heart for him: a snowstorm, a snow day from school, a stray dog taking off and getting lost, an accident that was bad but not too bad, the urgency of a U-Haul truck that needed to be packed. Oh, sure, she was dead by then—but let's face it, Blix wasn't the type to let a little change of address upset her plans. She stepped right in, and guided Patrick right smack into love.

And now . . . well, here we are again. While I haven't been paying attention, Patrick has gone off in the spaceship to his old familiar planet. I can feel this big old chunk of empty air where he used to be. No wonder my own faith in him has been wobbling; no wonder I've felt bereft as hell while I wait to see what happens. He's been out in space for too long.

Go to him. I hear her voice in my head. *Go find him. Show him again what it means to love.*

So, I square my shoulders and put on the equivalent of my own space suit, grab my oxygen tank, and walk over to bring him back to Earth.

CHAPTER THIRTY
MARNIE

His paintings are lined up in the front room. Ten of them, each one a fragile, heartbreaking meditation on desolation. Like the formless monsters that show up in your nightmares.

I stare at them for as long as I can stand it. It's not that they're sad—sadness I could take, I *respect* sadness. It's that they are so unspeakably bleak. Browny-green colors spread about in shapeless blobs. There is no Patrick in them.

I don't quite know what to say when he appears at the door, drying his hands on a towel.

"Don't even look at these," he says. "They're not going in the show."

"They're not?"

"No. Too awful. And speaking of awful, I suppose you saw the story." His voice is clipped, businesslike.

"Yeah."

"What did you think?" He's wearing an old black-and-blue plaid shirt and sweatpants, both of which seem to hang on him. The morning light makes him look haggard.

"Well, I know it wasn't what you hoped it would be. But the guy said a lot of nice things about you. *True* things even. You came out looking pretty good, in my humble opinion. It'll bring people in to the gallery, don't you think?"

"Yeah, well, in a perfect world, I'd say he didn't absolutely need to go mentioning the damn police report just to write about an art show, for God's sake. And all that hero stuff—bah!"

He scowls, and I see in his eyes that he's so much worse than he was a few weeks ago. He's not only boarded his old spaceship, he's already crash-landed back on the planet My Lover Died in the Fire, and he's built himself a fort there. My palms feel sweaty. He is looking at me as though from a long distance, but I am nothing if not determined to save him, and so I make myself meet his eyes.

"So . . . if you're not showing these paintings, does that mean you're canceling the show?"

"No," he says after a moment. "I have other work. Here. Come with me. I might as well show you what I've really been doing."

He leads me across the hall and opens the door and turns on the lamp, and we both stand there, blinking in the light. On the art table in the center of the room are a bunch of little sculptures—lifelike sculptures of a woman, all of them six to eight inches high. It takes me a moment to focus on them, to see what they really are, and then I have to take a deep, sharp breath.

They are Anneliese.

Some of the sculptures show only her face with its sensuous planes, her cheeks sloping into a half smile. I see her eyes, the carved lankiness of her hair.

"*This* is the art I'm entering in the show," he says. His voice trembles with . . . pride? Is that what I'm hearing?

I edge closer to them. There must be ten or twelve sculptures all lined up, like exquisite little dolls: some of them in which she's sitting or thinking, lying back on a pillow with one hand over her face. Here, she is standing with her arms held up to the sky, her legs spread apart, her face a mask of triumph. Another shows her body curled up on the floor in a fetal position, her face hidden, her legs drawn up tight to her body. There are another few that show her torso, the gentle flow of her arms outstretched.

They are beautiful. They are sexy, they are genuine, they are human. Exquisite expressions of energy and life. And they are, every single one of them, depictions of his love for Anneliese.

And not one of them is me. Something constricts in my chest.

"Yeah," he says softly. "You get it." He walks around the table, so he can look at each one of them more closely. "So, this," he says, "is what I've been trying to keep from you, that I've been reliving the whole experience with Anneliese." His voice is halting.

"Patrick," I say. I speak loudly, like maybe I can snap him out of this. "But why? What's the problem here? This isn't something shameful that you had to keep from me. Why are you acting like it was? We *know* each other. I'm on your side, remember?" I turn and look at him, but the air between us has taken on a dangerous feel. Like the crackling before a thunderstorm maybe.

He doesn't drag his eyes away from all the Annelieses. "No. It's not that simple. I've just been getting deeper and deeper. I feel like she's right here with me. She feels so real to me now. Directing me."

"Get real. She's not here directing you! You were thinking about her and you did some sculptures, and they're beautiful, and so you should show them."

He looks at me mournfully.

"I need to tell you something," he says. And I know, by the feel of the room, that he's going to break up with me. And I am not having that today.

"No, no. Really, let's skip it for now, and go in and have some soup. My mom made soup. You need to eat something. Look at you. You've been working so hard you're not even eating, are you?"

His eyes look hollow. "I am so sorry," he says, "but I can't do this anymore."

"Can't do what anymore? Make sculptures of *Anneliese*? Can't eat soup? Of course you can. You just need to come back to yourself. This is all *fine*."

Calm down, I say to myself. *None of this is real. He loves me. I love him. This is not how it ends. The magic is going to kick in any second now. Just don't let him say the final thing. Keep talking to him.*

But he's not feeling the magic. Yet. And so he holds up his hand to warn me away, and he says the Patrick version of the things guys say when they don't love you anymore. All that mishmash of stuff, so jumbled I can barely listen. Phrases jump out at me through the buzzing in my ears.

"I'm disappointing you . . . not any good to anyone . . . can't be a father to Fritzie . . . can't stand it that the place is full of teenagers half the time . . . hate chaos . . . need to be alone . . . need to take a break."

"Take a break?" I say. "What? No. We are not talking about this right now. I'm not having this. Because none of what's going on right now is permanent. You don't need to throw everything away when it's all going to change in a few months' time. Just wait it out."

"Marnie. Face it. It's not working."

"What are you talking about? It does work! This is the crazy talking, Patrick. We've been together for years now, and I *love* you. You're going to be okay! I know this more than I know anything else."

"It's not about love. I-I have to stay away, go back to the way things were before, being alone, living with Anneliese."

"Living with *Anneliese*?" I say. "Excuse me?"

He nods, almost imperceptibly.

"Anneliese who—forgive me for mentioning this—is dead?"

"She's dead, but she's still in my head," he says. He shifts his weight and looks out into the distance. I feel like snapping my fingers in front of him to bring him back to reality. Then I feel like hugging him, holding on to him for dear life. I wish I knew the emotional equivalent of CPR. But I just stand there.

"I do love you," he says, "but it doesn't mean anything when I'm still tormented by her, by what I did to her. I let her die, Marnie. I was standing right there, and I couldn't save her."

"You did not *let her die*," I say. "You tried to save her, but the fire was too big, and you couldn't. And you survived. But that doesn't make it your fault."

"No one understands."

"Okay then. Back up here a minute, and let me get this straight," I say. I decide to go for humor, of what might pass for humor. "Dude, am I seriously to believe that *you*, my boyfriend—a guy who says he loves me and who only recently emerged from his cave of doom to try to live a real life among the Family of Man—has now discovered a new *sub-cave* of doom, where you are secretly mind melding with a woman I have no chance of competing with? Is that what's going on? You can't see *us* together anymore because you're going to stay in this room while you think about this—once more, pardon the expression—*dead woman*? How does that make any sense? Tell me that."

"Technically," he says gloomily, "it's only an alcove of doom."

"I get it that she gets to be perfect because she's not here any longer, but the advantage of *me* is that I could still perhaps come up with some new, fantastic ways of being in your life and loving you, if you'd just open your eyes and let it in. The solution, it seems to me, is not in shutting life out again, but in letting yourself be loved. Maybe you could love life precisely *because* Anneliese can't. You know, like a tribute to love."

He's silent for a moment, looking at his fingers and thinking, and I'm holding my breath, sure that any second now he's going to turn to me and be regular, loving Patrick again.

But then he speaks. His voice sounds rusty and like something is hurting his throat, and he speaks so quietly, I have to lean in to hear him.

"There's more to this. I have to tell you something. I can't give you what you want."

"Oh, for God's sake, Patrick. What you're giving me—at least up until about Thanksgiving night at eight o'clock, when you moved into this stupid *alcove of doom*—has been just fine, thank you very much. And anyway, *I* get to say if it's enough for me or not. You don't get to say that. And I think we're good here."

He sighs and shakes his head. Then, in a very quiet voice, he says: "No. I can't give you babies."

The room goes so quiet, it's like all the air went out of it.

"Can't or won't?" I say at last.

"I-I'm sterile."

I feel like I'm underwater, and everything is coming in and out of focus. And then my brain clears. "But wait, that's not true. You already have a child! You're not sterile." I say this as though I'm a brilliant student, and I've located a loophole he hasn't thought of.

"I am. Sterile. From the fire," he says. "The damage from the fire—it happens."

"So . . . what then? You've been lying to me? All this time while I was trying to get pregnant? You couldn't ever do it, but you let me think—"

"No. It wasn't like that. I had forgotten."

I actually laugh. A high-pitched, strangled laugh. "What do you *mean*, you *forgot*? How does somebody forget something like that?"

He sighs. "I went to the doctor a couple of weeks ago to get my meds refilled. And I asked him about fertility, and he told me it's impossible, since the accident. He said he'd told me, but I didn't remember. Maybe I didn't really care back then so I didn't take it in. But the bottom line is that pregnancy is impossible. I'm sorry. You need to find someone else and get on with your life."

I stare at him. "You're not sorry! You never even wanted me to get pregnant. Don't act now like you're *sorry*. This is the most convenient thing that's ever happened to you and you know it."

"I'm sorry that you see it that way, because I don't think of this as convenient at all," he says.

"Ohhh! So *this* is why you want to break up?" I say. I'm angry now. "Basically, what you're saying is that because you can't give me babies, *you* get to decide for both of us that we shouldn't be together anymore. No asking me what I want. Or what I think. Maybe I would understand and prefer to have you in my life instead of babies, did you ever think of that? That that's what love might consist of? Working on a solution together? No other solution occurs to you except living in a cave, being miserable, you and your cat. Running over to Paco's for food and running back again. Except now, I'm pretty sure there won't be Paco's close by because no doubt you're not going to want to remain in this building, while I generate all this *chaos* around. That'd be weird for you, wouldn't it?"

He looks shaken, I'm pleased to see.

"So what *do* you envision happening?" I say. "What about Fritzie? Are you thinking that you and she are going to move somewhere else? Or are you going to fly her to Italy and give her back to her mom?"

He shrugs. "We'll have to work out some things," he says quietly.

I'm staring at the statues and there's a loud buzzing in my ears, and so I'm surprised to realize that he's still talking. Going on in a sad, defeated voice about how he'll try to come up with a workable solution, something that makes sense for all of us. He's not sure just yet what it will entail. For the time being, though, maybe he could stay in the studio? Out of my way?

Anger breaks over me in waves, a whole tsunami of fury. I have to make a fist to keep from picking up every one of those sculptures and hurling them at him. Patrick is so broken he doesn't even know how to break up properly. You're supposed to make it clean and respectful, state your position, and then get the hell out. Leave everybody a shred of dignity.

I need to get away from him. I don't want to stand here listening to his drifty talk about the next stages—the moving out, or what nebulous plan he has for Fritzie. It seems to me that a man who is orchestrating a freaking wimp-ass breakup like this should have thought of all that before.

Help! I think. *Blix, look at what's happening here! Remind him what's important.*

I give it a minute, just in case Blix has a little magic to contribute. A watery winter sunbeam is half-heartedly breaking through the dusty window, and I stare at the parallelogram it's forming on the oak floor. Blix is silent, the dust motes are silent, Patrick turns away, and the anger at the center of me is the only thing I can hold on to with any certainty.

And then I turn and walk out of his studio and slam the door behind me as hard as I can.

CHAPTER THIRTY-ONE
PATRICK

Patrick picks up two of the Annelieses who fell over when the door slammed and straightens them out, finds them a suitable location on the table where they'll be safe. The least he can do is keep the plaster Annelieses safe.

He certainly can't keep anything else safe, he thinks. He's crap at life right now.

But—despite the hollowness in the pit of his stomach, despite the fact that he might very well throw up any second, he knows he's done the right thing. Telling her. Breaking up with her was never going to be easy, but it was going to be far harder to carry on like this, watching her get progressively more disappointed.

She'll soon realize that she's still young enough now to find a guy who will want babies with her. She can go off to have all those things she once texted him she wanted—the Boppies and sippies and socks with lace and whatevers. Three years, tops, and she'll be a woman pushing a stroller with a baby and a diaper bag and a gorgeous husband trotting alongside looking pleased with himself. Looking so smug it'll be like they invented procreation.

And even though she's miserable right now, it's so much better that he did it this way, just *ripped that little bandage right off,* rather than letting things remain in a downward spiral, both of them thinking that love was going to be enough to see them through. When it wasn't. This was actually an act of kindness on his part, releasing her to the life she was meant for.

Someday, he'll be able to say the truth to her: "I broke up with you because I loved you and I wanted you to have the life you're truly meant for."

But for now, he'll just have to put up with her fury.

And of course he needs to start thinking about a plan. Maybe he'll suggest that he move back to the basement, when Ariana moves out. That way Fritzie's life will be disrupted as little as possible. In the meantime, he'll stay out of Marnie's way, be a polite houseguest who helps with dinner and the dishes, takes the dog for a walk, pays for things, and doesn't ruffle any feathers. He can be pleasant for—what? Five more months.

And then after that he'll get his own place. Alone. Somewhere.

He stands there looking at the collection of Annelieses, and he feels proud in a way he's not felt in a long time. It hurt his hands, forming them, which only served to make them more worthwhile. He hadn't thought he could ever do sculpture again. It wasn't going to be possible with all the nerve damage, with the scars. And even so, some days he hurt so bad that he had to get up in the middle of the night and wrap his hands in ice just so he could move his fingers. He lived on ibuprofen and some naturopathic salve he'd found at the health store.

But he'd worked through the pain. Again and again in his life, he's worked through pain. It's what he does. And now he can work through the pain of losing Marnie, too.

He thinks of Blix and how years ago she stormed down to his basement apartment and forced him to talk to her, and then—even more daringly—made him get up out of his chair and dance with her. He did *not* dance, he informed her. But she made him put on a Hawaiian shirt like hers, and she turned the music up loud, and she did this funny version of the hula, totally unselfconsciously, and pulled him out of himself. She wasn't afraid of anything.

She'd be proud of him for pushing through the pain. She'd made a huge mistake thinking Marnie and he belonged together, but that was probably because she didn't know that Marnie wanted her own kids. Even Blix would now see that breaking things off was actually a supreme act of love.

He remembers her saying one time, "Oh, don't be an idiot about love, Patrick! It's the only force that matters in the whole world. People say such foolish things in the name of love, but you've got to let yourself *live*—and to live, you've got to let yourself love."

Blix was a nice, eccentric wild woman who lived exactly the way she wanted to. And now that's what he's going to do, too. Surely she'd be proud of him for that.

CHAPTER THIRTY-TWO

MARNIE

When I leave Patrick's studio I go straight to my room, and I get in bed with all my clothes on, and I pull the cotton blanket, the down comforter, the quilt, and my twisted-up sheet over my head. I'm freezing cold, and my teeth are chattering, and also my arms and legs don't think they can work for me anymore.

I put the pillow over my head, too.

And that's when I let my heart break.

How can I love someone so much who is so damaged and hurting that he can't let himself have any joy? What the fuck happened that has made him run back to all that agony? I don't get it. We love each other.

I want to go over and yell it to him one more time. Maybe take him by the shoulders and shake him this time. But nothing would make a difference. I saw the look in his eyes while he was telling me about being sterile.

Somehow, when I wasn't paying attention, Patrick fell out of love with me. It wasn't like there was a *falling out* moment. It was seepage, is what it was. He seeped out of love for me, drip by drip by drip, while I was prancing around the house, entertaining my mother, getting to know the teenagers, helping Fritzie with her homework. The love all drained away, and I have to get over it. And what may be even harder is that I have to face the probable, likely fact that Blix was wrong about everything.

Eventually my mother comes to the edge of my bed. I can hear her breathing from my damp little cocoon.

"Are you all right?" she says. "What's going on with you?"

I start to cry all over again. "Patrick."

"What happened?"

"He's . . . not . . ." I just hope she gets the picture and will realize that I can't cope anymore, and that she needs to do everything for me from now on. I can't go on; really I can't.

"Come out from under the covers."

This is actually a good idea, because I've used up all the air under there. I'm still freezing, however. My feet feel like they are in danger of falling off. But I stick my head out and breathe in some real oxygen.

"Now tell me what happened," she says. She sits down on the bed and puts her hand on the bumps of the covers where my feet are.

I tell her that Patrick is breaking up with me, and then I tell her all the rest, too: that he's just remembered that he's sterile, and that means that he doesn't want me to stay with him because I want a baby too much. And also he's been over there making statues of Anneliese for the past few weeks, and that he's basically still in love with his dead girlfriend, and bottom line: he doesn't want to be with me anymore.

When I put it all out like this, it doesn't sound very good for Patrick. He sounds like a mental case, in fact, which is just what my mother thinks.

"I don't believe any of this. He's lost his mind," she says. I remember all too well now this side of her—the no-nonsense mom force-marching Natalie and me through any of our childhood traumas, using platitudes, commands, and whatever else she had at hand. It was part of her mom arsenal—an arsenal I realize now that I'll *never* need to develop. I'll never have my own child. I start to cry all over again.

"He hasn't lost his mind. He doesn't want to be with me, is all. It's not going to work. It doesn't matter what he's *saying* the reason is. He's just telling me every way he knows how that it's over."

She sighs. "I think the world of men has gone mad," she says. "Is it the full moon? Or, as you would say, is Mercury in retrograde?"

"It doesn't matter. He just doesn't love me anymore. He needs solitude all the damn time, and I keep creating chaos all around. So it's over. End of story." I pull the covers back over my head. Enough oxygen for now. I can't take the way my mother is looking at me, like I'm a project that's defeating her.

"You should have some soup. I'm going to bring you some soup."

"I don't want any soup."

"You need soup, and Patrick needs soup," she pronounces. She gets off the bed, and there's a cold patch of air hitting me now. "Both of you have gone completely bonkers here for no apparent reason, and soup is going to be just as good a cure as anything else. This is patently ridiculous of him. It's just the stress talking."

"Go tell *him* that. I need to be alone."

She's still standing next to my bed, breathing.

"Please," I say.

"I just want to ask you one thing, and I mean this with no disrespect," she says. "What good is all this magic stuff you're always talking about if you can have your whole outlook shattered in one day like this? Don't you have to have faith in it for it to work?"

If I had the strength, I would throw my pillow at her.

When Fritzie gets home from school, she comes in and sits on the edge of my bed. She's eating an apple. The crunching at first seems unbearable, and then feels like it might represent something holy and life-affirming. Eating! Like love, however, it is something for other people, not for me.

"Are you sick?"

"Yes."

"What have you got?"

"I don't know."

"Why are the covers and pillow on your head?"

"Because I'm freezing."

"Oh."

Crunches.

"Do you have homework?" I say after a while.

"Oh! Patrick says I should tell you he's not coming over for dinner."

"You should leave Patrick alone."

"I wasn't *bothering* him, Marnie. I just went to see if Roy wanted a cat treat."

"Do you have homework?" This is way more conversation than I want to be having.

"No."

Crunches.

"Marnie, can I ask you something?"

"Yes."

"Are you in bed because you're sad?"

"No. Yes. I'm a little bit sad."

I feel her little hand coming over to my shoulder, tentatively at first, and then patting me over and over again. A steady stream of little comforting pats.

That's when I know I should come out from under the covers—for her sake. Get up, start moving around the house. Life has to go on.

So I get up.

The next morning Patrick's in the kitchen with Fritzie when I get out of bed. He's made her breakfast—her latest favorite, a three-minute egg nestled on a piece of toast with a circular hole cut out of it. She examines it for precision; it's as though everything we do for her is a test of our commitment. This morning the hole is found to be a little lopsided, and to my surprise, he wearily agrees to make another one for her and to cut it more exactly.

He doesn't look in my direction.

"It's okay, Patrick," she says after a moment. "I'll eat it this way."

Normally he and I would have exchanged a look of triumph at a moment like this, but I don't look at him, and I can feel him not looking at me. My mother comes over from Lola's house, exclaiming about the snow that fell last night, and how it's slippery on the steps, so be careful.

"Shouldn't school be closed in these conditions?" she asks.

There's a silence, and then Patrick and I both start in at the same time, beginning to explain that Brooklyn doesn't usually have snow days. Embarrassed, we stop talking at the same time. And then worse, start up again at the same instant.

Fritzie laughs. My mother says, "Never mind. I get it." She gets herself a cup of coffee and goes out to the living room, shaking her head at us.

I do him the favor of disappearing back to my room. I hear him organizing Fritzie into Getting Ready to Leave—and although I'm the one who usually walks her to the bus stop these days, I don't go out there and offer today. It's painful to listen to—he doesn't know how to pack up the backpack, forgets and has to be reminded about the lunch, and then doesn't understand that her suede boots won't work in the snow. She needs the big fur-lined rubber ones. I lie on the bed and listen to his hopelessness as he learns these things. Serves him right.

"Patrick," I hear her say. "You are just a mess!"

And then they are gone.

We've almost made it through the first twenty-four hours. I can't even begin to think how awful my life is about to be. At some point, my mother will go back to Florida, the teenagers will move out and into their lives—and Patrick, whom I now detest, will take my sweet Fritzie away. And the house will be so quiet. So very horribly quiet.

I take a little mental inventory. And here's what we're left with. Magic doesn't work, love may not run the whole universe after all, and those little silken sacks with spell-casting herbs I've cultivated and carried around—well, maybe I shouldn't have wasted my time. Patrick and I were never meant to be together. Blix was wrong. I was wrong, and I am so sad that it takes everything to get up and face every new horrible day.

I fully expect all the couples I've insisted belong together to come, one by one, back into my life to point out that things didn't go so hot after all. Lola will phone and say that William Sullivan was her worst mistake to date. That couple from the restaurant, too. They'll be in, retracting everything. Dozens of people will all come shaking their fists at me and claiming I've misled them.

One morning I look over at the toaster on the counter and start to laugh. The toaster, even! Had I actually gotten myself to believe that Blix was a force who was still around, who flung toast out of the toaster to give me a message? Honest to God, I've been a lunatic! Dancing around through life, thinking the little sparkles in the air were evidence of love and that I could meddle in other people's lives! Who did I think I was?

There isn't any magic to me, and there never was.

As if to prove that, I get a text from him: *A proposal for going forward. In order to disrupt F's life as little as possible wondering if U wd be OK w/me living in the studio until school is out & she goes back to Tessa. I'll try to stay out of UR way. P.*

I think it's the abbreviations that hurt the most. He prides himself on typing out every word, on using proper punctuation. It was even a joke between us. Our thing.

"Can you believe this shit?" I say to my mom, who shrugs. "Dude writes me a note!"

"He doesn't dare talk to you in person because he loves you so much that he knows he'll break down and start sobbing," she says. "Already he's regretting what he's done."

"No, he's not," I say.

"I'm just saying he'll be back. You'll see."

But he does not come back.

And then one morning my mother and I are walking to Best Buds together and she looks at her phone and says, "Oh my God, your father's coming."

"O. M. G," I say. "He is? He's coming to visit you? Or is he coming to take you home with him?"

"Well, he's certainly not going to take me home with him!" she says emphatically. "Not unless he plans on kidnapping me. I don't really know what he expects to happen. That man! Honestly. He's made a reservation for two weeks from now. Why? *Why* is he coming here? I'm not ready for this."

I know why. He's coming because, after forty years of marriage, he at last senses some change in the marital air currents. My dad may be slow to catch on, but he's no fool. He's coming to reclaim his wife from the smarmy Randolph Greenleafs of the world. He's coming because he's sick of watching golf in Florida without her to ask him to change the channel.

And basically, he's coming because he's in love with my mother, and he knows through some unspoken deep connection they have, like a cable running between them from Florida to New York, that she's in love with him, and they need to be back together. Enough of this separation nonsense. I get it.

I get it, but I think my father is going to be stunned by the new Millie MacGraw. She's turned bold without him around to silence her with his disapproving sigh. There's no one to veto her purchases, to set his mouth in a line when she comes home with a new skirt, to say, "But did you *need* that?" There's no one to make her feel small or tentative, to question her choices.

Poor man: he thought it was his birthright to be the man of the family, to be the final, deep-voiced authority benevolently ruling over a small domestic kingdom. He did it well, too—with a chuckling demeanor most of the time, kind and loyal. He was accustomed to being obeyed, his fairness never coming into question. That coffee table? *That* vacation plan? No, no, no. *This* is how it's done. He had no reason to think he wouldn't spend his whole life that way.

But something happened, and his wife is a force now. If you ask me, she's turning into the Resident Crone and Wise Woman in the Frippery, and as her daughter, I'm alternately proud and horrified listening to the way she asserts her opinions.

For instance, I heard her tell Ariana the other day that she'd be so much more attractive to "a better class of young men" if she sat up straight. (Ariana didn't even get mad; she laughed and her eyes caught mine and she mouthed, "What the HECK?" and adjusted her posture just in case.)

"Millie," I said. "Ariana has Justin, and he is a wonderful class of young man."

"That's not what I'm saying," my mother said. "At her age, she needs to experience a *fuller* range of young men. That way she can see her way more clearly to what she really wants in life. We women don't have to settle for the ragtag group of guys we see right in front of us when we're teenagers, you know. In fact, with all due respect to your matchmaking powers, may I add that we may not need to settle for any man at all."

And now, having gotten Ariana to sit up straight, she's fired up to go on to fashion advice: pointing out that it's considered kind of mysterious and even classy when a woman doesn't quite show her midriff in every single outfit. And that leggings are perhaps not exactly the same thing as pants. To my surprise, the Amazings just take Millie's fashion advice as if it's something eccentric and adorable and worth following.

I almost can't stand being at the Frippery lately. I feel as though I'm just going through the motions, a person who has been forsaken by magic. Everything I believed in feels like it's been shown to be stupid and wrong-headed. Magic? Sparkles? *Oh, please.* I don't remember how it is that matchmaking happens. I look around for sparkles in the air, and even when I squint hard, I can't find them. And I can't even find the energy to participate in all the lively, bustling conversations taking place. Everything seems a little bit ridiculous, if you want to know the truth of it. I find myself yawning a lot, wanting to be in the back room adding up numbers into columns, filling out the forms for ordering. Kat, who told me she was sure this day would never come between Patrick and me, now looks at me with worry in her eyes and just shakes her head.

"Aren't you even going to mention the universe anymore?" she asked me one morning.

"What is this thing called the *universe*?" I said. "I don't know what crazy concept you could be referring to." And she came over and gave me a hug, which made my eyes fill up with tears. Again.

One day I hear my mother wading into the ongoing, ever-present Frippery discussion that should be called, "What Should We Think About Janelle." Janelle is the friend of the Amazings, the young woman who is pregnant and regretting it. Unlike Ariana, who is refusing to go to college, Janelle has already gotten an early acceptance and scholarship to Boston University, and baby or no baby, she wants to go there. But how can she? She doesn't have the money or childcare, or the time. It's an ongoing situation, and everybody who comes into the Frippery gets drawn into this conversation, it seems.

"She's steering that massive belly through the halls of the school," says Ariana. "Trying to get all her work done. But you can see how upset she is. Water just kind of leaks from her eyes these days."

"She's crying because of that scumbag who got her pregnant and then didn't stay with her," says Charmaine, but Ariana doesn't like that kind of talk. She starts waving her arms.

"No, no, no! Matt is not a scumbag. He's a normal guy with a normal life, and neither one of them thought there was going to be a pregnancy, so it's not like he went back on some promise he made. I get sick of people trashing him."

"But he gets to go to college, and she doesn't. That seems massively unfair," says Charmaine. "She's the one who has to suffer, while he gets off scot-free."

"Also, I think he should be required to stick by her at least while she's carrying his child, don't you think?" says Dahlia. "He certainly shouldn't be hooking up with Lulu."

"Who's to say he shouldn't be hooking up with somebody else?" Ariana wants to know. "Janelle and Matt are not technically a couple and if they ever were, it lasted about twenty minutes. And boom! She got pregnant and wanted to keep the kid, and he didn't have a say in it one way or the other—and now he's met somebody he's really into, and so what's the big deal?"

"What do you mean, they're not a couple? They're the very definition of a couple," points out my mother. "They are a couple that is actually, technically and physically, becoming a new person. Their DNA is mingling."

"I know that," says Ariana. "But it's not like it used to be. Back when couples had to get married because there was a kid on the way, whether you liked the person or not. And who's to say that Matt and

Janelle and the new girlfriend might not all figure out a way to raise this kid? You know?" She flings her arms out, describing a threesome with her hands in the air, a series of circles and gestures. "Stranger things have happened, you know. Maybe they'll all find an apartment near Boston University and Janelle can go to school, and the other two can, too, if they want, and everybody takes turns taking care of the baby. Big deal. That's a decent life for everybody."

I hear my mother get a bit louder, at full Millie MacGraw Force now. "That is patently ridiculous, and it's a pipe dream, and not the way humans are built. What *you* need to tell Janelle, if you want to be a good friend to her, is that she should consider putting the child up for adoption. There's no shame in that, none at all," she says. "Some of the finest people I know were adopted, including my husband."

I'm at the counter trimming flowers, and I keep my mouth shut, because I'm resigning from being the person who brings up seemingly impossible possibilities. I might not believe in those anymore. I also don't tell people anymore what they should do.

And to be honest, for self-preservation, I have to shut down part of myself when Janelle herself comes in, bloomingly pregnant and unhappy about it. She's a lovely, brown-haired girl-next-door type of girl, pale but shiny, with her gigantic winter coat and her Ugg boots, plodding through the winter waiting for a springtime baby she doesn't want. She floats in like a moony celebrity guest star—and the Amazings, including Justin and Mookie if they're around, give her hugs and kisses, and help her find a comfortable place to sit down. I hate it that I feel so acutely my own grief about the pregnancy I will probably never have. I look at her there, so morose and yet looking as though her body is on a brilliant mission, and I want to cry for both of us.

We always give her flowers, Kat and I, because she is in need of comfort. We give her raspberry tea, and we prop her feet up on the beanbag chairs, and we tell her she's beautiful and that she'll be fine, and that life will take care of everything. But I can't say I really believe any of that anymore, and sometimes when she's here, I find myself going into the back room and letting my tears fall, quietly, on the ledger sheets.

My mother, as far as I know, never does tell her about the adoption thing.

Which is just as well. If I were Janelle, I'm not sure I'd be looking for more people's opinions as to what I should do with my life.

CHAPTER
THIRTY-THREE
PATRICK

The morning of the gallery opening, Patrick girds himself for the worst and tells Marnie that he doesn't want her to come that evening. It's for her own good, of course. Not that he thinks she would come, in her newfound fury, but he wants to make sure. When he tells her, she takes a long moment to look at him like he's lost the last remaining bit of his mind. Then she goes back to clearing the table, dropping the silverware in the sink with a little more noisy force than he would have thought absolutely necessary.

"I'm just trying to be considerate of your feelings," he says. Because damn it, he is.

"Right. Thank you very much." She walks around him and gets the crumb-covered plates from the table, and he winces, thinking she'll fling them in the sink as well—or possibly at him—but she places them more carefully. He's grateful for that. She might be able to respond to reason.

He tries to appeal to that part of her. "I'm just thinking it might be awkward. Hell, I wish *I* didn't have to go."

"I wish you didn't have to also," she says without looking at him.

"Okay," he says. "Well. So that's it, then. You won't come."

She doesn't even answer him. She walks out of the room.

"Look," he calls after her. "I just don't want to hurt you anymore. I want this all to be over."

She comes back to the doorway. "Over?" she says. "Over? You want the gallery thing to be over, or you want our little domestic situation to be over, or you want all human life as we know it on this planet to be over? Which is it?"

"Um, all human life as we know it on this planet. Door number three," he says. Dark humor. Maybe she'll recognize that. *We are all suffering here, no good guys and bad guys. Just us, bumbling along.*

She stops now and looks at him, and he almost can't take the heartbreak in her eyes.

It snowed last night, and the white light coming through the windows is reflected on her face. She looks beautiful there, with her hair still uncombed from sleep, all jumbled up and halfway curly. Her eyes have no makeup yet, and they are looking at him straight on, plain and real. She reminds him of a deer he once saw in the woods in the wintertime, the way he and the deer both stopped and looked at each other, unblinking.

"Patrick," she says. "I'll be the one who decides whether or not I'm coming to the gallery tonight. Your daughter wants to see your work, as you might imagine, and so does my mother, and some of the Amazings. It would create much more of a statement if I don't go. So it's not really up to you."

"But I don't want you to be uncomfortable . . ." he says.

This time she does leave. "Noted," she calls back over her shoulder. "Do me a favor and don't worry about me anymore. I'm in charge of myself from now on. You don't even have to think about me, okay? In fact, *don't*."

He shouldn't have said that about not wanting her to be uncomfortable. You're not allowed to say routine, condescending things about someone's feelings when you're in the process of hurting them. He knows this. Even if you're scared shitless of the art opening you're about to have. Maybe especially if you're scared.

"I'm sorry," he calls after her as she leaves.

Everything makes it worse, so he goes back into the studio and closes the door.

Hi, says Anneliese. *You know, Patrick, none of this matters. We're all just specks in the universe, floating out there in time and space, with only a limited time to live. You can fight and shake your fists and yell, but the truth is that you are going to be gone, too, Patrick. Poof! It's over just like that.*

CHAPTER
THIRTY-FOUR
MARNIE

Patrick is a hit at the opening, despite everything. I can still feel all of his thoughts, so I can tell that he hates it, of course, hates that people are looking at him—hates hates *hates* that they see his scars. He's imagining that they're thinking with pity about the fire. But there he is, basking in his notoriety just the same—basking even in his disdain of it, being all artisty and wearing all black, and with his dark hair tousled and his big blue eyes cloudy and defensive.

Everybody here has surely read the story in *Inside Outside*, which Mr. Pierpont has thoughtfully blown up three copies of and posted on three walls in case anyone might have missed it. Everyone here knows what he's been through, and they hover for a long time around the little sculptures. The beauty of her form, the sensuousness of her limbs and her expressions.

Still, like it or not, I know him enough to feel his pain here. He stays in the back of the room as much as possible, avoiding talking to the general crowd of people, just the ones who venture over. Let Philip Pierpont do all the hullabaloo, talk to the strangers. I can feel him thinking that. I remain near the front, surrounding myself with the Amazings. Ariana stays close in a protective way, and so does my mother.

People keep streaming in from the street, welcomed by the warm, twinkling lights, the tinkle of piano music, the plates of cheese, and little plastic goblets of champagne being passed around by people dressed in black. Philip Pierpont is a dapper man, buzzing around in between people, with his hands always seeming to be clasped together, as though in prayer. He is praying for Patrick's success, and Patrick is bringing in a nice crowd, or at least what I think must be considered a nice crowd for a gallery opening. Good numbers.

I hear their enthusiasm. Muted, of course, because these are New York art people.

We leave early. I can only take so much. I see my mother watching my face curiously, wondering how I'm coping, probably ready to leap in and haul me out of there if the stress becomes too much. So after each of us has managed to have four pieces of cheese and a few crackers, and my mother and I each have a glass of champagne, we go. My mother is tired. The Amazings are drifty. There's not much to do. The freezing cold wind is blowing off the river, and I'm glad to be out of the weather by the time we get down into the subway. A man is playing the trumpet down inside the tiled fortress, people are hurrying. The lights are bright. I hold Fritzie's hand and she curls into me and starts sucking on a lock of her hair, a new habit. Lately she clings to me, which I kind of like.

"Do you miss your mom?" I asked her the other night as I was putting her to bed, and she was pouting and kicking at the blankets and telling me she was sick and tired of everything, and she didn't want to go to sleep.

"No," she said. "I miss my dad."

When we finally come out from the subway into the Brooklyn night, my phone throbs in my pocket. I look down and see that it's Natalie, so I press the button while we're walking. Ahead of me, Fritzie is doing her usual heart-stopping balancing act along a low wall, dodging the iron spikes that are embedded in it. I've gotten better at standing this, but it still makes my teeth hurt.

"Hi, Nat," I say tiredly. "You calling for Mom?"

There's a bunch of noise in the background. "No," she says. "I'm calling for you. Listen, Daddy's had a heart attack, and he's just gone to the hospital by ambulance. He's stable, they said. But they just took him away. With the sirens on."

"*What?* When did this happen?"

"It's *now*. It's happening right this minute, Marnie. I told you!"

"But what happened?" I don't know what else to say. I feel like if I can get her to tell me the story, then I can explain to her why it's all wrong. Our dad is healthy. In fact, he's coming to Brooklyn soon.

"Look. I don't know all of it, but he was alone in the house, and he started having chest pain and arm pain, and then he was out of breath, but he managed to call me. Why he didn't call 911 I don't know, but he didn't. So I called the ambulance, and then I drove over there to meet them. They worked on him for a while, and they just took him away. I'm about to follow in my car when I can get someone to come stay here. I've been trying to get Mom, but she's not answering her phone. So you tell her. I'll call you later, when I know more about what's going on."

"Wait. Did you say he's stable? You're sure? Did the paramedics—"

"Yes," she says. "He's stable. I've got to hang up and call Brian and find someone to watch the kids so I can go to the hospital."

I see my mother's head swing around, her eyes wide. The words *stable* and *paramedics* have a way of floating across the night air and bringing one's attention to what matters. She grabs for my phone, but Natalie has hung up. I stand there in the freezing night air, and I get very, very calm as I'm telling her the news. Fritzie manages to balance all the way to the end of the low little wall, and she only slips off when my mom lets out a cry and starts running down the sidewalk.

"Wait, Mom!" I say. "Millie, wait!"

I take Fritzie by the arm and run with her, but my mom is already so far ahead, running and running the blocks of Brooklyn.

She is brave and has always been fabulous whenever there's a crisis, unless it's something small like running out of potatoes when she wants some to mash this very minute, and then she panics. But as I run, I scroll back through tragedies I've known, and what I mostly can come up with is that when her mother was dying, she was cool and calm and orchestrated everything, only falling apart once the burial had taken place, and even then she discreetly took to her bed for two days and did her weeping in an organized, orderly way that anyone could understand.

She reaches Paco's and runs past, all the way to our stoop, where she stops and leans against the railing. Fritzie and I arrive there seconds later.

"I have to go to him," she says, and her voice is cold steel. "And I need you to come, too."

"Okay," I say. It's my father there in that ambulance, going fast to some hospital in Jacksonville, Florida, the sirens probably blaring, and him on a stretcher being tended by paramedics. People are trying to keep him calm. They've hooked him up to monitors and machines and fluids. Are his eyes open or closed? Is he in pain? Does he think he's going to die? I send him some energy. Some white light.

Hang on, I say to the air, and hope my words get to him.

"What about me?" says Fritzie. "You can't leave me. Marnie, I need you to be with me." And she starts to cry.

It's quite a night. My mother is on the phone to my sister four times, and she talks twice to the doctor on call in the emergency room and finally finds out they're admitting my father. Then she talks to the nurse in the Cardiac Care Unit. She talks to my father's brother, Joe, who lives in Cincinnati. She talks to Natalie's husband, Brian, who is home with the kids but who wants to reach out to my mom and see if there's anything he can do.

And then, at one in the morning, she talks to my dad, whose voice is fuzzy and sedated. He tells her he loves her. She tells him she's coming soon. He calls her Lumpkin, which is apparently a nickname from their honeymoon, something she never told me about.

I fall asleep thinking something I've never thought about before: my teenage mother and father off together on a honeymoon, children romping in the surf at Fort Lauderdale and making up silly nicknames. She was Lumpkin, and when I ask her, she smiles and says he was The Farteur.

For the first time in forever, I laugh. Perhaps I didn't need to know that.

CHAPTER THIRTY-FIVE
MARNIE

"How old is your father?"

"Um, he turns sixty in the spring."

"Sixty is old, right?" Fritzie is leaning against my arm, so close to me that I can barely type on the laptop. I'm trying to make airline reservations for my mother and me. I don't want to ask her to move, exactly, because it's Saturday morning and we are fighting a hefty layer of impending doom. There is packing to do and arrangements to make. My mother has been on the phone nearly all morning with all her relatives and friends and my father's golf acquaintances. The doctors have said that my father is out of danger for the most part; the heart attack wasn't very severe, and he's responding well to medication. But still, we need to go to him.

Fritzie smells like peanut butter and sleep and a skinned knee and last night's cheese and, also, deep down somewhere, no-more-tangles shampoo.

"Well," I say, "it's not *old* old, but it's getting up there in years."

"A person could die at sixty."

"Well, people die at all ages."

"But when they're sixty, nobody would be really surprised. Is that right?" She moves in even closer, if such a thing is possible.

"I think they would be surprised. They would say that person died too young."

"Huh. I wouldn't say that. I would say it's too bad, but I would say it was too young only if they were . . . twenty-eight."

"Okay, noted."

She scratches at her knee, which still has dried blood on it from last night's fall. "Did you know your dad your whole life?"

"Did I what?" I want to say that of course I did, but then I remember that for Fritzie, that's not something to take for granted. "Oh. Yes. I did."

"Not like me. I'll always have to tell people that I knew my dad only when I was eight. And if he gives me back to my mom, then I will also have to say that I only knew him for one year."

I type tomorrow's date into the computer. My mother wanted to go today, but I don't see how that's possible. And Natalie says it's fine. He's stable.

That word again: stable. It's only a word you use when somebody isn't really, really okay. I'm stable, for instance, but if I answered *stable* to the question *How are you?* people would think that I wasn't doing well at all.

American Airlines has no flights in the afternoon, just at 5:45 a.m., when I would rather not go.

"Are you making a reservation for me, too?" Fritzie asks.

"Honey, I can't. I'm sorry. Just my mom and I are going this time."

"I told you I wanted to go. Please take me."

"I know you did, and I'd like to, but it's just not going to work out. We're going to be spending so much time in the hospital, and it's not a place they let children come. And we've got things we're going to have to decide and all."

"Like what?"

Why did I say we had to decide things? "I'm not sure."

"Like whether he's going to die?"

"No. He's going to live."

"You don't know that."

"Well, I'm pretty sure."

"Pretty sure is not the same as sure. Just like I'm not sure if my mom is still alive in Italy. She probably is, but I didn't talk to her since Christmas because I don't like to talk on the phone with her, so I don't know. She could be dying right this minute, and I wouldn't know about it. Do you ever think of things like that? I think about that sometimes."

"Well," I say. "You're right. I suppose a lot of things in life are like that, you know. Things are probably good, because they're mostly always okay, but . . ."

"But we don't know for sure."

"I guess we can't."

"That's why I do my little things."

Sunday, 1:10 p.m. Delta from JFK. Only fifty million dollars. Sixty million if you want to check a bag. My mother is going to need to do that, but I probably don't.

"Let me see what you're doing," she says.

"Here, you can sit on my lap. See? I press this button here, and then it already has my mother's credit card information because she recently flew here . . . and . . ."

"So your mom is paying?"

"Yep. She's nice that way. So I press this, and voilà! We're reserved."

She hits me on the arm five times.

"Why do you always hit me?"

"It brings you good luck."

"Wait. Your hitting me brings me good luck? I think it brings me bruises."

"Nope." She smiles self-consciously. "I do that to bring you good luck for flying in the airplane. And last night I jumped on the bed five times so Patrick would have a good show. And sometimes I jump off the couch three times to help Ariana with her videos."

"Ah, Fritzie, Fritzie, Fritzie, I don't know what you're talking about, but I'm going to miss you when I'm gone. But it's only for a few days. You know that, right?" I hope it's only a few days. I probably shouldn't have said that, setting up expectations.

"I know."

"And you'll help Patrick take care of you?"

She nods and looks down at her hands.

Later, as I'm tucking her in bed after a tiresome argument about her theory that you can actually damage yourself by washing your hair two times in one week, she bursts into tears and clings to me, and tells me that my mom is nicer to her than I am, and that she hates the way I cook eggs, and that she didn't ever want to mention this but I look totally fat in the jeans I love the most. And for good measure she says, "And I hope you stay in Florida and never come back."

When I go out into the living room, to my surprise, Patrick is sitting there, scrolling through his phone. We haven't been talking, except for me to tell him about my father, which I managed to do in three short sentences before I turned on my heel and left the room. And now I say to him that he has his work cut out for him, keeping Fritzie.

"Does anyone really think I can do this?" he says, without looking at me.

"Who knows? You'll probably do better than I do with her," I say. "At least she won't tell you that you look fat in your jeans."

"Yeah, well. We'll see how it goes when I'm the only one she has left," he says.

It makes my heart hurt to look at him. And when I get back, I'm going to have to start planning for a life without him living here. Eventually it will be just me in this big old brownstone—and what then? Maybe I'll start renting out the apartments again—his studio and the basement. Get some new people. Invite some chaos in.

But no mental picture comes to mind.

My future feels blank. A scary, lonely blank canvas.

The next day Patrick rouses himself enough to be able to kiss me on the cheek, and he tells me that he's sorry about my dad and that I shouldn't worry about anything back here, and he'll call if he has any questions about the care and feeding of Fritzie. But I know he won't, so I tell him what she likes to take for school lunch and that he does not have to tolerate her walking backward on the low stone walls on the way to the bus stop, and also that he should call Maybelle if he has any questions about school. Ariana is also a very helpful person. For good measure, I tell him a parenting tip I've picked up on the playground: children kind of like it when you tell them no. Something about how it makes them feel more secure.

And then he hugs and kisses my mom, while I go upstairs to give the sullen and furious Fritzie a hug, and then the Uber is here, and it's time to go to Florida.

Patrick walks us out to the curb, carrying my mother's bags. "Call me and let me know how your father's doing," he says to me, and he gives me a limp hug.

"This is not the way I wanted to leave here," says my mom as we climb into the car.

"Me neither," I say, and I get a chill at how final everything sounds.

CHAPTER
THIRTY-SIX
PATRICK

The first thing that Fritzie does on Patrick's watch is go into the bathroom and cut off most of her hair.

She comes into the living room afterward nonchalantly, as if she'd always had hair that looked like patches of it had been unevenly chewed by raccoons to within an inch of her scalp. She goes over to where Bedford is lying on the floor and lies down on top of him, humming.

Patrick, who has not been able to settle into doing anything in the half hour since Marnie and Millie left, has basically been pacing around the apartment, straightening the artwork on the wall, thinking about how much work he should do now that he's officially back to being an artist, and also wondering what the hell is wrong with him that he doesn't want to do any of it. He flops down onto the couch to contemplate the ceiling and find out if it has any answers for him, and that's when he looks over at her.

At first he wants to burst out laughing, but then he realizes the true weirdness of the situation. Marnie has been gone for exactly thirty-five minutes and Fritzie already looks like a cross between a prisoner of war and Sinéad O'Connor. This is obviously a cry for help, and it's obviously outside of anything he knows how to handle.

"Fritzie?" he says mildly. "What have you done to your hair?"

"It's art, Patrick," she says. "I arted my hair. I'm surprised you don't know that. You're an artist, aren't you?"

Okay. So it's art. Fine. Statement hair. But oh God.

He supposes there's no point in yelling or getting hysterical. What's done is done. He'll have to watch her more carefully, that's all he can do, before she decides to *art* anything else. Add it to the list of things he can't fix.

This may be when he realizes something fundamental to his life in the near future: he must go it alone. He knows that Marnie would say that Ariana would be willing to help him out and that he should avail himself of her kindness and smarts. But he is not going to do it. He steels his jaw and makes up his mind to endure. He has plenty of practice at *enduring*, and endure he will.

They are at loose ends all day. He thinks he should clean out his studio a bit, but when he goes in there, he can't bear to tackle any of it. The sun coming through the windows is watery and noncommittal, and the studio is cold and he doesn't feel like making a fire in the fireplace. He doesn't feel like doing anything.

He wanders back into the apartment. He should probably return to sleeping over here now, now that he's in charge of Fritzie. The bedroom he and Marnie share, when he goes in there, feels off-limits somehow, like it's not his place anymore. The bed's unmade, which makes sense. Marnie's way of letting him know he should change the sheets. That's exactly the project he should take on now. Forward motion. He strips the sheets off and then the pillowcases. For a moment he is stopped dead in his tracks when he discovers that Marnie's pillow smells like her, the way her hair smells when she's lying next to him—kind of a floral scent, and something else that's just her. He'd know it anywhere.

"What are you doing?" Fritzie says from the doorway.

"I'm changing the sheets."

"No, you're not. You're smelling the pillow." She comes in, followed by Bedford, and the two of them get up on the bare mattress. She starts jumping up and down, higher each time, until Bedford can't take it anymore and gets down. Patrick can't take it anymore either, but he knows that if he asks her to stop, it'll end up being a whole discussion. She'll have facts at her disposal that prove mattress-jumping is good for the environment or for health or, God knows, even for mattresses. Living with her is like living with a pint-sized, eagle-eyed, hypermanic lawyer, somebody who knows where all the loopholes are and where all the bodies are buried.

Later he talks to Philip Pierpont on the phone. The numbers were good for the weekend. Successful show. Maybe now he'll do more work? People want to buy the sculptures.

"They're not for sale," says Patrick. "I want to keep them."

Pierpont starts in with wanting to negotiate. "None of them?"

None.

"Then do more, my good man. If you don't want to let these particular ones go, can't you copy them and do more of the same? You've got real feeling in these."

No. He can't even listen to this kind of talk. Copy them? Like he's some kind of hack? Doing this just for the bucks?

He takes Fritzie and Bedford to the park, and that feels almost like a hero's journey, just getting the two of them ready and then making their way along the sidewalk. Fritzie argues about wearing a hat, and he insists, especially now that she doesn't have any hair. He trudges along while the two of them—Bedford and Fritzie both—leap and cavort their way along in front of him. He'd never particularly thought about the word *cavort*, but there's no other description for this half skipping and half jumping they do. It starts to snow while they're at the park, the sky suddenly letting loose of all the cold it's been holding on to, and he stands shivering while flakes fall on his head and shoulders, and he watches while Bedford and Fritzie run back and forth, chasing a tennis ball, going further and further away. He walks along the path, sees them in the field, jumping and throwing and barking and running.

How many Januarys ago was it that he'd had to rescue Bedford after he got hit by a car, and then come to this very spot in the park to find Marnie to tell her? She'd been out searching for that mutt, who for some reason only known to his insane doggy mind, had left her at the park and headed for home by himself and then had gotten hit by a car. Patrick had been on the verge of leaving Brooklyn. Everything was ending for him here. That day he was packing up the truck. And yet . . . that day had been the turning point for them, he's heard her say when she tells their story. And it may be true. Certainly that was probably the day he figured out that he wasn't going to be able to live without loving her—or at least admitting it to himself. No other force could have pried him loose from his plan to stay a hermit and move to Wyoming. Nothing but love would have made him go out into the street and pick up her bleeding dog and carry him to a veterinary hospital, insist on them fixing him, and then go search for her when he couldn't reach her by cell phone.

It was love. He didn't choose it, he hadn't wanted to fall in love with her, but forces beyond his control seemed to set the whole love thing in motion, and he'd gone along. He had let life unthinkingly sweep him up in its moving current. Later that week, after the park incident, after he'd kissed her there in public, he'd moved upstairs to live with her, and he'd settled into the yin and yang and normality and laughter and strife and brooding and making up and kissing that comes with being part of a couple.

It turned out that love took over everything in life: who came to his house, what made him laugh, what his sleep was like. Love turned out to have power over even the sweatpants and shirts he wore, the smell of his sheets, over his opinions about cats and dogs, the pastries he baked and the music he listened to, his breathing and his heartbeats, the things he thought about in the shower . . . and the fears he kept secret because of how big they grew.

Now look at him. He's all out of love. Who knew it was a commodity and you could use it up?

He's cold. He stamps his feet and calls Fritzie and Bedford back. They've gotten yards and yards away by now out in the middle of the soccer field, and it's snowing harder.

"Patrick! Patrick! Patrick!" Fritzie is calling and jumping up and down.

He cups his hands around his mouth. "Come back!"

"Patrick! Patrick! Patrick!" She must say it seventy billion more times. Has any human ever used his name so many times in one day? He doesn't think so.

"Come! Back!" he hollers.

He looks for Bedford and doesn't see him. Shit. Is that damn dog lost again? He's going to have to go running through the field, isn't he, and into the woods, and out to the avenue to see just where this idiot mutt might have gotten himself to. He can't bear it. He simply cannot relive any of that.

"Patrick!" She is screaming it now, cupping her hands around her mouth.

"What?" he calls back. He starts to run toward her.

"I WANT PIZZA FOR DINNER!"

This is what she wanted to tell him? He slows down, catches his breath. He sees Bedford, galloping in that inelegant way of dogs, heading toward Fritzie with his ears flying straight out, looking like they could take him happily airborne if they had just a little more curve to them, a little bit of lift.

"PATRICK, CAN WE HAVE PIZZA FOR DINNER? CAN WE HAVE PIZZA FOR DINNER? CAN WE? CAN WE? CAN WE?"

There are going to need to be rules, he thinks. This sort of thing can't keep happening.

They decide upon some rules while they're eating dinner. And yes, it's pizza—takeout pizza. Patrick insists on taking it home, above all her objections. He knows he cannot sit in the brightly lit pizza parlor, which pretty much consists of a long counter and two tables. The place is taken up with teenagers, rough-talking kids milling around in knit caps and sweatshirts, cruising for things to point out, constantly saying variations of the word *yo*, while they share a paper plate filled with greasy garlic knots. Patrick does not want to be the subject of teenaged attention while he eats a pizza with a pint-sized POW.

She argues and argues, but he wins.

"It's because you're afraid the teenagers would talk to you," she says as they're walking home with the cardboard box of pizza, which is leaking grease onto his gloves.

"No, it isn't."

"Yes, it is. You hate talking to people, and you hate it more when people talk to you."

He makes himself stay silent. He wonders if he can make a rule that she is not to make any comments or observations about his character. She is stomping along next to him, with her jaw set in that way she has when she feels she's been wronged.

"Okay, we're going to have some rules," he says, once they're home at the kitchen table. Even though it's six o'clock, he's made himself a pot of coffee to try to give himself a modicum of energy to make it through the next few hours until her bedtime.

She slouches further into her chair and sticks out her tongue at him.

"Number one. No running away from me when we're out together."

"Okay, but what if—"

"Nope. You have to stay with me. At all times. I must be able to see you."

She slumps over, puts her head on her arm.

"And in the mornings, you need to get yourself ready for school. Clothing, shoes, homework, backpack. Can you do that?"

"What are you going to be doing?"

"I will be making your breakfast and your lunch."

"What if I want school lunch that day?"

"Then we'll talk about it, and you probably can. Now, next. What do you do after school? You go to an after-school program, am I right?"

"No. I got kicked out of it."

"Kicked out? What did you—never mind. So what do you do after school?"

She laughs. "You know literally nothing about my life, do you?"

"I've been a little preoccupied . . ."

She stands up and comes around to his side of the table and sticks out her hand to shake his. "Hello. Let me introduce myself. My name is Fritzie Peach Delaney. At least that's my new name for while I'm here. My real name, if you want to know, is Frances Elizabeth Farrell. And I'm eight years old, and I have two bio-parents who don't know anything about me. Thank you very much, and now I will sit down again." She takes a bow and goes back to her seat.

Fritzie Peach? The kid is named Peach? How did that get by him?

"Oh, and after school, I usually get met at the bus stop by a nice lady named Marnie MacGraw—maybe you remember her? And she usually takes me to her store, where they sell flowers and Marnie knows a lot about love, so she talks about love all day with people. People are always coming in and hugging her and kissing her and telling her things, and she tells them things, and sometimes everybody dances. There is a lot of talking. And yoga."

"Right," he says. He doesn't know why this makes his chest feel tight, but it does. When he can collect himself, he says, "Okay. So then after school, I, Patrick Delaney, will meet you at the bus stop and bring you here."

"Unless I get invited to go home with a friend."

"Unless you get invited to go home with a friend, correct. Which you will tell me about."

"I will try to remember."

"No, no. That's one of the rules. I *have* to know where you are. At all times."

"What if I'm downstairs with Ariana and her friends?"

"Then you'll tell me."

"What if I'm on the stoop with Bedford?"

"Then you'll tell me."

"What if I'm in the bathroom?"

"Fritzie."

"What?"

"You know you can go to the bathroom." He takes another slice of pizza. "By the way, is your name seriously Fritzie Peach?"

"Yep."

"And how did you happen to get that name?"

"I gave it to myself."

He laughs. "You're quite a piece of work, you know that?"

"I don't even know what that means."

He stands up and starts clearing the table. "It means . . . it means . . ." His phone buzzes in his pocket. It's Marnie. "Oh! I gotta take this," he says to Fritzie.

"Okay, but do we have a rule about getting my ears pierced?"

"We do," he says. "You're not to do it." And then he clicks the phone. "Hi."

Her voice is odd. At first he thinks that maybe the worst has happened, that she didn't make it to Florida in time to see her father before he passed away, but no. He realizes it's just her new, formal, dealing-with-Patrick voice. That kind of voice. Official.

"Just going up to see my father now in the Cardiac Care Unit. How's Fritzie?"

"She's fine."

"Good." Then there's a silence. He's supposed to say something else, so he says, "How are you?" even though she probably just covered that. Going up to see her father in CCU, right.

"Don't let Fritzie forget to put her homework in her backpack," she says.

"Fritzie, put your homework in your backpack," he says. Then: "How was the flight?"

"Good. A bit of turbulence, but nothing so bad."

He tells her it snowed and they went to the park. Which just about covers it if you don't want to go into the part about haircuts, dog nearly getting lost, Patrick's name being shouted seventy kazillion times. Just park, pizza, snow. He's fine. Bedford's fine. Fritzie's fine.

He looks over at Fritzie. Oh God, she is so un-fine. That hair. Now that he looks at it, really looks at it in the kitchen light, he sees that she seems less like a jaunty POW and more like she might have had a bad case of mange.

He decides it's best not to mention this on the phone. He doesn't feel he's qualified yet to explain the concept of arting one's hair. In fact, he's grateful when Marnie says she has to go, and they can stop talking.

The next day, after looking at Fritzie's hair and feeling like an abject failure at parenting, he invites Ariana upstairs for a hair consultation, with Fritzie's permission. In spite of himself. He has to ask for help, day two.

"We've had an incident of hair-arting, and I'm thinking you might be able to art it into something more . . ."

"Attractive?"

"Well, less like it was chewed off by rodents. More like it was done on purpose."

She does exactly that: snips and shapes, and she recommends a bit of hair gel for the mornings, something that would make it stick up ever so slightly.

"Thank you," Patrick and Fritzie say at exactly the same moment. For probably completely different reasons.

CHAPTER
THIRTY-SEVEN
MARNIE

"Just so you know, I'm not sorry," says my mother at the airport, out of the blue.

I look over at her. We've been sitting at Gate Eighteen with our cups of tea, waiting for the plane to board. Around us are a bunch of pale New Yorkers in flowered shirts laughing as though they're being freed from weather prison. My mother has mostly been grimly typing something on her phone, stopping to stare into space in an unfocused way, and then furiously typing again in response to a ding from her phone.

After a few attempts to make conversation with her about such neutral things as airport security lines, the taste of hot tea in Styrofoam cups versus cardboard cups, and annual snowfall amounts in Brooklyn, I too have fallen silent.

She puts her phone away and leans over closer to me. "I probably won't be talking about this much in the next few days, but I just wanted you to know that my time in Brooklyn was perfect the way it was," she says. "So thank you. And I don't feel guilty for being away, if that's what you're thinking."

That is what I'd been thinking. "Well," I say. "That's good. I'm glad. Guilt is sort of pointless."

"There are some things I didn't tell you that I might as well mention now," she says. "Just because I want you to know. I did have a little fling. I didn't tell you about him because I didn't want to burden you with all that. But I just texted him to tell him what's happening and that things are over."

"Oh, Mom," I say. I squeeze her hand.

"Yeah. I'm processing it all now, as you young folks say."

"Well, I guess so," I say. "You must have a lot of—"

"I don't know if you'll be able to understand this," she says, interrupting me, "which is why I'm going to tell you now so if you ever come up against this in your own life, maybe you'll handle it differently. I've realized that none of what I was feeling was about your father, not really. Sure, I felt neglected by him, and taken for granted, and ignored a lot of the time—but I now see that what was really happening was that I was the one taking the easy way out. I was being lazy with my own life. Not taking responsibility for my own happiness."

"Please. Don't even tell me that you're going to say it's your fault because you needed to try harder because he had lost interest in you."

Her eyes search mine. "No, that's not what I'm saying at all. Listen, because this is important. What I'm *saying* is that I expected him to provide all the excitement for me, all the praise, all the . . . attention. I didn't think of myself as a person who had any right to any restless feelings, or unpleasant feelings, or longings—so I just kept pretending and acting like I was perfect and happy, while I was burying my real self. And at the same time expecting him to come and excavate me. But it wasn't his job. Never was."

"I'm not sure . . ."

"Marnie, unlike you, I haven't ever done anything that's really hard. You've gotten married and divorced, you've broken off an engagement, you've moved far away and started your own business, you've decided to believe in magic, you've made a million new friends. And I . . . I've never upended anything. I got married young, I bought a house, had kids, threw dinner parties, joined the PTA, got my hair done every week, baked cookies and dusted the lamps, and basically just let myself go along a road that I never even looked at. I aced the big things, don't you see? I got myself a great husband and two daughters. He's nice to me and he makes a good living, and so what if he got grumpy sometimes? I just accepted everything about my life. I didn't ever do anything outside of what was expected. I didn't have to think about my life. Don't you see? Somehow I realized I never even ice-skated or kissed another man or went to the top of the Empire State Building or asked myself what wild and reckless thing I wanted to do with my life if I had the chance. I've never even lived alone, much less smoked dope or gotten really, really drunk, or bodysurfed in the ocean, or told anybody off or even disappointed anyone on purpose so I could suit myself."

"Oh, Mom."

"What? What are you thinking?"

"I don't know. It's just so sad. That that's what it comes down to."

"Well, it's less sad now. Because now I've done some of those things. And no matter what happens, I know I'm going to do more of them." She sits back in the black plastic airport seat and folds her hands across her purse. She smiles. "I'm no longer this upright person I was so smug about being. I've had a little extramarital fling—and I would thank you to *not* look shocked, young lady, but I did—and even more than that, I smoked some dope and I went to a Broadway show, and I went up to the top of the Empire State Building."

"Good lord, Mom."

"I had me some good, good days," she says. "I know you're the expert matchmaker and all, but I want to tell you one thing. I can see that things are broken between you and Patrick right now"—she holds up her hand to stop me when I start to protest—"and, let me finish, I don't know if you're going to be able to put things right between you or not. I hope you are if that's what you want, but whatever you do, I hope you'll never do what I did and narrow your life down to fit his. Or let yourself be so dependent on his attention that you pretzel yourself around to fit his view of how life should be. There are so many ways to live life. It's not only one way. We get ourselves thinking that we have to make something work because we've put so much time into it already . . . but you have free will. Remember that."

"He doesn't want to get back together, even if I asked him to," I say. "When the school year is over, he's told me he's going to move out."

She pats me on the hand. "I've seen what's happening. He's a wonderful man, Patrick is, but I know he's not easy." Her eyes search my face. "Do you want my advice?"

"Okay."

"My advice is—don't listen to anyone else's advice." She smiles. "No, really. I mean this. Trust yourself. No one knows whether you and Patrick can weather all this. This could be a trial you're in right now that will lead you to something deeper. Maybe it'll still work and maybe it won't. Don't think it's necessarily over. Love can survive worse than this."

"Not if one of the people doesn't want it to," I say.

"Well, that's true," she says. "But it sounded good, didn't it? And you can't give up on magic." Then she smiles and reaches into her carry-on bag. "Just so you know, I brought along Blix's spell book. Just in case you might need it."

She hands me the old, worn-out volume that I've checked and rechecked so many times, the book with the vines and flowers on the front that I've always kept nearby. Inside, I know, it's stuffed with handwritten pages that Blix wrote when she was thinking up spells for people. There's also a page in there on which she wrote *PATRICK AND MARNIE. PATRICK AND MARNIE. PATRICK AND MARNIE*, long before he and I knew of each other's existence.

Blix thought he was my destiny when she was writing that down. But she was wrong about a lot of things. And Patrick just may be one of them. He was my destiny for four years, maybe, but not beyond that. And I have to let it go.

I feel myself flush. "Thank you, but I don't want that stuff anymore."

"Take it," she says in her mom voice.

So I do. I shove it in my bag and roll my eyes at her. I'm not going to let it pull me in again, though. Magic didn't cure Blix's cancer, and it didn't save Patrick from the aftereffects of the fire. I think the evidence is in that it's not worth a whole hell of a lot.

There is no such thing as destiny or meant-to-be. We're just all out there, slogging through as best we can, and some of us aren't doing so well at it just now.

We find my father in the Cardiac Care Unit, sitting up in bed, looking like a grayer, tinier version of himself. He gets a big smile on his face when he sees us, and holds out his arms to my mother, who goes over to his bedside and leans down and kisses him on the forehead and holds his face in both hands as she kisses his cheeks and looks into his eyes.

"Look what I had to do to get you home!" he says. "God, I sure hope the insurance covers this, because otherwise it's been an awfully expensive way to get your wife back." Then he looks at me. "And, ducky, how are you doing, baby? Thank you for bringing her home to me and saving me from having to go up there and endure me some winter. I saw on the Weather Channel they got some snow up there today even."

And that's the way it goes conversationally: Weather Channel, hospital food, tests the hospital has done, the nurses' demeanor, the needles, the beeping machines. He's Ted, always the hearty salesman—jovial as he can be under the circumstances, glad to see his family, and making jokes when the nurse comes to adjust his IV and add some medication. Now that his wife is here, he tells them, he expects to be sent right home where the real good care is going to be. Not that he hasn't been getting excellent care from them, he hastens to add—but now he just needs the love cure.

"Can you imagine me—*me*—having this happen?" he says to me, his eyes wide with disbelief. "I'm the healthiest guy I know, and yet I'm the one getting the chest pains and the mild heart attack. Luckily the doc says it was just a mild one. Got one of those balloon things installed, and so I'm good to go. I tell everybody it was just that I missed my wife. My poor old heart was just sick of beating as one."

I look at my mother smiling and patting his arm, being his wife again. She's slipped right back into being who she always was, adjusting his sheets and his hospital gown, asking him if he wants a foot rub, or more water, or something from the cafeteria. Which nurse is his favorite, she wants to know, and how often has Natalie been in to see him? Any of the fellows from work come to visit? How's the house?

Only I see the shadow of the real person right there behind her eyes. The person who's sitting back for now but who has vowed not to disappear.

I leave my parents alone and take a walk through the hospital. The sun has gone down now, and the hospital is lit up like a shopping mall, with fountains and a gigantic atrium downstairs—palm trees and ferns lit up with spotlights. The only thing that differentiates this from your run-of-the-mill shopping plaza is that there are more wheelchairs than you'd perhaps normally see. And there's no kiosk selling sunglasses. I get a candy bar from a vending machine and think about calling Patrick back now that Fritzie has probably gone to bed.

But then I remember all the little sculptures of Anneliese in that studio, and his voice when he told me he loved her. I'm not the one he wants. Someday, maybe, I could be a stand-up comedian, and do a routine about how my ex-husband tried to break up with me at the altar on our wedding day—and then how the next guy left me to go back to his dead girlfriend. Would people laugh?

I wonder.

My father gets released two days later, and we take him home. We treat him like the invalid he hates being, lavishing him with attention and foot rubs and vegetable smoothies and lap blankets to protect him from "a possible chill" while he tries to bat us away and convince us he's as strong as ever. I sit outside with him on the patio and adjust the shade umbrella so that he doesn't get sun on his face. My mother gets to work making him healthy meals and going to the grocery store, lining up appointments, fixing up a sickroom for him. He has a whole sheaf of papers telling him what he can and cannot do, and we all read them and pass them around. He has written instructions on how he must change his life to prevent another heart attack.

"The next one, I might not be so lucky," he says.

"I know," I say. "It's good you're taking care of yourself."

He slaps his knee and laughs. "I'm just kidding you! There's not going to be another. I got my sweet better half back. I just needed me some of Millie's Marvelous Thursday Night Meat Loaf. This was just a fluke, trust me. Probably wasn't even a real heart attack. Just a warning."

"If it was a warning, it was a pretty serious one," I hear my mother say to him. "They don't put balloons in people for fake heart attacks, I don't think. You need to follow instructions and take it easy."

"But I feel like a million bucks," he says. He does not look like a million bucks. He looks like no more than one dollar and thirty-five cents. "I want to get out there on the golf course again. That's what eases my stress. That, and seeing you back at home, my dear. Hate to admit it, but I'm no good on my own."

When he and I are alone together, he lets down his guard and sinks down into himself, letting his chin rest on his chest, tapping his fingers on the plastic arms of the outdoor patio chairs. He says, "I didn't ever think she'd stay that long. What was she doing anyway? Who the hell goes to Brooklyn for the winter?"

"She was having a nice time," I say. "Went to the theater, talked to people in the flower shop. Helped out with Fritzie."

Went to the top of the Empire State Building. Rode the subway. Smoked pot. Dated some new men.

"I don't get it," he says. "Forty years married, and I guess I'll never figure women out."

"It's not too late," I say. And feeling bold, I add, "You don't have to figure all women out. All you have to do is love this one woman as hard as you can. Which I think it's in your power to do." Then, getting even crazy bold now, I say, "What if you tried listening to her like you really, really want to know what she's feeling and like you're on her side completely?"

"I am—" he says, but I hold up my hand to stop him.

"And stop talking to her in that fake way, like you're reading a bad sitcom script. The 'better half' and 'Millie's Marvelous Meat Loaf.' No one wants to hear that stuff. Be real."

I brace for what he would have said at any other time in my life, any time I tried to give any advice to him, the infallible Ted MacGraw, salesman extraordinaire, pillar of the community, good all-around nice guy. He would have said, "No one knows people like I do! I'm a people person, so don't go trying to tell me what's what. I'll talk to my wife the way I want!"

But now he just sits there in his pitiful white plastic lawn chair, looking out at the palm trees in their pots and the leaves from the ficus tree falling on the patio, and he says, "Yeah, you're right. I'm going to have to figure out how to listen to her better. Head this off so it doesn't happen again. I didn't even know she was unhappy." He looks up at me and laughs. "Not until that Thanksgiving dinner, that's for sure. I came back in the house after putting her in that taxi, and I sat there with that turkey leg, and I thought, 'Ted MacGraw, what the actual hell is this? Buddy, things have gone terribly, terribly wrong here. There's nobody sitting across the table. No smiling. No joy.'"

"Maybe this will usher in a whole new phase for you," I say.

He smiles and squeezes my hand. "It could, ducky. It could," he says. "I guess I gotta face that I'm in repair. Undergoing some renovations, both in my body and my personality. Gotta suck it up."

We both look up just then because there's a commotion at the door, and Natalie's arrived with her two kids. Amelia, who's four and perfect, runs over and climbs up on my dad, and Natalie swoops down and picks her up. "I told you, honey, you can't climb on PopPop. He's had an operation." She's got Louise on her hip—Louise chewing on a big plastic teething toy with little hard plastic bumps all over. Like a mace. Yet another thing I'll probably never need to know: why babies' gums require a medieval torture device.

"Well, nice to see you," Natalie says to me. "Good of you to bring Mom back."

I don't know why everything she says to me always seems hostile. We used to be best friends—or at least I thought we were. Patrick—and this is one of the reasons I loved him—says that I was never, ever, ever Natalie's best friend. At best, he says, I was her slave, sidekick, victim, and oppressed opposition. He's seen her operate—the former award-winning beauty queen/science champion/princess/overachieving mom/cancer researcher—and he points out that even today, when we're both adults, I regress in her presence to being a tongue-tied, unappreciated waif.

"And you're a million times nicer and smarter and more intuitive and prettier than she is!" he said once. "Why she thinks she's so much better is one of the great horrifying mysteries of modern life. It will be written up in textbooks, and scholars will puzzle over it in the centuries to come."

But I know the real answer. Natalie knows she's so much better because she has the paperwork to prove it. She's the one who, for our whole lives together, won all the awards, captured all the good grades, got her homework done on time, kept her room clean, ran around with the popular crowd, and dated all the great guys that everyone else wanted. I was the little sister in the corner, trying to design costumes that the neighborhood cats would wear for the weddings I was intent on staging in the backyard for them.

Now even as an adult, she has everything, all the showcase toys and rewards the universe hands out to its favorites: a husband who loves her and goes off to work at a well-paying and probably boring-as-hell corporate job that he is willing to do every single day, year after year after year, just to support her and their lifestyle, and she has two adorable little daughters, a 401(k), a house with a swimming pool, and a great job researching drugs that cure diseases, and . . . well, let's just say that no man is telling *her* that he doesn't quite see himself in the same life she's picturing. No man in her life is sitting up late at night making sculptures of a woman who died.

And if anyone happened to call Natalie's husband a hero—I know this guy—he would swell up with pride, and he'd tell everybody in the whole world who'd listen that *hell yeah*, he saved somebody's life, did everything he could, and he deserves whatever acclaim and applause and medals people might give for that. There would be medals on the mantel and hung on the walls. The situation would come up in at least 40 percent of all his conversations.

What it comes down to, it occurs to me, is that Natalie and Brian know they're awesome, while Patrick and I . . . well, we were still feeling our way along, like two blind people in a cave, using rusty instruments to try to figure out where we were and where we were heading.

And now, looking at my glorious blonde sister scolding our father for not taking better care of himself, and then turning her dazzling but angry smile onto me, asking where Mom is hiding out—I realize that Natalie has never had to ask a single question in her life about who she is or what she wants. Everything has simply come to her, and so she doesn't even know how the rest of us live and fret and struggle.

But then I realize something else, just as true. She's got plenty of insecurities and fears of her own. When I look at her talking to my dad and juggling her two children, I see behind her eyes that she's somebody who's so tense most of the time that she could chew off her own leg. Maybe she's got a successful marriage and a job she loves, but she doesn't get to hang out in the Frippery like I do, talking to people about love and helping them puzzle over what to say to the people they love and yearn to connect with. She's not seeing sparkles and running after people in restaurants because she's seen they belong together. And she hasn't gotten to hold Patrick's scarred, sweet hand at night or look into that luminous, but humble face. She hasn't seen what life looks like in the face of a person who's been broken a time or two.

In fact, now that I think about it, everybody I know and love has been broken a time or two. They've all had to climb out of darkness, to push back against the overwhelming, seek out the unknown comfort in a crisis. And sometimes they do it better than other times. Sometimes, like Patrick, they've had to stop moving forward temporarily and go back into the darkness. And we who love them have had to just wait outside the cave for the sight of their faint little light to come bumping along through the darkness and shine straight and steady again.

I feel my eyes fill up with tears, and I wipe them away. Patrick has decided not to come through the darkness. He wants to remain in the alcove of doom.

God, I have a pang of missing Patrick so much that I get dizzy for a moment. But I miss the old Patrick, the texting Patrick who resisted love and then fell so hard in love with me that I was bowled over with the sheer force of it. Before he started taking it all back.

And I miss Fritzie.

What will happen to us? I don't know. Maybe I have to bring myself to the point of loving Patrick enough to let him be wherever it is that he decides is home for him. It's his choice: the alcove of doom may be what he picks for good.

And I may just stay here in Florida, the place where my DNA knows all the home ground. I have to admit that, when I let myself stop being all angsty, I love how this feels. The sun shines on my skin, my father and I sit outside every day, drinking healthy smoothies and chatting about mundane things, and the humidity frizzes up my hair even while it's softening the dry-skin lines on my face.

A lot of people don't know that *Florida* is an old Spanish word that probably means "there are lots of flowers here even in winter, so just shut up and rest."

CHAPTER
THIRTY-EIGHT
PATRICK

Two weeks in, and with no end in sight, Patrick thinks his life as a father resembles a game of Whac-a-Mole.

Just as he thinks he's making some headway, that he's got this single-dad thing down, trouble flares up in a new place.

Fritzie has broken all the rules multiple times. Everything is subject to discussion, nothing simply gets taken care of without an argument: hair, homework, friends, playdates, as well as basic human things like getting clean and getting dressed. She makes everything an ordeal, and as far as he can see, she is doing it all out of a sense of glee. For fun. He comes to the conclusion, seeing the little quirky half smile on her face when she is torturing him, that she is having the best of times.

As if the hair-cutting incident thing wasn't bad enough, then a friend of Marnie's named Emily Turner called to tell him a story about

Fritzie letting kids rub her head for good luck—and charging them a quarter to do it. Apparently he is supposed to find this hilarious.

"She's a bold one," Emily Turner says, laughing. Then when he doesn't join in, she says, "Are you doing okay? Come for a drink sometime and meet my long-suffering husband. We'll commiserate by telling you all the vile and mercenary things *our* kids have done."

Of course he will not go. He intends to soldier on without reinforcements. Except for the repairing of Fritzie's haircut, he has resolutely not asked anyone else for help, even Ariana again, even when she pops in and out, offering assistance. It's just that he doesn't want to depend on anybody else. He needs to do this.

Still, he suspects he is losing more ground every day. Everything is so much more work than he ever imagined. Fritzie dances around the kitchen, teasing Bedford while Patrick is trying to get dinner ready. She goes on binges of asking him "Why?" after everything he says, until he's so exasperated he can barely think. And then she laughs at him. "Patrick, I'm just trying to see how many questions it takes until you get back to the whole creation of the universe as the reason," she says.

Then occasionally she'll declare it's Opposite Day, and with everything he says, she pretends he means just the reverse. "Oh, so you *don't* want me to take a bath then!" she'll crow. And, "Oh, you *hope* I'll stay awake all night and talk to you!"

And then there are the clingy times. She doesn't want to do her homework unless he agrees to sit there at the table with her the entire time. She says she shouldn't have to do it because it's boring unless he stays with her, and what if she started working on it and fell asleep and slid off the chair, hitting her head on the floor and dying of brain stuff?

All this companionship makes him crazy. He doesn't remember needing his parents to hang out with him for every little chore. She requires him to sing some nonsense song while she brushes her teeth. Sometimes he has to put a hand towel on his head—no, not that one, the blue one—and then he has to pretend to chase her down the hall to her room where he must pick out three stories to read to her before bed. And to sing her a song. And to tell her a story from his own life.

By the time he staggers back to the living room, he is exhausted, and then nine times out of ten, she's popped up again, saying she needs a glass of water, or she needs a new pillowcase because hers smells bad. Or she needs to talk about whether cats and dogs speak each other's languages. Something. Anything!

He doesn't get it. Why can't he just be allowed to be his old sad and incompetent self? Why does he have to talk to her all the time? He feels like his brain is being poked by sharp sticks about three-quarters of the time.

But worse—far, far worse—is that by the time February comes to an end, and Marnie has been gone for six weeks, Fritzie has neglected on five separate occasions to mention to him that she made other plans after school. He has been left standing at the bus stop while the bus discharges its non-Fritzie passengers.

Why, he wants to know, does she do this?

"Oh, I forgot. Sorry!" she'll say, looking surprised that he's mad, or maybe she'll come out with, "What difference does it make? I know where I am and how to get home!" And lately there's the more effective, "Well, Ricky, I did tell you where I was going, but you weren't listening to me! You never listen!"

Ricky?

Yes. Another baffling thing is that she has taken to giving him nicknames. Ricky! That one took him a bit to figure out. Then, of course: it's the last syllable in Patrick. Besides Ricky, she calls him Dude, Sad Guy, Art Man, Bio-Dad, and Spaceshot. He almost can't stand it.

"I was listening. I am always paying attention to when and where I'm supposed to pick you up," he says. "I know you didn't tell me."

She puts her hands on her hips. "The problem is, I need a phone," she says. "That way you won't have to worry that you lost me or that I died like that lady you loved, the one that was in the fire. Because you can't take it if anybody else dies, can you, Ricky?"

He must look shocked, because she comes over and stands next to him, breathing on him, and touching his face.

"If I have a phone, I will always be where you know I am," she says.

He pulls away and rubs his face. A phone! Ay yi yi. What universe is he living in where an eight-year-old should have a phone? But Emily Turner says they all have phones, and so he knows he is doomed.

One evening they go out and get her a phone. It's like a little rectangular insurance policy. Maybe now he can keep from waking up in the middle of the night terrified that somehow he has lost her.

This is no way to live. A phone is a small price to pay.

Tessa calls to FaceTime, as she does very occasionally, on Sunday morning. Patrick puts her on speakerphone because he's making pancakes. Behind her, he can see a café and some old-looking buildings, and all around her people are talking, which makes her have to lean into the phone at times. Suddenly her face fills the whole screen, scrunched up, trying to hear him.

He calls Fritzie, who comes charging in, bouncing around in excitement, spilling out all the news. "Mama! Hi, Mama! Listen, I got a phone! And Patrick bought me some new leggings with stars on them, and—oh, I got a sweatshirt and guess how they spell *girls* on it! Mama, it's *G-R-R-R-L-S*. And Marnie's gone because her dad got sick so it's just me and Patrick, and it's been sleeting here, even though it should be snowing instead. And did you know that sleet is like rain but it's ice at the same time? Kind of like when we had hail that time in England, remember, Mama?"

Patrick flips the pancakes over. He can't hear what Tessa said, but now Fritzie is demonstrating some incredibly complex gymnastic move on the floor, something involving spinning around on her butt and throwing her arms and legs in the air and then jumping up into place.

"I'm practicing doing a headstand flip, do you want to see me try to do that? Come on, watch me try to do that. Sometimes I can't do it, so it's *suspense*."

He sees in the phone that Tessa is looking elsewhere, gesturing to somebody. Not so interested apparently in the gymnastics displays or the breathless news from Brooklyn. Her eyes swerve back to the camera. She says, "Patrick? Are you still there?"

"Yes!" he calls.

"How's fatherhood treating you?" she says, and she smiles at the camera.

"Fine," he says. "You should watch Fritzie do this trick!" he says.

But Fritzie is shaking her head at him. She oozes her way along the wall, humming some tuneless thing, and then plops down on her back on the kitchen floor and puts her arm over her eyes. Bedford comes over to lick her face. Roy shows up, too, and Fritzie manages to pet both of them at the same time, still humming.

"Is she being good?" Tessa's voice rings out on the speaker. "Because—well, Richard and I were sort of interested in taking a bit more time when the semester's over, you know? Just feeling this out preliminarily . . . maybe . . . ?"

The phone signal glitches, but then Tessa starts talking again, mid-sentence, about a trip to Greece. Until the fall semester, he hears. And can they talk? Would he and Marnie be amenable to—

Fritzie scrambles to her feet and leaves the kitchen.

"Tessa," he says. There's a taste of iron in his mouth. How could she have this conversation in front of Fritzie like this? "I have to go. We'll talk soon."

And when he clicks the phone off, he goes off to fetch Fritzie, jolly her up, tell her funny jokes until he can get her to come back and eat her pancakes. He promises her a trip to ice-skate in Prospect Park. He feels like he's wearing his heart on the outside of his body, and every little breeze stuns it and makes it ache more.

CHAPTER
THIRTY-NINE
MARNIE

My father has gotten to the depressed stage of heart attack recovery. The internet thought that might happen.

"After a heart attack, even a mild one, many people experience depression and an awareness of their own mortality," it says on one website. "Contact your doctor if this becomes extreme."

Thank you, World Wide Web, for that piece of advice. I wonder if that description was written by Patrick, back when his job was to caution the world about the perils of being alive.

Speaking of Patrick and depression and the perils of being alive—he is being very circumspect about how things are going with Fritzie.

When I call his phone, Fritzie is the one who answers, and she is buzzing with news, all of it—complaints, announcements, gossip, exclamations—tumbling out accompanied by sighs and laughs and snorts and the kind of heavy breathing you only get when you're talking and jumping off of a bed at the same time. She's going to be in a spelling bee, she has to write a report about recycling, she went to a movie with Blanche Turner and it was sooo boring, she lost her hat but Patrick bought her another one, they had chicken for dinner *again*, Ariana has been too busy to come upstairs very much but it's very loud down there and Patrick thinks more people than just her are living there, but he doesn't want to go down and see, he says, because he's not the police. "That's what he said, Marnie. He is not the police."

"Well, that's true . . ." I say.

"So *I* went down there on Saturday. I wanted to know what was going on, and so I knocked on the door, and they let me in, and there were three girls there. Ariana, Charmaine, and that girl, Janelle, the one who's going to have a baby. And they had just gotten out of bed and they were still in their pajamas with their hair all messy, and they were drinking coffee and they were all doing some fortune-telling cards, they said, and they asked me if I wanted my fortune told, but I said no and went upstairs."

"Why didn't you want your fortune told?"

"I dunno."

"Maybe you didn't believe in it?"

"I . . . guess. There's some stuff I don't want to know," she says.

"What?"

"I don't want to know if . . ." I can hear her breathing into the phone, taking deep breaths. She taps on something nearby, tap tap tap. "I don't want to know . . . if I'm going to have to go back to live with my mum."

"Oh, honey," I say, and I close my eyes. How can I possibly protect her from heartbreak? I can't, is the truth of it. She's not mine, and Patrick is not mine, and despite the fact that I fall asleep every night thinking of him and wishing things were different, nothing has changed.

One day he sends a photo of him and Fritzie smiling into the camera, and I see that she has hardly any hair. Just a fuzz of brown on her head.

What happened to her hair? I text him.

He types: *#DIYHaircut. #Holymoly #GodHelpUs #HairArt #DontBeMadAtMe #IDidntKnow.*

I type back: *What the actual freaking hell is going on there?*

He sends an emoji of a man shrugging. *She says she "arted" her hair. Resembles POW. #GoodTimes #NeverADullMoment.*

And then . . . well, that's it.

No declarations of love, of missing me, of the hole in their lives without me. Because he is not my destiny. Because absence is *not* making his heart grow fonder. Someday his name won't make me smile, and the memories won't make me cry anymore, and I will heal up.

Because it's over.

One night, unable to sleep, I can't help myself, and I call Patrick up when I know Fritzie won't be the one to intercept the phone.

"I just want to ask you a question," I say when he answers.

"Um, okay."

"Why, if you knew that you couldn't father a child, were we using condoms all that time, for years?"

He sighs. "The reason we were using condoms is because I *didn't* know. After the fire, whether or not I could have a kid was the last thing on my mind, if you want to know the truth. I wasn't even sure I wanted to live."

"But you said the doctor told you."

"He says he did. But I don't remember it. It wasn't until I went to him recently and was telling him that you and I were trying—"

"Wait a minute. *Were* you trying? Because it didn't feel to me that you were. It felt like to me you were going along under duress, and you never even wanted to have sex anyway, so it was a moot point."

311

He's silent for a moment. "Wow. I wasn't expecting this."

"Patrick," I say after letting the silence between us grow heavier and heavier, almost unbearably heavy. "I have wanted a baby for a long time. I told you that I wanted a baby, and you built up a whole wall of nonsensical jokey excuses about school meetings and report card conferences. You did not once look me in the eye and say the truth, which was, 'You know something? I'm most likely infertile.'"

"Because I didn't remember being told that. What part of that are you not getting? And this is exactly why we can't be together anymore. Because you are always going to see this as my failure. You are always going to wish for that other life."

"Why can't I be the one to decide how important that is? There are other solutions, you know."

"Are there, though?"

"Well, at least we could have talked about it. You could have been honest about what was going on. You just let everything fall apart. Stopped loving me. Like, suddenly. Just stopped."

"Marnie, it's been a really rough few months. But you know that I loved you. I'll always love you."

"It's just not the kind of love that does anybody any good—is that it?" I say. "You said you didn't want to be a parent. Your whole argument was that you'd have to go in public, you'd have to talk to teachers and other parents, people would be thinking about your scars, on and on and on—and now look at you, Patrick, handling all that just fine."

He's silent.

"And it's doable, isn't it? And here's what *I'm* left with: the great love of your life turns out to be Anneliese, and even though she's dead, *she's* the woman who's been soaking up all your attention and love all these months—"

"I—"

"And the *child* you couldn't even consider having with me—it turns out you already had her! What do you know? She's here. Another

woman shows up with her! And so now you're being a dad—a temporary, one-year dad! Hooray for you! You get to have this whole *experience*
and then, ohhh, you'll get to miss her when she's gone just like you
missed Anneliese when she was gone. But as for me: I'm the real-life
woman standing right in front of you, yet I'm invisible to you."

"I cannot get you pregnant," he tells me in a steely voice I've never
heard from him before. "You can get mad about that all you want to,
but it doesn't change anything."

"Well, you certainly acted like you could and just didn't want to,"
I say. "It sounds to me like it's terribly convenient that *now* there's a
medical reason that shows up. That's all I'm saying."

"I'm sorry you feel that way."

"Yeah," I say. "Well, me too. It's actually kind of soul-crushingly
sad. And by the way, I do not happen to believe you love me. Nobody
acts like this to a person they love."

And then, because I can't stand hearing him say again that he loves
me, but in this teeny tiny way that can't exist except in some rarefied
air that only Patrick can appreciate and cultivate, I hang up. I want
love that you can see and feel and touch and eat dinner with and sleep
in the bed next to. I want love that shines through everything—all the
doubt and uncertainty. I want love that says, "So if we can't make a baby
together, what *can* we do to have a family?" And that is not something
Patrick can ever even imagine.

CHAPTER FORTY

PATRICK

One morning, Patrick wakes up to find Fritzie standing beside his bed. Staring at him. She has her phone flashlight on and is beaming it—not *at* his eyes directly, but around and around in circles close to his eyes. It hits his chest, head, and the wall behind his bed. Close enough to his eyeballs that they fly open, ready to usher in a full-body freak-out mode, if that's what's needed here. And it seems to be.

"WHA—what?" he says and sits bolt upright in the bed.

"I threw up."

"You threw up? Where?"

"In my bed."

He turns on the light. Thinks of swearing, then doesn't.

He's heard of this kind of thing—vomit in the middle of the night—and he knows that outside of drug arrests, sharp sticks in the eye, or car crashes, this is the bane of parenting. It's 3:22, according to the red numerals on his bedside clock, and he has no option but to get up. She smells horrible. Dealing with this situation cannot be put off.

"Okay," he says. He swings his legs over the side of the bed. She's standing there, looking decidedly unfresh. Perhaps even with a shade of green to her face, although that could simply be the bad lighting. He sees that she'll need new pajamas.

Okay.

So . . . what he will need to do . . . go to the bed where the *stuff* is, strip the sheets off the bed, then throw them into the washing machine, find new sheets (oh please, oh please let them be washed and dried in the linen closet) and remake the bed. (Possibly he will have to keep himself from . . . also . . . hurling, due to the sight and the smell.) There will be a need for new pajamas, toothpaste, assurances, resettlement. He looks over at her, slumped now against the wall. Poor little kid. He knows that look. She looks like someone who is possibly going to have to have another go-round . . . or maybe twelve more go-rounds. Depends on which nightmare scenario they are in.

An indeterminate amount of time later—the sun has come up, gone away again, snow fell then turned to sleet and then rain, continents formed and were swallowed by the Earth's oceans—he can report with some confidence that they have entered the dreaded "twelve more go-rounds" nightmare. Great. Every hour throughout the day it happens again. She has a fever, too, and when he looks into her sad little face, he thinks that her eyes are hollowed out, that she's possibly a zombie, and that if it wouldn't make her even sicker, she would probably be intent on eating his brains.

She sleeps in fits and starts, tossing back and forth in her bed, moaning, and then she lifts her head up, leans over the side of the bed for the trash can he's provided for her deposits, makes terrible noises, and flops back down. Groans.

The doctor's office says to give her small sips of sugar water. Or ginger ale. Popsicles. And no, they don't wish to see her. It's a virus. The flu. It's going around. He should wash his hands a lot and drink plenty of fluids himself. And good luck to him. Call if her temperature goes over 105 or if she goes into convulsions.

Convulsions!

Thanks, he says. Thanks loads.

She is unwilling to take a sip of anything, which is bad. He decides she is baking from the inside out. If she drank water, it would probably boil inside her. She's that hot. So he figures out ways to coax her.

"You know who would be so silly not to drink anything when she's sick?" he says. "Ariel the Little Mermaid. Anybody who would give their voice away would think it was a great idea not to drink anything! Luckily you're smarter than that."

She looks at him through hollow eyes. Not going to buy it.

Bedford and Roy seem to be of the opinion that death is imminent. Bedford deals by staying close by the bed, watching intently, while Roy begs to be allowed to go back and live in the studio. They both look at Patrick with expressions of disgust. *Are you just going to let this happen, man? Come to your senses and stop this! And also, I need to be fed.*

It goes on like this for three miserable days, which he wouldn't have thought even possible. She gets up for only minutes each day, leaning on him to hobble to the bathroom and then to hobble her way back. Her little arms feel like sticks to him, and when he helps her change her pajamas, he feels heartbroken at the sight of those sharp little shoulder blades. Did they always stick up so much? How do children make it through life when they have so little meat on their bones?

He should ask for help. Ariana, maybe. Or Emily Turner. Marnie might even know what to do. But the truth is: he knows what to do. He was the goddamned medical writer; he knows every symptom and what it means. Fluids, sleep, bites of food. Keep the fever down.

Be vigilant, says his brain.

He feeds her minuscule pieces of crackers and holds a cup of ginger ale to her lips and urges her to sip, only sip, don't gulp. But drink the whole cupful. He sends out for popsicles and brings those to her like an offering. He and Bedford take their place beside her bed for hours at a time. After day two, Patrick brings in his laptop and stretches out next to her on the bed and shows her movies. They watch everything Pixar ever thought about. Then he shows her *Forrest Gump*, *The Unsinkable Molly Brown*, *Heidi*, *The Three Stooges*. He cries when Forrest Gump's mother dies. And when the *Titanic* sinks. When he even cries over Moe getting hit on the head, he has to go into the bathroom and splash water on his face and have a talk with himself.

He brings cloths for her head. He holds her hand. He sings, at her insistence, "What Do You Do with a Drunken Sailor," and she gazes at him with those enormous, red-rimmed eyes, and she says, "Thank you, Patwick." It breaks him.

He falls asleep on the floor beside her bed at night, after dragging in his comforter and pillow. Lying on the floor this way, he thinks he can hear the thumping of drums or the low thrum of a bass from downstairs. The hordes of teenagers are playing music. He concentrates on watching the moon through her window.

He'd forgotten about the moon and the sky. It seems he needs to keep track of them so he doesn't forget them again.

And then, five days after it started, it's over. One morning at five o'clock, he is startled awake by her voice. "Patrick! Patrick! Hey, Art Man! Ricky! Wake up! What the heck are you doing sleeping on the floor? Let's go have some ice cream."

Ice cream? *Ice cream?*

He looks at her through his bleary eyes. She's perfectly fine, as if the last five days had been a figment of his imagination, as if she hadn't looked for days like she might die. She has come roaring back to life. Wants to take a shower, go outside, walk to Paco's. Can they go to Best Buds, see their old friends? What if they went in his studio and did an art project? Maybe he could make some more of those things he was making, the sculptures that everybody liked so much. She was dreaming of how to make them. She could probably make them, too. She's bouncing on the bed. Her eyes are bright. He thinks that haircut, radical as it was, actually looks cute on her. Brings out her eyes.

He gets up off the floor. His body is stiff and sore, but for the first time in forever, he can't stop smiling.

The return of health—who knew it could be like the end of the apocalypse, when the zombies return to their graves and the sun shines and people turn out to be not out to eat your brains after all? That you could go from hating food and drink and even light bulbs and televisions to thinking that something as mundane as cleaning the bathtub is truly a miracle.

He buys doughnuts and flowers at Paco's. The day Fritzie goes back to school, he goes into his studio—a major test of the will, something he couldn't have done even as recently as three days ago—and yes, there is a huge mess, there are the vestiges of sculpture, paints, canvases, wires, scalpels, and blowtorches, but he can look at all of it and not want to jump out of the window.

Anneliese doesn't seem to be in there.

How can he explain that? Maybe he loaded her up when he loaded up all the artwork and took it to the Pierpont Gallery. Maybe when he came home that night after the opening, she didn't come back with him. She may be still there in the gallery, greeting art patrons and keeping Pierpont company.

He starts putting things away, but then he stops. It's all different in here somehow. Like there's more air and space. He takes off the sheets and folds up the futon.

Then he looks at all the paints and clay and rags and canvases. There are things he wants to make. He grabs some clay and a putty knife. The sun is shining through the window, and he turns on music, and he lets the studio fill up with the Motown stylings of Marvin Gaye.

And then he just puts his brain aside and lets his hands take over and he makes stuff.

"Okay, so I have some questions for you," Fritzie says. He's washing the dishes, and she's wandering around in a circle in the kitchen, making herself dizzy. This is how you know somebody's well, he thinks. They don't mind getting dizzy once again.

"Is this an interview?" he says.

"Nope. Just questions."

"Okay, shoot."

She is spinning around with her arms out, faster and faster, punctuating each spin with a word. "What. Happens. To. Kids. Who. Are. Really. Really. Bad. And. Nobody. Wants. Them?"

"I don't know any kids like that," he says.

"What if a kid ran away, would that be a really bad kid, do you think?"

"Wow. That's a tough one. I guess I'd have to know *why* the kid ran away. Do you know a kid who's done that?"

"Okay, another question then. Why is Marnie still gone for so long when her dad is better?"

"Um, because she . . . is helping her mom and dad get settled again, I think." *Because she's furious with me.*

"It's March, Patrick. *Is* she coming back here?"

"She is."

"When? I said *when* is she coming back here?"

"That I'm not sure about."

"Is it tomorrow?"

"No."

"The next day?"

"No."

"The day after that?"

"I don't really know."

"You don't ask her?"

"I, um, try to let her make her own decisions, and not pressure her."

"Ah. You don't want to *pressure* her."

"Yep. I'm nice that way."

"Patrick, we have to get Marnie to come back," she says. "Here, I'm going to help you dry the dishes." She gets a dish towel out and stands on her tiptoes and gets one of the plates out of the dish drainer and very carefully dries it. "This isn't all that good here with her gone."

"What? We're doing okay, aren't we?"

She laughs. "Patrick! We are *not* doing okay!"

"Wait. I'm hurt. We eat good meals, we play games sometimes, we keep the house pretty clean."

"Nope, nope, nope," she says. "We are not that good without Marnie. I think you should beg her to come back. Have you even asked her?"

"No," he says. "It's up to her."

"Oh, Patrick."

"You don't know how it works," he says.

"Okay, my last question," she says. "This is a tough one, I gotta warn you."

"I'm warned."

"If my mum doesn't want to come back, what's going to happen to me?" She puts the dried plate very carefully on the kitchen table, centering it so it's not too near the edge. He is touched by the fact that she won't look at him and the precision with which she places the plate just so.

"Listen," he says. He turns off the water. His voice might be shaking a little. "The adults in your life are going to figure things out. You don't have to worry. It's going to be okay. We're all talking about what to do."

"Okay," she says, and her voice is quivering a bit, too. "Because when my mum called, you know, she said she's not ready . . . she wants me to stay longer . . ."

"I know," he says. He might be growling when he says it.

"Richard doesn't really like me, you know. It's okay and all that, but he doesn't."

"He's an idiot then," says Patrick, and then he's shocked at himself. But he means it. She laughs a little bit and trots off to play with Bedford.

Later, after she's gone to bed, he goes in and sits down next to her bed the way he did for so many nights when she was sick. God, what is wrong with him? The sight of her eyelashes on her cheeks makes him feel like crying.

Here's what it is: he knows something he didn't know before, that he's going to figure out how to keep her. He doesn't want to send her back to Tessa. In fact, he *can't*.

He gets up and paces around the room. He woke up last night in the middle of the night thinking about Anneliese, and for the first time she wasn't screaming, and he wasn't feeling guilty toward her. She wafted away.

The streetlight is shining in the window, making a patch of light on the floor. The windows rattle like they're rattling his bones. Why, he finds himself wondering, has he wasted so much time on guilt? Hell, he *ran* toward her in the fire, didn't he? He tried to save her. He gave his utmost in that effort. What if . . . what if, like everybody kept saying to him, it really wasn't his fault?

It wasn't my fault, he thinks, experimentally. He sits down. *I didn't do anything wrong. I am a survivor.*

He says the words again: *I tried to save her.*

He holds out his arms and looks at them. They look strong and capable, these hands, even with their scars and their uneven coloring. He remembers back before, before the fire, when he thought of himself as strong. He's been contemptuous the last few years, thinking of that guy—but he was a good guy. He got stuff done.

He doesn't have to hate himself for who he is.

He was strong for Blix when she was dying. And then he was strong for Marnie when she needed him, back when she first moved here, and through all the months of figuring out how to be a Brooklynite. He smiles, remembering how she acted like she'd come to a quaint but baffling foreign country or something, a place filled with mysterious hipsters and subways and scary radiators clanging in the darkness.

He looks down at Fritzie, who turns over in her sleep, curls herself up. He wipes his eyes. What the hell is happening to him? Love has sneaked up on him and zapped him so hard that he's down for the count. He's got some fairly serious demons to stare down. He needs to say good-bye to Anneliese. Send her away.

And call Marnie. The thought of that makes his head hurt. He's been such an idiot.

Before he does that, though, there is a thing. Some unfinished business he needs to take care of, something that he'd avoided for too long. He needs to call Anneliese's parents. Just to talk to them. To let them say whatever it is they need to say to him. They should hear from him that he loved her, that he tried to save her, that he hopes they've found peace.

Tomorrow.

That's what he'll do tomorrow. He still has their phone number in with his things that he's kept and moved from place to place. Grace and Kerwin will probably cry, and maybe he will, too. But he owes them this.

Fritzie Peach. He looks down at her sleeping and smiles, shaking his head at that name.

"My daughter," he says.

And then—well, after he talks to Grace and Kerwin, then he'll figure out how to call Marnie. See if he can make things right.

If Marnie doesn't come back, if she can't love him anymore—well, that's unimaginable. He'll grovel. But if he has to, he'll raise this girl alone. He listens to her breathing for a long, long time and then he tiptoes away and closes the door. He feels like he wants to sit outside the door with a shotgun, if need be, keeping anybody out who's going to try to take her away from him. And meanwhile, he'll think of what to say to Marnie.

Grace is surprised to hear his voice on the phone.

"Patrick," she says, and he tries to gauge by the way she says his name if she's angry that he waited so long. But then when he stammers out his apology, she says, "Oh, Patrick! No, no, no! No apology necessary. It is so good to hear your voice. We so hoped you'd call when you were ready. You've been through so much, my love."

She always called people "my love." He remembers that—and her warm brown eyes. She puts Kerwin on speaker, and they tell him they live in California now, with their other daughter. They trade off telling him things: They are grandparents now. They have a little shrine to Anneliese and they talk about her every day, they say. They've told their grandchildren about her. She stays alive in their house, and with her artwork and her stories.

The Anneliese who visits *them* is their loving daughter, he realizes.

But what surprises him even more is that they are grateful to know that he's well, that his life has continued. He remembers hearing that they had visited him in the hospital when he was in a coma. They have said prayers for him, Kerwin tells him.

"It's so good to hear from you, Patrick," says Grace before they hang up. He apologizes again for not calling sooner, and she says, "We've often wondered where you are, if you've healed. It's lovely to hear that you're moving on with your life. I'm so relieved, my love."

After he hangs up, he takes Bedford for a walk in the cold air and crunchy snow. Funny thing: he hadn't told them he was moving on with his life. They just knew that that's what people do. Because they are healthy and loving, they didn't want to think of him suffering any longer. Funny how that thought had never occurred to him before.

"You're different somehow," says Ariana to him the next evening. "What's happened to you?" She is studying him, squinting her eyes and chewing on her lip. Thinking hard about him. He meets her scrutiny with a good-natured shrug, a first for him.

"Hey, I'm just cleaning the house is all," he says. "That's not so out of character for me, is it? I'm a clean guy most of the time."

He had invited her for dinner earlier, when he'd seen her out on the sidewalk. A spontaneous invitation for dinner. Something he can't remember ever wanting to do before.

"Nooo, I don't think that's it," she says. "You've got like something else going on. It's like you disappeared for months into that studio, and then you emerged as a big old grouch—excuse me for saying it, but it's true. And now you're like normal again."

"I'm never all that normal," he says.

"Hey, by the way, thanks for not giving me a hard time when I let Janelle move in. She's going through some heavy shit."

He's in such a good mood that he doesn't feel the need to point out that he didn't even know that Janelle had officially moved in. He's just assumed the basement apartment is filled up all the time with tons of kids.

"Just a ballpark estimate, how many would you say are living down there these days?"

She laughs and shakes her head. "Basically there's just the two of us. Janelle and me. Although occasionally somebody else might need a night away from home, you know."

"Everybody staying safe and legal?"

She laughs again. Just then Janelle shows up at the door to the kitchen. She has dark brown hair, a blue plaid shirt and jeans leggings, and an enormous belly sticking out in front of her.

"Hi, Patrick," she says. She has a stricken expression on her face, and she's telegraphing something to Ariana with her eyes.

"Wow. Won't be long now!" Patrick says, which is the line he always uses upon sightings of pregnant bellies. He has hoped that it conveys the perfect amount of observation, respect, and even perhaps a sense of optimism.

"Sorry to interrupt. Ari, can I talk to you?"

"Oh, God. Who is it this time—your father or Matt?" Ariana says. "Come on in and sit down. You can tell me about it with Patrick here. He's not a typical guy. He knows how awful men are."

"What?" says Patrick. "Is that supposed to be a compliment?" He looks over at Janelle. "Come on in and have a seat. I just made some tea. You look like you could use a cup of tea."

Naturally she bursts into tears.

"Oh dear, oh dear," he says, but Ariana says, "It's okay, Patrick. She cries all the time, don't you, Janelle? It's a combination of pregnancy hormones and also the fact that her parents are being kind of shitty about things. And Matt wants her to put the baby up for adoption and for neither of them to ever see it again. And this is *after* he said he'd help her raise it."

"Okay," Patrick says. "Tell me the whole thing." He feels he owes it to the universe to listen to any story a woman wants to tell him about pregnancy.

Janelle sinks down in the kitchen chair he holds out for her and sticks her legs out as far as they will go. "Well, so even though we're not really a couple anymore, we had decided we were going to do this cool experimental thing, where we'd live together. It was going to be Matt and his girlfriend and me, and we'd all raise the baby together in Boston while the three of us took turns working and going to school—"

"But the girlfriend, Lulu, now doesn't think this whole arrangement works for her," supplies Ariana. "Which we are not judging her for, are we, Janelle? It would be a tough go if you only later found out she wasn't really into it."

Patrick doesn't say what he's thinking—that this whole plan sounds insane. Like off the charts insane. Not that he's a poster boy for good relationship tips or anything.

Janelle is still weeping softly. He remembers what Marnie had told him about her—that weeping is her default setting.

He pours her a cup of tea, and she says, "I might be judging her. And then my mom said *she* and my dad would keep the baby while I went to school. So okay. But I just got off the phone with her and now *she* said that she's not going to be my Plan B. She told me that she and my dad had a big talk, and they realized they have never gotten to do anything they wanted, and they want to travel. They don't want to be tied down."

"Which we are also not judging," says Ariana.

"Nooo, but why did she then have to start yelling at me? She was saying that I can't look to other people to clean up the mess I've made of my life, and it's time I grew up and realized that I have to *choose* which life I'm going to have: saddling myself with a dependent that I can't really care for, which means turning down my scholarship from BU, or finding people who will adopt my baby and getting on with my life." It takes her forever to get this story out, because she has to keep stopping to cry. Patrick feels his own breath high in his chest. He cracks his knuckles.

"I categorically reject the two-choice view of life," says Ariana. She gets up and goes over and gives Janelle a hug.

"Yeah, well," says Janelle. "Tell my mom that." Patrick hands her a fistful of paper napkins, and she blows her nose. He sips his tea and tries to think of something to say.

Janelle sits there for a few moments, contemplating the tabletop, and then she says, "Well, maybe there is another way. I met this woman on the subway the other day, and she's a counselor, and she said maybe I should look into open adoption, which is a system where I could pick the parents I wanted for the baby, and then I could arrange with them to be part of my baby's life. I could visit and make sure she had a good family life. It's better . . . maybe. At least I wouldn't feel like I was just throwing her away."

"By the way, it's a girl," Ariana says to Patrick, and he nods.

"Are there . . . agencies . . . for this?" Patrick says. His voice sounds like it's coming from far away.

"I'm going to find out. I'm a little bit exhausted by the whole idea. It's already March, and she's due at the end of May, and I'm in school so I don't have a lot of time to interview people." She puts her head down on the table, resting on her arm. "I'm just so tired of it all. Not knowing what's going to happen."

"Hell, I'll take her myself," says Ariana. "*You* can go to school, and Justin and I can take her out on the road with us this summer and we'd videotape people holding her. How would that be?" Ariana gets up and paces around the room, cracking her knuckles.

Patrick says, "Well, *that* seems like a horrible idea!" and Ariana says, "I was *just kidding*, Patrick! Where's your sarcasm gene?"

"It's gotten thrashed out of me," he says. "It wasn't working for me so well with the parenthood gig."

Janelle bursts into a fresh round of tears. Maybe he shouldn't have said the word *parenthood*. She buries her face and lets go with all the sobs. Patrick doesn't know if it would seem creepy to get up and give her a hug, but he can't seem to help himself. He stands up and moves toward her, feeling like he's being carried along by a current that's taking him away somewhere. It's as though some part of him has forgotten that he's not a hugger.

It seems everywhere he looks people are suffering and fighting, experiencing the collateral damage of being alive. Here is this teenager crying in his kitchen, knowing she doesn't have what she needs to raise a baby. And here is Ariana, hurting from her parents' disapproval of her plan for her life. And Fritzie—dear little rebellious, resistant Fritzie—scared of being abandoned, feeling that she has to push the boundaries every single day, to test out whether she can still be loved. That chin of hers, thrust out, and the POW haircut, the lower lip that sticks out and trembles and breaks his heart.

And Marnie. Oh God, Marnie. He thinks maybe he should send her a funny text: *Hey, Marnie. I sent that artsty, angsty guy packing, and regular Patrick is back. Wonders where you are.*

No, that wouldn't work. He has to do better.

He's been crap at being in the world. Looking at all the wrong things. Letting himself seize up with fear. Building guardrails all around himself, using his scars and his sarcasm to scare off any interlopers. Never paying attention to what mattered.

He gazes down, looks at the grain of the wood of Blix's old table, thinks of all the dinners he's had here, first with Blix and her friends, and then with Marnie and all the people she brought in.

Blix had said once to him: "Maybe everything that frightens you, Patrick, is really something helpless in you that needs you to love it."

A thought hits him, like it's the missing piece to a puzzle he didn't even know he was working on.

He could be the dad to Janelle's baby. He and Marnie could adopt her. Maybe.

Could that work? Is he insane? He feels that steady humming in his ears that means he's getting some kind of feeling he's not going to be able to block out. He checks with himself again. He wants this baby. Does he, though? He has never even entertained such a thought before in his life. He rubs his face, hard with both hands. Makes a little sound.

The two girls look up at him absently, then Ariana swivels her head back to Janelle. "We can find you a family, just the right family," she says.

Oh God. He. Wants. This. Baby. He wants the baby and he wants Fritzie and Marnie—all of them here with him, being a family. A put-together family. He feels such a sudden pang of longing, so sharp it's like heartburn. Maybe he should go look for an antacid and ask himself again later if this is really what he wants. Lie down until the feeling passes.

That thought makes him smile. This isn't going to go away. A baby! He feels excited when he thinks about it instead of abject, pull-the-blanket-over-his-head fear. What would it have been like to have known Fritzie as a baby, to see that little flame of humanness in its beginnings? That spunk she has: What did it look like at four weeks of age? At age two? And how did love first show up in her eyes? What would it have felt like to have her stop crying and hold out her arms at the sight of him?

Dude, something says, *you've been wise to be wary of babies. Think of their paraphernalia. Their screaming fits and their drooly chins. The diapers alone are scary as hell.*

But another part of him answers quickly. *Bring it on.* He wants the whole happy catastrophe: mostly he wants Marnie back, but he also wants kids, the dog, the cat, strollers in the hallway, Legos on the stairs, the rows of little shoes, the diaper bag . . . and he can see himself and Marnie in bed with the two children curled around them, sunshine coming through the window, their faces tilted up to his.

He wants Marnie and her laughter and her funny little dances and her genius for magic, and he wants it all so much that his heart is aching. He wants Mercury in retrograde and the universe and Toaster Blix and the homeless people she loves.

"But I want to be able to see her sometime," Janelle is saying. "I want her to have people who will love both of us, you know?"

He looks at her, forgetting that she can't read his thoughts. She doesn't see the yes that's running through him, pinging his nerve endings. She doesn't know yet that he could love her baby and love her, too.

The silence in the room roars in his ears. It's like the time at YMCA camp when he was at the top of the diving board, staring down at the water so impossibly far away. Everybody else had already dived, and it was his turn. He wanted so badly to turn back, to crawl down the ladder. But the longer he stood there, the clearer it was that he was going to have to dive. It was as though he was being pulled toward the water by a force that was stronger than any fear he had. But that moment before the dive—now *that* was the moment. When you could still turn back, but you knew you weren't going to. That's when the courage attached itself to you.

That's what this is.

"Janelle," he says quietly. He has to interrupt their conversation. Both sets of eyes turn to him, questioning. "I need to talk with Marnie, but let me just ask you something . . ." he begins.

And then he says the thing he needs to say. The thing that's going to change his life.

CHAPTER FORTY-ONE

PATRICK

Later, he'll wonder why he didn't see the whole thing coming. He'll go over the day in his mind, the way people always do after a tragedy or a near-tragedy. "What were the signs I missed?" they ask themselves. "Why didn't I look a little more closely?"

But for now, the morning is just a regular morning, perhaps even a happier than normal morning. He made a huge decision last night, and he still feels the high of possibility. He makes breakfast for Fritzie and himself—toast and oatmeal. The toast does not fly out of the toaster and land on the floor, which makes him smile. Also: Fritzie gets herself completely dressed all on her own, and she comes out of her room on time with her backpack already filled up with everything she needs for the day.

She has her homework, and she's brushed her teeth, and she has her pencils and her notebook, and her phone, and her shoes are tied. She shows him that she's even wearing matching socks. She has a big smile on her face. When he lifts her backpack off the table, when it's time to leave, he says, "Whoa, this is heavy."

Later, that will be a clue.

Another clue will be that when the bus comes rumbling down the street, she clings to him for a long moment. She kisses him on both cheeks, and then she does a butterfly kiss, where she flutters her eyelashes against his eyelashes.

And when she gets on the bus, she sits by the window and looks down at him, waving and smiling. "Thank you, Patrick!" she yells out the window.

Thank you?

He walks back to the house, taking out his phone while he walks. It's time to get Marnie back, and he is so ready.

He's decided to start off by texting her. Funny, humble, clever texts. That's the way he won her over in the first place, so it's bound to work now. She'll see that he's back to being his old self and that he loves her. Then he'll beg her to come back home, where he will show her how much he's changed.

Marnie, he types. *There are people here in Brooklyn who are not meeting their soul mates because you are not here to run across the park (or restaurant, or wherever) and introduce them. Mayor is declaring state of emergency. #LoveEmergency*

There is no answer. Of course there's no answer. It's the stupidest text ever.

Ten minutes later, he writes: *That didn't sound like what I meant to say. The truth is that the #LoveEmergency is happening in our kitchen.*

Nothing. Nada. He types a heart and sends that.

He makes himself a cup of coffee, does some knee bends and boxing moves. Feeds the cat and dog. Washes up the breakfast dishes. Stares out of the window. Wonders if she'll want to get one of those deluxe strollers, or if she'll want the tiny, foldable kind that looks like an umbrella. That is just one of *hundreds* of discussions they'll have.

He types: *(Clearing throat here, beginning again.) I miss you so much. I don't think I can go on without you. People here in this house think eight weeks is too long without you. #Me #Fritzie #Bedford #Roy*

It may sound selfish, but we voted and we think we need you more than your dad does at this point, he types. That was risky. Maybe her dad has had a relapse.

And anyway she's not going to answer him. She's mad. She may be actually done with him.

I love you, and I'm sorry, he writes.

But now he has to stop this. Step away from the phone. But he can't help himself from typing one more:

Please forgive me.

He slips the phone into his pocket, and then to his surprise, it makes a beeping sound, and he leaps in midair. Feels his pulse quicken. There's a voice message from a missed call. He can't imagine how he missed a call when he's been standing right here, holding the thing in his hand. But there it is. He's shaking as he presses the buttons to hear the message. It's got to be her.

But it's not her. It's the Brooklyn Kind School. Maybelle's voice. "Hi, Patrick. Just wanted to check in with you this morning to see if Fritzie is sick again. You didn't call in this morning to report her absent. Sure hope she's not having another bout of flu. Let her know we miss her."

And that's it: he thinks he might die right then and there.

Fritzie didn't show up at school, and nothing that has ever happened to him before has prepared him for this moment. The air has gone out of him.

His fingers punch in Marnie's phone number, and to his surprise, she answers.

"Patrick, what in the *hell* is going on with you? These texts!" she says. Not even "hello."

"It's Fritzie," he says, all in a rush. "She never made it to school today. I put her on the bus, and then Maybelle called and said she isn't there."

Marnie is silent for a moment. "Is this for real?"

"Yes! God. Yes."

"Listen. Call Maybelle. Maybe there's a mistake when they did the attendance. That must happen sometimes. Don't panic yet."

Right. Of course, he thinks. He hangs up and calls Maybelle, who says she'll make sure and call back—and sure enough, she calls back five minutes later and tells him there is no Fritzie at Brooklyn Kind School today.

"Where might she have gone?" she asks him. "She's impulsive, so we should try to think of something she might have decided on her own."

"I'm calling the police," he says, and Maybelle says, "Right. That's a good idea."

He gets off the phone and thinks to call Fritzie's cell phone first. His breathing matches each thrumming sound as it rings. Two times . . . three times . . . four . . . five . . . There's no answer, which of course there wouldn't be, because most likely the kidnappers who have taken her have thrown her phone into the East River to hide any evidence. He thinks he's going to throw up.

Marnie calls him back. "So? Is she at school after all?"

"No. She's not."

"Okay, Patrick. I think you should call the police. And we have to think good thoughts. Not go into a huge panic. This is Fritzie, after all. She'd fight off anybody who tried to kidnap her. She's most likely had some crazy idea and has gone off to do it—"

"Marnie, I-I'm flattened by this." He's surprised at how calm his voice sounds to his own ears, even though his whole brain seems to have gone on red alert. He remembers this feeling. He's moving through a fog. It's as though the world has so many sharp edges, and the worst thing are the edges he can't see to focus on.

"I know."

"Please, can you come back home?" he hears himself say from very far away. "Not just for this! For *everything*. Marnie, I can't tell—I mean, this isn't the time to tell you how much I love you and how much you mean to me, because I have to call the police now. But—could you come?"

"Call the police, Patrick."

"Wait," he says. Something is beeping in his ear. "There's a call on the other line."

"This is Officer Timothy Pettigrew with the Kennedy Airport police unit," says the voice on the phone when Patrick clicks over. "To whom am I speaking?"

He tries to explain who he is, says it all too fast, has to repeat it. Tongue is suddenly all too thick. Can't remember how it is a person can breathe and talk at the same time. The police are calling *him*? *Kennedy Airport—what? So . . . kidnappers? Traffickers, then? IS SHE ALIVE?*

"We have your daughter, Fritzie Delaney, here in custody, and we're requesting that you come down . . ."

"The *airport*?" he says. His breath is high in his chest. "Oh my God. Is she all right?" So it *was* kidnappers. Traffickers. Smuggling her somewhere. His breath leaves his body.

The officer seems to be talking to someone else. He can hear the muffled sounds of voices; some kind of explaining is going on.

Patrick has died three times by now. He's surprised to realize that he's now slumped on the floor. Bedford has come over to investigate. "Is she all right?" he says again, yelling this time, and then Officer Whoever the Hell His Name Is returns to the phone and says, "She's fine, sir. A little scared, but she's all right. She was trying to get on a flight, but she got stopped in the security line. She was pretending to be with a family of four, but when they went through security, they told the TSA worker that she wasn't with them, so our officer went over and took her into custody."

So no kidnappers. Or maybe the family of four *was* the kidnappers, and then Fritzie outsmarted—

"I'll be there," says Patrick. "May I talk to her?"

"Fritzie," says the officer. "Your father is on his way, but first he wants to talk to you."

There's the squawking of radios in the background, and then he hears her say quite clearly, "I don't want to talk to him."

"What?" he says to the cop. "Why not?"

"It's just what she says," says the cop. Then he lowers his voice, changes his tone. "I've got kids like this myself. Especially one of them. If I had to guess, I'd say she's embarrassed right now. This was a pretty big mistake. Guess she thought she was going to see her mom maybe? Had her plans wrecked. She'll be real happy to see you when you're here."

Her mom. Fritzie was heading to *Italy*? He has so many questions he needs to have answered this second. He's tempted to ask the cop, but he knows he can't. How had she planned all this? Did she have a ticket? And how did she get to the airport in the first place? And why, why, why was she thinking that going to see Tessa was going to solve anything? Is that who she's been pining for? Do kids always run back to the neglectful parent?

"So, Mr. Delaney, if you'll bring her birth certificate with you when you come. Just so we know we're releasing her to the right person."

Her birth certificate.

Does he even have that? After he hangs up, he calls Marnie back. She listens silently as he tells her the whole story.

"Okay," she says when he finally winds down.

"I thought we were doing so well," he says. "I thought I could do this job. We did homework, bedtimes, guessing games, playtime. We cooked. It was all good. She was sick—so sick for days and days, and I didn't sleep, I stayed by her side—"

"Patrick," she says, interrupting him. "I'm sure you've been brilliant at all this. And I'm coming. I already made a reservation, and I'll get in tonight. But you have to know something: I'm not coming because you asked me to. I know we're not together anymore. I'm coming because I want to see Fritzie. And I'm probably going to come right back here. Just so you know."

"Okay," he says. He wonders if she was being sarcastic about the brilliant part. "Thank you for that."

"Not a problem," she says crisply. "I want to see her."

"Do you happen to know where her birth certificate might be?"

She says it's in the top drawer in the kitchen, the one near the toaster. Like this was something she had told him before. She keeps some important stuff there. He finds the envelope containing it while he's still on the phone with her. His guts feel like they're in a knot. He can't seem to bring himself to hang up the phone.

"I love you," he says. "Thank you for helping me through this. And I don't think I can live without you."

"Patrick, I am really, really mad at you."

"I know. I know you are."

"I guess she really has been missing her mom all this time," Marnie says. "I hope Tessa steps up here. Otherwise this is just going to be so sad."

"It is sad," says Patrick. "Now would you please go get on that plane? I think if you miss it, I might actually die."

The airport police office has a big counter and uncomfortable plastic chairs and officers coming in and out, some filling out paperwork, while others are drinking coffee or talking. One cop is standing with his foot up on his desk chair while he talks on a cell phone. Radios are crackling, cutting in and out with the static news of police business. A German shepherd, all harnessed up for duty, lies on the floor with his eyes open. He raises his head when Patrick comes in.

Fritzie is sitting in a black plastic chair, with her feet in their scuffed-up boots not touching the ground, her legs swinging back and forth. Patrick can't believe how tiny she looks. She is such a force in his life, so loud and powerful that he is shocked to see that she's really such a little girl, so small in that busy, government-business room, with her crazy haircut. Big saucer eyes, fingers in her mouth, looking around at all the activity. Waiting for him with an empty granola wrapper next to her on the chair.

When she sees Patrick rounding the corner, her lower lip starts to tremble, and then she puts her face in her hands and brings her knees up and scoots backward in the chair.

He makes his way over to her, squats down next to her, and puts his arms around her. After a moment of hesitation, she buries her head in his neck. He feels her shaking, and her tears are wet against his skin.

"Hey. It's okay, it's okay," he says. His own eyes are watering, too.

She's whispering. "I'm sorry, I'm sorry, I'm sorry."

"Sssh," he says. "It's okay. I'm here now."

He sees a police officer approaching them and then backing off, letting them be. Patrick is grateful for that. He's not sure he can compose himself just yet.

"What were you doing?" he whispers. He rubs his thumb against her cheek.

"I just wanted to find Marnie for you."

He pulls back and looks at her face. "You were trying to get to Marnie? I thought you were trying to go to Italy."

"No. I wanted to go get Marnie back. For you." She looks down at her fingers and starts pulling at them. "You weren't going to get her to come back. You know you weren't."

"Ahhh, Fritzie, that wasn't your job. Not your job at all." He takes her hand. "You—you scared me so much. I've been out of my mind with worrying about you! You know that, right? I was terrified when I heard you'd gone to the airport."

"I had to do it."

"No, you didn't have to do it. You should have told me how you felt. We're a team, remember? We agreed to talk everything over. How did you think I was going to feel when I discovered you were gone?"

"I knew you'd be worried, but then it would all work out okay because Marnie would call you and say I was there with her, and then we would come back together."

"No," he says. "That's not how that works." He sits back on his haunches and looks at her.

"Are you gonna keep me?" Her eyes are enormous, all black pupils, boring into his.

"Am I going to . . . *keep you*?"

"Yeah. Are you gonna take me back home with you and keep me?"

"Fritzie." Her face is smeared with snot and tears and something that he hopes is granola pieces. "Of course I'm going to keep you. Did you think I was going to leave you here?"

She sticks her fingers in her mouth. "I thought you might be so mad at me."

"Look at me. I don't *get* mad. And I wouldn't ever be that mad."

"Yes. Patrick, do you remember when you first met me, and you didn't love me? You didn't want to keep me, and I was your daughter, but you didn't want me there."

He shakes his head, runs his hands through his hair, entertains an irrational hope that the cop isn't hearing all this. "Yeah, well, I'm— Fritzie, wait. You really thought I'd just leave you *here* at the airport?"

"Marnie loved me, and I miss her, and *you* miss her, and you were *not* doing it right, Patrick. You know you weren't saying the things to get her to come back!"

"Never mind all that. Did you get a plane ticket for this, or were you just going to charm your way onto the plane?"

339

"Yes. I had a ticket. The policeman took it."

"But how—how did you get it? You're *eight*."

"On the computer. I saw her do the buying on the computer, and I went in and did it, too."

"On her credit card . . . ?"

"I saw that in her drawer."

"Oh, Fritzie."

"I know. That was bad, wasn't it?"

"Not the best, I guess," he says. He lets out a long breath, tries to think of what to do.

She's chewing on her lip, looking around the police station. "The dog here is pretty nice."

"Yeah." He looks over at the German shepherd lying ominously on the floor, pretending to be resting but obviously at high alert. If Patrick made one false move, he has no doubt that dog would have him in its jaws. Leave it to Fritzie to have made friends with it. He stands up and his knees make a creaking sound. "Well, let's get out of here. See what we have to do to get them to release you." He hopes this next part is going to be easy, but he doesn't hold out a lot of hope, knowing what he does about airports, security, rules, and children's welfare.

"Does . . . Marnie know?" she says. "What I did?"

"Yeah. She knows. She's already got a ticket to come home tonight."

She claps her hands and then evidently remembers she's on shaky ground and says meekly, "Is she mad?"

"Nobody's mad. You act like we're these angry monsters. We're shocked, yes. But we're glad you're safe. We were scared. There's a big difference."

The police officer comes over. Officer Pettigrew, it says on the tag. "Quite an adventurous day for you, missy," he says. "You're lucky to have this guy as your daddy, I'll tell you that." He shakes his head, and Patrick's afraid they're now going to have to hear tales of things Officer Pettigrew has seen in this job, but at the last instant, Pettigrew seems to think better of it. Patrick knows he's probably relieved that this particular story has an okay ending: nobody's raging, the kid is wanted, and security managed to do its job and not let her fly across country unaccompanied. Nevertheless, for a moment Patrick fears that there is going to be other questioning, talk of fraud and child neglect—who knows what could be drummed up?

And here it comes. "Sir, I'll just need to see your identification and the birth certificate of the child. And then you can sign these forms."

He gets the birth certificate out of his pocket and then remembers it's not going to have his name on it. He starts a bumbling explanation about how he's not married to the mother—but the cop looks around and then quietly says it's okay. "I can see you two belong together. Same eyes and hair. Same blubbering tears." He smiles and pretends to wipe away nonexistent tears from his own face.

Patrick opens the envelope and hands him the birth certificate anyway . . . and there, on the line where it says *Father*, there he sees his own name. Typed there. *Patrick Delaney.*

And just like that, there's a crack in the awful, and he feels the flood of . . . something . . . love, maybe, hope . . . rushing in.

Fritzie holds his hand as they walk out of the airport to catch their Uber. By the time they get there, he's actually kind of glad to see she looks spunky and defiant again.

"Don't ever do this kind of thing again," he says. "Okay?" His voice comes out all croaky. "Please?"

She squeezes his hand. "I hope not, Patrick."

Which, for some reason, makes him smile so big. He squeezes her hand.

CHAPTER
FORTY-TWO
MARNIE

I have had nineteen separate talks with myself since I talked to Patrick on the phone. All designed to harden myself up. Which is what you have to do when you've gotten yourself all entangled with a man who can't love.

He's been terrible, really. And I can't afford to be hurt like this all the time. A dead woman has his heart, and no matter what he says, he's not really interested in coming back to life, not on any kind of permanent basis. He doesn't want children, or parties, or public displays of affection, or random conversations with people on the subway. He has to be dragged into any social interaction—and so what if he then likes them okay? So what if he's now proven he can cope with parenthood on his own for weeks at a time? So the hell what? It proves nothing except that when he is cornered, when he is *forced* to endure something, he can do it. But oh, how he fights it. He doesn't want to do anything outside of his comfort zone, anything the rest of the population thinks of as regular, ordinary life. And somehow that makes it worse, that he *can do* it, but won't unless he's made to.

And—I may have to face the fact that although I got to have a little four-year-long adventure in Brooklyn, I may well belong here in Florida. Best Buds is doing fine without me. Kat was always the one who could keep the business part going, and Ariana is running the Frippery, according to all reports. They are fine.

And . . . there are some advantages to being back at home. It's definitely warm here, unlike March in New York. And Natalie is being nicer to me, and it's great to be with my nieces again. Built-in access to children who know the best uses of an auntie. (When they get a little older, I'll be the one who brings them gum. I know the auntie rules.)

And my parents. They are working their way back to a happy marriage, it seems. I don't want to say I see sparkles around them, because that would be a lie; I don't see sparkles at all anymore. But when they're together, it just feels right again, like something in the world is set back on its rightful perch. My mother is still bloomingly herself, not hiding from my father's opinion of her or her purchases or her dinner choices, any of it. He's stopped criticizing her. They have both stopped bickering, and I see them sometimes holding hands.

At night, we three play a cutthroat game of triple solitaire to see who has to get up and do the dishes. My father usually loses—probably because he had a little surgery and can't move his arms so fast, but my mother says it's fine, we *should* let him do the dishes. He has about forty years of dishwashing responsibilities to catch up on.

I could stay here in my old childhood room for a while, and then decide what to do. See what my heart really wants, where it wants to take me next.

Maybe the lesson I got from Blix ends up being that you have to learn to listen to your own dear heart, go where it takes you.

And another thing I now know is that I am not constitutionally able to be with a man who's aloof. I need someone who loves me day in and day out, who isn't hauling around a whole sack of reasons for not being with me. I need someone who wants a big, big life with me, who's not trying to shrink life down to its smallest, most manageable component. I don't want a life that is so small it could fit in your back pocket.

"I'll be back," I say to my parents and to Natalie and the girls.

Then, as I'm just about to go through security, my mother slips me Blix's book of spells to take with me on the plane.

I look at the book and sigh. "This doesn't matter," I say. "I've read every one of those spells and all of Blix's notes, too, and I'm done here."

Her face looks very, very serious all of a sudden. "Listen to me. Don't count out magic," she says. She takes me by the shoulders and stares right into my eyes. "I don't know what the hell is wrong with you right now, but this could be your moment."

Believe me, it isn't lost on me that *my mother* is the one pushing me toward magic, and that I'm the one looking at the book of spells like it's something that isn't going to fit in my carry-on bag.

I take it anyway, and I read it again on the plane.

Here's my unbiased review of the book of spells, delivered at long last: it's an entertaining read, with some remarkable concoctions, seemingly designed to test one's determination and patience more than anything else. And Blix's notes, sprinkled throughout the book? Well, they show a colorful, lovely, joyful, optimistic, and halfway-crazy woman who lived in the real world with all the rest of us, but who perhaps possessed an outsized dose of hope that I simply don't share. No one does.

End of story.

By the time I get off the plane, tired and full of salty airline pretzels, Coca-Cola, and shortbread cookies, and limping along under the cloud of a big headache, I am tired and sad.

But then I get to the baggage claim area, and to my astonishment, there are Patrick and Fritzie, both of them jumping up and down, being ridiculous. I'd texted him my flight time, but I never thought he'd show up for it. Much less bring Fritzie! She's doing her straight-up-and-down jumps, like she's spring-loaded from the ground, and he's standing right behind her, smiling and imitating her. They look like a matched set of something. Salt and pepper shakers, maybe. Father and daughter.

"We came to meet you!" yells Fritzie. "I was just here today already, because I wanted to fly on an airplane, but then we left, and when we were at home, Patrick said we should come back to get you as a surprise, so you wouldn't have to take an Uber! We were just going to text you to tell you in case you were about to call Uber yourself! And then I said, 'Here she is!'"

I hold myself tight when he sweeps me up in a big hug, and rocks me back and forth, and says close into my ear, "Oh my God, she never stops talking for one second." He's laughing his deep Patricky chuckle that I haven't heard in about forever, while Fritzie grasps my hand and pats my arm. It feels like it's been so very long since I've seen these two characters, and at first I can barely handle looking at them. It hurts, like staring at the sun. And then I just want to slow down time and walk around them and look at the myriad ways they aren't the same people I left behind. She's got hardly any hair and looks like she's grown about five inches taller and maybe ten times more sure of herself, and he's all mushy and clearly has had the bejesus scared out of him, as my mother used to say.

I am so mad at him, even though he keeps smiling and taking my hand and saying funny things. It turns out that Fritzie *wasn't* trying to get to Italy to see Tessa, they both tell me, talking a mile a minute. It was me.

Me.

"I was going to Florida! I wanted to go to Florida!" she says while we're waiting for my bag to come along on the baggage carousel, and then, "Look at me, Marnie, how I've learned to do a cartwheel even better than before." She holds her arms in midair and is about to flip herself over, but Patrick catches her arm and, laughing, tells her maybe not in the baggage claim area. At home. Cartwheels coming up at home.

"Anyway, Marnie, Patrick wanted you back so much, and you know how I knew it? Because he was sad about you and also he was smelling your pillow all the time! Every time I'd go into your room, he would have *your* pillow over his head—"

I look at him.

"Wait a minute!" says Patrick. "I did not!"

"You did that. You know you did!" She is jumping up and down again. "Anyway, he wasn't doing *anything* right to get you to come back home! And so I decided that *I* would come and tell you myself!"

"But that wasn't so smart, and you'll never do anything like that again," he says.

She smiles at me and takes my hand while he goes off to grab my suitcase. "It was a little bit smart," she whispers. "Because here you are."

CHAPTER
FORTY-THREE
PATRICK

It's nearly eleven o'clock at night by the time Patrick's heart stops beating at metronome speed. She's here now, back with him, and he's got a lot of work to do with her. He can tell by the way she looks sort of muted—surprised and muted, both. Like she's holding back 93 percent of her personality. So unlike her. Did he break her? Maybe he broke her. He vacillates between hope and despair that he has the skills to fix this. Him, and his bad personality.

For the last hour, after eating delivery pizza in the kitchen, the three of them have been lying on what used to be his and Marnie's bed—and every now and then the thought flickers through his brain that he might be consigned back to the futon tonight, the futon he folded up. They've been talking very, very carefully about everything that went on while they were apart: all the gentle, easy-to-talk-about things, that is. Patrick keeps steering the conversation away from minefields. Marnie's suitcase is still packed, on the floor, and she's propped up on the pillows while Fritzie lies alongside her, scratching Bedford's exposed belly. Bedford is exhausted after his welcoming dog-love dance, when he zipped through the apartment like he couldn't contain his joy in one place, in what Marnie called a "perfect puppy blowout."

"So," says Fritzie. "Now that we're in a family meeting, I've been thinking, and I've decided we should all three get married to each other. What do you think, guys? Let's have a vote."

Patrick clears his throat. "Marnie and I will take it from here, Fritzie. It's time for you to go to bed."

"But we should talk about this!" Fritzie says. "I know how to make a whole bunch of things happen, so I want to be in the talking."

"Nope, not tonight. To bed, Fritz," he says.

She rolls around on the bed, pretending she's gone unconscious, and Bedford stands up over her and starts licking her face, and she laughs and kicks and waggles her head back and forth. Marnie has to get up to keep her glass of wine from being knocked over.

"Come on, come on," Patrick says. "It's late. We'll hang out tomorrow."

He can feel Marnie watching him as he scoops Fritzie up into his arms and carries her into her room.

"Marnie!" Fritzie calls over his shoulder. "Tell him you want me to stay up and do some more talking! Insist on it!"

Marnie laughs, and hearing that sound again hits him so hard right between his ribs, right at the solar plexus, that for a moment it takes everything for him not to fall to the floor. He tucks Fritzie into bed, kisses her good night, and turns out the light.

"Don't make her mad, Patrick," she whispers to him.

"You're off duty now, sport," he says. "Go to sleep."

And then he stops outside the door and closes his eyes for just a moment before he goes back to Marnie, who is no longer in the bedroom. Of course.

He finds her in the kitchen folding up the pizza box for the recycling bin.

"That was some exemplary bedtime maneuvering," she says.

"Yeah, she's a weasel."

"No." She laughs. "I meant you. You were kind of . . . parent-like."

"Yep. That's me. I'm thinking of starting a parenting podcast called *The Most Clueless Dad Ever*, where I explain that children *like it* when you make them go to bed. Did you know?" He's smiling his teasing smile. "Kids like boundaries. Boundary after boundary after boundary. You gotta become a regular boundary factory these days to have a happy kid."

"Uh-huh. This said by a man whose kid just today tried to get on a plane by herself."

"Yep. Exactly. That's what makes it real. I've been in the trenches, baby! Another podcast episode would feature the news that if your child cuts all her hair off, you need to ask yourself if it's a fashion statement or a cry for more boundaries."

"Interesting."

"And if they take off for the airport one morning when you put them on the bus to school . . ." He moves toward her, cautiously. She's not exactly inviting him to hold her. But who could blame her?

"Yes?" she says. "What does that signify? Boundaries again?"

"That," he says, "was the culmination of the fun Let's Test Patrick's Sanity program we had going on around here for about a month."

"She is certainly . . ."

He waits, but she doesn't seem interested in finishing that sentence. She turns and puts the forks and knives in the sink.

"Yes," he says. "She certainly is. She's all of it: brave and smart and kind and loving and generous and funny as hell, and she's going to need about forty years of therapy, I think, to recover from this childhood. And lots of loving kindness. And stability. Loads and loads of stability. Bedtimes and you and me both here. Probably we'll need to keep a close watch on the scissors as time goes on. And the computer. And the credit cards. Probably more stuff I haven't thought of yet."

"Really," says Marnie.

"So, um, how would you say this is going?" he says.

"This?"

"Marnie, I'm dying. I'm falling at your feet. I sent you the stupidest texts in the world this morning—which seems like a lifetime ago now—all because I thought I could be clever and funny and maybe you'd remember what you used to love about me. But now I know that I don't want to text you anymore. I want to look at you face-to-face, and I want to hold you, and hear your voice telling me every single thing you're thinking and feeling and everything about your parents and your sister and all your matchmaking projects, and I don't want to keep talking nonsense, so please stop me, and *you* start. Tell me how you feel. Start there and just keep going. Please."

"Well, first of all, I don't have matchmaking projects anymore," she says slowly. "That turns out to be a bit of a mistake, I think it's safe to say. All that Blix-thinking-I-was-magic stuff."

"Please," he whispers. "The toaster can hear you. It would be devastated to hear you're not matchmaking anymore."

To his surprise, she laughs. And then their eyes meet. The way her eyes linger on his makes him shiver.

Emboldened, he says, "I was kind of wondering if we might move this discussion to the bathtub. This is presumptuous of me, perhaps, but I don't know if you recall that our establishment here features a gigantic, claw-footed tub that I've taken the liberty of outfitting with some bubble bath and about a hundred tea light candles. I recall we've had some of our best staff meetings in there. Would you consider it too forward if I suggested we adjourn to there?"

She looks a little hesitant, he thinks, but then she swallows and says, "Well. I guess so. Especially if your tub is all that you say it is. Really, claw feet?"

"Really claw feet," he says. "Much like my own." He sticks out one foot, which he only recently groomed, so he knows the toenails are exemplary. "And not to try to make a whole bunch of decisions in one night . . ." he says, "but since you've agreed to the tub thing, I was also sort of hoping after that you might marry me."

She looks wary but amused, which is not exactly what he was hoping for, but it's not the worst thing either. "Hmm," she says. "A fascinating question, but even in the best of cases—which this is totally *not*—I think it might be too late tonight to get an officiant over here."

"That probably wasn't the most romantic proposal anybody ever offered," he says. "I really should have thought of something more elegant."

"Noooo," she says. "I thought it was very Patricky, actually. Completely out of left field and without much context."

"Ha ha," he says. He goes tentatively toward her and holds out his hands, and she comes into his arms. It's awkward at first, and then he pulls her closer, and after a beat of hesitation, she responds, and so he kisses her soft, warm, familiar mouth, and then reaches up to touch her hair. And then, at last, he closes his eyes.

When he can speak again, he says, "Um, why isn't this the best of cases?"

"Well, obviously because this proposal is coming from you missing me so much. Which may be simply a temporary state." She whispers in his ear, "It's not really real."

"It is real. It's not temporary. I'm a beaten man. I know that I can't go on without you."

"Maybe I don't want a beaten man," she says lightly.

"Okay, rephrasing. I'm a changed man."

"What's gotten into you, Patrick? What changed you?" She pulls back and looks at him closely. "Really. What happened? Are you just sick of doing childcare? Are you lonely at last?"

"Could we adjourn to the tub? It's kind of a long story. I'm going to need to have my clothes off for this one."

"You are, huh?" she says.

She goes with him, and he helps her unbutton and unsnap and unzip everything, which she allows—but he can tell she's still holding back. She doesn't lean into him. She keeps her eyes open, fastened on the ceiling. He loses his breath at the sight of her naked in front of him, has to take a deep breath. Maybe the bath wasn't such a great idea. He may wreck everything by jumping on her. And it's too soon for that. Her wariness hasn't gone away, and he doesn't blame her, but he also has no freaking idea how to shift the mood, except maybe he needs to stop being so jokey and tell her everything. So he does.

It starts like a rickety train going up a mountain. He tells her he loves her. And then he tells her the rest: how the horror of the fire never left him; how he would wake up in the middle of the night hearing Anneliese screaming; how in some kind of really screwed up way, the more he let himself fall in love with Marnie the louder those screams became. How scared he was that he was a man who wouldn't ever be able to love.

Real, true words. And now he has to get to the hard part.

CHAPTER FORTY-FOUR

MARNIE

Rule Number One of Seeing a Man You're Broken Up With: do not agree to take a bath with him.

That should be obvious, I know. Probably the dating rule books don't even mention it as a caution. Any ninny would know that you need to keep your clothes on so you have your wits about you. Bad enough that he's looking at you and *looking at you*, and that you know him well enough to read all that love on his face. And on his body. It takes everything to keep reminding yourself that what he's feeling is *love now*, not love he'll remember next time when he's unhappy, or when his dead girlfriend rises up in his head and marches him back to the spaceship.

But here we are anyway, climbing in the tub, our old place of comfort, and he's determined to tell me a bunch of stuff, which judging from the urgent look in his eyes, I probably need to hear. He sits in the back of the tub, and I lean back against him. Too much of my skin is touching too much of his, I think. It's affecting my ability to focus on what he's saying.

And the more he talks, the more I get irritated. I turn my head around and glare at him. "Why didn't you trust me to talk about it with me? That's what I don't get," I say.

"Because . . . because, damn it, I came from people who settled the West and plowed the fields and minded their own business and didn't know how to talk about their feelings and so never showed me how that was done, and because I thought I was supposed to always be strong, and because I knew it was time I got over this, and because I loved you so much, and because I *knew* at some level it was ridiculous, and that I had so much to be grateful for, and why couldn't I let myself feel it?"

"Okayyyy," I say. I lean back again. "Believe it or not, Patrick, I actually have the capacity to understand all that."

"And then . . . well, it got so much worse. I was being dragged under. It was like being crazy. Voices inside my head, blaming me." He swallows and drags his hand through the bathwater, as an illustration. His hand grazes my breast, and I jump. I have to bite my lip, and he moves his hand away. "I think . . . I think that completing those paintings—and those sculptures—although it didn't feel like it at the time, now I think maybe it was me healing. Only to do it, I lost sight of everything that was important."

He leans down and kisses my neck.

I pull away and turn and look at him, mad all over again. "I couldn't reach you. What good is love that goes away when there's a big problem? That's what I want to know."

"Marnie, I swear to you it didn't go away. You were always the important thing I was trying to fight my way back to. You're so different from anyone I've ever known. You're Christmas morning and a Fourth of July parade both happening at once, and you have so much optimism and joy and love. You always think the best of everybody, and you want the tallest Christmas tree and the biggest crowds around the table, and the creamiest ice cream cones, and the longest, sweetest, slowest kisses—and for some reason, you see sparkles when you look at me, so how could I possibly tell you how far down I had fallen? And how fucked up I was? I'd look at you living life and making plans and I would feel like I was at the bottom of a well. Don't you get it? You're a happiness genius."

"A happiness genius? I don't think that's a thing." I lean back against him.

"A happiness genius is obviously a thing. And I was a happiness school dropout. And when I realized that I had pushed you away, and that it was totally my fault that I had to live without you, I was . . . well, I lost my mind. I can't do that. I can't go back there."

The tap is dripping slowly. *Plink. Plink. Plink.*

We're silent for a while, and then I say, "How can I possibly believe in this?"

"I guess I just need you to trust me. I'm willing to wait for as long as it takes. I'll do my time in love jail, if you want." He swirls his hands through the bathwater again, turns on the tap with his toe to warm it up. In a different voice, he says, "I've been through worse. Like, while you were gone, Fritzie got really, really sick—the kind of sick where I, at least, thought she might die. Like really, seriously die."

"What? You didn't tell me that part."

"I couldn't tell you. It took all of me to take care of her. I sat by her bed trying to get her to drink liquids. I *literally* thought I'd snuffed out another person I loved. And I think Bedford and Roy might have agreed; they sat right there, too. Days of it. And when she didn't die—I don't know, I guess part of the relief I felt was that I'm not a toxic human-destroying monster who should be forced to wear a warning label on his back. Also, I figured out that absolutely everything is going to be lost at some time in the future—all of this, even Blix's wonderful bathtub—and that I can't let myself live in total fear of that happening.

Turns out I'm one of the survivors. And as you pointed out one time, that's a good thing, surviving. I could see my life again. I can take care of us, Marnie. I can do my share and more. When you let me out of the love jail, of course."

I shiver, suddenly aroused by him, and he feels it, and smiles.

"Um, we'll get to that in a minute," he says. "A couple more things you need to know. I never stopped loving you. I just stopped feeling like my love could make you happy. But I'm ready to feel pleasure in things again. I'd like to sign up for a few remedial courses from the happiness genius. And—" He sucks in his breath, waits a beat, and then says, "Well, maybe I'm a big idiot to mention this now, when it's so soon, but I'm thinking I'd like to tell Tessa I want to keep Fritzie full-time. Would you . . . want to be here with me for that? I mean, could we raise her together, do you think?"

I turn to look at his eyes. They are holding mine, like this is the most important question ever.

"You really think we could keep her?" I say.

"I think Tessa would be only too happy to have that be the case. I know this is going to feel like a complete reversal for me, but I'm ready for a family. I don't think I can give her up at this point. *And* I think I want the whole nine yards—the boppers and the sippies and the stroller and the . . ."

"Fritzie is too old for a sippy cup."

"I know," he says. "Funny you should mention that. Because there's something else I want to talk to you about." He turns me around gently now so I'm facing him. I can see his Adam's apple going up and down. He puts his hands on my shoulders and looks into my eyes so hard that I can't look away. His beautiful, luminous face—the face I've missed so much—brings tears to my eyes.

"This is the thing I want to tell you," he says. "I love you, Marnie MacGraw, and I want to spend my life with you, and I want us to have a baby. But seeing as we can't have our own DNA do that little trick for us, I have another plan." He swallows, closes his eyes. "Sooo I talked to Janelle . . ."

I can barely breathe. "Janelle," I say.

"Yes, and she wants to give us her baby in an open adoption—that is, if you want to do that," he says. "She and I have talked about it, and we've already got somebody in mind who can help us draw up the papers—that is, if you agree. This is all a big shock, I know, and maybe you want to think about it. We have some time. Her baby isn't due until May . . ." He goes on for a bit about the legality and how he came to this decision, and what it might mean for Janelle and what it would mean for us. But my head is spinning, and all my thoughts are so loud that I can't take in all this extraneous stuff because I'm thinking, *I am going to be the mother of a baby.* Patrick and I are going to have a baby.

He finally stops talking because I'm crying so hard and hugging him, and he puts his forehead against mine and we stare into each other's eyes, except we're so close it looks like he has one giant eyeball. One giant, all-seeing, all-knowing, unblinking eyeball.

"Are you *sure*?" I whisper, unable to stop crying and unable to pull away and blow my nose, so my whole face is ridiculously gross.

"Are *you* sure?" he whispers back. "Because I also think we should make ourselves official and get married . . . if we're going to have all these children, you know."

"But, Patrick, there's just one thing that makes us not quite the perfect fit," I say. I wipe my nose on the washcloth.

He groans. "Name it. Please."

"Perhaps you're not aware that I'm going to need a wedding that has actual people attending it."

"*I* want that," he says, so quickly that I laugh.

"And not just a ceremony at city hall. I want a wedding on our rooftop."

"Yes."

"With guests. And lots of different kinds of cakes."

"All the people we want who can fit on our rooftop. Or, wait, would you rather hold it at Yankee Stadium?"

"Our rooftop will be sufficient."

"And how many cakes? A hundred?"

"Just sixteen. I want sixteen cakes, and I want everybody we know to come and dance with us. Will you dance?"

"I will dance. Can one of the cakes be a banana cream pie, and that's the one you and I will eat together after everyone has gone?"

"Are you serious? Because I am very, very serious about this."

He shrugs. "As long as we're dreaming, I didn't think it would hurt to get in there that I want banana cream pie, too. With a little bride and groom standing in the whipped cream."

"Well, sure. I want them up to their knees in whipped cream."

He kisses me for a long time. "Anything else?"

"Yes. Can we adjourn this official meeting and get on with the *important stuff* in our bed right this second?"

Indeed, he says, we can. He thought I'd never ask.

And, well, after the important stuff—which, believe me, could not have waited thirty more seconds—well, we lie together, my head on his shoulder, until very late, talking about babies and little girls and what it's going to feel like to cuddle our daughters—our *daughters*, plural!—and we talk about everything we can think of. The big stuff and the little stuff, down to what kind of stroller makes the most sense and which of us should make the Saturday morning pancakes, and at some point we're so tired and delirious that the words all flow together, and *then* we get so tired we can't even form sentences anymore, and I fall asleep hearing my heart calling out into the darkness, and being answered back: yes yes yes yes.

CHAPTER
FORTY-FIVE
MARNIE

Blix told me over and over again that I was going to have a big, big life.

I never knew what that meant, of course. Was I supposed to be working at the United Nations or becoming an ambassador to some third world country? Was I meant to join the space program? Perform miracles? What the heck would be considered big?

All I ever wanted, I told her, was a husband and children, a house, some bikes and strollers in the front hall, maybe some mittens I'd knit when I learned how. That didn't sound like a life anybody might describe with even one *big*—much less two.

But now—well, now I know what a big life is. It's a feeling more than a *thing*. You don't have to go up in space or even stand on a big stage or run for office. It can be something as small as seeing shimmers in the air and convincing two strangers they need to get to know each other. And it can be as routine as a man rubbing your toes in a claw-foot bathtub, a child drawing pictures at the kitchen table, and a baby girl sleeping on your chest. Throw in some music playing in the background, the sound of people walking by in the street, and the fragrance of a Thursday night meat loaf in the oven—and that's about all the miracles I need.

It's a year later, and I guess I should explain what's happened.

Fritzie was delighted when we asked if she'd like to live with us full-time, and armed with the knowledge that we were doing the right thing for everybody, we easily worked out details with Tessa and Richard, who decided they wanted to stay in Europe for another year anyway before coming back to the States. She'll go visit them, and they're making arrangements to come and stay with us for a week sometime soon. Patrick says they've unwittingly become part of my plan to turn everybody I know into one big, happy family, and that I won't be content until I have all my loved ones under one roof for every single holiday.

Patrick and I got married in a crazy big May wedding on our rooftop with, yes, sixteen cakes and one secret banana cream pie with a plastic bride and groom standing up to their knees in whipped cream. There was a mariachi band and people dancing under the full moon. Everybody wore wonderful boho clothes, and Patrick found a tiara for me that he said belonged to Blix and that she'd worn when she threw her own Irish wake, because only Blix would have thought of putting on her own wake so she could get to comfort the mourners herself. And only she would have worn a tiara for it.

Fritzie stood up next to us while we read our vows, and she said her own, in which she promised to love our family and to notice if we were falling away from all the things we promised that day, particularly the one about always having ice cream in the house, which was her idea. She also said she'd pick up trash on the street and thank people on the subway when she saw them giving up their seats for pregnant women or old people, and people clapped—and even though that didn't really have anything to do with our marriage vows, the clapping was a nice touch, and Fritzie, I think, needs a full amount of clapping. Years of clapping!

For my part, I promised to clap for her and love her and make sure she gets a lot of time to be a kid and I promised to remind her that she doesn't have to worry about parenting the grown-ups around her.

Talk about interesting speeches, my mother got up and said that her dearest wish for us was that we shake up our marriage at least once every five years—that we should just throw out all the rules and break loose into doing completely new things.

"It's great to be in a couple, and most people will tell you that you have to sacrifice everything for the marriage and *work hard* at it, but I say you should *play hard* at it, and don't sacrifice a thing. Most of all, be brave enough *not* to give up on your own personal self," she said. "Also, if you hate making meat loaf every Thursday night, don't do it. *Do not do it.*"

My dad called out, "Could we have it on Wednesday sometimes, maybe, every once in a while?" and everybody laughed, and Paco yelled out that he'd give my dad some meat loaf to take home, and also give him the recipe so *he* could make it himself. That line drew some applause. My wedding was becoming like a group conversation.

You know what was the best part, though?

Well, first let me tell you that all the people from the Frippery came: Anxious Toby, Kat, Ernst the Screenplay Guy—and all the Amazings, which was like having precious swans show up. Lola and William Sullivan were there, and Lola kept dabbing her eyes and telling me that she knew that Blix was right here with us, enjoying immensely the whole idea that her plan for Patrick and me had worked out after all.

"That's the thing about Blix's plans," she said. "Just when you give up on them and think they're not coming true, then everything kind of works out just the way she said it would."

I pointed to the tiara. "She's right here," I said. "Narrating the whole thing."

So right there on that rooftop was everything I've ever loved about weddings: tears and applause and laughing and family and food and dancing and children and a fire in the firepit. Nobody jilted me at the altar this time or said he didn't think he could go through with it.

But now I need to get to the best part.

After we'd said the vows, and after everybody had gotten their plates of food and the sun was starting to go down, Patrick came over and tapped me on the shoulder. I was chatting with my sister about Brooklyn kid events, and my nieces, Amelia and Louise, were running in circles around us.

"Marnie," he said in a low voice. "It's time. She's pushing."

"Oh!" I said. I stood up and put my plate on the table nearby. I felt like my cheeks were flushed.

"Should we put somebody in charge of this wedding while we're gone, or will it just run along on its own power?"

I looked around. It seemed like a wedding that had enough oomph for a few more hours at least. Mariachis were lining up to play after a break, and there were still a whole bunch of cakes to be introduced.

My sister thought that we should stay at our wedding—"It's *your* moment!" she said—but we thanked her for that observation, and kissed and hugged everybody and said we were off to have a baby.

Janelle had been very clear that she wanted us to come. We were supposed to be there for her whole labor, but she'd known we were getting married today, so she had her mom call us at the pushing stage instead. We hadn't even known she'd been in labor since it was a whole week early.

Three hours later, I sat in Janelle's hospital room, and Patrick and I held on to our new little daughter, and all of us cried. She was beautiful and pink and perfect, with curled-up little fists and big, soulful navy-blue eyes that gazed right up into mine. She was swaddled up in one of those white hospital blankets with the pink-and-blue stripes, and she was wearing a jaunty little knit cap that Fritzie said was so cute that we should all make some for ourselves.

Yes, Fritzie was there with us. She insisted on coming along to meet her new sister, and make sure we didn't name her anything stupid, she said. Her eyes were glowing, I noticed, and she kept saying, "Now my daddy has *two* little girls."

At Janelle's request, I stayed with her after Patrick and Fritzie left and went back to the wedding. I think she wanted me there for fortification when Matt came to see her. The reluctant father of the baby.

He looked like a cowboy, striding into that room, bringing in an air of testosterone and defensiveness, and I didn't like it one bit. When he asked me if they could have some privacy, I looked at her, and she nodded so I left the two of them alone and went down to the cafeteria to have a cup of tea and walk around. People looked at me and smiled, and maybe it was because I was wearing my wedding dress, which was dragging along the ground, all that lace and colorful silk—but maybe it was because I couldn't stop hugging myself, since I was having two very intense and opposing feelings at once. I was so excited and happy in the main part of myself, but there was this other little section that was, I have to admit, a little bit scared that maybe Matt was going to say he'd changed his mind, and that *he* wanted to raise his baby girl with Janelle after all.

You know these things can happen.

So I asked the universe for a little sign. The universe and I hadn't been communicating so much lately, to tell you the truth. I'd gotten a little bit more practical, maybe, and things were humming nicely along on their own, without me doing spells.

But sure enough, ten minutes later I saw a nurse's aide come in and sit down at a table with a sheaf of papers and a tired, worn-out expression. She started reading her papers, and fidgeting—and a few minutes later, a man in a uniform came in. I saw him look over at her and then look away. And look again and look away again. She was completely unaware of him until about the third time he looked at her, this time from three tables away—and then their eyes met, and guess what I saw.

Yep, sparkles. It had been so long since I'd seen any. But there they were, shimmering as beautifully as the sparklers we used to run around with on the Fourth of July. I closed my eyes, but the stars didn't go away. They stayed there, plain as anything, like they were reaching out to touch us all.

As I was leaving to go back upstairs, I knew what I had to do. I stopped by the nurse's aide's table and I leaned down and whispered to her, "Don't let him get away. Go sit with him."

She laughed. "No way. He looks at me every day, and he has to come talk to me."

"Sometimes," I said, "it happens that he provides the spark, but then you have to make the next move. I know this might sound crazy, but I wouldn't risk letting him get away if I were you. You and he are going to be great together."

She looked at me, just the way people do when I'm telling them something that's true and unbelievable, and something that's also going to change their lives. "Okay," she said, but I didn't know if she really would. I didn't want to tell her that the fate of the world depended on what she did just then, but that's how it felt.

Janelle texted me just then, so I went back to her room.

Matt had left, although there was a smear of him lingering—a slight ruffledness to the air—so I closed the door to her room, and then I stretched out beside her on the bed, with the baby sleeping between us. I held her hand. Around us was the gentleness of the baby's soft breathing, and Janelle's slight sniffling.

I wanted to be there with her when the sadness came for her, when the hugeness of her gift knocked her over. I didn't want to tell her stupid stuff like it was all going to be fine, or that she was doing the right thing. Instead, I told her the truest things I knew.

That sometimes love doesn't look like what you had in mind.

That sometimes, even when we are doing everything right, our lives can start to look like a pieced-together bundle of problems, and we're sure a terrible mistake was made in our paperwork and we got assigned to the wrong people.

I said there was mercy to be found in a good night's sleep, a good cry, a hot bath, a cup of tea, and dancing alone in your room with the music turned up as loud as you can.

There is love out there for all of us, I said. Your heart may be broken right now, but as the great philosopher Blix Holliday said—the woman for whom this little baby will be named—love runs the universe. And because of that, it's out there for us all. You just have to be braver than you want to be. The person offering it might not have been your very first choice.

I kissed her on the forehead. And I stayed there, holding her hand, until she fell asleep.

I put little Blix into her bassinet and I stood there looking at her for the longest time, blinking in gratitude as I took in the soft pink cheeks, the little fringe of dark hair, the sweet little hands that looked like tiny little starfish. So new to the world, so fresh and sweet-smelling, and with such a full life ahead of her. A life that I was going to help her launch. I'm here on the ground floor of this new, splendid life, I thought, and I was so happy to be in this moment.

So I leaned down and whispered to her that I'd come back for her tomorrow, and I would be her mama forever.

And that's what is happening. She's made us all a family, with her giant slobbery smiles and those wet openmouthed baby kisses. We're not getting any sleep anymore, Patrick and I, but we don't care. It's May again, and in the early evenings, we sit on the rooftop with our girls, and we sing songs and tell stories, and he and Fritzie make little sculptures out of toothpicks and popsicle sticks.

The thing I now know for sure—and that Patrick is learning, too— is that no matter how dark it gets, how many times you fall down, love steps in to save us, over and over and over again. Oh, and that spirits can live in the toaster. Or anywhere you need them to be.

ACKNOWLEDGMENTS

One of the best things about writing a book is that, for quite a while, you get to live a whole other life. Once you think it up, writing a book is like taking a little vacation to another world where YOU get to control the situations. (Or a lot of them, at least. Characters do argue from time to time. I'm looking at you, Patrick!) Best of all, you get to enter this world each day and then leave again, closing the door on your characters and the situations you've put them in and returning to the world of friends, family, and figuring out what to cook for dinner.

I always become a little bit obsessed when I'm writing a book. And over the past year, Patrick and Marnie talked so incessantly and so much to me that I had difficulty simply walking away from them when it was time to try to be back in my so-called "real" life.

I owe a huge debt of gratitude to those who have put up with me. To those who have helped me by listening to drafts, giving me feedback, encouraging me, cooking me meals, writing me letters, blogging, or leaving reviews on Amazon, I have been truly humbled by your attention and kindness. To all the readers who have contacted me and sent me their own stories of love and magic and heartbreak, who have welcomed Blix and Marnie and Patrick into their lives—thank you so very much.

I also must thank Kim Steffen and Nancy Antle and Leslie Connor and Beth Levine for reading early drafts and making suggestions. My writing workshop—Marcia Winter, Grace Pauls, Linda Balestracci, Sharon Wise, Laurie Ruderfer, Michellee Speirs, P. B. Baraket, Mary Ann Emswiler, Mimi Lines, Marji Shapiro, Robin Favello, and Sue Richman—helped me remember the advice I always tell them: *Don't be afraid to write badly at first. You can't edit a blank page.* Judy Theise let me spend many afternoons with my laptop in her beautiful living room and fed me cheese and grapes while I typed. Susanne Davis has listened to endless plot points. And Holly Robinson makes me laugh and keeps me sane when I'm going crazy. Alice Mattison, who is a master of fiction writing, helps me sort myself out again and again whenever I'm writing a book—and our conversations about our novels over sushi every month are *everything*.

My Lake Union author friends have been lovely and generous with their ideas and counsel and encouragement. There are too many of them to name, but I especially want to thank Kerry Schafer, Barbara O'Neal, Nancy Star, Marilyn Simon Rothstein, Catherine McKenzie, and Bette Lee Crosby for all their wonderful stories and generosity. Also, the Blue Sky Book Club has been the best fun!

I am so lucky to have Jodi Warshaw as my editor at Lake Union. She always knows exactly what needs to be done with a plot or a character, and she makes everything I write so much more clear. Besides that, she's so much fun to talk to! Nancy Yost, my agent, is a whirlwind (in the best possible way) of energy and ideas, and keeps me on track and makes me laugh. Many thanks also to Danielle Marshall and Dennelle Catlett and Gabriella Dumpit of Amazon Publishing, who have been unfailingly kind and helpful and have helped me believe in magic again and again.

I also want to thank my kids, Ben, Allie, and Stephanie, and their spouses, Amy, Mike, and Alex, for reading and listening—and endless thanks to Charlie, Josh, Miles, and Emma, who remind me that writing isn't the only thing that exists in the whole world. (There's also mini-golf, soccer, baseball, Legos, guitars, ukuleles, hammocks, Minecraft, and pugs.) And of course, all my love to Jim, whose love makes everything possible, always.

BOOK CLUB QUESTIONS

1. Marnie and Patrick have what he calls the perfect life—they love each other, and they can do anything they want whenever they want. But she wants a baby and thinks she can't live without being a mom. What advice would you give to a couple navigating their way through this kind of basic disagreement?

2. Marnie is a matchmaker who sees sparkles in the air when people might be a good match for each other. Have you ever successfully brought any couples together? If so, how did you know they were meant for each other?

3. Patrick has what he considers airtight reasons for not wanting to bring a child into the world, including his disabilities due to the fire. Was he correct to be worried about how his child would experience his limitations?

4. Tessa decides to leave Fritzie with Patrick soon after she locates him. She had never let him know that he had fathered a child with her nine years ago. What long-term effect do you think this would have on a child?

5. Fritzie is a handful, getting herself into trouble and causing headaches for Marnie and Patrick. Yet she seems able to draw people to her when she needs to. What qualities did she possess that make Marnie, and then Patrick, start to love her?

6. Marnie believes in magic. She believes in signs, and she thinks she hears from Blix if she stands near the toaster. She feels that magic might have been responsible for bringing Fritzie into her life, the same way magic brought Patrick to her. Have you ever believed in magic? Do you think there are energetic forces that we don't fully understand?

7. Marnie's mother has been married for over forty years and now feels she can't go on any longer with a man who simply wants to watch the golf channel and not communicate with her. Marnie thinks her parents still love each other and should remain together. Have you known people who have this late-in-life urge to separate? Were you sympathetic toward Millie's feeling that she's no longer necessary now that her kids are grown and gone?

8. Patrick has a change of heart during the time he is responsible for Fritzie. What led to the realization he came to during Marnie's absence? Is this a transformation that you think will stick?

9. Blix had a mantra that Marnie also tries to follow. It's "whatever happens, love that." What do you think this really means, and how does Marnie—and finally Patrick—put that mantra to work in their own lives?

ABOUT THE AUTHOR

Photo © 2018 Dan Mims

Maddie Dawson grew up in the South, born into a family of outrageous storytellers. Her various careers as a substitute English teacher, department-store clerk, medical-records typist, waitress, cat sitter, wedding-invitation-company receptionist, nanny, day care worker, electrocardiogram technician, and Taco Bell taco maker were made bearable by thinking up stories as she worked. Today Maddie lives in Guilford, Connecticut, with her husband. She's the bestselling author of six previous novels: *Matchmaking for Beginners, The Survivor's Guide to Family Happiness, The Opposite of Maybe, The Stuff That Never Happened, Kissing Games of the World,* and *A Piece of Normal.*